Marriage wasn't in their plans, but these handsome men are about to meet the women they can't live without!

Will He Ask Her to be His Bride?

Three emotional novels from favourite authors Catherine George, Trish Wylie and Patricia Thayer

Will He Ask Her to be His Bride?

CATHERINE GEORGE

TRISH WYLIE

PATRICIA THAYER

First published in Great Britain 2012
by Mills & Boon, an imprint of Harlequin (UK) Limited,
Eton House, 18-24 Paradise Road, Richmond, Surrey TW9 1SR

WILL HE ASK HER TO BE HIS BRIDE?
© by Harlequin Enterprises II B.V./S.à.r.l 2012

The Millionaire''s *Convenient Bride, The Millionaire's Proposal* and *Texas Ranger Takes a Bride* were first published in Great Britain by Harlequin (UK) Limited.

The Millionaire's Convenient Bride © Catherine George 2007
The Millionaire's Proposal © Trish Wylie 2008
Texas Ranger Takes a Bride © Patricia Wright 2008

ISBN: 978 0 263 89696 1
ebook ISBN: 978 1 408 97062 1

05-0812

Printed and bound in Spain
by Blackprint CPI, Barcelona

THE MILLIONAIRE'S CONVENIENT BRIDE

BY

CATHERINE GEORGE

Dear Reader,

The Millionaire's Convenient Bride involves Connah, a handsome, brooding Welsh hero, with a voice like Richard Burton and a name derived from an ancient Celtic tribe. He engages Hester to look after his ten-year-old child. She met him fleetingly ten years before and, though at this point he doesn't know it, he has haunted her dreams ever since. Add to the mix a beautiful Georgian house and a holiday in a romantic villa in Tuscany, then negotiate some twists and turns in the plot before reaching a happy ending for everyone.

In all my books I enjoy developing the relationship between a man and a woman, and conveying the way they warm to each other both emotionally and physically. But I take equal pleasure in writing about children, as previous readers of my novels will know. Lowri, the young girl in this story, bears more than a passing resemblance to a ten-year-old closely related to me, so I had a lump in my throat when I was describing Lowri's longing for a mother.

For readers who know my work, and for those who are new to it, I hope you enjoy this story and wish you happy reading always.

Love to you all,

Catherine

Catherine George was born in Wales and early on developed a passion for reading, which eventually fuelled her compulsion to write. Marriage to an engineer led to nine years in Brazil, but on his later travels the education of her son and daughter kept her in the UK. And instead of constant reading to pass her lonely evenings she began to write the first of her romantic novels. When not writing and reading she loves to cook, listen to opera and browse in antiques shops.

To Howard, with my love.

CHAPTER ONE

HESTER'S excitement escalated as she neared her goal. She checked the address again, then mounted the steps of one of the tall houses which lined three sides of leafy Albany Square. She rang the bell, gave her name over an intercom and, after a pause, the door was opened by a man who was obviously an employee of some kind, but nothing like her idea of a butler.

He smiled at her pleasantly. 'Good morning, Miss Ward. Come this way.'

Hester followed him along a high-ceilinged hall and up a flight of Bath stone stairs to a large, book-lined study. He held out the chair in front of the desk, told her his employer would be with her shortly and left her alone. Her anticipation at fever pitch, Hester sat, tense, on the edge of the chair. Her preliminary interview had been over coffee in a hotel lounge with John Austin, personal assistant of the owner of this house, but now she was about to meet the man himself.

On the desk a solitary framed photograph faced the window. She hesitated a moment, then turned it towards her and felt a rush of pure adrenaline. Her hunch had been right! The man she'd come to see really *was* her mysterious Mr Jones. And one look at that striking face, with its knife-edge cheekbones and intense dark eyes, sent her straight back to her first encounter with the man smiling down at a child in the photograph.

She had been packing that cold January night when her mother rushed in, radiating urgency.

'Give me a hand, darling. We've got guests.'

Hester stared at her in disbelief. '*What?* At this time of night?'

'I just couldn't say no. It's snowing, and they look exhausted.'

'Honestly, Mother! We're supposed to be closed for the entire month. You should have put the No Vacancies sign out.'

Moira Ward gave her a stern look. 'I want help, please, not a lecture.'

'Right away!' Hester hurried after her mother, down the back stairs to the kitchen. 'Where are they?'

Moira began taking food from the refrigerator. 'Settling into their rooms while I whip up a snack. Mr Jones accepted my offer of sandwiches with such enthusiasm I think it's a long time since either of them had a meal.'

Hester shook her head in disapproval as she buttered bread. 'You're too soft-hearted by half.'

'But not soft-headed,' returned Moira tartly. 'I don't turn away paying guests who offer cash in advance.' She sighed. 'Besides, the poor girl looked ready to drop. I couldn't turn them away.'

'Of course you couldn't!' Hester blew her a kiss. 'What shall I put in these?'

'Slice some of the roast ham from supper, and I'll heat up the rest of my vegetable soup. The girl looked frozen.'

'You want me to take the tray up?'

'Yes, please, darling. I'd rather they knew I'm not alone in the house.'

Hester laughed. 'I doubt that my presence will make much difference if Mr Jones has anything sinister in mind.' Her eyes narrowed. 'Wait a minute. Did you say rooms plural?'

Moira nodded. 'The connecting rooms at the front.'

'So we not only feed these people supper as well as breakfast, we clean the two largest rooms in the house after they've gone!'

'For which I've been paid a handsome sum in advance,' her mother reminded her, and, with a triumphant smile, played her trump card. 'You can have half of it to take back to college.'

Hester laughed as she gave her mother a hug. 'Brilliant! Thanks, Ma. Why aren't they sleeping together, do you think?'

'Ours is not to reason why.' Moira added a tureen of steaming soup to the tray and sent her daughter on her way.

Hester bore her burden with care up the wide staircase, eager to take a look at the couple who'd appealed to her mother's hospitable heart.

The man who opened the first of the garden view rooms smiled as he took the tray and one look at the handsome, haggard face took Hester's breath away.

'Thank you.' His voice was deep, with a timbre that sent shivers down her spine. 'Would you tell Mrs Ward we're deeply grateful?'

'I will,' she said with effort, and pulled herself together. 'You'll find biscuits, coffee, tea and kettle on the desk, and I've brought fresh milk. Can I get you anything else?'

He shook his head as he inspected the tray's contents. 'This is wonderful—and much appreciated.'

'No trouble at all,' she assured him fervently. 'What time would you like breakfast?'

He glanced at the closed connecting door. 'We need to be on our way first thing. Would toast and coffee be possible about seven-thirty?'

'Of course. I'll bring it up.' And bring it willingly if it meant another encounter with the knee-trembling Mr Jones. Plus no dining room to clean afterwards.

Hester went back downstairs in a pink haze. That, she thought reverently, was one mouth-watering male specimen if you liked your men tall, dark and masterful. Which she did. Or would if she knew any. She sighed enviously. The lady with him was very lucky. Her man had charisma in spades.

Moira was drinking tea at the table when Hester went back to the kitchen. 'Everything all right?'

'With the *über*-gorgeous Mr Jones, yes. The connecting door was half closed so I didn't see his lady.'

'If you had, you'd have seen for yourself why I couldn't turn them away. She looks like a ghost, poor thing.'

Hester poured milk into a mug, stirred in squares of chocolate and put it in the microwave to heat. 'He wants breakfast at seven thirty, so I said I'd take it up. But what on earth were they doing out here in January at this time of night? We don't normally do much with passing trade.'

This was true. Most of their customers came via tourist agencies and the Internet.

'Mr Jones said he'd meant to drive overnight,' said her mother, 'but his companion began feeling ill about the time it started to snow. At which point he spotted our sign on the main road and turned up here on the off chance that we had room.'

Hester fluttered her eyelashes. 'I thought Smith was the alias of choice for secret getaways. Do you think Jones is his real name?'

'That's how he signed the register.'

'Pretty anonymous. He could have murdered the woman's husband to run off with her for all we know.'

Moira shook her head. 'I somehow doubt that! But they'll both be gone in the morning, so we'll never know.'

Never say never, thought Hester, her excitement back in full force as she heard footsteps on the stairs. The clock struck the hour in a nearby church steeple to mark the occasion as she rose to face the man who'd made such an impression on her ten years ago that she'd never forgotten him.

Tall and impressive in a formal suit, he looked older and more remote, but the thick black Celtic hair and ink dark eyes were unmistakable—and had exactly the same effect as the first time they'd met. He came towards her, hand outstretched, a slight smile softening the hard, imperious features. 'Connah Carey Jones. I apologise for keeping you waiting.'

Hester took the hand and felt a jolt of heat rush through her like an electric shock. Heart thumping in startled response to the contact, she returned the smile with determined composure. 'Not at all, I was early.'

He waved her back to her chair, then seated himself behind the desk, looking at her in narrow-eyed silence for a long moment before turning to her application.

She tensed. Could he have remembered her? But if he did he made no mention of it as he read through her CV.

'You look young to have so much experience in childcare,' he said at last.

'But, as you see, I'm twenty-seven.' She hesitated. 'Mr Carey Jones, to avoid any possible waste of your time, could you confirm that the post is purely temporary?'

'Certainly. It's for the summer vacation only.' The dark eyes looked up to connect with hers. 'However, there is a complication. Lowri went away to school when she was eight, and would hotly resent the idea of having a nanny again. To get round this, I've told her I'm hiring a temporary house-keeper. Sam Cooper, the man who let you in, actually runs our all male household, but during the school holiday I need a woman on hand to provide Lowri's meals, see to her personal laundry and take her out during the day. Her evenings would be spent with me.'

'I see.' Not that Hester did, entirely. Once she'd discovered the name of her prospective employer, and began wondering if he was the same Mr Jones, she'd put out some feelers through a journalist contact on the *Financial Times* to find out if her hunch was right. But Angus had drawn a blank on personal details. Known as the Welsh Wizard due to his phenomenal success in the world of finance, Connah Carey Jones kept his private life so strictly private there'd been no mention of a wife and child.

He returned to her application. 'Would a Norland-trained nanny with such glowing references object to posing as a house-keeper, Miss Ward?'

'Not in the slightest,' she assured him. 'I have experience in that field too, Mr Carey Jones. After my father died, my mother turned the family home into a successful bed and breakfast operation. I was involved at every level right from the start. I enjoy cooking and did a certain amount of it in my previous post, as I explained to Mr Austin.'

'It would certainly help in this instance,' he agreed, 'but my priority is finding someone trustworthy and competent, who is also young enough to be company for my daughter. It would be necessary to live in for the period of employment, also to furnish the requisite references and agree to a security check.'

'Of course.'

He mentioned the very generous salary offer and looked at her in enquiry. 'Now that you're clear about my requirements, Miss Ward, would you accept the post if it were offered?'

Like a shot.

'Yes, Mr Carey Jones, I would,' she said firmly.

'Thank you for being so straightforward. I'll be in touch as soon as possible.' And, instead of ringing for his butler, he surprised her by accompanying her downstairs to see her out.

Buzzing from her encounter with Mr Jones, Hester set off at a brisk pace to walk back to the house on the hilly outskirts of town. She waved, smiling, when her stepfather threw open the front door before she was halfway up the steep path to the house. 'Hi, Robert.'

He hurried her inside, his kind face expectant. 'How did it go?'

'Quite well, I think, but I'll have to wait to see if I beat the opposition.'

'Of course you will! Moira's popped out for something

missing from the lunch menu, but we'll eat in the garden as soon as she gets back.'

Hester kissed his cheek affectionately, then went out to climb the fire escape stairs to the garage flat Robert Marshall had redecorated to her taste. Hester's chosen career required her to live in with whatever family she worked for, and now the family home had been sold she was deeply grateful to Robert for providing her with the security of a private, self-contained apartment as a base. She gazed out over his steep, beautifully tended garden as she changed into shorts and a halter-neck top, wondering if a second interview was likely. Having met Connor Carey Jones again, she fervently hoped so.

When Moira came back with her shopping, her jaw dropped when Hester, not without drama, announced that her interview had been with the man who'd made such an impression on them both all those years ago.

'I had an idea it might be him, Ma,' she said, smiling triumphantly, 'but I didn't say anything because it sounded so far-fetched. But I was right. The man in need of a temporary nanny for his daughter really is our mysterious Mr Jones.'

'*Amazing!* How did you react when you saw him?'

'Luckily there was a photograph of him with a little girl on his desk, to give me advance warning.'

Moira shook her head in wonder. 'Did he recognise you?'

'Of course not. I've changed a lot since then. Besides, you saw far more of him than I did. They didn't end up leaving early in the morning as they'd planned and I had to get back to college before they left—so I never did meet his lady.'

'He was worried in case she had something infectious. She didn't, as it happened, but she was far too ill to travel, so I let them stay on for a few days until she was better.' Moira smiled reminiscently. 'Mr Jones was very appreciative. He sent me the most wonderful flowers afterwards.'

'Now you've solved your mystery, would you like the job, Hester?' asked Robert.

She nodded fervently. 'I certainly would. But apparently the daughter would object to having a nanny again, so if I did get it I'd have to pose as the temporary housekeeper.'

'No problem for you, darling,' said Moira promptly. 'You've had far more experience of housekeeping than most girls your age.'

'I think the age bit might be the problem. I got the impression he wanted someone a bit older.'

Hester found out sooner than expected. During the evening John Austin rang, asking if it was convenient for her to call back at the house in Albany Square to meet his employer at noon the next day. She raced into the garden to break the news.

'First hurdle over, folks. I've got a second interview tomorrow.'

Hester felt nervous as she mounted the steps to the elegant house in Albany Square the following morning. Which was silly. It wouldn't be the end of the world if she didn't get the job. But, having met Mr Jones again, she was very keen to work for the man she'd had such a crush on when she was a teenager. And the bonus of six weeks generous salary while she was filling in time wouldn't hurt, either. The original plan for the gap between jobs had been a holiday in the South of France, but she'd kept that secret in case it fell through at the last minute. Which it had.

The butler gave her a friendly smile as he opened the door. 'Good morning, Miss Ward. I'll show you straight upstairs.'

This time Connah Carey Jones was waiting at the open study door to greet her.

'Thank you for coming again at short notice.' He led her to the chair in front of the desk. 'To get straight to the point, your credentials tick all the boxes, Miss Ward. I notice you even live here in town.'

'Yes. Though it's actually my stepfather's house.'

His eyes sharpened. 'You don't feel welcome there?'

She shook her head. 'On the contrary, Robert couldn't be kinder.'

When his phone rang he glanced at it, then, with a word of apology, left the room. Hester's tension mounted as she waited for him to come back. It looked as though the job was hers. But first she had to tell him that they'd met before. He obviously didn't remember her. No surprise there. He'd been so worried about his lady at the time he'd had no attention to spare for a chubby teenager with heavy eye make-up and yards of blonde corkscrew curls. She was ten years older now, twenty pounds lighter, and her smooth coiled hair and discreet cosmetics were more in keeping with her job.

Connah Carey Jones came back into the room shortly afterwards and sat behind the desk. 'John has checked your references, Miss Ward, and has also run a security check on your background—'

'Before you go on,' she said, bracing herself, 'I must tell you that we've already met.'

He sat back in his chair, nodding slowly as he trained his eyes on her face. 'I thought you looked familiar, but I couldn't pinpoint why.'

'Until I saw you yesterday,' she said quickly, 'I didn't know we'd met before. I'd read about you in the press, but I'd never seen a photograph—'

'Because I make very sure I keep out of the limelight,' he assured her. 'I'm not a social animal, so where exactly did we meet, Miss Ward?'

'You came knocking on the door of our B & B one night, looking for accommodation.'

He stared at her, arrested. 'That was *your* home?'

'Yes. We were supposed to be closed, but it was snowing, so my mother hadn't the heart to turn you away.'

'And I thanked God for it. I've never forgotten her kindness.' He frowned. 'But I'm afraid I don't remember you.'

'I was the one who brought your trays up.'

'The teenager with yards of hair?' He smiled, surprised. 'You look very different now.'

'Ten years is a long time,' she said wryly.

'It is indeed.' He looked at her in silence for a moment. 'Right. Let's get down to brass tacks, Miss Ward. You and your mother were so kind I'm only too glad to return the favour in some small way. If you want this job, it's yours.'

She smiled warmly. 'Thank you. I promise to take good care of your daughter.'

'Good. Talking of Lowri, you need some details about her.' He looked at his watch. 'Let me give you some lunch while I put you in the picture.'

The meal was served under a vine-covered pergola overlooking a suntrap patio garden at the back of the house.

'May I give you some wine?' asked Connah.

'Thank you. I'm walking today; my car's in for service.'

'You won't need your own car while you're here,' he informed her as he filled glasses. 'Sam Cooper will drive you wherever you need to go. His official job description is butler, but he's a great deal more than that. While Lowri is here with me, his priority is security.'

Hester eyed him, startled. 'You're afraid of kidnap?'

'Afraid isn't the exact term. Let's say I keep a constant guard against the possibility.'

'Does Lowri know this?'

'No.' The handsome face set in grim lines. 'Nor, if humanly possible, do I intend her to find out.'

'But how do you manage when she's at school?'

'I chose one with security as one of its top priorities.'

'But she had a nanny up to that point?'

He nodded. 'Her mother died when she was born, and my

mother brought her up with the help of a girl from the village. When Lowri went away to school Alice stayed on to help my mother for a while, but she got married recently; hence the problem for the school holiday. My mother's recovering from heart surgery and can't take care of Lowri this time.'

Hester looked thoughtful as she helped herself to salad. 'Does Lowri like boarding school?'

'She took to it like a duck to water, thank God. Now,' he added briskly, 'down to business.'

Connah Carey Jones made his requirements very plain. Without letting his daughter feel she was being watched every minute of the day, Lowri's safety was to be Hester's main concern.

'Sam will drive you to the park, or into town for shopping. This last, by the way, is urgent. Lowri needs new clothes. She's growing rapidly, particularly her feet. But you can leave school shoes until the end of the holiday,' he added, with an unexpected touch of economy.

'I shall do my best for her,' she assured him.

He nodded briskly. 'I feel sure you will, Miss Ward. In this household, by the way, we're all on first name terms. Are you happy with that?'

'Of course.'

'Good.' He smiled briefly. 'I hope you enjoy your stay with us. Feel free to ask me for anything you need.' He looked up as Sam appeared with a coffee tray. 'Hester has agreed to work with us during Lowri's school holiday, Sam. I've put your many and varied services at her disposal.'

'Right you are.' Sam gave Hester a friendly smile and set the tray down in front of her. 'I live in the basement flat, so I'm always on hand.'

'Thank you.' Hester smiled at him warmly. 'I'll depend on you to show me the ropes.'

'You can run Hester home later, Sam,' said Connah. 'I'll give you a call when she's ready.' He leaned back, relaxed, as Hester dealt with the coffee. 'This is pleasant. I should eat out here more often.'

'Does Lowri share your evening meal, or should I make supper earlier for her?'

'When I'm home we eat together, to make the most of each other's company. But I'll let you know in good time if I can't make it.'

'Thank you.' She smiled. 'It would also help if you could give me an idea of Lowri's tastes. At her age I was a bit picky.'

He shrugged. 'Lowri will coax for fast food because the school doesn't allow it. Indulge her now and again as a treat, but otherwise just make sure she keeps to a balanced diet. Sam normally shops online, but Lowri might enjoy looking round a supermarket. Choose what you want, pay in cash, and Sam will carry the bags. And right now he'll give you a tour of the house before you leave.' Connah downed his coffee and got up. 'I collect Lowri on Friday, Hester. Are you free to start on Monday morning?'

'Yes. What time shall I come?'

'About eight-thirty. Unfortunately I need to be in London afterwards for a day or two so I'm throwing you in at the deep end. But Sam has my contact numbers.'

'Mr Carey Jones—'

'Connah,' he reminded her.

'I just wanted to ask after your mother.'

'She had a triple heart bypass and her convalescence is worryingly slow. When I fetch Lowri we'll spend time with her before coming back here.' He glanced at his watch and collected his jacket. 'I must be off.'

'Thank you for lunch,' said Hester, as they went back into the house.

'My pleasure.' He beckoned as Sam appeared. 'Show Hester round, then drive her wherever she wants to go. I'll see you on

Monday, Hester. All right, John,' he said, resigned, as his assistant opened the study door. 'Put your whip away, I'm coming.'

'If you're ready, Hester, we'll start at the bottom with my quarters and work up,' Sam suggested.

She followed him down a short flight of stairs to a compact, orderly basement flat. His sitting room doubled as an office, with electronic equipment to screen visitors, and the control panels of a very complicated alarm system.

'Connah's very hot on security,' he explained.

'So I gather. Have you worked for him long?'

'Since I left the military. The lower stairs lead to a cellar Connah converted into a double garage,' Sam added as he led her up to the ground floor into a kitchen with tall sash windows and a door that opened on to the back patio. 'My quarters used to be the kitchen and scullery, and this was the original dining room,' he explained. 'The old butler's pantry leads off it—very handy for the freezer and washing machine and so on.'

'Very nice indeed,' she commented. The large kitchen was fitted with every modern appliance possible, including a state-of-the-art electric range. 'You'll have to give me a teach-in on that before I start producing meals.'

Sam chuckled. 'If I get a share in the result sometimes, no problem. I'm a dab hand with a potato peeler.'

'I'll remember that!' They went up to the next floor and passed by the closed study door to enter a drawing room furnished with the emphasis on comfort and lit by the multi-paned windows typical of Regency architecture. The adjoining dining room was more formal and painted an authentic shade of pale green Hester found cold. The master bedroom on the next floor was part of a suite with a bathroom, dressing room and guest room, Sam informed Hester as they passed by on the way to the top floor.

'You're up here, next to Lowri,' he said, leading the way to two adjoining bedrooms, each with a small bathroom and a view over the trees in the square to the hills encircling the town. 'You wouldn't think so now, but these were the attics at one time. Suit you all right?' added Sam.

Hester nodded, impressed. 'But how is it so cool up here on a hot day like this?'

'Air-conditioning.'

Sam's phone rang as they went downstairs. 'Right you are, Connah. Coming down now. He wants to see you again before you go, Hester,' he added.

Connah looked up as she put her head round the study door. 'Come in and sit down. Is your room satisfactory?'

'Very much so.'

'Good.' He consulted a list. 'Next on the agenda, time off. You're free to go out some evenings when I'm home, Sundays are your own, also the occasional Saturday from noon onwards. You'll have to ring the doorbell to gain entry, but Sam will either be with you or waiting for you, so it's not a problem.' He paused, as though gauging her reaction. 'Or is it?'

'Of course not,' said Hester, though it was, a little. 'Otherwise I'd need the code for your impressive security system.'

'Other than myself, only Sam knows that.'

'Not even Mr Austin?'

'No. John's London based so he isn't here very much, but when he is he rings the bell.' He paused, giving her a very direct look. 'One last point. In your application you say you're single but precisely how single are you?'

Hester felt her hackles rise as she met the intent dark eyes. 'For the time being, totally. There's no danger of gentleman callers, Mr Carey Jones.'

CHAPTER TWO

'I'VE been pronounced fit to take care of Connah Carey Jones's ewe lamb, but not to drive her anywhere myself, nor to be trusted with a key to the house,' Hester announced when she got home. 'Security is a religion with the man. If that's what it means to have loads of money, I'll pass.'

'You can't blame him for wanting to keep his child safe,' said her mother, and shook her head in wonder. 'I'm still amazed that he's the man who turned up on our doorstep in the snow all those years ago. You were very taken with him at the time!'

'You must have been too, to volunteer full board for a few days,' Hester retorted.

'I liked him, yes,' said Moira, and smiled wickedly. 'But I wasn't moonstruck like you, darling.'

'I've been reading up on him,' said Robert, the peacemaker. 'He's one of the new hedge fund breed. He made a packet with an asset management firm he set up with a partner, but eventually sold off his share in the firm to "pursue other interests", but these weren't specified.'

Hester nodded. 'I heard that much from Angus Duff, my journalist chum. Of course I didn't know if the CC Jones he researched was our man, but I somehow had this gut feeling that he might be.'

Moira eyed her narrowly. 'Was that why you were so keen to apply?'

'Of course not. I replied to a box number. It was only when John Austin told me the name of his employer that I had this wild idea that Mr CC Jones might just possibly be our mystery man. But even then my only reason for applying was to earn some extra money before I go to the Rutherfords in October.' Hester smiled in satisfaction. 'While I'm living in Albany Square I'll spend very little, which will do wonders for my rainy day fund.'

'How about time off?' asked Robert.

'Every Sunday, the occasional Saturday, and some evenings when the big white chief is at home.'

'You sound as though you're not so enamoured with him this time round,' said her mother.

'His looks still pack the same punch for me, I admit, but I was rather put off when I found he wasn't willing to trust me with a key to the house,' said Hester tartly. 'He also got a bit personal about my social life.'

'Understandable, with someone as attractive as you,' said Robert.

She smiled at him affectionately. 'But I assured him there would be no gentleman callers—'

'Surely you didn't say that!' exclaimed Moira, rolling her eyes. 'You're not an Edwardian parlourmaid, girl!'

'For a moment he made me feel like one,' admitted Hester, eyes kindling.

'What's he like?' asked Robert curiously.

'Tall, dark and formidable, with hard black eyes that pin you down.'

'Are you *sure* you want to work for him?' demanded Moira.

'Don't worry, Mother, I'm sure I can play Jane Eyre to his Rochester for six weeks, whether I like him or not,' Hester assured her, then grinned. 'And I know he doesn't have a mad wife in the attic because that's where I sleep.'

* * *

Robert drove Hester to the house in Albany Square just before eight thirty on her first day and not only insisted on carrying her luggage up the steps to the front door, but on waiting with her until Sam Cooper appeared.

'Good morning, Sam,' said Hester, smiling. 'This is my step-father, Robert Marshall.'

Sam held out a hand to Robert. 'Sam Cooper, sir.'

Robert gave him a straight look as he took it, then smiled, obviously satisfied with what he saw. 'Glad to meet you. I'm sure I leave Hester in good hands.' He kissed her, reminded her to ring her mother later, and went back down to the car, waving as he drove off.

'Your stepdad's obviously fond of you,' commented Sam as he took the suitcases inside.

'He is, luckily for me,' said Hester affectionately. 'He's never had children of his own and tends to be protective where I'm concerned.'

Sam nodded in approval. 'Sounds like a good relationship. I'll just take this lot up to your room. Connah and Lowri stayed with Connah's mother over the weekend and they're not back yet, so you've got time to settle in before they arrive for lunch.'

'Talking of lunch, will you put this in the refrigerator for me?' Hester handed him a package. 'Or am I required to cook something hot?'

'Just soup and sandwiches, and Connah told me to stock you up for a cold meal tonight for supper.' Sam grinned. 'No need for a frontal assault on the cooker until tomorrow.'

'That's a relief! I brought a cold roast chicken just in case, but I can use some of that for sandwiches. After I've unpacked will you show me where everything's kept?'

'I'll give you a guided tour through the cupboards later,' promised Sam, and took her luggage upstairs.

Hester followed him, relieved that Sam Cooper seemed to like her. She unpacked rapidly and put her belongings away, then went downstairs to the kitchen. With Sam's guidance, she explored the cupboards and found them well stocked with everything she could possibly need.

'Has Connah lived here long?' she asked.

'No. The house was only finished properly a few weeks before we moved in. There was a hell of a lot to do. It dates from about eighteen-hundred and because it's a listed building it couldn't be hurried. Connah's main place is a penthouse flat in London but he's got business interests in this area, so when this house came on the market he snapped it up. Tomato is Lowri's favourite,' he added, as Hester surveyed the ranks of soup tins.

'Thank you. By the way, were there many other applicants for my job?'

'Three.'

But Connah had chosen her.

Sam answered her question before she asked it. 'Apparently the others were older and obviously set in their ways. Connah wanted a companion for Lowri, not a starchy, no-nonsense nanny.'

Hester began making sandwiches with the speed and efficiency of long practice. 'But officially I'm a housekeeper, not a nanny, remember.'

'Lowri will be glad of someone your age for company, whatever the job description,' Sam assured her. 'Normally she spends the holidays with her grandma at Bryn Derwen, but now Alice is married it's lonely there for her.' He munched appreciatively. 'These are first class.'

'I hope I haven't made them too soon.'

He shook his head. 'Connah said midday, so that's when he'll be here—' He broke off as his phone rang. 'Told you,' he said, checking the caller ID. 'Yes, Boss.' After a brief exchange, he disconnected. 'ETA twelve noon, Hester, and Lowri wants lunch in the garden. I'll help you take it out.'

Feeling far more nervous than before her interview with Connah, Hester put the soup to heat and prepared a tray.

'Lay for three,' said Sam. 'Connah expects you to join them for lunch.'

'Oh, right.' Hester hastily added a third setting. 'What does Lowri drink?'

'Fizzy stuff if allowed, milk or juice if not.'

'There wasn't time to make a pudding. Will ice cream do? Or fruit, maybe?'

Sam smiled reassuringly. 'Ask when you see her. Don't worry, Hester. She's a nice kid.'

Lowri's resemblance to her father was only slight. She showed promise of height like Connah's and her mouth was a smaller version of his, but her long straight hair was shades lighter and her eyes a striking cornflower blue.

'Hello,' she said, holding out her hand politely.

Hester took the hand. 'Nice to meet you.'

The bright eyes regarded Hester with frank curiosity. 'Daddy says you're going to look after us during the holidays. I thought you'd be like Mrs Powell, Grandma's housekeeper, but you're really young.'

Connah gave his daughter a warning look. 'Mind your manners, young lady. Remember what Grandma said. We must make Hester's stay here as pleasant as possible.'

'And I have to behave myself,' said Lowri, resigned, and gave him a smile so brimming with mischief that he laughed and gave her a hug.

'Hard work, I know, but you can do it.'

'Of course I can,' she said loftily, and beamed at Sam as he came into the kitchen. 'Did you bring my rucksack from the car?'

'It's in your room with the rest of your stuff.'

'Thanks, Sam.' She looked at Hester hopefully. 'I'm starving. Is it time for lunch soon?'

'Right away. Sam's already taken the tray into the garden, so if you go ahead I'll bring the food out.'

'You'll join us, of course,' said Connah courteously.

'Thank you.' Hester poured hot soup into a thermal jug, took the covered platter of sandwiches from the refrigerator and followed him into the garden.

Lowri polished off a bowl of soup with relish, despite the heat of the day, but Connah kept to sandwiches.

'Excellent chicken,' he commented. 'From the local delicatessen?'

Hester shook her head. 'I cooked it at home alongside my mother's Sunday roast. I wasn't sure what would be required for lunch today, so I made sure I had something ready.'

'You must let me reimburse you,' said Connah promptly.

'If you wish.' Hester smiled at Lowri. 'I asked Sam what you liked, so I put cheese and crispy bacon bits in some and just plain old ham in others. You can tell me what else you like as we go along.'

Lowri nodded, downing a sandwich at top speed. 'Yummy,' she said indistinctly, then shot a sparkling look at Hester. 'Though almost anything would be after school food.'

'Try the chicken, *cariad*,' advised Connah.

She made a face. 'They do that a lot in school.'

'Not like this,' he assured her, and with a martyred look Lowri took a minuscule bite.

Hester felt absurdly gratified when the blue eyes lit up.

'Wow! This is nothing like rubber school chicken. I *love* the stuffing.'

'How is your grandma?' asked Hester.

The blue eyes shadowed. 'She was very tired.'

'But getting stronger slowly,' Connah assured her.

Lowri gave her father a worried look. 'She doesn't look stronger. I didn't know she needed a nurse to look after her.'

'I insisted on hiring one for a while. At Grandma's age it takes time to get over surgery,' he told her. 'Don't worry. She'll soon pick up now she's beginning to eat normally again.'

'I hope so. Will she be well enough for us to have Christmas at Bryn Derwen?'

'Good Lord, yes.' He ruffled her hair. 'There's an entire term at school to get through before then.'

Lowri smiled as Sam approached with a coffee tray and a jug of orange juice. 'Is that for me?'

'Yes. Have you finished your lunch?' he demanded.

She smiled smugly at the empty platter. 'Every crumb.'

'No sarnies left for me?' he teased, then relented as she looked stricken. 'Only joking, pet. I ate mine before you arrived.'

'Did you have some with chicken?' she asked eagerly.

'I certainly did.' Sam put the tray down and bowed in Hester's direction. 'Best I've ever tasted.'

Connah finished his coffee and got up to follow Sam into the house. 'Thank you for lunch, Hester. Be good, Lowri; I'll see you ladies at dinner.'

Lowri heaved a sigh as she watched him go. 'Daddy's always so busy,' she said disconsolately. 'And he's got to go to London tomorrow. He said it's urgent or he wouldn't.'

'We'll have to think of things to do while he's away,' said Hester, pouring more juice.

'Thank you.' Lowri drank some of it, eyeing Hester over the glass. 'But won't you be too busy housekeeping?'

'No,' said Hester firmly. 'With Sam's help, it won't take long. The rest of the time I'll spend with you.'

Lowri gave her a very adult look. 'Will you tell me the truth?'

Help, thought Hester. 'I'll try. What do you want to know?'

'Are you really a housekeeper, and not some kind of nanny?'

'Hey, do I look like Mary Poppins?' Hester demanded, resorting to indignation to avoid a direct lie.

'No. But you don't look like a housekeeper either.' Lowri giggled, then sighed gustily. 'Anyway, Mary Poppins had two children to look after, and I'm only one. I'd just love to have a baby sister—even a baby brother would do.'

'Maybe that will happen one day.'

'I don't think so,' Lowri said forlornly, then brightened. 'But I've made lots of friends in school.'

'That's good. Your father says you really like it there.'

'I don't like all the lessons, but otherwise it's great. Some girls get homesick, but I don't.'

Because you don't have a mother, thought Hester with compassion. 'Right, I must get these things indoors. Would you carry the jug, please?'

Once the kitchen was tidy, Hester said it was time to unpack. Lowri made a face. 'The trunk will be a mess. I'm rubbish at packing.'

'Then let's attack it right away. You can tell me where to put everything.'

'I don't really know. I've only been here once, and that wasn't to sleep,' said Lowri. 'I usually go back to Grandma's for school holidays, but last half-term I went to stay with Chloe Martin. It was brilliant. She's got two brothers and a little sister and her mother's very nice.'

'Is her father nice too?' asked Hester as they went upstairs together.

'Oh, yes, but I didn't see him much. He's in the police. A deputy something.'

No wonder Lowri was allowed to stay there. 'Deputy Chief Constable?'

'That's right.' The child scowled at the trunk beside her bed. 'I just hate this part.' She looked guilty as Hester raised the lid. 'I've got some clean things in my backpack, but it's all got a bit jumbled in here.' She sighed. 'If you *were* Mary Poppins you could make everything fly into the drawers.'

'Since I'm not, you can hang the things up from your back-pack and I'll take this lot down to be washed. Your blazer and skirt must go to the dry cleaners.' Hester cast an assessing eye at the tall, slender child. 'But I think you need new ones. You've grown out of these.'

'*Yes!*' Lowri punched the air in triumph. 'How soon can we go shopping? I want new jeans, lots of tops, trainers, a miniskirt like Chloe's—'

'Hold on,' said Hester, laughing. 'I need a chat with your father first.'

Hester loaded the washing machine then suggested they take a stroll in Victoria Park, but, with Connah's instructions fresh in her mind, she asked Sam to drive them there.

'I'll wait here, Hester,' he said as he parked near the entrance gates. He took a paperback thriller from the glove compartment. 'I'm well prepared.'

'Are you sure about this, Sam?' asked Hester.

'If you mean is it OK with the boss, yes. Just press my button and I'll come after you at the double if you need me. Not,' he added, looking round the peaceful, sunlit park, 'that I think you will.'

'I don't either.' She smiled wryly. 'But I'd rather not break any rules on my first day.'

Hester's previous charges had all been toddlers with limited conversation and it was a refreshing change to listen to Lowri talk about her friends in school and the boy from the farm near her grandmother's home.

'I used to go there to buy eggs with Alice—she was my nanny when I was little. Owen's twelve, but he's only a bit taller than me,' she said with satisfaction. 'He's nice. He helps on the farm after school and his father pays him wages. I just get pocket money.' Lowri looked at Hester hopefully. 'I've got some left. I could treat you to an ice cream from the park café. May I?'

'I don't see why not. I'll have a vanilla cone, please.'

Lowri's long legs covered the short distance to the café at top speed.

'Thank you,' said Hester, accepting her ice cream. 'Do you want to walk or sit while we eat these?'

'Walk, please!' Lowri cast Hester a glance as she licked. 'Do you live here in the town?'

'When I'm not working in other people's houses, yes. I have a flat all to myself at my stepfather's home.'

'One of my friends has a stepfather and she doesn't like him.'

'How sad for her! I'm lucky. Robert's a darling. He had my flat redecorated just for me. If your father agrees,' Hester added, 'I could take you to see it one day, if you like.'

Lowri's eyes widened. 'Go to your house? *Could* I?'

'We'll ask your father this evening. If he gives permission, I'll get my mother to make cakes. She's a great cook.'

'I hope Daddy says yes,' said Lowri wistfully. 'I never go to other people's houses, except to play with Owen sometimes.'

'You stayed with your friend Chloe,' Hester reminded her.

'Only because Grandma was too ill to have me for half-term.'

As they strolled back to the car, Hester hoped she hadn't raised hopes that Connah Carey Jones would dash. But he'd not only met her mother, he had good reason to be grateful to her. His daughter would come to no harm in the Marshall household.

As soon as they got back, Hester provided Lowri with milk and biscuits, then took a tea tray up to the study.

Connah looked up at her in surprise. 'Hester! Sam could have done this.'

'I'm supposed to be the housekeeper,' she reminded him. 'Lowri chose the biscuits, so please eat one or two.'

He stared down at the plate, bemused. 'Oh. Right. Thank you.'

'If you can spare a few minutes, I'd like to talk to you later,' she informed him.

'Problems?' he said sharply.

'None at all, so far. But I need instructions. You're obviously busy right now, so perhaps you'll let me know when it's convenient.' She smiled politely and went from the room, closing the door behind her.

She found Lowri glued to a cooking programme on the kitchen television, and Sam got up to go, eyeing Hester with something like diffidence. 'I eat my dinner downstairs on my own in peace, by the way.'

'Then I'll make a plate up for you. Any dislikes?'

'You serve it, I'll eat it,' he assured her. 'Thanks, that would be great, Hester. Connah eats at seven when Lowri's with him, so I'll collect mine a few minutes beforehand, if that suits.'

'Of course. I'll ring down when it's ready.'

Lowri tore her eyes away from the television when he'd gone. 'This programme's making me hungry.'

'Then let's see what's on the menu for dinner,' said Hester and went off to the giant refrigerator to find that Sam had ordered every conceivable kind of food necessary to serve a cold supper.

'Can we have more of your chicken?' said Lowri eagerly.

'We certainly can. I'll lay the dining room table.'

'Can't we eat here?'

Hester shook her head. 'I'm sure your father would prefer the dining room.' At least she hoped he would, then, like Sam, she could relax with her own meal in peace.

'I'll ask him!' Lowri shot out of the room before Hester could stop her and went running from the kitchen to make for the study.

Hester thought about following her to apologise, then shrugged. If Connah disapproved he could tell her in private later. She collected some potatoes and had scraped several by the time Lowri came back, tongue between her teeth as she concentrated on the tray she was carrying.

'Daddy said he only uses the dining room for visitors, and would you please put supper in here for the three of us.'

So that was another question answered. 'Thank you, Lowri. And before we eat we must have a bath and change our clothes.' Sometimes one just had to be nanny. 'But first I'll finish these potatoes, then wash some salad greens and boil some eggs. I'll show you how to devil them, if you like.'

Lowri nodded eagerly. 'Chloe's mother let us help her in the kitchen and make scones and things, but Mrs Powell does Grandma's cooking and she hates mess, so I don't go in the kitchen much in Bryn Derwen.'

'We'll do some baking some time, if you like,' offered Hester. 'And if you make a mess, you clean it up. Deal?'

'Deal!' said Lowri, beaming.

Sam had departed, with grateful thanks for his appetising meal, and Hester was decanting buttered, herb-scattered potatoes into a serving dish when Connah came into the kitchen in jeans and open-necked shirt, his hair still damp from a shower. And looked so much more like the man who'd taken her breath ten years ago that Hester's pulse went into overdrive as the scent of warm, clean male skin stood every hormone she possessed to attention.

'You look nice, Daddy,' said Lowri, running to him.

'Thank you, *cariad*, so do you.' He gave her a hug, smiling at Hester over the shining dark head of his child. 'Good evening.' He cast an eye over the dishes on the table. 'Tempting display.'

Get a grip, she ordered herself fiercely. 'Thank you. Lowri helped prepare it.' She smiled as the child launched into the list of things she'd done for the meal, including laying the table and devilling the eggs.

'You mash the yolks with butter and pepper sauce, Daddy,' she informed him. 'They're yummy.'

'I'm sure they are. And such a splendid feast deserves some wine,' Connah told her. 'Would you fetch three wineglasses from the cupboard over there? You can have lemonade in yours, and Hester and I will drink some New Zealand white.'

She certainly knew exactly where she stood with Connah Carey Jones, thought Hester as they sat down to the meal. But thank God he had no idea that she'd ever carried a torch for him—and still did, heaven help her.

'Hester said I can do some baking with her some time,' said Lowri, as she helped herself to potatoes.

'Brave Hester,' her father said dryly.

'Oh, it's all right, Daddy,' Lowri assured him. 'If I make a mess, Hester said I just clear it up afterwards.'

Connah smiled across at Hester with respect. 'An excellent policy.'

Lowri chattered nineteen to the dozen while they ate, but even so Hester found it hard to relax in the company of her new employer, who might still have the same effect on her hormones, but was nevertheless very different from the man she'd romanticised in her teenage dreams. However courteous and polite he might be, these days there was a remote, untouchable quality about Connah Carey Jones that only warmed when he was interacting with his daughter. As a result, Hester ate sparingly and, though she enjoyed the intense fruit flavour of the wine, refused a second glass when Connah offered it, and could see he approved.

'Tomorrow I'll make a pudding,' she said, as she began clearing away their empty plates. 'But tonight it's a choice of fruit or cheese.'

'I think Lowri's full, for once in her life,' said Connah, 'and I'll forgo the cheese in favour of coffee.'

'Certainly. I'll bring a tray up to you.'

'Better still, I'll wait while you make the coffee, then take it up myself,' said Connah firmly.

Hester thanked him and switched on the coffee-maker, glad that it was a make she was familiar with, since she had an audience for the process.

'When the coffee's ready, Lowri, we'll leave Hester in peace for a while,' said Connah. 'How about a game of chess?'

She nodded fervently. 'Can you play chess, Hester?'

'I can, but sadly I'm out of practice.' She turned to smile at the child. 'You can bring me up to speed on a rainy day some time.'

'Incidentally, Hester,' said Connah, 'I like Lowri to be in bed by nine normally, but she can have an extension tonight. Put a glass of milk on the tray, then she'll be ready for bed when you come to fetch her.'

'Hester made me drink milk at teatime. Do I have to drink it again?' complained Lowri.

He ruffled her hair. 'Yes, you do.'

Hester heaved a sigh of relief when they'd gone, envying Sam his solitary dinner. It was a draining experience to spend time in Connah's company without betraying by the flicker of an eyelash how much it affected her. She glanced at the clock, found she had almost an hour's grace, and got to work. When the kitchen was tidy, Hester went up to her room to make repairs to her face, then sat down in the buttoned velvet armchair by the window to do absolutely nothing for a few minutes, well aware that at seventeen she would have been on cloud nine at the mere thought of living in the same house as the man of her dreams. Especially a house like this one. Neither of her previous jobs had provided her with such appealing private quarters.

Unlike Lowri's, which had pink flowers trailing down the wallpaper and a hammock suspended over the bed to house the soft toys she'd brought with her, Hester's room had cinnamon walls and carpet and white curtains and bedcover, all of it brand-new, including a writing desk and a combination television and DVD player. Everything was bound to be new, of course, if the house had only just been redecorated, or restored, or whatever. Doing up a listed house of this age had to be a huge undertaking. At the mere thought of the permits required, Hester yawned widely, wishing she could just crawl into the tempting brass bed. With a sigh, she got up, tucked her white shirt into her narrow black skirt, then went downstairs to knock on the study door.

Lowri opened it, smiling all over her face. 'I'm beating Daddy,' she said with triumph, pulling Hester over to the desk.

Connah looked up from the chessboard with a wry smile. 'You've snatched me from the jaws of defeat, Hester.'

'You haven't lost yet,' Lowri comforted him. 'We can go on with the game when you get back and maybe you'll win in the end.'

She obviously thought this so unlikely that Connah laughed. 'Off to bed with you, champ. Give me a kiss.'

Lowri threw her arms round his neck and he pulled her on to his knee to kiss her.

'Goodnight, Daddy.'

'Goodnight, *cariad*, sleep well.' He stood up and set her on her feet. 'I'll be off early in the morning, Hester, so if you need to speak to me, see Lowri settled then come back down.'

CHAPTER THREE

WHEN Hester went downstairs again Connah motioned her to one of the sofas facing each other across the fireplace.

'Did Lowri settle down happily?'

'Yes. She was tired enough to welcome going to bed.'

'It's been a long day for her,' agreed Connah and sat opposite, eyeing her closely. 'So, Hester, Lowri seems to have taken to you. Do you think you'll enjoy spending time with her?'

'I will, very much. She's a delightful child—remarkably adult in some ways, yet still a little girl in others.' Hester smiled. 'Up to now I've worked with under-fives, so it's quite a revelation to be with someone of Lowri's age. There was one sticky moment, though,' she added. 'She asked me point-blank if I was a nanny.'

He raised an eyebrow. 'And how did you answer?'

'To avoid the direct lie, I asked—very indignantly—if I looked like Mary Poppins.' Hester gave him a straight look. 'But if she brings it up again I prefer not to lie.'

'She probably won't. It's just that Alice—her former nanny—was never required to cook meals.' He paused. 'Thank you again for dinner. I normally eat out or have it sent in. But I don't expect you to cook for all of us on a regular basis.'

'I have no problem with that. I like cooking. I'm no cordon bleu chef, but my mother's a very good cook and taught me well. And Lowri likes helping in the kitchen so it's a good way of keeping her occupied.'

'And will do her in good stead when she has to fend for herself one day. Thank you, Hester. I'll adjust your salary, of course.' He eyed her expectantly. 'So what did you want to talk about?'

'First on the list, clothes. Before I take Lowri shopping, I need a clear idea of what you want—and don't want—for her.'

Connah looked taken aback. 'I thought you'd know more about that than me.'

Hester smiled. 'For starters, she wants jeans, tops and trainers and—I warn you—a miniskirt like Chloe's.'

He laughed. 'Then buy her one. She'll look cute in it.' He gave her an impersonal, assessing look. 'Judging by your taste in clothes, she's in good hands.'

Hester felt a warm sensation inside at his comment on her appearance. 'Thank you. The list is pretty extensive. When I unpacked her trunk I found that Lowri's outgrown practically everything, including her uniform.'

Connah got up to go over to the desk. 'I order that through the school. I'll give you the number and you can get on to that right away. They add it to the bill for fees.' He came back with a thick roll of notes. 'For shopping here in town I'd rather you used cash, Hester.'

'As you wish. I'll keep a list of what I spend.' She paused. 'Talking of clothes, I dressed soberly today, for obvious reasons. But for walks and picnics and so on I'd be more comfortable in something casual, if you're happy with that.'

'Wear what you like,' he said, surprised. 'In fact, the less you dress like a nanny the better.'

'Thank you.' She looked at him in appeal. 'Now I have a favour to ask. Could I have your permission to take Lowri home to see my mother one day? When I broached the subject, Lowri was very enthusiastic.'

For a moment Hester was sure that he was going to refuse point-blank. Then he smiled wearily. 'I must seem like an ogre to you, keeping my child shut away from the world.'

'I'm sure you have good reason.'

'I do. But Lowri would enjoy a visit to your home. I remember your mother very well.' His eyes softened. 'Is she up to entertaining a lively ten-year-old?'

'She'll just love it. So will Robert, my stepfather. You can check with Sam about him, if you like. They met when Robert insisted on delivering me here this morning.'

'I already have. Your family was cleared when John ran the security check on you.' Connah got up to cross to a drinks tray. 'Have a nightcap before you go up, Hester.'

'I won't, thank you.' She got up, battening down her resentment. 'I'll look in on Lowri, then take myself to bed.'

'In that case, I'll say goodnight.' He walked with her to the door. 'I won't see you in the morning, but if you need to speak to me at any time while I'm away, Sam will know where to find me.'

'Thank you. Goodnight.'

'Goodnight, Hester.'

She forced herself to walk slowly upstairs instead of running up to burn off some of her annoyance. Connah Carey Jones might be paying her well for her services but he was getting good value for every penny. She was an experienced, highly qualified nanny, who could also cook and keep house. And, as the icing on the cake, her family had unknowingly passed John Austin's security check with flying colours. It was the unknowing part that really hacked her off, no matter what her hormones felt about him.

Lowri was fast asleep. Hester drew the covers higher and went to her own room to ring her mother to report on her first day in the Carey Jones household. Moira was full of eager questions, which Hester answered in detail before mentioning the proposed visit with Lowri. This received such an enthusiastic response that Hester promised to bring the child round for tea as soon as possible.

'We've got some shopping to do first, Ma. Lowri needs clothes, and I must have a session at the supermarket.'

'Come on Wednesday afternoon, then. I'll bake.'

'I told Lowri you would!'

Hester woke next morning at six as usual, and got up to shower before Lowri surfaced. Leaving the sleeping child to the luxury of a lie-in, Hester went silently downstairs to the kitchen to make herself a cup of tea, and almost turned tail and went out again when she found Connah there before her, drinking coffee, dressed ready to leave and looking so much the embodiment of every dream she'd ever had that Hester was struck dumb for a moment.

'Good morning, Hester,' he said, surprised. 'You're an early riser.'

She pulled herself together, irritated by the effect he had on her. It was too much to cope with at this time of day. 'Good morning. Babies and toddlers wake early, so it's a habit I can't break. Lowri is still asleep, so I left her in peace for a while.'

He gave her one of his piercingly direct looks. 'Actually I'm pleased to have caught you before leaving. Last night I could tell that you were unhappy about having your family investigated, Hester, but where Lowri is concerned you must appreciate that I can't take risks.'

'And now you know that my stepfather is a recently retired headmaster and my mother the daughter of a clergyman, you'll be happy to leave Lowri in my care,' she said without inflection, and moved past him to fill the kettle.

'From your point of view, I was sure of that the moment I saw you with John at the Chesterton,' he said, surprising her.

She swung round in surprise. 'You were there when he interviewed me?'

'Beforehand, not during. I sat outside in the lounge behind a newspaper.' He shrugged. 'I was beginning to despair by the time you arrived. The other three might have been suitable carers for small babies, I suppose, but much too old to be a companion for Lowri.'

'So my age was your main reason for employing me?'

'It was part of it, yes.' He gave her a sudden disarming smile. 'But watching you talk to John as he saw you out, I knew Lowri would take to you. And, to be candid, I'm sure the others would have marched off in high dudgeon if asked to pose as my housekeeper.'

'But you thought I'd take it in my stride?'

'I think you take most things in your stride, Hester.'

She smiled a little. 'After years of looking after other people's children, I should have the knack by now.'

Connah smiled back as he put his empty cup in the sink. 'Am I forgiven for the security check?'

When he smiled like that she could forgive him anything. 'I expected one for myself as a matter of course. But no one's ever checked up on my family before.'

'Will you do me a great favour?' he asked, surprising her.

'If I can,' she said cautiously.

'I assume that your mother knows I'm the man who came knocking on her door in the snow all those years ago?'

'Of course. I rushed home to tell her after the first interview—' Hester halted. 'By the way, if you saw me at the Chesterton, may I ask why you interviewed me twice?'

'The first time was to make sure that my first impression was right, and you were exactly what I was looking for. But I had to wait for the security check before I could call you back to offer you the job.'

'I see.' She held the look steadily. 'So what favour do you need?'

'Have you told your family I had them investigated?'

'Certainly not.'

'Good. In that case, could you keep it to yourself? Your stepfather would probably just be furious, but your mother would be hurt. I don't want that any more than you do, Hester.'

'Then I won't tell her.' She glanced at the clock. 'Can I cook you some breakfast?'

'Coals of fire?' Connah smiled crookedly. 'It's a tempting thought, but no, thanks. I must be on my way. If you need to speak to me while I'm away, ring me.'

'I hope I won't.'

'I know you do,' he said, and left her to her tea.

'Good morning,' said Sam, coming into the kitchen a few minutes later. 'Did you see the boss before he left?'

'Yes, I did. Good morning, Sam.' She finished her tea. 'There's more in the pot if you want. I'd better check on Lowri. She was out for the count when I got up.'

Hester smiled wryly as she went up to Lowri. The job had an unexpected benefit. Three flights of stairs would do wonders for her personal fitness.

Lowri was still out for the count. Hester eyed the sleeping face for a moment, then scribbled a note to ask Lowri to come down for breakfast when she woke. With the radio for company, Hester had ironed half the contents of the trunk by the time the yawning child finally trailed into the kitchen in her dressing gown.

'Good morning,' said Hester, smiling. 'How about scrambled eggs?'

Lowri nodded sleepily. 'Yes, please.' She slid into a chair at the table, watching as Hester folded the ironing board. 'Has Daddy gone?'

'Yes, he left very early.'

'Do you know when he's coming back?'

'He didn't say.' Hester poured orange juice into Lowri's glass. 'But cheer up. He said yes to a visit to my mother and Robert.'

Lowri's face lit up like a Christmas tree. 'When? Today?'

'No, tomorrow for tea. Today we go shopping for clothes.

Then we have some lunch and shop for food. How's that for a programme?'

'At last!' said Lowri when Hester emerged from her own room later in a navy cotton shirt and white denim skirt. 'You look nice. Can I buzz Sam now and say we're ready to go?'

The morning was tiring but very entertaining. Let loose in a shopping mall packed with chain stores full of clothes that sent her into raptures, Lowri looked through every last bit of merchandise in each shop they went into, it seemed to Hester, before she made her final choices. But though Connah had handed over a generous sum of money, Hester firmly steered her charge past shops that sold expensive designer clothes.

'You'll be tired of them or have grown out of them, long before you get your money's worth,' she said practically. 'And with those long legs everything will look good on you, anyway. With shoes it's different, no economising there.'

'Trainers?' said Lowri hopefully.

'Of course. And something less sporty too.'

'Not school shoes!'

'No. At least not yet. We leave those until the end of the holiday.'

They loaded their packages on to a patient Sam, then made for a café to wait while he stowed everything in the car.

Not sure of the protocol, Hester was relieved to hear that Sam had always lunched with Lowri and Alice during shopping trips near Bryn Derwen.

'But Alice is married now, to Owen's father,' said Lowri as she downed her drink thirstily. 'Owen's mother died when he was little, and his grandma brought him up, just like me. But she's got arthritis now, so Mr Griffiths married Alice.'

'That's nice for Owen,' said Hester.

Lowri nodded sagely. 'Alice used to take me to the farm a lot, so Owen's known her for ages. He thinks she's cool. It's a very good arrangement, Grandma says.'

Not least for Mr Griffiths, thought Hester, and looked up with a smile as Sam came in to join them.

'Good,' said Lowri. 'Let's eat!'

When Hester finally got to bed that night she stretched out with a sigh of relief, confident that she'd made a reasonable start with Lowri. There'd been an awkward moment at suppertime when the child had wanted Sam to stay and eat his lasagna in the kitchen with them, but he'd refused, saying he liked to read the paper while he ate his dinner and, in any case, he couldn't leave the monitors that long.

'You leave them when you come out with us,' Lowri had pointed out mutinously, but he told her that was different and he had to get going or his dinner would be cold.

It was different, Hester could have told Lowri, because when he was out with them, Sam had Lowri under his watchful eye all the time. Here in the house, his job was to keep unwanted visitors away for the same reason. But Hester also had an idea that Sam refused to cross a line he saw as clearly defined. Connah thought a great deal of Sam Cooper, it was obvious, but the relationship on both sides was still very much employer and valued employee. And, since Connah had elected to dine in the kitchen when he was at home, it would have been awkward if Lowri had expected Sam to join them.

We'd have made an ill-assorted quartet, thought Hester wryly. In her former job, the question of eating with her employers had never arisen. They were both successful actors with working hours that varied according to the film or television series they were involved in. It was Hester who'd made the children's supper. The three-year-old Herrick twins, Sebastian and Viola, were engaging children Hester had been very fond of. But when their parents won lead roles in an American television series, nothing they could say would persuade Hester to accompany the family to Los Angeles.

Hester sighed as she stared through the window at the stars. After a job in a theatrical household, her next post would be very different. George Rutherford, her new employer, owned a very successful haulage firm. His wife Sarah was still helping him run it, seven months into her first pregnancy at the age of forty-one, and had every intention of going back to work after the birth, leaving Hester very literally holding the baby.

But, before all that, Hester reminded herself, she had six weeks in Connah Carey Jones's home, which was not only a dream come true on one level, but a very pleasant way of earning some money before she moved on to pastures new. One of the downsides to her job was parting with her charges when the time came. She sighed in the darkness. She'd known Lowri for only a very short time, but she already knew that it would be no easier to part with her after six weeks than it had been with the other children after several years. And this time there would also be the painful wrench of parting with Lowri's father.

CHAPTER FOUR

HESTER'S phone jolted her awake next morning.

'Connah here. Good morning.'

Heart thumping for various reasons, not least the sound of his voice, she took a deep breath. 'Hello. Is something wrong?'

'A bad case of guilt. I had a totally manic day yesterday. By the time I had a moment free, it was too late to ring either Lowri or you. Was she upset?'

'If she was she didn't say so. She had a wonderful day. After the shopping spree, she was quite sleepy after supper and settled down in bed shortly after nine. Shall I get her for you now?'

'No, don't wake her. When she gets up, tell her I apologise. Was the shopping trip a success?'

'Very much so. Brace yourself for an itemised—and very long—list of her new clothes when you see her. I'm taking her to tea with my mother this afternoon, by the way.'

'I only wish I could gatecrash the party. Please give your mother my regards.'

'I will. Goodbye.'

Hester snapped her phone shut and slid out of bed to make for the bathroom. Half an hour later she looked in on a deeply sleeping Lowri and went down to the kitchen to enjoy a peaceful—and very early—breakfast. It had been a mistake to tell Connah she was an early riser. If it hadn't been for his phone call, she could have stayed in bed a little longer for once. And, more importantly, without the fright of thinking something was wrong at home.

After a late breakfast Lowri spent a happy hour sending texts to friends on her treasured phone, while Hester saw to the minimal duties necessary to preserve the fiction that she was a housekeeper before she took her charge off to the park for some exercise.

Lowri was all for it, provided she could wear her new combat trousers. 'Perfect for a run,' she announced, doing a twirl for Sam in the kitchen.

This time, rather to Hester's surprise, Sam elected to accompany them into the park. 'I like a run myself now and then,' he announced.

Lowri eyed him doubtfully. 'I run fast,' she warned.

'Run a bit slower today then, so Sam can keep up,' said Hester, giving him a sly grin.

When they got back to the house later, Sam went down to his own quarters to make himself some lunch and Hester and Lowri ate alone.

'Just one sandwich,' said Hester. 'We must leave room for my mother's tea.'

'It must be lovely having a mother,' sighed Lowri. 'Or even a stepmother like Alice. Owen's so lucky.'

'Did you see them over the weekend?'

'Yes. Daddy took me down to the farm to get eggs, and we all had tea and fruitcake. Alice baked it. She asked Owen's grandma for the recipe.'

Good move, Alice, approved Hester.

Lowri was ready well before time to leave in a new denim miniskirt and pink T-shirt to match her new pink and white trainers.

'How do I look?' she asked Sam.

'Very grown-up!'

She smiled ecstatically. 'I can't wait to show Chloe my new things.'

Lowri's excitement visibly mounted as Hester gave Sam directions on the journey. When they reached the house Robert was waiting at the gate. He opened the rear door of the car and gave the passengers his gentle, irresistible smile.

'Hello. I'm Robert and you must be Lowri. Welcome.' He held out his hand to help her out and Lowri smiled back at him shyly.

'Hello. It's very nice of you to ask me to your house.'

Well done, thought Hester, and gave her stepfather a hug. 'Hi, Robert. You've met Sam, of course.'

Sam shook hands, then asked Hester what time he should return to fetch them, but Robert shook his head.

'We insist you stay to tea, Sam. My wife has spent most of the day baking.'

Hester grinned. 'And she'll be mortally offended if you don't stay to eat some of it.'

Moira waved from the open doorway as they climbed the steep path to the house. She hugged her daughter, then turned to Lowri with a warm smile and held out her arms. 'Could I possibly have a hug from you too, darling?'

Lowri was only too happy to be hugged. Then she remembered her manners and introduced Sam, and Moira led the way through the house into the back garden, where tea was laid under a large umbrella on a table surrounded by a selection of odd garden chairs.

'What a lovely garden,' said Lowri rapturously. 'We've just got a sort of patio in the townhouse.'

'This must be hard work,' commented Sam with respect, and Robert nodded.

'But I enjoy gardening, and so, thank God, does my wife.'

'That's why he married me,' said Moira, exchanging a sparkling look with her husband. 'Now we'll leave you men to set the world to rights while we do the tea. Will you help me carry the food out, Lowri?'

'Yes, *please*!' She went into the house with Moira, chattering about devilled eggs and the baking she was going to do with Hester.

'That's one very happy little girl,' said Sam, watching, and Robert nodded, his eyes fond as they followed his wife.

'Moira has the knack of making people happy. I'm a fortunate man.'

How fortunate was soon demonstrated by the quantity of cakes and savoury delicacies covering the table.

'If you eat like this, how do you stay so fit, sir?' asked Sam, awed.

'A steep garden on several different levels takes care of that,' Robert assured him wryly. 'Besides, this is a special occasion, not everyday fare.'

The tea party was a great success. And since the adults took pains to include Lowri in the general conversation, her delight in the occasion was a pleasure to see.

'And now,' said Hester later, when they'd helped Moira clear away, 'I'll take you to see my own private lair, Lowri, but be careful on the steps.'

Lowri followed Hester up the open-tread iron staircase eagerly, her eyes round as they entered the flat. 'This is so *cool*! Is it just this one big room?'

'More or less. There's a small bathroom through that door at the end.'

'It's perfect,' sighed Lowri rapturously. 'I'd love a place of my own like this one day. Could I bring Daddy to see it?'

'Do you think he'd want to?' said Hester doubtfully, not sure she wanted Connah's overpoweringly male presence invading her private space.

'I want him to see what I'd like.'

'Time we went back to the others,' said Hester firmly. 'Careful on the stairs!'

It was late that evening before Lowri said her goodbyes and

thanked her hosts very prettily for having her. 'I've had such a lovely time.'

'So have we. You must come again soon, darling,' said Moira, and handed Lowri a large box. 'I've put a few cakes in there for your tea tomorrow.'

'Oh, *thank* you!' Lowri reached up spontaneously and kissed Moira's cheek, at which point Robert demanded a kiss too.

'Right then, folks,' said Hester. 'I'll give you a ring later in the week. Thank you for this.'

'My thanks also,' said Sam. 'It was an unexpected treat, and much appreciated.'

When they were in the car on the way back into town, Lowri heaved a great sigh. 'What a darling house. It must be so lovely to live there, Hester.'

'It is, but actually I'm not there very much. In my kind of job I live in the house where I'm—employed. I don't get home here nearly as often as I'd like.'

'You must get very homesick.'

'I miss my mother, certainly.'

To Hester's dismay, tears suddenly slid down Lowri's flushed cheeks. 'If I had a mummy like yours I would too,' she said, so forlornly that Hester put an arm round the child and held her close in wordless comfort all the way home.

It was so late by the time they arrived that Lowri was only too happy to go straight to bed. She fell asleep so quickly that Hester turned off the DVD player, left a night light on and went down to the kitchen. If Connah wanted to talk to his daughter tonight he was out of luck. But, as she sat down at the table with the daily paper and a mug of tea, it dawned on Hester that, unlike Lowri, a sandwich and one of her mother's cakes had been her entire food intake for the day.

Hester toasted two slices of sourdough bread, spread them

with butter and marmalade and sat down to enjoy her snack while she caught up on the day's news. She was making a second pot of tea later when she heard footsteps on the stone stairs leading up from the basement and turned with a smile, expecting Sam. Her heart gave a deafening thump when Connah strolled into the kitchen instead, smudges of fatigue under eyes which lit with such involuntary pleasure at the sight of her that Hester sat, transfixed.

'Hello,' she said at last, breaking the spell.

'Good evening, Hester,' he said, clearing his throat, and dumped down his briefcase. 'Sam thought you'd gone to bed.'

'Not yet. Though Lowri's asleep,' she said, getting a grip. She gestured towards the teapot. 'I've just made a fresh pot. Would you like some tea?'

He slung his jacket on the back of a chair and sat down at the table. 'I had my sights set on a shot or two of whisky, but now you've mentioned it I think maybe I would like some tea. First, anyway.'

'I didn't realise you were coming back today,' said Hester, shaken by her delight at his unexpected appearance.

Connah raked a weary hand through his hair. 'When I spoke to you this morning it wasn't on the agenda. But things went better than I expected, so I thought why the hell am I going back to a lonely flat tonight when I can be home with my daughter in a couple of hours?' He smiled. 'Of course Lowri's asleep now, but at least I'll be with her first thing in the morning.'

'She'll be thrilled. Have you had dinner? I could cook you something.'

'I had a cholesterol-heavy lunch, so thanks for the kind thought but I won't trouble you to cook tonight, Hester.' He eyed her expectantly. 'Maybe you could rustle up a biscuit or two?'

'Of course.' She opened the box containing her mother's cakes. 'Or perhaps you'd like one or two of these.' She put a selection on a plate and put it in front of him. 'My mother sent them home with Lowri.'

Connah bit into an almond tart with enthusiasm. 'Delicious,' he said indistinctly. 'So how did the tea party go?'

'Huge success.' Hester smiled. 'But I'll let Lowri tell you all about it tomorrow. I had a job to tear her away—it was late when we left.'

'I hope your mother wasn't too exhausted!'

'She enjoyed it enormously, so did Robert. Sam, too, by the way,' she added. 'He was all for depositing us there and collecting us later, but my parents wouldn't hear of it.'

'Knowing your mother even as little as I do, I can well believe that.' He shrugged. 'I suppose I should have made things clearer for you from the start where Sam is concerned, Hester, but his role in the household is somewhat hard to define.'

'It's not a problem because Sam himself is totally clear about it. So he joined us for lunch on the shopping trip, and for tea today, but dines alone—in peace as he puts it—in his own quarters.' Hester looked at him levelly. 'I was quite prepared to do the same, until you instructed otherwise.'

He stared. 'It's utterly pointless for you to eat alone in here, while Lowri and I dine in solitary splendour in the dining room— which is the only room in the house I dislike, by the way. You might take a look at it tomorrow and tell me where I went wrong.'

Not sure she would dare to do that, Hester sat down with her own tea. 'Did you use an interior designer?'

'Originally, yes, but the woman had ideas so bizarrely different from mine we soon parted company. The study, the dining room and the master suite are down to me. Your room too,' he added, 'which is why it's a touch stark.'

'Not to me. It's exactly to my taste.'

'Good. By the way, did you apologise to Lowri for me?'

'Yes, but I didn't say you'd ring in case something prevented that.' She eyed him thoughtfully. 'She was a bit blue on the way home tonight.'

He frowned. 'Why?'

'Seeing me with my mother emphasized the lack of one herself.' In for a penny, in for a pound, thought Hester. 'She would like a baby sister. Even a baby brother would do.'

Connah stared, thunderstruck. 'She told you that?'

'Oh, yes. She's madly envious of her friend Owen because he's acquired a stepmother.' Hester's lips twitched. 'Be warned. She'd like one of those too.'

'Good God!' He held out his cup for more tea, looking poleaxed. 'She's never said a word to me.'

'It's woman to woman stuff. Please don't let on that I told you.'

'I won't, but I'm glad you warned me. I try to give her most things she wants, but in this case she'll just have to deal with disappointment.'

Influenced by the intimacy of the situation and the lateness of the hour, Hester found herself asking a question so personal she regretted it the moment it was out of her mouth. 'You have no plans to marry again?'

She held her breath, certain that Connah would tell her it was nothing to do with the woman he was employing to look after his daughter, but, to her immense relief, he merely shook his head.

'Not even for Lowri will I marry just to provide her with a stepmother, Hester. She'll have to find something else to wish for.' His mouth turned down. 'But at the weekend my mother informed me that Alice is expecting a baby, so in view of what you've just told me I suppose I can expect fireworks from Lowri when she hears that piece of news. Apparently Owen doesn't know yet, but I doubt that a boy of his age will be thrilled.'

'He might be if Lowri envies him.'

'True.' Connah eyed the empty plate in surprise. 'I seem to have eaten all the cakes.'

'There's plenty more in the box. Are you sure you wouldn't like me to cook you something?'

He shook his head and got up with gratifying reluctance. 'I'd better take myself off to the study for some of that whisky I mentioned.' He gave her the smile that had bowled her over when she was seventeen and was doing pretty much the same right now, all the more potent because it was the first time she'd witnessed it at full power since then. 'You must be desperate to get to bed. Tomorrow I'll get something sent in for once to give you the evening off. And I'll put Lowri to bed myself,' he added, collecting his briefcase. 'Don't mention that I'm home when she wakes in the morning. I want to surprise her.'

'Of course. Goodnight.'

Hester cleared away, then went straight upstairs to check on Lowri. Later, armed with a paperback thriller her mother had given her, she settled down in bed in a glow of well-being which soon faded when she traced it not only to Connah's return but because he'd seemed as pleased to see her as she was to see him. She sighed. This was something to be nipped in the bud right now. He was a very different man from the mysterious Mr Jones who'd set her teenage pulse fluttering. But, although he still had much the same effect on her ten years on, no way was she getting involved again with someone related to a child in her care.

Lowri was utterly delighted when Connah walked into the kitchen during breakfast next morning.

'Daddy! I didn't know you were home,' she cried, jumping up to hug him.

'I came late last night and asked Hester not to tell you so I could give you a surprise,' he said, taking her on his knee. He kissed her and smiled down into the sparkling eyes. 'You're getting so big I won't be able to do this much longer. I won't have room on my lap.'

She beamed up at him. 'Did Hester tell you what a great time I had at her house yesterday?'

'Not yet; she said you'd want to tell me yourself.'

'Before Lowri starts on her saga,' said Hester quickly, 'what would you like for breakfast?'

Connah smiled at her warmly. 'Oh, just toast and coffee, please.'

While Lowri launched into her account of the tea party, Hester made a pot of coffee, poured orange juice, filled a silver rack with wholemeal toast and put it all on the tray she'd laid ready for the breakfast Sam had told her Connah ate in the study while he caught up with world news and the state of the stock market. Hester took the tray upstairs and left it on the desk, but Connah frowned as he came into the room with Lowri. 'I could have brought that up myself, but thank you, Hester.'

'Not at all. It's my job. Lowri can tell me when you've finished.'

'I was just telling Daddy about your flat, Hester,' said the child eagerly. 'I can't wait for him to see it.'

'We can't intrude on Hester's home, *cariad*,' Connah told her, and gave Hester a questioning look.

'You're welcome to any time,' she said casually. 'Not that there's much to see.' She left father and daughter together and went back to the kitchen to make herself a cup of coffee she could drink in peace on her own. She wondered why Connah had objected when she's taken his breakfast up to the study. After all, it was what housekeepers did. Or would he have preferred Sam to do it, as presumably he'd done before she arrived on the scene? If the appropriate moment presented itself, she would ask to save further embarrassment. It presented itself sooner than expected when Lowri came to tell her that her father had finished his breakfast.

'He wouldn't let me bring the tray down myself,' she said crossly.

'Only because he didn't want you to slip on those stone stairs and hurt yourself,' said Hester briskly. 'Now, you think about what you'd like to do today while I fetch it.'

Connah turned from his computer screen as Hester knocked on the study door. 'Come in. Sit down.'

She took the chair in front of the desk and looked at him warily.

'Lowri may be unaware of your true role in this house, but I am not,' said Connah bluntly. 'Which means I don't expect you to fetch and carry for *me*, Hester.'

'You obviously prefer Sam to do it.'

He frowned. 'I wouldn't put it that way exactly; I just think he should. You were engaged to look after Lowri, not wait on me. The fact that you also cook for us is more than enough.'

'As you wish,' she said, feeling rebuffed, and got up. 'But I'll take the tray since I'm here.'

All through the day, while she was making lunch and walking with Lowri in the park, Hester found herself wondering why Connah's edict had annoyed her. Any Norland-trained nanny worth her salt should have been glad that he refused to have her wait on him. But she felt hurt that he didn't want her in and out of his study on a regular basis. The rapport of the night before had obviously been a figment of her imagination.

'What's the matter, Hester?' asked Lowri, eyeing her anxiously.

'Nothing, why?'

'You were frowning.'

'The sun's strong today.'

'I know. I'm hot! Can I buy us some ice creams again, please?'

'Of course.' Hester fished in her purse for change. 'Only this time let's sit down to eat them.'

'OK.' Lowri ran off to the café, but before Hester could find an empty bench she spotted a man speaking to Lowri and raced towards them, pressing the button on her phone for Sam as she went, by which time Lowri was in possession of two ice cream cones and the man was nowhere to be seen.

'Who was that man, Lowri?' gasped Hester, her heart in her throat.

'I don't know. He wanted to buy me an ice cream.' Lowri grinned at Hester's look of outrage as she handed one to her. 'Don't worry, I said no, thank you—very politely—and he went away. It's all right,' she added soothingly, 'that kind of thing's hammered into us in school.'

'What kind of thing?' demanded Hester.

'Never to talk to strangers, and never, ever, let them sell you anything or buy anything for you.'

'So you know the drill. Good,' said Hester, fighting for calm. 'What did the man say?'

'He asked if you were my mother—wow, Sam's in a hurry,' Lowri added as he sprinted to join them.

'What's up?' he demanded, and Hester explained while Lowri demolished her ice cream.

'Before we go back to the car,' said Sam, his eyes hard, 'how about we take a walk through the park, Lowri? If you see the man, point him out to us.'

She shrugged. 'I didn't take much notice of him, Sam. But he had smart clothes. He was rather nice.'

'What's the matter?' Hester asked, as Lowri sighed heavily.

'I suppose you'll stick to me like glue from now on.'

'You'd better believe it!'

The child's mouth drooped. 'If you tell Daddy, you won't have to—he won't even let me come in the park any more.'

Or sack the nanny on the spot.

But Connah was surprisingly calm when Hester reported the incident the minute they got home. 'Did you know the man?'

'No.'

'Would you know him again?'

'I doubt it. I took one look, and ran to break it up. But he'd disappeared by the time I reached them. I do apologise. I'll know better another time.' Hester looked at him squarely. 'If there's to be another time. For me, I mean.'

'Of course there will,' he said, surprised. 'My daughter's become attached to you so quickly there'd be hell to pay if I tried to replace you.'

'And I to her,' Hester assured him. 'In the circumstances, perhaps Sam could take us further afield for our walk tomorrow.'

'Good idea. Take a picnic lunch.' Connah's eyes softened slightly. 'Relax, Hester. There was no actual harm done.'

She sighed. 'I suppose not. But in future I'll be doubly vigilant.'

Connah Carey Jones took so long to get his daughter to bed that night, he felt respect for Hester and for Alice before her, who, like his mother, managed the process so effortlessly. When it became obvious that Lowri was drawing it out to see how far she could go before he lost patience, he kissed her one last time and told her to go to sleep, or else.

'Or else what, Daddy?' she said, smiling at him.

'Try it and find out,' he growled, and Lowri, knowing she'd pushed the envelope far enough, blew him a kiss and settled down.

Connah smiled to himself as he closed the door. Lowri was growing up fast. The thought gave him a sharp pang as he went downstairs. All too soon she would be a teenager, with all the problems that entailed. Problems he would have to deal with single-handed.

As he passed the lower landing window, he caught sight of Hester's graceful, athletic figure coming into view and stood still, watching her walk towards the house, suddenly aware of how empty it had felt without her for a few hours. He raised a sardonic eyebrow. Empty, with Lowri and Sam in residence? Lacking, then, rather than empty. After only a matter of days, Miss Hester Ward had become a vitally necessary part of life in Albany Square. To him, he admitted, as well as to Lowri. Which was preposterous in such a short time. But a fact, just the same. He wanted more of Hester's company than just at mealtimes with Lowri, or a few minutes when the child was in bed. With sudden decision he thought of the ideal way to achieve it, then his eyes narrowed as he saw Hester pause at the foot of the steps to speak to a man who'd been following her along the pavement. Connah craned his neck, but the man was just out of view. After a moment or two Hester ran up the steps to ring the bell and he hurried downstairs to intercept her as she made for the kitchen.

'You're home early,' he commented.

She smiled at him. 'There's a film on television I missed at the cinema, so I left after supper to walk back in good time. Robert wanted to drive me, but I felt like the exercise—always a good move after one of my mother's little suppers.'

'I saw you from the landing window,' Connah informed her.

'You were watching for me?' The dark blue eyes frosted over. 'Am I late?'

'Of course not. I happened to be passing the landing window when I noticed a man following you. Was he someone you know?'

'No. Just someone asking directions to Chester Gardens,' she said coolly, and went past him into the kitchen.

'If you're making coffee, I'd like some too,' he said, feeling wrong-footed as he made the request. She was in his employ, dammit. He had the right to ask her to make him a cup of coffee. His jaw set as she promptly laid a tray with a solitary cup and saucer. 'I want your company while you drink it,' he informed her crisply.

Hester looked at him for a long moment, then nodded. 'Very well.'

'Put another cup on the tray and come up to the study with me. Please. I want to talk something over with you.'

Connah took the tray from Hester and waved her ahead of him up the stairs.

'Is it something about Lowri?' she asked, then regretted it. What else could it possibly be?

'Actually, it's about Sam. Sit down, Hester.' Connah put the tray down and sat on the sofa opposite to watch her pour. 'He's long overdue for a holiday. If he knew Lowri was safe with me, Sam might agree to take a few days off.'

Her face cleared. 'In which case, I could make sure she didn't disturb you when you were working, if that's your problem.'

'It's not.' Connah gave her a searching look. 'Hester, had you ever seen the man before?'

'Which man?'

'The one asking directions just now.'

She tensed as she saw where this was leading. 'You think it might have been the man in the park?'

'Do you?'

Hester gave it some thought. 'I honestly don't know. I only saw him fleetingly. He was gone by the time I reached Lowri.'

'Describe the man tonight.'

'Tallish, slim, well-dressed, about your age, maybe—' She put her coffee down untouched. 'He *could* have been the same man, but I can't swear to it.'

'You probably think I'm paranoid on this subject, but I dislike coincidences.' Connah drained his cup and sat back. 'Let's go back to Sam's time off.'

Hester shook her head. 'If Sam feels the same about coincidences, he'll refuse point-blank to take any.'

'I know, so I won't bring it up.' Connah gave her a very direct look as he played his trump card. 'But if you and I take Lowri on holiday, Hester, we'll be well away from this mystery man, whoever he is, and Sam could enjoy some R and R with no worries. Lowri would be delighted,' he added. And her father could spend a great deal more time in Hester's company than was feasible in Albany Square.

She returned the look steadily, wondering if he realised how much the idea appealed. 'Do you normally take Lowri away during her summer vacation?'

'Yes. My mother comes with us.'

'But I was a complete stranger until a few days ago,' she pointed out, playing devil's advocate. 'Are you sure you want me along? Wouldn't you prefer to be on your own with Lowri?'

Connah shook his head. 'Lowri wouldn't go unless you came too, Hester. You were the main topic of conversation tonight.'

'How boring for you,' she said lightly. 'More coffee?'

'Thank you.' Connah sat back with his refilled cup, his eyes on Hester's face. 'So will you come?'

Of course she would. Anywhere. 'Do you have somewhere in mind?'

'Italy. A friend of mine owns a villa in Chianti country in Tuscany. I'll have a chat with him and hope by some miracle that the house is free for a couple of weeks. It's a picturesque place, with terraced gardens and a pool with a view. Lowri would love it.'

Me too, thought Hester. After the South of France fiasco, a holiday in Tuscany with Connah and Lowri was the stuff of dreams. 'It sounds idyllic.'

'Then you agree,' Connah said with satisfaction. 'You own a current passport?'

'Of course. Does Lowri know about this?'

He shook his head. 'I consulted you first. No point in getting her hopes up if you refused to come.'

As if! 'You engaged me to work for you for six weeks,' said Hester, smiling, 'but you didn't specify where, so I have no right to refuse—even if I wanted to, which I don't. Thank you. I'd love to come.'

'Good. That's settled, then. I'll talk to Jay.' Connah got up and went over to the drinks tray. 'How about a nightcap first?'

Hester got up quickly. 'I won't, thanks.'

He swung round to face her. 'Of course, I forgot. You rushed back to see a film.'

'Yes,' she agreed. 'I can still catch most of it.'

Connah walked to the door and opened it for her. 'Goodnight, Hester. Not a word to Lowri in the morning about the holiday, in case it doesn't come off. And if it does I'd like to break the glad news to her myself.'

'Of course. Goodnight.' Hester went slowly up to her room, wishing she could have stayed talking to Connah for a while. But she was attracted to him so strongly it was getting harder and harder to hide the fact from him. And because he also paid her salary it was necessary to keep to a strictly professional level of employer and employee between them. Not that Connah had the least idea that she thought of their relationship in any other light. And resisting the temptation of a tête-à-tête with him at this time of the night had been one way of making sure he kept thinking that way.

CHAPTER FIVE

LOWRI was so enraptured with the idea of a holiday which included Hester, she talked non-stop over the breakfast her father shared with her at the kitchen table for once to tell her that his friend, Jay Anderson, was happy for them to stay at his villa in Tuscany, not just for a fortnight but for a whole month.

Four whole weeks, thought Hester.

'Can Hester take me shopping again before we go, Daddy?' Lowri demanded, after a pause to draw breath.

He smiled and ruffled her hair. 'You didn't buy enough clothes last time?'

'Hester didn't buy me a new swimming costume!'

'How remiss of you, Hester,' said Connah dryly. 'In that case, you two can raid the shops again today with Sam while I take a trip to Bryn Derwen to tell my mother what's happening.'

Lowri looked worried. 'Shouldn't I go too?'

'Not this time. We'll visit her when we get back.'

'Hester too, so I can take her to see Alice and Owen.'

Connah ruffled his daughter's hair. 'After a holiday chasing after you in Tuscany. Hester will be glad of a break. Besides,' he added, 'she'll want to visit her own mother as soon as she gets back from Italy.'

Which could mean that he didn't want her to visit his, thought

Hester, trying not to feel hurt. 'Then when you get back from Grandma's, Lowri,' she said briskly, 'we'll be busy getting you ready for school before I leave.'

Lowri's face fell. 'Then I suppose you'll be someone else's housekeeper.'

Hester avoided Connah's eyes. 'I have another job to go to, yes.'

'Where is your next post, Hester?' asked Connah.

'Yorkshire.'

Lowri's mouth drooped. 'Is that too far to come home on your day off?'

'I'm afraid so,' said Hester with regret.

Lowri brightened. 'But when you come home to see your mother and Robert, couldn't you do it at half-term? Then you could see me too.'

'You'll be spending next half-term with your grandma,' Hester reminded her.

'True,' said Connah, and got up. 'But you're welcome to visit Lowri there any time you fancy a trip into Wales during the school holiday, Hester.'

She thanked him politely, sure that this was merely a courtesy to soothe his disconsolate daughter. 'I'll just clear away, then we'll get ready to go shopping, Lowri.'

'And I,' said Connah, pulling his daughter to her feet to hug her, 'must be off on my travels to get to Bryn Derwen in time for lunch.'

'Are you coming home again today?' demanded Lowri.

'Yes,' he assured her, 'but not before your bedtime. If you're asleep, I'll see you in the morning. Now, give me a kiss, then you run upstairs and tidy your room while Hester finishes down here.'

'OK. Give Grandma a big kiss for me.'

When the child had gone, Connah gave Hester a wry smile. 'She's grown very attached to you.'

'It's mutual,' admitted Hester, shutting the dishwasher. 'This is the hardest part of my job. It's so painful to say goodbye to the children I care for.'

He watched her in silence for a while as she moved round the room, putting things away. 'Have you never thought of having children of your own?' he asked at last.

She shot him a startled look. 'Of course, but only in the abstract.'

His eyes glinted. 'By which I take it you've never met someone you consider suitable to father these children?'

Hester's chin tilted. 'That's a very cold way to look at it.'

'Ah! You mean you'd have to be in love with the prospective father first.'

'He would have to be someone I cared for, certainly,' she said stiffly. 'And vice versa. It makes for security for the child. You should understand that. You're a very loving father.'

He sobered. 'The loving part is easy, but I have to function as both parents to Lowri, which is difficult sometimes. So tell me, Hester, do I shape up to the other fathers you've met in your line of work?'

'Admirably.' Hester gave the counters an unnecessary sponge-down. Something about Connah in his present mood was unsettling.

'You've never asked me about Lowri's mother.' Connah's eyes took on an absent look, as though he was gazing far back into the past. 'When she died I felt as though half of me had died with her and I never want to feel that way again.'

Hester stared at him, aghast, shocked that he should tell her something so intensely private.

He looked at his watch, suddenly very much back in the present. 'I'm late. I'll call in on Sam on the way down to the garage and tell him to shape up for another shopping session with Lowri. He has the Bryn Derwen number if you need to contact me.'

Why couldn't she be trusted with the number herself? Hester smiled politely. 'Have a good trip. I hope you find your mother better.'

'Thank you. By the way, since this holiday is entirely my idea, please use some of the money I gave you for yourself.'

She shook her head. 'That's very kind of you, but I already have everything I need.'

'What an independent soul you are, Hester.' He gave her a mocking smile. 'See you tonight.'

Hester went upstairs to Lowri after Connah had gone, her mind still reeling—not only from shock about the revelation itself, but the fact that he'd confided something so personal to her. She wished he hadn't. The unexpected glimpse into Connah Carey Jones's private life left her with severe qualms about their next encounter.

Lowri's mood improved enormously once they were back at the shopping mall, though she was disappointed when Hester refused to buy a new swimsuit.

'I don't need one, Lowri. Honestly. Let's concentrate on you.'

'And this time,' said Sam firmly, 'I come in every last shop with you.'

'I hope you can keep up, then,' said Lowri, giving him a cheeky grin.

After a couple of hours of intensive shopping Sam took charge of the bags Lowri and Hester loaded on to him but, instead of taking them up to the car park, stayed with them when they went to look for lunch.

'Daddy told you to stick to us every minute, I suppose,' sighed Lowri, as she studied a menu in the café they chose.

'That's right,' agreed Sam cheerfully. 'Now, what shall we eat?'

'I'll order a salad, then pop into the pharmacy over there while you choose yours,' said Hester. 'I forgot to buy more sunblock.'

'We'll stay put then, Lowri,' said Sam, and gave Hester a straight look. 'Don't be long.'

Leaving her companions wrangling about their choices, Hester walked swiftly across the mall to make her purchases.

When she hurried from the shop afterwards she collided with a man who apologised profusely as he picked up the packages she'd dropped.

'Did I hurt you?' he demanded.

'Not in the least,' she said firmly, taking her parcels.

'Let me buy you a cup of coffee to make amends.'

'No, thank you. I have someone waiting for me.'

'Of course you have,' he said with regret and, when she pointedly waited for him to go, he gave her a wry little salute and walked away.

Hester gazed after him with narrowed eyes. She wished she could have taken him up on his offer so Sam could vet him. Because she was pretty sure he was the man who'd asked for directions in Albany Square, and therefore possibly the man in the park as well. But she couldn't risk letting him anywhere near Lowri. She hurried back to the café to find Sam and Lowri making inroads into their lunch.

'A good thing you ordered a salad,' said Sam. 'We wondered where you were.'

'Sorry, folks. The shop was busy. Is your pizza good, Miss Jones?'

Lowri nodded with enthusiasm. 'It's yummy! Sam said it was all right to start or it would get cold.'

'Of course. I'm ready for mine too.'

When they got back to the house, Hester sent Lowri up to her room with some of the bags and told Sam about the incident, which was assuming alarming proportions in retrospect.

'I thought something was up when you took so long,' he said grimly. 'You'd recognise him again, then?'

'Yes.' Hester frowned. 'Odd thing—there's something familiar about him.'

'Bound to be if you saw him last night.'

'No. Other than that. Yet I'm sure I've never met him before.'

'Could he be the guy in the park?'

'Possibly. But I wouldn't swear to it.' She grimaced. 'Shall I tell Connah or will you?'

'Your shout, Hester. You actually saw him, so you can give him a proper description.'

'Or the entire thing could be a coincidence.'

Sam looked her in the eye. 'I don't believe in coincidences.'

'Neither does Connah,' she said glumly, and picked up the rest of the shopping. 'You'll be glad when we're safely on our way. Are you going somewhere exciting?'

Sam laughed. 'My mother used to say that her idea of a holiday was for my dad and me to go away and leave her in peace for a week, and now I see what she means. So when you three go I'll stay put, Hester, to make sure nothing goes amiss with this place. I'll have a nice little holiday with nothing to do but answer the door, keep my phone charged and take down any messages. A few DVDs, a good book or two and a list of numbers to phone for whatever cuisine takes my fancy—what more can a man ask?'

'Company?'

'The occasional pint down the pub will take care of that.' He patted her hand. 'You enjoy yourself in Italy with Lowri and the boss. I'll be fine.'

Hester's worries about feeling awkward with Connah were unnecessary. He arrived home earlier than expected, his manner matter-of-fact as he announced that he was so hot after the long drive he fancied eating supper outside on the patio.

'It's a beautiful evening. Can you do something cold, Hester? Or I could get a meal sent in—'

'I've got the makings for a Caesar salad, if you'd like that.'

'Sounds good to me.'

'How was your mother?'

'She's not recuperating nearly as rapidly as I'd like,' he said, frowning. 'It's going to take time and patience before she's back to normal. Where's Lowri?'

'She was a bit tired and hot after our shopping trip, so she had a bath and said she fancied watching television in the study. As of five minutes ago, she was still doing that.'

'I'll go and see her, then take off for a shower.' Connah smiled at her. 'What an efficient creature you are, Hester. Nothing seems to throw you off balance.'

He was wrong there, she thought grimly. He'd done that very effectively just this morning. And the incident with the stranger in the shopping mall had made it twice in one day. But Connah could learn about that later, when Lowri was asleep.

The treat of supper in the garden was welcomed with great enthusiasm by Lowri.

'It's just like a picnic,' she said happily, when her father sent her down to the kitchen, 'only we've got a proper meal instead of sandwiches. I'll help you carry things while Daddy's in the shower, Hester.'

'Thank you. If you'll ring down for Sam, he can come to collect his meal before we take the salads out.'

When Sam arrived he put the supper Hester had ready for him in the refrigerator. 'Before I eat I'll take whatever you want out to the patio.'

With Sam and Lowri helping it was a simple matter for Hester to get a meal ready in minutes on the marble table under the vines. The only task left for Connah, when he appeared a few minutes after Sam went downstairs with his own meal, was to open the bottle of white wine keeping cool in an ice bucket in the shade.

Connah removed the cork, filled two glasses, poured lemonade for his daughter and sank down with a sigh of pleasure at the table. 'This is just what I need. We'll be able to eat outside all the time at Casa Girasole.'

'Even breakfast?' said Lowri, eyes shining.

'Even breakfast,' Connah agreed. 'But I hope you bought plenty of sun cream today. There'll be no venturing outside without it once we get there, young lady.'

'Hester bought extra while Sam and I were waiting for our lunch,' Lowri informed him.

'Of course she did,' said Connah, smiling at Hester, and helped himself to the salad. 'So how many bathing suits did you buy, Lowri?'

'Only three, Daddy. A plain blue one, and a really cool yellow bikini, and a sort of top with little matching shorts.'

'You must show them to me later. How about you, Hester?' added Connah. 'Was sun cream your only purchase?'

'No, indeed. I also bought a floppy white hat, two paperback novels and topped up my first aid box.'

'So we are now prepared for all eventualities,' he said, smiling at her. 'Excellent salad, by the way. Just the thing for an evening like this.'

'Thank you.' She put some on her plate. 'After supper I'd like to visit my mother, if that's all right with you. I need to collect some things from my flat.'

'Of course.'

'Can I come?' said Lowri eagerly, then sighed mutinously when her father shook his head.

'Let Hester have a quiet hour with her mother.'

'I'll take you there when we come back,' promised Hester. 'Then you can tell my mother and Robert all about your Italian holiday. They went there for their honeymoon four years ago, so they'll enjoy that.'

'Only four years ago?' said Lowri, diverted. 'I thought they'd been married for ages.' She thought about it. 'Do older people have honeymoons when they get married, then?'

'Certainly,' said Connah. 'Alice did when she married Mal Griffiths, remember.'

Lowri nodded. 'They went to Paris on the Eurostar. Alice bought me a silver Eiffel Tower charm for my bracelet.'

Hester smiled at her. 'Robert took my mother off to Italy for a month.'

'If they were away that long you must have missed them an awful lot,' said Lowri with sympathy.

'Not really, because I was working. Though I had time off for their wedding, of course, which was a lovely, happy occasion. I was their bridesmaid.'

The blue eyes widened. 'Really? Did you have one of those puffy dresses with a big skirt?'

'Afraid not,' said Hester apologetically. 'Mine was short and quite plain, but it *was* silk.'

'Have you got pictures?'

'Of course. I'll bring some back with me tonight.'

'Talking of which,' said Connah, 'leave all this, Hester. Give Sam a buzz. He can drive you to your parents' home.'

'No need. It's a lovely evening. I can walk—'

'No, Hester,' he said with finality. 'Sam will give you a lift. He can fetch you again later.'

And much as she wanted to protest, Hester gave in rather than upset Lowri by arguing.

'Though this wasn't necessary,' she told Sam on the short journey.

'If this joker's on the watch for you, it might be,' he reminded her. 'And, although it could be just your big blue eyes that draw him, Hester, if he's the man in the park it's likely he sees you as a way of getting to Lowri.'

Hester eyed him with horror. 'To kidnap her?'

'Or he could just be a paedophile attracted to *her* big blue eyes. Either way, it's not going to happen if I can help it. So I'll drop you at the garden gate, then come back an hour later. In the meantime, I'll clear your supper things from the patio.'

'Sam, you're a star!'

'I know.' He gave her a sidelong grin. 'Don't worry. Connah pays me well.'

Hester eyed his profile thoughtfully as they reached the house, wondering what regiment he'd been in. 'Thank you, Sam. See you in an hour, then.'

Hester found Moira and Robert sitting at the table in the garden with glasses of wine. They were delighted to see her, but surprised when Hester told them she was off to Italy with Lowri and her father for a whole month.

'This is a bit sudden, darling,' said her mother.

'Connah's idea. I could have rung you, but I thought it better to come and see you instead.'

'Much better,' said Robert. 'Have a drink. We opened a very nice red for dinner.'

'Yes, please. Will you shudder if I ask for lemonade in it?'

'You can have whatever you want,' said Robert, and went into the house to fetch it.

'Are you looking forward to the trip?' said Moira, eyeing her thoughtfully.

Hester nodded. 'Of course. I took Lowri shopping for bathing suits today. She's very excited.'

'She's a delightful little girl. Our Mr Jones has done very well with her.'

'True, but he's had his mother's invaluable help until recently. She's taking a long time to recover from heart surgery, poor lady. Which, of course, is why I'm looking after Lowri. And a trip to Tuscany's not to be sneezed at. I'll be able to send you postcards from some of the places you visited.' She grinned at Robert as he came back with the lemonade. 'Lowri was surprised to hear you and Mother had a honeymoon, by the way.'

He chuckled. 'Thought we were too old, of course,' he said, and kissed his wife's hand.

'I promised to take her the wedding pictures,' said Hester. 'Could you dig them out while I round up my holiday gear from the flat?'

'Drink your wine first,' said Moira. 'Relax for a while and let us enjoy your company, darling, while we can.'

Hester smiled and sat back. 'Right. So tell me what you've both been up to lately.'

'Gardening,' they said in laughing unison.

The time flew by as Hester sat, relaxed, in the cool of the evening. In the end it was an effort to heave herself out of her chair to go up to her flat to collect the clothes bought for the French holiday that never was. When she was carrying her suitcase down the steps from the flat later, she stopped dead as she heard a new male voice. Connah, not Sam, had come to drive her back to Albany Square. And it was pointless to deny that she was utterly delighted about it.

CHAPTER SIX

CONNAH crossed the lawn to take Hester's suitcase. 'Sam is playing chess with Lowri,' he informed her, smiling. 'So, because I'm spiriting you out of the country, I came to renew my acquaintance with your mother and introduce myself to your stepfather at the same time.'

'Come and sit down, Hester,' said Moira. 'Connah's having a drink before driving you back.'

'Tonic only,' he assured her.

Hester sat down and let Robert refill her glass, knocked off her stride for the third time that day. 'This is a surprise,' she remarked.

'I came to assure your parents that I'll take good care of you in Italy,' he said smoothly.

'And we're very pleased you did.' Moira smiled warmly at Connah. 'I'm so glad to see you again. I thought about you such a lot after your stay with us.'

'I've never forgotten how kind you were,' he said sombrely, then changed the subject and turned to Robert. 'Is this garden all your work, sir?'

'No, indeed. My lady wife works as hard as I do.'

'And I've got the hands to prove it,' said Moira, holding them up. 'You have a delightful daughter, by the way, Mr—I mean Connah.' She smiled wryly. 'I confess I still tend to think of you as our mysterious Mr Jones.'

He grinned and glanced at Hester. 'You, too?'

'At first, but I grew out of it,' she lied, flushing. 'By the way, Mother, Lowri would like to visit you and Robert again when we come back, to tell you about her travels.'

'We'll look forward to that,' said Robert, and patted his wife's hand. 'Just give Moira a couple of hours' notice to make cakes.'

'My daughter never stops talking about the wonderful time she had here,' said Connah. 'She keeps telling me she's set her heart on a flat of her own like Hester's one day.'

'I know,' said Moira, laughing. 'She wanted you to come and see it. So now you're here you may as well. Robert's rather proud of it because he did the decorating himself.'

'In that case I can hardly leave without taking a look,' said Connah promptly. 'With your permission, of course, Hester.'

'Come this way,' she said, resigned, and led the way across the garden and up the steps. 'As I told you, there's not much to see.'

Connah followed her into the long, uncluttered space, filling it, just as she'd feared, with his dominant male presence. 'I can see why you feel at home in your room in Albany Square,' he commented after a while. 'This is remarkably similar.'

'I'm very lucky to have it,' Hester assured him, annoyed because she sounded breathless. 'I chose the paint and the furniture while I was here for a weekend, and next time I came home, here it was, beautifully decorated by Robert and ready for occupation. Mother put up a couple of watercolours from my old room at home, and insisted on buying a few cushions to make this one look less spartan, but otherwise it's all my own taste.'

'I can see why Lowri likes it so much.' Connah smiled wryly. 'On the other hand, if you'd gone for carpet and wallpaper awash with cabbage roses she'd probably feel the same, just because it's yours, Hester. She thinks the world of you.'

'And I of her.' Which was worrying, because in a few weeks' time they'd have to part.

'You can always come back and visit her in the future,' he said softly, reading her mind, and held her eyes. 'Your welcome would be warm, I promise.'

Hester controlled the urge to back away. 'Thank you. But now I'd better get back to put Lowri to bed.'

The drive home was achieved in silence which neither broke until Connah turned into the private road behind the house in Albany Square.

'You thought I was intruding tonight, Hester?' he asked abruptly.

'Of course not. Mother was delighted to meet you again.'

'I had the feeling you were not.'

'I was surprised,' she said sedately, as the car glided into place beside Sam's in the garage. 'I was expecting Sam.'

'Would you have preferred that?' he questioned hastily.

Hester eyed him in surprise as she got out of the car. 'Not particularly.' Her eyes narrowed. 'You disapprove of fraternisation among the hired help?'

Connah threw back his head and laughed. 'So there is some fire inside that cool shell. Come off it, Hester. You don't look on yourself and Sam as hired help any more than I do. To me, Sam is both friend and employee, while you—' he paused, thinking it over '—I'm not sure how to categorise you, exactly. I find it difficult to think of you as either nanny or housekeeper.'

She eyed him in alarm. 'You mean my work isn't satisfactory?'

'God, no, quite the reverse.' Connah leaned on the roof of his car, eyeing her across it. 'You take good care of my child, you cook well and you're not only easy to look at, I'm very comfortable in your company. The hard part is thinking of you as an employee.'

'Nevertheless, I am,' she said matter-of-factly, 'and right now I must do what you pay me for and put your daughter to bed.' She turned as he followed her up the stairs to Sam's level. 'Once she's settled for the night, I need to talk to you.'

'Why do I get worried when you say that, Hester?' he said,

sighing. 'All right. Do what you have to do, then come down and have a drink. And this time don't say no. Serious discussion goes better over a glass of wine.'

Lowri's reception was so warm that Connah laughed as he reminded the child she'd been parted from Hester for only hours, not weeks.

'It seemed like a long time. And I would have so liked to go with Hester to see her mother and Robert,' said Lowri, sighing heavily.

'They sent their love, and said they look forward to seeing you when you get back. And while you're at the villa perhaps you'd like to send them postcards of the local scenery to show where you are,' said Hester, and smiled at Connah. 'Thank you for the lift.'

'My pleasure. Goodnight, sleep tight, Lowri.'

'Goodnight, Daddy.' Lowri gave him a careless wave and slipped her hand into Hester's. 'Will you watch some television with me for a while? It's early yet.'

'It's not early, young lady,' said her father, 'but Hester can stay with you for half an hour after she takes you up. But then you must get to sleep or you'll be too tired to travel tomorrow.'

Lowri brightened and jumped to her feet, full of questions about Hester's parents as they made for the door.

'Half an hour,' called Connah. 'Then I need Hester myself.'

His choice of words had an unsettling effect that Hester couldn't get rid of as she sat on her usual chair by Lowri's bed to show her the wedding photographs she'd brought. Of course Connah hadn't meant the words literally. But it would be good to be needed by someone like him as a woman, instead of as someone suitable to look after his daughter. Not just good—wonderful. And as much a fantasy as any of the dreams she'd woven about him when she was seventeen. Hester shook herself out of her reverie when she saw Lowri had fallen asleep.

She went downstairs to knock on the study door and found

Connah reading the *Financial Times*, a half empty glass on the table in front of him. He got up with a smile and went to the drinks tray.

'What will you have, Hester?'

'Tonic water, please. Lowri fell asleep quite quickly, by the way.'

'No prizes for guessing why. Once you were there to settle her down, she was fine.' Connah poured the drink, added ice and slices of lime and handed it to her, his eyes sombre. 'She's going to take it hard when you leave us.'

'She'll soon adjust when she's back in school. She likes it there, she told me.'

'Yes, thank God. Now sit down and tell me why you need to speak to me.'

Hester described the incident outside the pharmacy. 'It was the same man who asked directions the other night.'

'Was it, by God?' Connah's face set in grim lines. 'What did you do?'

'I refused his help politely and stood my ground until he moved off. I would have liked Sam to get a look at him, but I couldn't risk letting him anywhere near Lowri.'

'Maybe it was quite innocent and the man was just trying to pick you up,' said Connah and smiled, his eyes gleaming. 'Who could blame him?'

She flushed. 'Possibly. But he looked familiar, which worried me. Though I'm sure I'd never seen him before the other night, unless he is the man in the park. I didn't get a good enough look that day to be able to tell.'

'But if you met this one again, you'd recognise him?'

'Definitely. I was so pointed about not moving until he did, I had time for a good look at his face, also of his back view as he walked away. He was wearing casual clothes, but they were the expensive, designer kind, like his shoes. And he wore a Rolex watch,' added Hester.

Connah gazed at her with respect. 'You're very observant.'

'In this case only because I thought it was necessary. I doubt I'd have noticed any of that in ordinary circumstances.' She gave him a worried look. 'I'm really glad we're going away tomorrow. Whoever this man is, we'll be out of his reach.'

'Which was part of my reason for organising the holiday.' Connah finished his drink, then sat back. 'Right then, Hester, with that thought in mind, I want you to forget about the man and relax while we're away. The house is a mile or so from the village, so there aren't many people around to bother us. It has a private pool, a maid to do the housework and shopping, so you have nothing to do except keep Lowri entertained. No small task, as I know to my cost, even though you make it look easy.'

'In my last post I looked after three-year-old twins,' she reminded him. 'After my stint with Seb and Viola, sweet children though they are, taking care of Lowri is a breeze.'

'A theatrical household must have been interesting,' he commented, leaning back.

'It was.'

'Did you meet many famous thespians?'

'One or two, yes. But Leo and Julia, the twins' parents, were on stage in different theatres during the last few months I was there, so I spent most of my time with only the twins for company.'

'Quite a responsibility.'

'True,' agreed Hester, 'but it's what I was trained for. I was in at the deep end right from the start of my first job. I had to complete nine months of satisfactory work with the children of the first family who engaged me before I could actually qualify as a Norland-trained nanny.'

'Which you did, of course, though I can't remember your CV in detail. Were you with the first people long?'

'Three years, until the family went to Australia. Beforehand they had recommended me to their friend, Julia Herrick, and I went straight to Julia a month before she gave birth to the twins.'

'And when you leave us you're going off to Yorkshire,' said Connah, his eyes sombre. 'I'm already dreading the day you part with Lowri.'

So was Hester. 'As I said before, it's the part of my job I don't enjoy.' She finished her drink and stood up. 'But now I'd better finish packing.'

Lowri was fast asleep, with her head on Hester's shoulder, missing the incredible views as Connah drove along the final stage of their journey on the Chiantigiana, the famous road that meandered through the hills and vineyards of Tuscany. The air-conditioning in the car was fighting a losing battle with the heat of the day and Hester felt hot and weary by the time they were in sight of the sleepy little village they were heading for. To her disappointment, Connah turned off without entering it and took a narrow, stony road that curved up through umbrella pines and ranks of tall cypresses towards high pink walls at the top of a hill.

'Is that Casa Girasole?'

'It certainly is.'

Connah nosed the car through high wrought iron gates and drew up in the courtyard of a pink-washed house with Juliet balconies at the upper windows. Hester gazed in delight, drinking in heat and sun and flowers growing in profusion in rich hot earth. Tiny pink roses twined in the greenery, curling round the pillars of the loggia, and three descending tiers of flower beds held drifts of white jasmine among scarlet and pink geraniums and the cheery faces of the sunflowers that gave the house its name.

He turned round in his seat to smile at Hester. 'Well?'

'It's absolutely lovely,' she said softly, and Lowri stirred and sat up, rubbing eyes which suddenly opened wide in delight.

'Are we here? Is that the house? Gosh, it's pretty! Why didn't you wake me?'

'You're awake now,' said her father, and got out to open the passenger door. 'Out you get. Hester must be squashed and very hot. You started snoring on her shoulder as soon as we left Florence.'

'I don't snore!' said Lowri indignantly, then her eyes lit up as she spotted a blue glint in the distance. 'Wow! Is that the pool? Can we have a swim before supper?'

'After you've unpacked, yes.' Connah helped Hester out of the car. 'First we find Flavia, otherwise we can't get in.'

'*Signore!*' Right on cue, a plump young woman came hurrying round the corner of the house and let out a cry of delight as she saw Lowri. No translation was needed for her flow of liquid welcome as she expressed her pleasure to see them. Shooing them before her like a hen with chicks, she ushered them across the loggia into a living room with a shining terracotta tiled floor and furniture covered in sunny yellow chintz.

'What's she saying, Daddy?' demanded Lowri, smiling helplessly in response to the lava-flow of conversation.

'We must sit and have drinks, while Flavia takes our luggage upstairs, only I'm not going to let her do that,' said Connah firmly and, with creditable fluency, told Flavia in her own tongue that refreshments would be welcome, but he himself would carry the bags up to the bedrooms.

'I'll carry my own,' said Hester at once, but Connah waved her away.

'For once, you will just sit there,' he said with such firmness that Lowri laughed.

'When Daddy talks like that you have to do as he says or he gets cross, Hester.'

'And you wouldn't want that, Hester, would you?' mocked Connah.

Hester smiled, defeated, secretly only too glad to subside on the sofa in the blessedly cool room.

Connah relieved Flavia of a huge tray and brought it to a glass-topped table in front of Hester.

'How do you say thank you, Daddy?' asked Lowri, her eye caught by a plate of little cakes.

'*Grazie*,' said Connor, and went out to unpack the car.

'*Grazie*, Flavia,' said Lowri, and the woman beamed, patted the child's hand and pointed to a teapot.

'*Tè*,' she said, then indicated the other pot and a tall jug clinking with ice. '*Caffè, limonata*.' Then, with a determined look on her face, she left the room to follow Connah.

'I think she's going to help with the luggage,' said Lowri, examining the rest of the tray. 'Daddy won't be cross with *her*.'

'No,' agreed Hester. 'I'm sure he won't.'

'Why are there two jugs of milk?'

'I expect one's hot for the coffee and the other's cold for tea.' Hester grinned as she heard sounds of altercation outside. 'Who do you think is winning?'

'Daddy always wins,' said Lowri positively, but for once she was wrong.

Connah came into the room later, looking unusually hot and bothered.

'Flavia insisted on helping you?' asked Hester, smiling.

He nodded ruefully. 'When I tried arguing, she pretended she couldn't understand me.'

'Have some coffee, Daddy,' consoled his daughter. 'I left you some cakes.'

'Thank you, *cariad*. What are you having, Hester?'

'Tea. And very welcome it is,' she said fervently, pouring coffee for him.

'Once we've recovered, we'll explore,' said Connah. 'Apparently Flavia normally leaves at five, but stayed later tonight to welcome us. She showed me the cold supper she left for us, and promises to cook whatever we want for lunch tomorrow.'

Lowri was thrilled with everything about the villa, from her airy bedroom next to Hester's to the big, bright kitchen big enough for three of them to eat meals at the table at one end, and outside the arcaded loggia with table and chairs for the outdoor meals her father had promised. But best of all were the beautiful terraced gardens, which led down in tiers to the crowning glory, an oval pool surrounded by well-tended grass and comfortable garden furniture with shady umbrellas and a view of Tuscan hills that begged to be photographed.

Connah smiled indulgently as he watched Lowri running about in delight to explore everything.

'Your friends have great taste,' commented Hester, impressed.

'And the money to indulge it. Jay Anderson was my partner until I sold him my share of the asset management firm we founded together. I still keep a stake in it, but these days I spend some of my time—and money—on restoration of properties like the house in Albany Square. I bought it with the intention of using it as my headquarters in the Midlands. But the house feels so much like home to me now that I'm not so sure I want to do that.'

'You could still use it for meetings,' suggested Hester. 'The dining room certainly feels like a boardroom, with all those chairs and that long table. Meals could easily be served there if you have business lunches.'

Connah eyed her with respect. 'You're right. The room could be a lot more useful that way than for dinner parties.'

'Can we have a swim?' demanded Lowri, running towards them. 'It's still lovely and warm.'

'What do you think, Hester?' asked Connah.

'Just for a few minutes, then. We'll unpack the swimming things, but afterwards we must hang up the rest of our clothes before we have supper.'

Lowri was ready to agree to anything as long as she could go in the pool, but Connah declined her invitation to join them.

'I,' he said virtuously, 'will go up to my aerie on the top floor and unpack, then have a shower. I shall join you later for supper.'

Hester was glad to hear it. Her swimsuit was the plain black one she'd worn to teach the twins to swim, and she'd long since lost the puppy fat of her first encounter with Connah. Nevertheless, she preferred to enjoy her first swim with just Lowri for company.

Lowri was out of her clothes and into her bathing suit at the speed of light and harried Hester to get ready quickly before it was too late.

'The pool will still be there tomorrow,' said Hester, laughing, as she collected towels.

The pool was set in natural stone and constructed with such skill that it looked as though it had always been there rather than man-made. The water was silken and warm on Hester's skin as she sat on the edge to dip her feet in it, and she smiled indulgently as Lowri jumped in with a terrific splash at the other end and swam towards her like a small torpedo. She stood up, waist deep, when she reached Hester, pushing her wet hair back from her beaming face.

'Isn't this *gorgeous*?' she gasped. 'I just love it here. Come on in. I'll race you to the other end.'

Lowri counted to three, then they set off for the far end, Hester careful not to overtake the child. They swam several lengths, then Hester called a halt as she saw Connah stroll up to watch them.

'Did you see us, Daddy?' said Lowri as she held up a hand. 'I think Hester let me beat her.'

Connah pulled her out, then held out a hand to Hester. 'You both looked far too energetic for me.' He handed a towel to Hester, then enveloped his daughter in the other. 'Hurry up and get showered and dressed, you two. I'm hungry.'

'If you'll give me half an hour, I'll put supper on,' said Hester breathlessly. So much for avoiding Connah in her swimsuit.

'I'll help,' said Lowri, hurrying up the steps in front of them.

'We'll all help,' said Connah firmly. 'This is Hester's holiday too.'

By the time Lowri and Hester were both dry and dressed and the cases had been unpacked it was rather more than half an hour, and Connah had pre-empted Hester by taking their supper out to the loggia himself.

'It's just cold turkey and spiced ham, and tomatoes and bread and cheese and so on tonight, as I asked,' he said, looking pleased with himself. 'Plus a pudding Flavia made for us.'

'Thank you,' said Hester, taken aback by this reversal of their usual roles.

'My pleasure.'

As they sat down to their meal the sun began to set and Connah lit the shaded lamp on the table. He filled two glasses with sparkling white wine, and one with *limonata,* then raised his glass in a toast. 'Happy holiday, ladies.'

'You too, Daddy,' said Lowri happily.

'Yes, indeed,' agreed Hester. 'Thank you very much for inviting me.'

Lowri stared at her blankly. 'We couldn't have come without you!'

'If we had, Hester,' said Connah wryly, 'I'd be a broken man by the time we got back if I had to cope with Lowri on my own for four weeks.'

'I'm not that bad!' protested his daughter. 'Oh, look. The stars are coming out and there's a little moon at the edge of the sky over there by the pool.'

'All laid on specially for you,' teased her father.

It was a magical evening, not least because Connah Carey Jones was a very different man on holiday. He treated Hester as though they were just two people enjoying the company of the child and each other, with no hint of employer and employee. The impression grew stronger when Connah insisted that he and Lowri would remove dishes and fetch the pudding while Hester just sat there and counted stars.

'I will also make the coffee,' he announced as he came back with a dish of *pannacotta*, the national favourite, for dessert.

'There's a caramel sauce underneath the creamy bit,' Hester told the child. 'Shall I spoon it over yours?'

'Yes, *please*,' said Lowri, licking her lips. 'Are you having some, Daddy?'

He shook his head. 'Not for me. I'll stick with *pecorino* and another hunk of this wonderful bread.'

They lingered at the table while the sky grew dark and the stars grew brighter. The warm air was fragrant with flowers and new-cut grass and some other scent Connah told Hester came from a herb bed under the kitchen window.

'Jay Anderson planted it for his wife, and Flavia is only too delighted to make use of it. The scent is a mixture of rosemary, thyme, sage—and basil, of course, and probably a few other things I've never heard of.' Connah leaned back, relaxed. 'I must tell Jay that if ever he feels like selling the place to think of me first.'

Lowri gazed at him, round-eyed. 'Would you really buy it, Daddy?'

'In the unlikely event that Jay and Stella would want to sell, yes. But they won't part with it, *cariad*. And who could blame them?'

Jay Anderson had installed a large television and DVD player in the sitting room, but for once Lowri made no protest when Connah said it was late and she must go straight to bed so that Hester could come back downstairs and relax for a while in the warm night air.

'You can read another chapter of that book you're devouring,' said Hester.

The child embraced her father with enthusiasm, but a yawn overtook her as she went inside with Hester. 'I quite fancy going to bed in that dear little room next to yours,' she admitted sleepily. 'I was too excited to sleep much last night.'

Within minutes the face-washing and teeth-brushing routine was over and Lowri was tucked under the snow-white covers on the bed. 'I'm too tired to read tonight,' she said, yawning. 'Will you kiss me goodnight, Hester?'

Touched, Hester bent to kiss the smooth, flushed cheek, brushed a hand over the silky dark hair, then said goodnight and went quietly from the room to go downstairs to Connah.

As always, his requirements had been clearly stated. Otherwise, since this was a different situation, in a different country, Hester would have been uncertain what to do once Lowri was in bed. She felt a *frisson* of pure pleasure at spending time alone with Connah in these circumstances, as she took a few minutes in her room to brush her hair and touch a lipstick to her mouth. Her thin cotton dress was an old one, but the gentian-blue shade deepened the colour of her eyes and the wide skirt was more holiday-friendly than the clothes she wore in Albany Square. The face that looked back at her from the mirror was flushed from the sun and the swim and the sheer pleasure of the evening. Four weeks, she told it firmly. After that it would nearly be time to leave Connah and Lowri and go on to pastures new in Yorkshire. Where she would miss Lowri badly when she was looking after a newborn baby. She would miss Lowri's father even more. She took in a deep breath and smiled at her reflection. Instead of anticipating future pain, right now it was time to join Connah—and make the most of present pleasure.

CHAPTER SEVEN

CONNAH was waiting impatiently when Hester joined him on the loggia. 'At last! Did Lowri con you into reading the book to her, instead?'

'No, she was too tired.' She smiled. 'By the time I'd finished tidying her room she was asleep.'

'You were a long time coming down,' he commented, pulling out a chair for her. 'I thought you might have had second thoughts and gone to bed.'

'Not without saying goodnight!'

'Goodnight, Connah,' he ordered. 'We're supposed to be on first name terms, but so far, Hester, I've yet to hear mine from you.'

'I find it difficult,' she said awkwardly.

'Why?'

'For obvious reasons.'

He eyed her challengingly. 'How did you address your last employers?'

'As Leo and Julia,' she admitted, 'but it was a very informal household.'

'So is mine. From now on you say Connah, or I shall address you as Miss Ward.' He smiled suddenly. 'Loosen up, Hester. This is a holiday. Forget your scruples and enjoy the break from humdrum routine in Albany Square.'

Hester couldn't help laughing. 'During my brief but eventful time in Albany Square, life has been anything but humdrum.'

'That's better—you should laugh more often,' he approved. 'Have a glass of wine.'

Oh, why not? thought Hester. 'Thank you,' she said sedately.

After a comfortable silence Connor asked what she would like to do the next day. 'The local shops will be shut on a Sunday, but we could drive somewhere, if you like.'

'Speaking in professional nanny mode,' said Hester, 'I think a day of doing nothing much at all would be good for Lowri after the journey today. She can swim and sunbathe, maybe watch a DVD or even take a nap when the sun gets hot, and if she gets restless I can take her for a walk later when it's cooler. Then, maybe, on Monday you could drive us into Greve and drink coffee in the square while Lowri and I look round the shops.'

'I'll come shopping with you,' said Connah, surprising her. 'And afterwards I'll take you to lunch somewhere.'

'Thank you. Lowri would adore that.' So would Hester. 'By the way, when you need time to yourself with your laptop, just say the word and I'll keep Lowri occupied.'

Connah stretched out in his chair with a sigh of pleasure. 'At the moment the thought of even opening my laptop is too much effort. Maybe I'll just stick to lotus-eating for a while. God knows, this is the ideal place for it.'

'You said you'd stayed here before?'

'Twice. But on both occasions the house was packed with the Anderson family and various friends. Great fun, but definitely not peaceful.' He turned to look at her. 'I'll join you and Lowri to laze the day away tomorrow—including the daily swim.'

Hester liked his programme very much. Even the swim.

'Tell me,' he said idly, as though the answer were of no particular importance, 'why was there such a gap between your last job and the next one, Hester?'

'It wasn't planned. When Leo and Julia won the leads in a new television series in LA, I looked for another post right away and sorted the one in Yorkshire quite quickly. But the Herricks were needed in LA weeks sooner than expected and the Rutherford baby isn't due until early October, so a temporary job seemed the ideal way to fill in the time.'

'Wouldn't you have liked a holiday before getting down to work again?'

Hester was silent for a while. 'I'd been asked to go to the South of France,' she said at last, gazing out at the starlit garden, 'but the holiday fell through at the last minute.'

'So what went wrong?'

'The friend who invited me cancelled at the eleventh hour.'

'Why?'

'He received a sudden job offer and barely had time to apologise before boarding the plane to head west for fame and fortune.'

Connah shot her a searching glance. 'Were you unhappy about that, Hester?'

She shook her head. 'Only where the cancelled holiday was concerned.'

'You mentioned fame and fortune, so I take it the man is an actor. Would I know him?'

She shrugged. 'You might. He played a psychopath in one of those film *noir* type thrillers recently. It won him rave reviews, which led to a role as Julia's wicked brother in the American series she's starring in with Leo. Though the fact that he really is Julia's little brother probably helped with that.'

'What's his name?'

'Keir McBride.'

Connah shook his head. 'Never heard of him.'

Hester chuckled. 'He'd be mortified if he knew.'

'Is he very pretty?'

'Very. He's fair, like Julia, with bright blue eyes and angelic good looks. They made his psychotic performance all the more chilling.'

Connah's face looked stern in the dim light. 'Had you known him long?'

'Off and on for the three years I worked for his sister. But in the period before the Herricks' big break he was out of a job and came to "rest" for a while at their house. Leo and Julia were out in the evenings, performing in their respective shows, so Keir took to spending time with me most evenings after I put the twins to bed. We got on so well he asked if I fancied a holiday with him in the Herricks' farmhouse in the Dordogne once Julia and Leo left for LA. But then, out of the blue, he got the offer of a lifetime, so no holiday.'

'Will you see him again?' said Connor, seized with a sudden desire to rearrange the actor's angelic face.

'I doubt it. If Keir makes a success of his part in the series—which he will because, pretty face or not, he's a brilliant actor—he's bound to get more offers over there. If things go well for him, I doubt that he'll come back to this country any time soon.' Hester smiled crookedly. 'Believe me, it was no romance. Keir was out of work, short of funds and I was right there, captive company for him every evening. The bird in the hand.'

Connah gave her a searching look. 'If you'd gone with the Herricks to LA you could have gone on seeing McBride. Why did you refuse?'

'It was too far away from my family. Also, at that stage Keir was based in the UK and wanted us to see something of each other now and then. But in the end he went off to LA too.' Hester shrugged. 'At which point I answered a couple of advertisements for temporary summer jobs and one of them was yours.'

'Which is my great good fortune—and Lowri's.' He frowned. 'You do so much more than just look after her, I should be paying you a far larger salary than I do.'

'Certainly not,' she said promptly. 'A free holiday in a place like this is recompense enough.'

'I wouldn't call it free exactly,' he said dryly. 'Looking after Lowri is no sinecure.'

'But I enjoy it. If I didn't, I'd be in the wrong job, Connah!'

'At last,' he said in triumph. 'You finally brought yourself to say my name.'

She hadn't brought herself to it at all. His name had tripped off her tongue all too easily. Probably because here in this starlit, scented garden the world they'd left behind could have been on another planet.

'I wonder how Sam's getting on,' she said idly.

'After I rang my mother to tell her we'd arrived I gave Sam a call while you were putting Lowri to bed. All's well in the house and Sam was about to take a stroll down to his local for a pint. I thought he'd have seized the chance of a holiday abroad somewhere, but apparently he had his fill of globe-trotting when he was in the army. He prefers Albany Square in peace and quiet on his own.'

'So he told me.' To her embarrassment, Hester was suddenly overwhelmed by a huge yawn.

Connah smiled. 'You're tired. I'm sorry to lose your company, but I think it's time you went to bed, Hester. You'll have a full day tomorrow—as usual.'

Hester rose at once to assert herself in housekeeper role before she lost sight of why she was really here. 'I'll take these glasses into the kitchen on my way. Goodnight.'

'Goodnight, Connah,' he corrected.

'Goodnight, Connah,' she repeated obediently.

'Much better,' he said, and gave her the smile which knocked her defences flat.

The following day was spent as planned—swimming, reading or just lazing in the sun. Connah joined Hester and Lowri for their morning swim, then retreated to his room afterwards to ring his mother again. She assured him she was feeling better and asked to speak to Lowri. He beckoned from his balcony and the child came running upstairs to chatter happily to her grandmother about the Casa Girasole and the wonderful time she was having with Daddy and Hester.

'Lowri sounds very happy, Connah,' said his mother, when Lowri had raced back down to the garden. 'Miss Ward is obviously doing an excellent job with her.'

'So much so that I'm not looking forward to the day she leaves us.'

'Lowri will be in school soon after that. And next school holiday, God willing, I shall be fit enough to take charge of my granddaughter myself.'

'Of course you will,' he said firmly, and wished he could believe it. 'With that in mind, take good care of yourself, Mother. I'll talk to you again tomorrow.'

Connah returned to his small balcony to look down at the pool. Hester was lying back in a garden chair under an umbrella, listening as Lowri perched at her feet to read aloud from one of the books provided by the school for the summer holiday. He smiled wryly. He wouldn't have thought of bringing the books with them, but Hester had produced one straight after the morning swim. And Lowri had begun reading without the slightest protest. Whatever Hester wanted, Lowri would do, Connah realised. It was a disturbing thought. He rubbed his chin, frowning. Lowri had been fond of Alice, who had been a fixture all her young life and taken for granted. But because Lowri had settled to life away at school so well there'd been no problem when Alice left to get married.

The situation with Hester was very different. Lowri had grown attached to her so quickly she would miss Hester desperately when the time came to part. And so, by God, would he! Thrusting the thought from his mind, Connah put the phone in his pocket and went downstairs to tell Flavia that she could take the following day off; they would bring food home with them from Greve for supper. Flavia thanked him, beaming, explaining that the unexpected holiday gave her the opportunity to visit her niece. Connah then went out to the pool to tell Lowri about the proposed outing.

'Brilliant,' said his daughter, delighted. 'I can buy postcards to send to Grandma, and Moira and Robert, and Chloe and Sam. Gosh, my throat's dry. I've been reading so long I'm thirsty.'

'I'll get you a drink,' said Hester, getting up, but Lowri pushed her back in her chair.

'I can get it myself, and practice my Italian on Flavia at the same time.' She ran off, long legs flying, and Connah took her place beside Hester.

'She's growing up before my eyes. It's frightening. But should she be on first name terms with your parents?'

'It was their idea,' Hester assured him.

'Good. By the way, I told Flavia to take the day off tomorrow.'

'No problem. I can cook.'

'No cooking. We'll buy food for a cold supper while we're in Greve.'

Hester smiled her thanks. 'Is that the kind of thing you did when your mother shared your holiday?'

Connah shook his head. 'Mother's holiday of choice is a fully-catered hotel in Devon or Tenby in Wales. She doesn't like flying. And we rarely stayed more than ten days or so.'

Hester sat up, surprised. 'But Lowri told me she'd been to France last year.'

'That was a school trip. My mother thought she was far too young to go, but I find it hard to refuse Lowri anything. So far her demands have been easy to meet.' His face darkened. 'As she gets older, things will change.'

'Don't worry too much. I think Lowri knows exactly where to draw the line.'

He smiled crookedly. 'I discovered that for myself last week when you were out. She played me like a fish at bedtime until I blew the whistle.'

Lowri came racing back to tell them Flavia said lunch would be ready in ten minutes.

'How did you understand what she said?' asked Connah, amused.

'I'm picking up a word or two, so lunch will be at *mezzo-giorno*,' she said with a flourish. 'That's midday, and it's in ten minutes. Eight now,' she added, looking at her watch. 'It's spaghetti with yummy red sauce—Flavia let me taste it. And for supper tonight it's *pollo cacciatore*. That's some kind of chicken. It just has to be heated up when we need it, and it's all in one pot and smells gorgeous.'

Her father chuckled. 'One way to get fluent in a foreign language!'

Hester got up. 'Right then, Lowri. Just time for a wash and tidy-up before lunch.'

'You sound just like Alice sometimes,' remarked Lowri as they walked up the garden.

Something to watch, thought Hester, biting her lip.

'You're not a bit like her in other ways, though,' added Lowri. 'Alice is pretty, but she's not slim like you. She's very smiley and cuddly, though.'

'And I'm not?'

Lowri eyed Hester objectively as they went upstairs. 'When you smile it sort of lights up your face, and I notice it more because you don't smile all the time. And you use make-up and scent, you have a great haircut, and your clothes are sort of plain but always look just right, like Chloe's mother. And you're young,' she added as the final accolade. 'Mrs Powell said Alice was very lucky to catch a husband at her age.'

Poor old Alice, thought Hester. 'And what age would that be?'

'I'm not sure. More than thirty, anyway.' Lowri looked at her curiously as they went into the bathroom. 'How old are you, Hester?'

'Twenty-seven—and I'm hungry, so let's hurry it up.'

After Flavia's excellent lunch, all three were a little somnolent as they sat at the table on the loggia.

'Lord knows I don't feel like it, but I must do some work this afternoon,' announced Connah, yawning.

'I feel sleepy too,' said Lowri, surprised.

'Then why not have a nap on your bed and leave Hester in peace for a couple of hours?'

'Later we'll have a swim,' promised Hester.

'OK,' said Lowri, getting up. 'I'll read for a while. You don't have to come up with me,' she added, but Hester was already on her feet.

'I want my book. I fancy a nice peaceful read by the pool.'

'Make sure you keep under an umbrella,' advised Connah.

'Alice can't sit in the sun, she gets all red and shiny,' said Lowri as they went upstairs. 'But you don't, Hester.'

'Genetics—olive skin like my father. Right, then. When you've had a rest, get into your bikini and join me by the pool.'

'Have you got a bikini?' asked Lowri as she began to undress.

'Yes.'

'Wear it this afternoon!'

'I'll see.'

'Oh, please, Hester. I bet you look really cool in it.'

'I'll think about it. Enjoy your book, and I'll see you later.'

In her own room Hester exchanged her shorts and T-shirt for a sea-green bikini bought for France. She eyed herself in the mirror and thought why not? She added the long filmy shirt bought to go with it, collected her book, hat and sunglasses and the tote bag that held everything else and went downstairs to compliment Flavia on their lunch. The afternoon sun was hot as she made for the pool and she was grateful for the shade of an umbrella as she settled down with the book she'd started in bed the night before. The bed had been supremely comfortable and the room cool and airy, but sleep had been elusive. The sounds of the night through the open windows had made her restless because, added to the mix, she knew Connah was sitting alone on the loggia.

Hester was absorbed in the novel when a shadow fell across her book and she looked up with a smile, expecting Connah. But a complete stranger stood smiling back at her. A handsome Italian stranger at that.

She shot upright, pulling her shirt together.

'*Perdoneme*, I startled you,' he said apologetically. 'I thought you were the Signora Anderson. Permit me to introduce myself. I am Pierluigi Martinelli.'

'Hester Ward,' she said formally. 'How do you do?'

'*Piacere*. You are here on holiday?'

'Yes.' Hester cast a look back at the house, relieved to see Connah about to join them, hand outstretched to the visitor.

'Hello, Luigi. I didn't know you were here.'

'Connah, *come estai*!' The two men shook hands. 'I have just arrived. I came through the woods and along the private path into your garden. I am at the *Castello* for a while.'

'Have you met Hester?'

'We introduced ourselves, yes,' said Luigi, smiling at her. 'Are the Andersons here?'

'No. Just Hester, myself and my daughter.' Connah took Hester's hand. 'Darling, would you be an angel and ask Flavia to bring us some coffee?'

Darling? Hester gathered up her belongings. 'I'll get Lowri up while I'm there.'

Grateful for the long, filmy shirt which veiled most of her from the Italian's appreciative gaze, Hester went quickly up the garden and into the house to announce, as best she could, that they had a visitor.

'*Caffè, per favore, Flavia, per* signore Martinelli.'

The name had a dramatic effect on the plump little woman. '*Il Conte? Maddonnina mia—subito, subito!*' Flavia went into overdrive as she began laying a silver tray with the Andersons' best china.

Amused, Hester went upstairs to find Lowri already changed for her swim. 'Your father has a visitor, so put a shirt on top. I won't be a moment. I'm going to change.'

The glowing face fell. 'But you said you were going to swim with me!'

'And I will, later, but right now I'm going to get dressed.'

Lowri gave an admiring look at the sea-green bikini. 'Do you have to?'

'Yes, I do. Go on down and meet the visitor, if you like. I'll be five minutes.'

'I'll wait for you,' offered Lowri.

'Flavia's making coffee for the visitor. Why not run down and ask if you can carry something to the pool for her?'

'OK. But don't be long.'

Hester pulled on a white cotton jersey shift at top speed, the word 'darling' reverberating in her head. At last, her hair caught up in a careless knot, gold thong sandals on her feet, dark glasses in place, she went downstairs to the kitchen where, with many apologies and much hand-waving, Flavia explained that the cakes meant for dessert after supper had been served to *Il Conte* with his coffee.

'*Non importa,*' said Hester airily, and took the ice-filled jug of lemonade Flavia handed to her.

As she strolled down the descending tiers of flower beds towards the pool, Hester watched the two men standing together, with Lowri between them like a small referee. They were both dark, mature men, but Signor Martinelli, or *Il Conte* as Flavia called him, was unmistakably Latin. He wore elegant casual clothes, as expensively cut as his glossy black hair, and had an air of swagger about him even in repose. Connah's darkness of hair and eye were, at least to Hester's eye, unmistakably Celt. He was the taller of the two, with a hint of toughness and power about his broad-shouldered physique which appealed to Hester far more than the grace of the urbane Italian.

'Ah, Hester,' Connah said, smiling, as he took the jug from her. 'Perhaps you'll pour for us while Lowri hands round the cakes?'

'Certainly.' She looked enquiringly at Luigi Martinelli, who promptly took the seat beside her as she sat down. 'You like your coffee black?'

'*Grazie.*' He eyed her with open appreciation. 'And how do you like my homeland, Miss Hester? You have travelled here before?'

'Not here exactly. I've been to Venice, but this is my first time in Tuscany, which is so beautiful, how could I not like it? Please, have one of Flavia's cakes.'

He took one from the plate Lowri was offering, smiling fondly at the child. 'And how old are you, *carina*?'

'Ten,' she said quietly, shy in the presence of this exotic visitor.

'You are a tall lady for ten,' he said with admiration.

'Is Sophia with you?' asked Connah.

'No. My wife is in Rome. Where else? She does not care for the *campagna*.' Luigi shrugged. 'But from time to time I experience *la nostalgia* for the tranquillity of my old home. When I heard that Casa Girasole was occupied I assumed that the Andersons were here and came to invite them to dinner tonight. But I would count it a great privilege, Connah, if you and your ladies would honour me with your company instead.'

Connah shook his head decisively. 'Sorry, Luigi. We keep early hours here to suit my daughter. Another time, perhaps.'

'Of course.' Luigi drained his cup and stood up. 'It was a great pleasure to meet you, Miss Hester, also you, Miss Lowri. A charming name,' he added. 'I have never heard it before.'

'It's Welsh for Laura,' she volunteered shyly.

He startled the child by bowing gracefully over her hand before bidding the others goodbye. 'I hope to see you again soon. Ciao.'

Luigi Martinelli strolled off the way he'd come, knowing— and probably enjoying the fact—that three pairs of eyes watched him go.

'What a nice man,' said Lowri, taking the chair next to Hester. 'Can I have some *limonata*, please?'

Connah raised an eyebrow at Hester as she poured it. 'What did you think of our local sprig of nobility? I should have introduced him as Count Pierluigi Martinelli. The local *Castello* has been in his family for centuries.'

'Flavia mentioned the title as she rushed to make coffee for him.' Hester smiled. 'You note that the Andersons' best china was produced for *Il Conte*.'

'Flavia has lived here all her life. In her mind, she numbers God, the local priest and Luigi as most important in the local pecking order—though not necessarily in that order. As a girl she was a maid up at the *Castello*, and Nico, her husband, is Luigi's gardener.'

'Is it a real castle with turrets and things?' asked Lowri, fascinated. 'I would have liked to see it, Daddy.'

He smiled ruefully. 'Sorry, *cariad*, I should have consulted you before turning Luigi down.'

'We couldn't have gone tonight anyway,' she reminded him. 'We've got Flavia's special chicken dinner.'

'So we have.' Connah picked up the tray. 'I'll leave the lemonade, but I'll take the rest in for Flavia, then I think I'll change and have a swim.'

'Me too,' said Lowri promptly, stripping off her shirt. 'Are you going to change back into your bikini, Hester?'

'I don't think so. You can have your swim with your father,' said Hester, avoiding Connah's eye.

'Spoilsport,' he murmured as his daughter jumped into the pool.

Hester was happy to sit where she was, watching as father and daughter played in the pool. Connah's muscular body was broad in the shoulder and slim-hipped, also deeply tanned, probably, thought Hester, by some other foreign sun, in striking contrast to his daughter, whose fair skin was already acquiring a glow, courtesy of the Tuscan sun, but it was a different tone from her father's. Lowri's eyes and skin obviously came from her mother and, as she often did, Hester wondered about the woman Connah had cared for so deeply. After the one startling incident when he'd showed his emotions on the subject, he hadn't mentioned her again. And why should he? Theirs was a professional, working relationship, she reminded herself. On Connah's side, anyway.

Eventually, after much splashing and laughter, father and daughter went in the house to shower and dress. When Connah announced that he was going to do some work before dinner Lowri asked him if she could walk to the village with Hester.

'Flavia says they have good *gelato* in the shop there,' she said eagerly.

'How you do love your ice cream,' he mocked. 'But I'd rather you didn't go without me, and I can't come right now. We'll all walk there another time.'

Lowri pouted a little, but brightened when Hester suggested that instead they ask Flavia for instructions about heating her *pollo cacciatore*. 'We'll ask her to teach us the Italian words for things in the kitchen.'

This programme met with warm approval and a lively hour was spent in the kitchen with a delighted Flavia, who enjoyed the impromptu Italian lesson as much as her students. Afterwards she said her farewells, wished them a happy time in Greve the next day and set off down the road on her bicycle with all the panache of a competitor in the Tour de France.

'She's so jolly and nice,' said Lowri, and gave Hester an impish grin. 'A lot different from Grandma's Mrs Powell.'

Since Flavia had already laid the table on the loggia and the pot of chicken merely needed heating when they were ready to eat, Hester suggested it might be a good idea to sit quietly in the *salone* with a book until it was time for supper.

'Will you sit with me?' said Lowri quickly.

'Of course.' But as they settled down together Hester felt troubled. Lowri was becoming far too dependent on her. Which was delightful in one way, because Hester was very fond of the child. But when the day came to say goodbye, as it always did, the parting would be even more painful than in the past. The other children she'd cared for had cried bitterly when she'd left, but unlike Lowri they'd had their mothers to comfort them. Although Lowri had Connah and her grandmother, Hester consoled herself. Children were resilient. She would soon recover once she was back in school with Chloe and all her friends.

The supper was a great success. On instruction from Flavia, Hester served a first course of Parma ham with ripe figs bursting with juice. The savoury *cacciatore* that followed tasted as delicious as its aroma, but it was so substantial that when Hester offered the depleted selection of cakes for dessert not even Lowri had room for one.

'Gosh, I'm full,' she said, yawning.

'In that case, to let your supper go down you'd better stroll round the garden for a while with Daddy while I clear away,' said Hester, collecting plates. 'You can watch the moon rise over the pool.'

'I'll make coffee when you come down after Lowri's in bed, Hester,' said Connah. 'Come on then, *cariad*,' he said, holding out his hand to his daughter. 'Quick march.'

Later, when the kitchen was tidy and Lowri seen safely to bed, Hester went down to join Connah. The scent of freshly made coffee mingled deliciously with the garden scents of the night and she resumed her chair with a sigh of pleasure.

'How beautiful it is here.'

'But it gets cold in the winter when the *tramontana* blows,' said Connah, pouring coffee. 'I was here once with the Andersons for New Year's Eve. By the way, that was a very meaningful look you gave me regarding the stroll in the garden with Lowri.'

'Yes.' Hester braced herself. 'Forgive me if I'm overstepping the mark, but I think you should spend more time with her on your own. Not,' she added hastily, 'because I want time off or because I don't enjoy her company. I do. So much that Lowri won't be the only one to feel sad when we say goodbye. But instead of always having me around I think, or at least I'm suggesting, that you should take her out now and again on your own, just the two of you. Maybe take her to visit the *Castello*, or walk with her into the village.'

'Is that why you seemed abstracted over our wonderful dinner?'

'Yes. She wouldn't sit and read earlier unless I did too.' Hester raised worried eyes to his. 'If she's with me all the time, it will be even more painful when I leave. As I know from bitter experience. The Herrick twins sobbed so much when I left it tore me in pieces. Julia had chickened out of telling them I wasn't going with them to America, so when they found out at the very last minute it was rough on all of us.'

Connah sat in silence for a while, sipping his coffee. 'If,' he said at last, 'you find this part of your job so painful, isn't it time you found some other way to earn a living?'

'I've been thinking of it quite a lot lately, but though I'm top of the tree at what I do, I'm not qualified for anything else. Besides,' she added with a sigh, 'it was always a vocation for me rather than just a way of earning my living.'

'So that's the reason for your sober mood tonight? I thought it was something quite different,' said Connah casually. 'Like being addressed as "darling" this afternoon, maybe.'

CHAPTER EIGHT

THE silence which followed this statement grew too long for comfort. Hester drained her coffee cup and set it down, then refilled it. 'More for you?' she asked politely.

'Thank you. So tell me. Were you annoyed?' Connah said bluntly.

'Surprised, not annoyed.' She shrugged as she poured his coffee. 'You don't strike me as someone who bandies meaningless endearments about, so I assumed you had a practical reason.'

'You assumed right.' Connah leaned back in his chair, watching her, his long legs crossed at the ankles. 'I didn't like the way Luigi Martinelli was looking at you.'

Hester stared at him blankly. 'How *was* he looking at me?'

'You were wearing a few bits of green silk and a transparent shirt. How do you think he was looking at you? He's a man, for God's sake, and Italian at that.'

Hester was glad the covering darkness hid the rush of indignant colour in her face. 'I would remind you that I was not expecting a stranger to appear in the garden when Lowri coaxed me to wear the bikini.' Her chin lifted. 'Don't worry, it won't happen again!'

'Pity. That green colour looks spectacular against your tan. No wonder Luigi couldn't take his eyes off you. But you won't have any trouble from him,' Connah added with satisfaction. 'He knows the rules.'

'Which are?' she demanded.

'No mention was made of your official role in the household so now, naturally, he thinks the role is more personal—'

'Than the one I'm paid for,' she said stonily.

'Are you saying you'd have welcomed Luigi's attentions?'

She glared at him. 'Certainly not. He's a total stranger, also married. You mentioned his wife, remember.'

'Mainly because he'd rather forget he has one,' said Connah, shrugging. 'Luigi possesses a meaningless title but a very old name and impeccable lineage. Sophia inherited a pile of money from her wheeler-dealer Papa. She wanted Luigi's aristocratic pedigree and he needed her cash, which just about sums up the relationship, according to Jay Anderson. Since the birth of their son, they lead separate lives.'

'How sad.'

He shot her a look. 'You, I assume, would only marry for love.'

Hester was silenced for a moment. 'The subject has never really come up,' she said at last, 'but if it did, respect and rapport would be my priorities. Loving someone to desperation is not for me.'

'But you were willing to spend a holiday in the South of France with the actor.'

Hester nodded serenely. 'The offer was too tempting to turn down.'

'Then I gave you the chance of one in Tuscany instead. And there was no backing out of this one at the last minute,' he added.

'But that's different,' she protested.

'Why?'

'It's my job. I'm very grateful you asked me to come here with you and Lowri, of course, but you're paying me to work for you wherever we are.'

'A very cold-blooded way to look at it,' he said morosely and shot her a look she didn't care for. 'If the trip to France had come off, would you have shared bed as well as board with your Romeo?'

Hester stood up and put the cups on the coffee tray. 'The fact that I work for you, Mr Carey Jones, doesn't give you the right to ask personal questions.'

'I disagree. The moral welfare of my daughter gives me every right,' he retorted, getting to his feet.

'I was not looking after your daughter at the time,' she reminded him, dangerously quiet. 'Not counting breaks at home, the only holiday I've had in years was a package trip to Spain with school friends in my teens. Once I started work, I went straight from my first job to the Herricks. And looking after babies means constant responsibility, long, irregular hours and a lot of broken sleep. So yes. I was human enough to accept the offer of a free holiday in the sun before starting work in Yorkshire.'

'A long speech, but you still haven't answered my question, Hester.'

She gave him a haughty look. 'I don't intend to. Goodnight.' She picked up the tray and took it into the kitchen to wash up and with supreme effort did so quietly, instead of bashing dishes about in a rage.

'I apologise, Hester,' said Connah, coming up behind her so quietly that she almost dropped the cup she was drying.

'You startled me,' she said tightly.

'Come out again and have a glass of wine. It's too early to go to bed.'

'No, thank you.'

Connah looked down at her, his hard eyes wry. 'I've obviously offended you past all forgiveness.'

'I work for you,' she said shortly. 'I can't afford to be offended.'

'Dammit, Hester, that's hitting below the belt! I know damn well I have no right to probe into your private life.' He took the cup from her and put it on the tray, then fetched a bottle of wine from the refrigerator and gave her a smile she tried hard to resist. 'It's a pity to go to bed so early on a night like this. Can you honestly say you'll sleep if you do?'

'I'll read.'

'You can do that later. Come out and talk for a while.'

Because Hester had no real desire to go to bed, she swallowed her pride, went back outside and even accepted the glass of wine Connah poured for her.

'So what do you want in Greve tomorrow?' he asked.

'Postcards, some food for supper. Real local fare from small grocery shops rather than a supermarket,' she added.

'Whatever you want, as long as it doesn't involve cooking. I meant what I said. This must be a holiday for you before you go on to your next job. Particularly in the light of our recent discussion,' he added dryly. 'Will you enjoy looking after a newborn baby?'

Hester shrugged, resigned. 'I've done it before in my last post, twins at that. But, much as I love babies, it's a lot easier to look after someone like Lowri. And not just because she dresses and feeds herself,' she added with a chuckle. 'She's such fun and good company. And she sleeps all night!'

Connah laughed. 'Ah, yes, the broken nights. That's one part you can't be looking forward to.'

'I won't be doing it alone. Sarah Rutherford intends to feed the baby herself if she can, but I'll be on hand to see to the rest. At least there's just one to look after this time.'

'I don't know how you do it,' he said, grimacing. 'I wasn't around much when Lowri was at that stage. My mother and Alice bore the brunt of it.'

Because he'd had to cope with his wife's death, thought Hester with compassion, then eyed him quizzically when he gave a sudden chuckle.

'Talking of Alice, I wonder how Mal and Owen will cope when the baby arrives.'

'With someone of Alice's experience, perfectly well, I imagine. By the way, Lowri told me that Alice isn't at all like me.'

He let out a bark of laughter. 'God, no. Nice, sweet creature though she is, I wouldn't be sitting here with her like this.'

'Why not?'

'She's very nervous around me, for a start. In the unlikely event that I asked her to sit and chat over a glass of wine, she'd run a mile.' He shot a look at Hester. 'Alice is a sweet, ordinary young woman from the village near Bryn Derwen and I'll always be grateful to her because she came to us at a time when we needed her so desperately. I will never forget that. But she's very different from you, Hester.'

'In what way?'

'You're good looking, well read, and your qualifications are impeccable. Alice has no professional qualifications, other than willingness to work and her unbounded love of children.'

'Then I salute her, because Lowri is a credit to her—and to your mother, of course,' said Hester, and looked across at Connah. 'And last, but very definitely not least, to you—the most important person in her life.'

'I know,' he said soberly. 'And it's a huge responsibility.' He got up to refill her glass, but she shook her head.

'No more, thanks.'

Connah sat down again, looking out over the starlit garden. 'A pity we can't do this by the pool.'

'It's too far away from the house—and Lowri.'

'Exactly. I've been thinking about you a lot lately,' he added, startling her. 'I've tried hard to remember you as you were when I first saw you all those years ago. But all I can bring to mind is a teenager with long blonde curls and huge eyes.'

'The curls were courtesy of a perm and the eyes looked huge

because I was into heavy-duty eye make-up at the time.' She laughed. 'I was also rather chubby, but you've been kind enough to gloss over that.'

'From the fleeting glimpse I had of you by the pool this afternoon, it's not a word that applies any more.' He raised an eyebrow. 'As a matter of interest, would you have stayed in the bikini if I'd been there alone with you and Lowri?'

'Yes,' she said honestly. 'Lowri pleaded so I wore it.'

'Then wear it again, when we're safe from intruders.'

'I don't think so.'

'You mean it's not approved nanny wear?'

She nodded. 'Or housekeeper wear.'

He chuckled. 'A bit different from the archetypal Mrs Danvers.'

'So you've read Rebecca too.'

'Afraid not—I saw the film. It's one of the few films I've ever seen. I'm not a movie buff.'

Hester eyed him in surprise. 'You must have watched one of Lowri's DVDs with her?'

'No. I keep to chess,' Connah admitted.

'A suitable film is another good way to keep her company while she spends a quiet hour out of the sun. Try watching one with her some time. She'd love it.'

'Yes, Nanny.'

Hester chuckled. 'Sorry.'

Connah shook his head. 'Don't be. I'll take all the advice I can get. Pity the single male parent of a girl child.'

'Speaking professionally, I think you make an excellent job of it.'

'Thank you. But it's going to get harder as she gets older.' He sighed deeply. 'And my mother's convalescence is much slower than I'd hoped. It's going to be some time before she's in any kind of shape to look after an energetic child like Lowri.' He shot a look at her. 'I know the original agreement was six weeks, but if you're not due in Yorkshire until October, Hester, would you consider staying on with us for an extra week or two to get Lowri ready to go back to school?'

'Yes, of course,' she said without hesitation. 'If it helps you out, I'll be happy to.' More happy than he knew.

Connah smiled at her in relief. 'Thank you, Hester. That should take us up to the middle of September when Lowri starts back. Can you do that?'

'Yes. The Rutherford baby isn't due until mid-October. I promised to start there two weeks beforehand, to help Mrs Rutherford get ready for the big day, so it works in quite well and still gives me time to spend with my mother and Robert first.'

'That's a great load off my mind,' he said, smiling at her. 'But that's a long way off, so until then let's enjoy our summer in sunny Italy. I've never indulged in so much leisure time, so I might as well make the most of it.'

'Everyone needs to unwind now and then.' Hester got up. 'Time I went to bed.'

Connah rose immediately and put a hand on hers. 'Hester, forgive me for my transgression earlier.'

'Of course,' she said lightly, and smiled at him. 'Goodnight.'

The trip to Greve was a huge success. The sun-drenched piazza had originally been square, Connah informed them, but over time buildings with porticos and loggias had encroached on it until now it was a triangle pointing to the church of Santa Croce.

'The church has paintings of the school of Fra Angelico,' he added, then grinned as his daughter made a face. 'All right, don't panic. We'll just look round the shops and buy some postcards since it's your first day in town. Then we'll have some lunch and when Greve wakes up again afterwards we'll buy food for supper.'

For Hester it was hard to remember that this was part of a job she was being paid for as she strolled through the sunlit town with

Connah and Lowri. Never in her wildest dreams of the mysterious Mr Jones when she was young had she imagined a scenario like the one being played out right now. She could almost believe...

'Penny for them,' murmured Connah as Lowri went through every postcard on display before making her choice.

'They're worth far more than that!' Hester assured him.

Lunch was eaten in a restaurant with stone arches and terracotta floors, and best of all to Lowri, a vine-covered pergola with a panoramic view of the sunlit countryside of Chianti.

'Can we eat outside, Daddy?' she asked eagerly.

'Of course, *cariad*.' He turned to Hester. 'Unless you're too hot and would prefer to eat indoors?'

'No, indeed. I'll take all the sun and fresh air I can get.'

Connah had eaten at the restaurant before and, on his recommendation, they all chose light-as-air gnocchi with a sage and butter sauce as a first course, followed by pork roasted with rosemary and served with porcini mushrooms.

'They're just like little pillows,' said Lowri in delight as she tasted the gnocchi. Hester smiled at her lovingly, then flushed when she saw Connah watching her and applied herself to her own meal.

Full of good food, they lingered afterwards in the pergola, the waiters only too pleased to supply them with as much mineral water and coffee as they wanted.

'They take food very seriously here,' said Hester lazily, 'yet they seem quite happy for us to linger as long as we like. There's no rushing to clear away so that someone else can take our place.'

'Not their style at all. Besides, they have enough tables to make that unnecessary,' said Connah, and took his drowsy daughter on his lap. 'Sit quietly for a while, *cariad*, before we make for the shops again. They won't be open for a while, anyway.'

Lowri yawned widely. 'OK.' She snuggled her head into his shoulder and her father smoothed the length of silky hair with a stroking hand as she dozed off.

'I rang my mother last night,' said Hester quietly after a peaceful interval. 'She sent her regards.'

'Return the compliment when you speak to her again.' Connah looked at her across the shining dark head on his shoulder. 'Did your mother ever talk about my companion?'

'Only to say that she was ill. Mother was only too happy for you to stay until the lady was well enough to leave.'

'To my immense gratitude.' His eyes turned towards the sunlit view of vine-covered hillsides. 'I went back to your house a few years later to see your mother, but she was no longer there, of course. And the new owners very rightly felt they weren't at liberty to give me her address.'

'Is that why you came to fetch me the other night? To meet Mother again?'

'Partly.' The dark, intent eyes turned back to hers as though he was about to explain further, but Lowri stirred and sat up, yawning.

'I'm just like a baby, having naps all the time,' she complained.

'This one was very short,' her father said, kissing her nose. 'You go off with Hester to wash your face, then we'll wander round the town again—maybe we'll even force you to explore the church if the shops aren't open yet.'

Lowri slid off his lap at once as Hester got up. 'Do you like churches, Hester?' she asked, sighing.

'I'd like to look round this one. Then we can both write about it on our postcards.'

After a leisurely stroll back to the Santa Croce to admire its neo-classical façade, they went inside to look at the paintings. But Lowri grew restive in the dark interior and they soon went outside again into the sunlight, discussing what food to buy in one of the *alimentares*, the various grocery stores beginning to reopen after their long lunch break.

'We'll definitely get your local fare in one of these, Hester,' said Connah. 'We might as well stock up while we're here.'

Lowri was consulted on every purchase as they bought a great bag of tomatoes, another of peaches, crusty Tuscan bread, ricotta cheese and glossy green spinach.

'Though I'll leave Flavia to deal with the last two,' said Hester, smiling. 'Perhaps she'll make ravioli for us tomorrow.'

'I'll ask her,' said Lowri promptly. 'She likes me.'

'Does she really?' teased Connah. 'Now it's my turn to choose. I want some of those fennel flavoured sausages, and salami, and thin slices of roast turkey breast and ham, and more pecorino cheese. What about you, Hester?'

'Mozzarella and fresh basil, anchovies and olives, and some of those gorgeous baby lettuces, please.'

'Anything else? Speak now while I'm in a good mood, and willing to carry all this stuff to the car.'

'I'll help,' said Lowri promptly.

'I was only teasing, *cariad*. I'm happy to carry anything Hester wants.' Connah grinned. 'After all, she's going to make supper for us tonight.'

It was the kind of day, thought Hester, as they drove back to the Casa Girasole, that she would keep in her mind like a snapshot to look back at and sigh over during a cold Yorkshire winter. But the day wasn't over yet, she consoled herself, and once they were back at the house she sent Lowri off to have a swim with her father while she put the food away.

'If we all help with that, you can swim too,' said Connah, but Hester shook her head.

'That's my job. Besides, I have more idea where everything goes. Then I'll have a shower and start getting supper ready.'

'Can I help?' said Lowri eagerly.

'Of course,' said Hester.

'No cooking,' Connah reminded her.

'My choices were made with that in mind!'

Lowri's swim with her father was surprisingly brief.

'It wasn't the same for her without you,' said Connah as his daughter ran upstairs to shower. He rubbed at his hair with the sleeve of his towelling robe, his smile wry. 'I begin to see what you mean. Tomorrow morning I'll walk into the village with her while you do anything you want.'

'Laundry,' said Hester promptly.

He laughed. 'I was thinking more of a book by the pool with a long drink.'

'I can do that later, when you come back.'

Connah looked back at her as he made for the stairs. 'Did you enjoy the day, Hester?'

'Enormously.' She smiled cheerfully. 'Once Lowri comes down I'll get supper ready. Though after lunch I couldn't imagine wanting to eat another thing today.'

'Well, I can, easily, so be generous.' He paused. 'Not that I need to say that, Hester. Generosity comes naturally to you.' His dark eyes held hers. 'It was a lucky day for me when you came back into my life.'

Hester flushed, deprived of speech for a moment. He held the look a moment longer, then smiled and carried on up the stairs. Hester pulled herself together and went up to check on Lowri's progress and found her wrapped in her robe, gazing out of her window at the view. She turned with a sigh.

'I wish Mr Anderson would sell this house to Daddy. I just love it here. I'm sure Grandma would love it too.' She frowned. 'But she doesn't like flying—perhaps Daddy could bring her here by train if we have another holiday here.'

'In the meantime,' said Hester practically, 'let's get that hair dry so you can dress and help me put supper on.'

One of the many attractions about the holiday for Hester was the lack of hurry about everything. There was no rush to make supper and if Lowri went to bed later than usual it didn't matter in the slightest, because next morning she could sleep until she woke naturally.

'I thought we'd have *bruschetta* first,' said Hester, when a very clean and shining Lowri reported for duty. 'That's thick slices of the bread we bought, with a sprinkling of olive oil and some of those gorgeous tomatoes chopped and topped with basil, anchovies and olives.'

'I've never had anchovies,' said Lowri, inspecting them. 'They're all furry. How can you have furry fish?'

'Magic. But you can have yours without, if you like.'

'Does Daddy like them?'

'I don't know. So we'll just go as far as the tomatoes and basil, and put the olives and anchovies in little pots to add as required.'

'I'll do that, then,' said Lowri promptly. 'What else are we having?'

'Turkey, ham and salami. I'll whip some lemon juice and this wonderful olive oil together for a dressing for the lettuces, and you can get the cheese out.'

Connah crossed the hall later and paused in the kitchen doorway, unnoticed for a moment as he watched Hester and Lowri working together, the gleaming fair head bent to the shiny dark one. Then Hester looked up and smiled and the idea that had germinated in Albany Square, and had been growing in strength ever since, crystallized into certainty.

'It's a hive of activity in here,' he commented, smiling, and Lowri whirled round to beam at him.

'Supper's almost ready, Daddy.'

CHAPTER NINE

AFTER their trip to Greve, all three of them were content to stay at the house the next day. After a leisurely breakfast Connah went indoors to contact John Austin, but Lowri was perfectly happy to take her morning swim with only Hester for company. They played a splashing, noisy game with a ball, with rules that Lowri made up with screams of laughter as she went along until Hester called time at last. While they were towelling themselves dry on the edge of the pool, Lowri stiffened and nudged Hester.

'Look!'

A boy stood watching them from the area where the woods of Martinelli territory edged the grounds of Casa Girasole.

Hester pulled her towelling robe on quickly, wondering if she should call Connah, then heard someone in the distance shouting 'Andrea!' and Luigi Martinelli came racing through the trees with a younger man close behind. He clasped the boy in passionate relief but the boy pushed him away, embarrassed, and spoke urgently to him. Luigi spun round, saw they were being watched, then dismissed the young man with him and brought the boy towards the pool.

'I am intruder again,' he apologised breathlessly as he drew near. '*Buon giorno*, Miss Hester, Miss Lowri, allow me to present my son, Andrea, who has been missing long enough to cause much anxiety. He heard sounds of laughter from your pool and came to investigate.'

'*Piacere*,' said the boy, with a bow that won him a stare from Lowri.

'Hello, Andrea,' said Hester, smiling. 'You like swimming?'

'Very much, *signora*, but we have no pool at the *Castello*,' he said in English more heavily accented than his father's. He turned to an unusually silent Lowri. 'You like to swim?'

She nodded briefly and looked up uncertainly at Hester, who smiled at her reassuringly.

'Why not run and tell Daddy that the Count is here with his son?'

'OK.' Lowri took another look at the boy, then went running up the garden to the house.

'We have interrupted your swim,' apologised Luigi, watching with a wry smile as Connah emerged from the house and strode towards them. '*Buon giorno*. I regret that you have not one but two trespassers today.'

'Good morning.' Connah put his arm round Hester as he smiled at the boy making every nerve in her body tingle in response. 'Hello, there. I'm Connah Carey Jones.'

The slim, dark boy bowed again. 'Andrea Martinelli. Where is the girl, *signore*?'

'My daughter's getting dressed.' Connah smiled down into Hester's face. 'Would you like to do the same, darling? Ask Flavia to bring some coffee to the loggia.'

'Of course.' Hester excused herself and went up the garden into the house, to find that Flavia was already in a fever of activity to provide *Il Conte* and his son with refreshments.

'*Poverino*,' she said as she laid the tray.

With no hope of understanding the answer if she asked why Flavia pitied the boy, Hester went upstairs to change and found Lowri at her window, pulling on shorts and T-shirt as she cast a wary eye at the visitors.

'Are they staying?' she demanded.

'Only for coffee. I'll just throw some clothes on, then we'll go down and show off our exceedingly good manners.' Hester grinned and, after a moment, Lowri grinned back reluctantly.

'OK! I'll wait for you.'

Hester tied up her damp hair with a ribbon and pulled on white linen trousers and blue shirt, hoping that next time she met the Count, if there was a next time, she would be fully dressed from the start. 'Ready?' she asked as she looked into Lowri's room.

'I suppose so. Why has that boy got a girl's name?'

'It's not a girl's name here. It's Italian for Andrew.'

'I hope he doesn't stay long.'

'I thought he looked lonely, standing there by himself. Perhaps he just wants some company.'

Lowri heaved a sigh and followed Hester downstairs. 'He's got a funny accent,' she commented.

The atmosphere on the loggia was much more cordial than on the previous occasion, Hester noted as she sat down to pour coffee.

'Luigi says that young Andrea heard you playing in the pool and couldn't resist coming to have a look,' said Connah, pulling his chair close to Hester's.

'Will you have coffee or lemonade, Andrea?' she asked.

'Lemonade, if you please, *signora*,' he said formally, and Hester filled a glass for Lowri to pass to him. '*Grazie*,' he said, smiling at her.

'So how are you enjoying your holiday, Hester?' asked Luigi.

'Very much. We went to Greve yesterday. It's a delightful town.'

'A pity you are not here in September for the wine fair, which is Chianti's largest,' he commented, accepting a cup of coffee. 'Connah came last year with the Andersons.'

'That was one of the visits I mentioned, Hester,' said Connah. 'Lowri, why not take Andrea for a walk round the garden?'

His daughter shot a bright, accusing look at him, but after another at Hester she got up reluctantly and went off with the boy.

'They are like two little animals, prowling round each other ready to bite,' said Luigi, smiling after them indulgently. His eyes darkened. 'My son gave me a very bad fright earlier when he could not be found.'

Connah nodded. 'I can appreciate that. Don't you have someone to keep watch over him?'

'Of course, his *precettore*, his tutor. But the poor fellow went into the house to answer a call of nature—*scusi*, Hester— and when he came back Andrea had vanished. He ran off in anger because I had just told him I must return to Rome for a day or two tomorrow on business and wish him to stay here while I am away.'

'Is there no one for him to play with at the *Castello*?' asked Hester.

'Apart from the servants, there is only Guido. But I will be away only a short time. It is better he stays here than endure the journey to Rome and back.'

Connah nodded absently, watching the boy dabbling his hands in the pool while Lowri looked on, telling him something he was listening to intently. 'They seem to be getting on well enough now.'

Hester could see that. Andrea appeared to be nodding in enthusiastic agreement to something Lowri was saying, then the boy brushed the water from his hands and the pair ran up the garden together.

'Daddy,' said Lowri, 'can Andrea have lunch here? I told him Flavia was making ravioli. He likes that.'

Hester could tell by the look on Connah's face that he was desperate to laugh, but he nodded gravely. 'We'd be delighted, Andrea. You too, of course, Luigi.'

'Alas, I cannot, I must leave soon.' Luigi beckoned his son close and, with a word of apology to the others, spoke to him at length in rapid Italian, which the boy responded to with much enthusiastic nodding.

'Don't worry, we'll take good care of him, Luigi,' said Connah.

'I have no doubt of that. I was merely telling him to behave well and to make no argument when Guido comes for him later.' Luigi bowed over Hester's hand. 'It was a great pleasure once more. I trust my son did not startle you too much.'

'No, indeed.' Hester smiled warmly at the boy, who responded in kind, his eyes sparkling. 'We'll be glad to have your company, Andrea.'

'*Grazie, signora.*'

Lowri leaned against Hester's shoulder as father and son took leave of each other, watching as Luigi hugged and kissed his son, then came to smile down at her. 'Thank you for inviting Andrea, Miss Lowri. You are very kind.'

'No problem,' she said casually. 'He can watch one of my DVDs with me after lunch, if he likes.'

'He is a very fortunate boy!' Luigi took his leave all round, embraced his son again and walked off quickly through the garden to the woods bordering his own property.

'Right then, Andrea, let's help get the lunch,' said Hester, astonishing him.

'You have no servant for that, *signora*?'

'Flavia does the cooking, but we take the tray with the knives and forks and plates and we set the table on the loggia,' said Lowri.

'*Bene.* I will help,' he assured her manfully and followed her into the kitchen, where it was plain from the ensuing flood of Italian that Flavia was shocked to have the son of *Il Conte* involved in any way with lunch other than to eat it.

'Do the boy good,' said Connah, grinning. 'While the battle rages, stroll round the garden with me, Hester, and enlighten me about the mystery that is woman.'

She laughed at him as they strolled down towards the pool. 'You mean Lowri?'

'Absolutely. One minute she's snarling at the boy, then suddenly she wants him to stay to lunch.'

'These Italian men can be very charming,' said Hester demurely.

Connah threw out his hands. 'This one's only eleven, for heaven's sake.'

'But very much a chip off the old block. And very good-looking.'

'Then why was Lowri so hostile to start with?'

'He was invading her territory. Once she made it plain that this is her patch, and he's only here on her say-so, she relented. She's sorry for him because he looked so lonely standing there when we first spotted him.' Hester grinned at him. 'Like a junior Adam expelled from Eden.'

Connah led her to a chair under one of the umbrellas. 'His arrival has one advantage. If you're worried because Lowri clings to you too much, Andrea's advent could change that. This tutor of his could give you some time off if he looks after both children now and again.'

Hester stared at him, affronted. 'Certainly not. Lowri is my responsibility.'

'Even so, it won't do any harm for this Guido to watch over them at the pool for an hour or two—talk of the devil,' Connah added, as a young man appeared through the woods. He hurried towards them with a holdall.

'*Signore, signora.*' He bowed. 'I am Guido Berni. *Il Conte* told me to bring Andrea's swimming suit.'

'Excellent,' said Connah. 'Have you brought your own?'

'*Si, signore. Il Conte* wishes me to stay to make sure Andrea is no trouble for you—if you permit.'

'We'd be delighted,' Connah assured him. 'Here comes my daughter with Andrea now.'

Andrea was not at all delighted, obviously thinking that Guido had come to fetch him home, but when the tutor explained the boy's face cleared.

'He has to stay to take me back,' he explained to Lowri, then introduced her with quaint formality to his tutor, who bowed over her hand in a way which won her over completely.

'Are you staying to lunch too?' she asked. 'It's ravioli today.'

The young man flushed with embarrassment, but Hester smiled at him reassuringly.

'Of course you must stay.'

At first Andrea was not at all happy to have his tutor included in the lunch invitation. But he brightened considerably when Connah and Hester left the younger members to their own company as they talked to Guido, who was a very likeable young man from a local Greve family.

'I am a law student at the University of Padua,' he confided, relaxing as he began to eat Flavia's unrivalled ravioli. '*Il Conte* hired me to be with Andrea during the summer vacation.'

Connah smiled as he watched Andrea listening to Lowri with rapt attention as he did his best to understand everything she said. 'He doesn't strike me as needing much tuition, unless it's to polish his English,' he commented.

'*E vero,*' said Guido with feeling. 'He is very clever. But I am not really employed to teach Andrea. He has no need of extra tuition. *Il Conte*'s need is for someone to be with his son always. As *sicurezza*—for safety, you understand.'

'Oh, yes, we understand very well,' said Hester with feeling, and the young man nodded soberly.

'Of course, with so beautiful a young daughter.'

'Exactly,' said Connah, and touched Hester's hand to forestall any explanation about relationships.

After lunch Guido sat outside on the loggia with a textbook while Lowri and Andrea watched a DVD in the shady *salone*.

Connah excused himself to do some work and Hester, suddenly at a loose end, went out to sit under an umbrella by the pool.

She would enjoy the blessed peace while she could, she decided, since her presence would be demanded in the pool once Lowri had enough of sitting still. But Hester was wrong. When Lowri came running to join her, already changed into her swimming things, she announced that Daddy said she could go in the pool with Andrea and Guido.

'We're going to play games,' she said, her eyes shining.

'Sounds good to me,' said Hester, and turned with a smile as Andrea raced to join them, with Guido following at a more sedate rate with towels and wraps.

'Will you not join us in the pool, *signora*?' asked Andrea politely.

'No, thank you. I shall be very happy to sit here and watch.'

Guido, decided Hester as she watched, was a godsend. He was not only a strong swimmer, he made up a complicated game of tag with a ball, and when the youngsters tired of that he organised races and roped in Hester as referee when there were heated arguments over the winners.

Eventually she got up and said it was time everyone got dressed and had something to drink. 'You come upstairs with me, Lowri, while Andrea and Guido change in the downstairs bathroom.'

Connah met them outside Lowri's door. 'From what I heard, you were having a wonderful time out there, *cariad*.'

Lowri beamed at him. 'It was great. Guido's so cool. Are you coming down to have tea with us?'

'Of course. I'll go down and give Flavia your orders.'

While Connah was making his request in the kitchen, Andrea, dried, dressed and sleek of hair, knocked at the door.

'Thank you for letting us use your pool, *signore*,' he said punctiliously as Guido joined them to express his own thanks.

'My pleasure,' Connah assured them. 'Now, you gentlemen can carry the trays out to the pool for Flavia.'

Flavia was so delighted to serve the son of *Il Conte* that she brought out the *torta* made for dessert for the evening meal, but when Guido and Andrea insisted on carrying the trays to the pool for her she was clearly reluctant to allow them to perform such menial tasks and only submitted when Connah advised her to accept their help.

'I'll help too,' said Lowri, running down the stairs, and Hester, coming behind, eyed Connah questioningly.

'What am I required to do?'

'Just sit under an umbrella and let us look at you,' he said in a tone which won him a searching look from his daughter.

From then on the holiday took a new turn. Next day was a repeat performance, with Andrea spending most of the day at the Casa Girasole with Guido in attendance, but Luigi Martinelli returned from Rome the day after and came early to thank Connah and Hester for being so kind to his son.

'In return, perhaps you will allow your daughter to spend time at the *Castello* today,' he suggested. 'Andrea has a little work to do this morning before he may play again. But afterwards he is most eager to have Lowri's company for the day. You need not fear. Both Guido and I will take great care of her.'

'That's very kind of you, Luigi. Lowri's upstairs, getting dressed.' Connah exchanged a look with Hester. 'Would you go up to pass on Luigi's invitation, darling?'

'Of course.' She turned to Luigi. 'Are there women servants at the Castello?'

'Yes. I promise Lowri will not lack for motherly care!' He smiled at Connah. 'And you will wish to accompany us there, to make sure you leave her in safe hands.'

Reassured, Hester went up to consult with Lowri, who, as anticipated, was wild with excitement at the idea.

'Are you coming too?' she demanded, eyes sparkling.

'No. The invitation's just for you. But Daddy's going to walk there with you and any time you want to come home, just tell Andrea's father and he'll bring you back.'

'Am I going to have lunch there?'

'Yes. So I'll put a clean T-shirt in your backpack just in case— a comb too.' Hester gave her a sudden hug. 'Have fun, darling.'

Lowri hugged her back tightly. 'I wish you were coming too.'

'Nonsense. You'll have much more fun without me.'

The child gave her a very adult look. 'I'll miss you, just the same.'

Hester swallowed a lump in her throat. 'I'll miss you too. Think how quiet it will be without you.'

But once Connah and Lowri had gone off with Luigi, the house could hardly be called quiet since Flavia was singing at the top of her voice while she whipped it into shape. After informing her, not without difficulty, that numbers were reduced for lunch, Hester learned that *Signore Connah* had already informed Flavia of this, also that she could have the rest of the day off and was leaving soon after preparing a cold supper in readiness for the evening.

'*Bene*,' said Hester, surprised, and went off to the pool with her book.

Later Flavia appeared with a coffee tray, announced that she was ready to leave and, after a cheery, '*A domani*,' she hurried into the house.

After half an hour of peaceful solitude Hester was tired of it and felt a leap of pleasure as she saw Connah emerge from the trees to take the path towards the pool. 'Was Lowri happy at being left?' she demanded.

'Couldn't wait to get rid of me,' he said, taking the chair beside her. 'Last seen climbing the tower staircase at the *Castello* with Andrea, Guido panting after them in hot pursuit.'

'I told her to tell Luigi the moment she'd had enough and wanted to come home.'

Connah chuckled as he lay back, long legs outstretched. 'It won't be any time soon.' He turned to peer under the brim of her hat, a look in his eyes which made her pulse leap. 'Has Flavia gone?'

Hester nodded silently.

'Then we're alone at last, Miss Ward.'

'Would you like some coffee?' she said, preparing to get up, but he caught her wrist.

'No coffee. Relax.'

Not easy in these circumstances, thought Hester, subsiding. 'Please don't think you have to keep me company if you have work to do.'

'I have no intention of wasting such a golden opportunity, Hester. Work can wait.'

Her mouth dried. 'Have you spoken to your mother this morning?'

'Yes. I mentioned it before I went out.'

'So you did. Sorry.'

Connah gave her a wolfish grin. 'Are you by any chance nervous now we're alone, Hester?'

She felt her colour rise. 'Of course not.'

'Then I'll just take this tray up to the house and collect a book I've been trying to finish for weeks. Don't go away.'

Hester sat very still when he'd gone. Connah was right. She was nervous—just a little. To be suddenly alone with him felt so dangerous that it took her a while to realise that her phone was ringing from the depths of her tote bag. She fished it out and eyed the caller's name in surprise.

When Connah returned a few minutes later, he looked at her with concern. 'Hester, what is it? Don't you feel well?'

'I'm fine, but I've just had a phone call.'

'From your mother?' he said quickly. 'Something wrong at home?'

'No, in Yorkshire. The call was from George Rutherford in Ilkley. His wife had a fall at the works yesterday and had to be rushed to hospital. Sarah lost the baby and she's inconsolable, poor woman. So is he.' Hester took in a deep breath and tried to smile. 'I feel horribly selfish for thinking of myself in the circumstances, when the Rutherfords are so devastated, but it means I'm out of a job. As soon as we get back I'll have to find another post.'

Connah looked down at her in silence for a moment, then held out his hand to help her up. 'I might be able to do something about that. Come inside for a while, Hester, and I'll explain.'

She took the hand, eyeing him blankly. 'You know someone who needs a Norland nanny?'

'No,' he said as they walked up the garden. 'But I know someone who needs *you*, Hester.'

'You can't mean Lowri,' she said, puzzled. 'She doesn't need a nanny any more.'

Once they reached the *salone*, Connah took her hands in his. 'I know Lowri doesn't need a nanny, exactly. But she desperately needs a woman in her life who can take care of her. And, after talking to my mother this morning, it's obvious that she can no longer take care of Lowri without help.'

Hester gazed into the eyes holding hers. 'I'm not perfectly sure what you mean.'

'You told me yourself, Hester, that Lowri would like a stepmother, and you're the perfect choice. Lowri loves you, Hester. And, unless I'm much mistaken, you feel the same about her.'

She swallowed hard, trying to control the heart that had leapt, beating wildly, to her throat. 'I do love her. But to become her stepmother—'

'You would be obliged to marry me.' He smiled crookedly. 'Is that so impossible to imagine?'

'Yes,' she said after a tense pause. 'I thought you were offering me a job.'

'I was proposing marriage, but I obviously made a hash of it.' His hands tightened on hers.

'You must love Lowri very much.'

'I do. But I care for you too. Although we met for the first time years ago, we've known each other for a relatively short time since fate brought you back into my life, but I'd miss you like hell if you left us now. You're part of our lives now, Lowri's and mine. We need you, Hester.'

She gave him a troubled look. 'But I can't forget what you said about Lowri's mother, Connah. That you never wanted to feel that way about anyone again. No marriage would stand much hope of success on those terms.'

'When the holiday's over and Lowri's back in school I'll tell you all about her mother,' he promised. 'But for now, while we have this unexpected interlude of peace and privacy, I want you to think hard about my proposal.'

As if she'd be likely to think about anything else! 'It seems a pretty drastic solution to the problem of school holidays, Connah,' she pointed out. 'When I marry I expect it to be a permanent arrangement, not some kind of business transaction that can be cancelled if it doesn't work out.'

The dark eyes hardened. 'Is that what you think I'm suggesting?'

'That's what it sounds like.' She gave him a bleak little smile. 'I must be a closet romantic after all. Much as I love Lowri— and you're perfectly right, I do love her—I can't marry you just to provide her with the stepmother she yearns for.'

'As must be patently obvious, Hester, it's not just any stepmother she yearns for. She wants you.' Connah's eyes smouldered suddenly. 'And, just so you're not in any doubt, so do I.'

CHAPTER TEN

'IS THAT so hard for you to take in?' demanded Connah, after seconds ticked away with no response from Hester.

'Yes, it is,' she said at last, when she could trust her voice. 'Did you mean it?'

His eyes lit with a disquieting gleam. 'Of course I meant it. Marrying you would obviously fulfil Lowri's need for a mother, but it would also fulfil certain needs of my own. This is no fictional marriage of convenience we're discussing. I expect it to be normal in every way.'

'That's if I agree to it,' she said, surprising him. 'I don't think you've thought this through. You don't have to resort to something as drastic as marriage, Connah. There is another solution.'

He dropped her hands abruptly. 'Explain.'

Hester stood back, her arms folded across her chest. 'When Lowri went away to school, Alice stayed on with your mother to be on hand during school holidays. You could employ me in the same way, if you think your mother might like me enough to make that feasible.'

'You'd prefer that to marrying me?' he demanded incredulously.

Of course she didn't!

'Marriage is difficult enough—so I'm told,' said Hester crisply, 'when both parties are madly in love. It's certain to be a lot more so as a mere solution to a problem.'

Connah was silent long enough to make her edgy.

'Would you have preferred me to say yes without giving a thought to the pitfalls involved?'

'Hell, yes.' He scowled, looking so much like Lowri when things went wrong that Hester's lips twitched. 'What's so funny?' he demanded.

'You looked exactly like Lowri then.'

Connah flung away to walk to the long doors leading into the garden, one hand raking his hair back as he stared out at the profusion of colour. Hester gazed at his powerful shoulders and tapering back, her eyes moving down to his long muscular legs as she wondered if she'd just made the biggest mistake of her life. Her brief encounter with him in her teens had left her dreaming about him for years. Yet now she was turning down a proposal she'd never in her wildest moment imagined in those dreams, merely because the love of her life had made it for the wrong reasons. How stupid was that? He turned round suddenly and gave her the rare, blinding smile that made nonsense of her high-flown principles. But, before she could tell him her answer was yes to anything he wanted, Connah pre-empted her.

'This is what we do, Hester. We go on with our holiday, spending time together as a family, and if by the end of it your answer's still no, I'll go with your alternative. It's not what I want, but it's a damn sight better than letting you disappear out of Lowri's life—and mine—to bring up someone else's child.' He smiled wryly. 'Though keeping you on as Mother's companion will be an extravagance. You're a lot more expensive than Alice.'

'But I'm worth it,' she said lightly, to cover her disappointment. If he really wanted to marry her, surely he could have tried a bit more persuasion.

'Oh, yes,' he said softly, 'you're worth it, Hester.'

* * *

To Hester's chagrin, Connah kept very firmly to his plan for the rest of the holiday. Lowri spent some days with Andrea at the *Castello*, which meant that Hester was often alone with Connah for hours at a time. But, although he constantly reminded her in unspoken, subtle ways that their relationship had changed, he never took advantage of their time alone together to plead his cause. Which served her right, she thought irritably. Connah had said this was what they'd do, and that was that.

From then on Hester's underlying tension, far from spoiling her holiday, merely added a *frisson* of excitement to both the tranquil lazy days and the various expeditions to explore Tuscany. These outings were usually planned for the days when Flavia's husband Nico came to augment his job at the *Castello* by working in the garden at Casa Girasole. On one of Nico's days they were invited to lunch at the *Castello* and, because Guido had been given time off to visit his family, Connah remained with the children in the gardens while Hester accompanied their host on a brief tour of the turrets and towers of his ancient mediaeval home, marvelling that it was in such excellent repair.

'Since it was her reason for marrying me,' said Luigi, 'my wife considers her dowry well spent on maintenance of the *Castello*.'

Hester smiled at her spectacularly handsome host. 'I can't believe it was her only reason.'

He bowed, smiling cynically. 'At the time, possibly not, but it is the only reason which now survives. Are you going to marry Connah?' he added abruptly. 'He behaves like the dog with the bone over you. I am amazed he allowed you to tour my home alone with me.'

'I don't care for the word *allow*,' said Hester without heat, and he smiled ruefully.

'Forgive me. I do not express myself well in your language.'

She laughed. 'I think you do it very well.'

Again the bow. '*Mille grazie*, Hester. Now, let us join Connah before he comes to murder me.'

On one level it was a truly glorious holiday, with day trips to the ancient towers of San Gimignano and the great fan-shaped square of Siena and, last but not least, a triumphantly successful outing to Florence. After queuing to marvel at Michelangelo's David in the Accademia, they went on a tour of the wonderful shops before settling down to a long, lazy lunch. Lowri liked this outing best of all because Andrea went with them, which gave her a lot to write about on the postcards she sent off at regular intervals. But she wrote sealed letters to Chloe, Hester noted, amused. Detailed information about Andrea was obviously not to be trusted to a postcard anyone could read.

But on another level the holiday was a subtle waiting game that Connah indicated very plainly he intended to win.

The day before they were due to fly home, Andrea invited Lowri to a farewell lunch at the *Castello*. Connah walked there with her in the morning and then stayed to drink coffee with Luigi while Hester remained at the villa to finish off as much packing as possible. The house was more peaceful than usual because Flavia had been given the day off to make up for the extra hours she would put in after they left to prepare the house for the next visit of the Andersons.

Satisfied that the packing was complete other than last minute additions, Hester laid the table outside, then settled down there with the last of her supply of books. But she soon gave up trying to read and just sat, gazing out at the sunlit vista of flower-filled garden and the pool and hills beyond. She sighed, depressed. It would probably be raining when they got home tomorrow and life would return to normal, whatever normal might be in future. Back in Albany Square, Connah might even revert to remote employer again for the short time before Lowri went back to school.

'Why are you scowling?'

Hester looked up, startled, to find Connah standing over her. 'I didn't notice you coming through the garden.'

'I walked back via the village to post Lowri's letter.' He raked his dark hair back from his sweating forehead. 'Mad idea at this time of day. I need a drink. Can I get you one?'

She shook her head. 'I'll come in now to start lunch.'

'Then I'll sit at the kitchen table and watch.'

Hester put a pan of water to heat for the pasta and lit a low flame under the sauce Flavia had left ready the day before. Connah settled at the kitchen table with a bottle of mineral water, long legs outstretched, his eyes following every move while she put the simple meal together.

'If you need to wash, this will be ready in five minutes,' Hester told him, her tone tart because her fingers had turned to thumbs under the intent dark gaze.

'Yes, Nanny,' he mocked and retired to the ground floor bathroom.

She looked after him, biting her lip. His walk had put him in an odd mood. Which was a pity, when this would be their last lunch alone together. At least it would taste good. She drained the pasta, poured hot sauce over it and, because her appetite had taken a sudden nosedive, gave Connah the lion's share. She carried the tray out to the loggia, determined to be pleasant and conversational even if it choked her.

'That smells good,' said Connah as she set a bowl in front of him.

She nodded. 'I'll miss Flavia's cooking when we get back.'

'Yours is equally good, Hester.'

'Thank you. How was Lowri when you left?'

'About to embark on a treasure hunt in the *Castello* with Andrea, armed with clues in verse composed in two languages by Guido—a young man of many talents.' Connah smiled at her as he twirled his fork expertly in his pasta. 'Life will seem so flat for Lowri in Albany Square. I'll take her to visit my mother as soon as we get back so she can brag to Owen about her holiday.'

Hester smiled. 'She bought him a belt in Florence. Is he the kind of boy who'll appreciate something like that?'

Connah nodded. 'He's a good kid. Even if he doesn't like it, he'll thank her politely. Grandma Griffiths brought him up well. But if he's been told about Alice's baby he'll be able to trump Lowri's holiday news pretty effectively.'

Hester was finding it easier to sip water than eat, and Connah noticed. He noticed everything, she thought crossly.

'Aren't you hungry, Hester?' he asked, so gently she had a sudden, absurd desire to cry.

She smiled at him instead. 'Not terribly. It's so hot today.'

He poured her a glass of wine. 'Have some of this, then.'

Hester rarely drank wine at lunch time because it made her drowsy in the heat. But she fancied it just this once, she thought morosely. Afterwards she'd go up to her room for a nap. She would take her book to bed and doze the time away until Connah fetched his daughter home—because home for Lowri meant Connah. Something Hester could relate to all too easily.

'That's a strange look, Hester,' said Connah.

'The house is always so quiet without Lowri.'

'Peaceful, rather.' He looked at her bowl. 'You haven't eaten much.'

'No.' She got up to put the dishes on the tray. 'I'll just put these in the dishwasher, then I'll go up to read on my bed for a while.'

'No coffee?'

'Not for me, but I'll make some for you—'

'No.' He took the tray from her. 'I'll see to these.'

Hester thanked him very formally and went up to her room, deliberately depriving herself of a post-lunch hour alone with Connah. It was only prolonging the agony, she thought bitterly.

It was almost the end of the holiday and he'd made no actual reference to the proposal again. The days of lotus-eating at the Casa Girasole were over.

Hester stretched out on the bed in her cool, airy room and watched the filmy white curtains moving slightly in the faint warm breeze as she wondered what Lowri was doing right now. But, between them, Luigi and Guido would see that she came to no harm.

Quite sure that she'd lie awake all afternoon, Hester dozed a little eventually, but woke with a start to see Connah leaning in the open doorway, his lean torso and long legs tanned by this time to a shade of bronze which contrasted darkly with the white towel slung round his hips. Her stomach muscles tightened at the look in his eyes as he lounged away from the lintel and strolled towards the bed.

'This has gone on long enough, Hester.' He stood looking down at her in silence, a pulse throbbing at the corner of his mouth. Slowly he put a knee on the edge of the bed and leaned over her, his eyes smouldering down into hers for a second before he took her mouth with a kiss that made her head reel.

'Weeks ago you seemed to doubt that I wanted you,' he said in a tone which sent fire streaking down her spine as he pulled her against him. 'It's time you learned that I meant it.'

Held so close to him that she had trouble breathing, Hester knew very well that he wanted her. But, much as her body urged her to, she wasn't ready to surrender that easily. Summoning every last scrap of self-control, she pushed at him until her hands, flat against his chest, held him away a fraction.

'You're teaching me a lesson?' she demanded unevenly.

Connah flicked her hands away and pulled her close again. 'A lesson in love,' he whispered and kissed her again with a heat and passion intended to remove all possible doubt. When he raised his head at last his eyes glittered in triumphant possession as he tossed the sheet aside to look at her.

Hester felt her entire body grow taut in response to the eyes which moved over her in a scrutiny as tactile as a long drawn out caress. At last he pulled her into his arms, his mouth possessing hers with such fierce tenderness that everything was suddenly simple. He wanted her. And she wanted him. It was utterly pointless to pretend otherwise. She wreathed her hands round his neck, responding hotly to his lips and tongue and subtle, provoking hands. One of them slid into her hair to hold her head back as his mouth slid down her throat to linger on the throbbing pulse there, before it continued on a tantalisingly slow journey downward, tasting every inch of her before his mouth closed on each nipple in turn, his grazing teeth sending darts of fire to melt her into hot, liquid response. He uttered a growl of pure male satisfaction as his exploring fingers discovered her readiness, causing turbulence which mounted to fever pitch when his tongue replaced them. She went wild as he caressed the taut little bud he found with unerring aim. She gasped, her hair tossing back and forth on the pillows until he gave in to the demand of her frenzied hands on his shoulders and slid up over her and inside her to rocket them both on a tumultuous race with an engulfing, shattering orgasm as the prize.

Before Hester could even breathe normally again, Connah heaved himself up on his hands to look down into her stunned eyes. 'Are you angry?' he panted.

'Not—angry,' she gasped. Shattered in several pieces, possibly, but not angry.

'Good,' said Connah with satisfaction, and let himself down beside her. 'That means I won.'

Her eyes narrowed as she fought to breathe normally. 'Won what?'

'My gamble. I took a chance that this was the right way to convince you that we'd be good together. Not just good—spectacular,' he amended, kissing her swiftly. 'But it was a risk. I could have alienated you completely.'

She surveyed him, narrow-eyed. 'It's quite obvious that you won. You must have noticed I'm not complaining.'

He stared at her. 'Hester, you could have said no at any stage—'

'Oh, I know that,' she said impatiently. 'I meant there was no need for your gamble. If you hadn't insisted on your plan, I would have said yes long ago.'

Connah's eyes narrowed in menace. 'You mean you've kept me on a string all this time as some kind of dressage?'

'Certainly not. You made the rules. I kept to them,' she said sweetly.

He laughed and pulled her into his arms. 'So you'll marry me, then.'

Her lips twitched. 'You could try phrasing it a little more gracefully!'

He looked deep into her eyes for a long, sober moment. 'Will you do me the honour of becoming my wife, Miss Ward? I strongly advise you to say yes. If you don't, I'll keep you here in this bed until you do.'

Did he really doubt her answer? Hester pretended to think it over. 'Since it's nearly time for you to fetch Lowri home, I don't have much choice. So the answer's yes, Mr Carey Jones, I will.'

'Good,' he said with satisfaction. 'We'll get married right away.'

She blinked. 'Why the rush?'

His eyes gleamed implacably. 'I want it signed and sealed as soon as possible.'

Hester pushed him away and sat up, pulling the sheet up to her chin. 'Why, Connah?'

'Because, once having set something in motion, I like to see it through to completion with all possible speed.' He shrugged. 'I'm no good at flowery speeches, Hester, but I'm deeply grateful to you for taking Lowri and me on for life. Because that's what saying yes means. You do understand that?'

'Perfectly,' she assured him.

He eased her back down beside him. 'You said that respect and rapport were your main requirements in a relationship and, God knows, I respect you, Hester. I also like you enormously and enjoy your company, and I felt a strong rapport with you from the first moment we met up again. Now we've proved beyond all doubt that it's physical as well as mental, we have the basis for a very successful marriage.'

Not quite, thought Hester, her face buried against his shoulder. One major emotion was missing from his list. But she'd known that in advance. His capacity for love had been expended on Lowri's mother. But she was dead, poor lady, while Hester Ward was not only very much alive, but fiercely determined that Connah's feelings for her would eventually change into something a whole lot hotter than mere liking and respect.

She raised her head as she felt his body tense. 'What's the matter?'

Connah rubbed his cheek against hers. 'The magnitude of the risk just struck me.'

Hester eyed him curiously. 'Risk?'

'How would I have faced Lowri if you'd refused to come back to Albany Square with us?'

'I wouldn't have hurt Lowri by refusing to do that.'

He raised a sardonic eyebrow. 'Wouldn't you care about hurting me?'

'I hope,' she said primly, 'that I'd care about hurting anyone. But this is all hypothetical so it doesn't apply. You won your gamble.'

'In the most ravishing way possible!' He kissed her again, then sat up with a heavy sigh. 'If I didn't have to fetch Lowri we could repeat the experience, just to make sure.'

'Sure of what?'

'That you're completely clear on what I expect from our

marriage.' He reached for the discarded towel, then turned to look down at her.

'Not quite, Connah. Could you clarify things a little more?' she said demurely and smiled at him, her eyes dancing.

His eyes blazed in response as he reached for her phone.

'Luigi? Would you mind keeping Lowri a little longer? I've got something I need to see to here before I fetch her.' He paused. 'Wonderful. In an hour, then. *Grazie.*'

He dived back into bed, laughing against Hester's open mouth as he began making love to her all over again, this time with such slow, tormenting attention to every part of her that the hour was almost up before Connah could force himself to get out of bed.

'I need a shower,' he said, kissing her, and grinned. 'If I wasn't pushed for time, I'd suggest we had one together.'

Hester smiled drowsily. 'I'll take a rain check.'

Connah bent to touch a finger to her bottom lip. 'I'll remind you of that soon. Very soon. Ciao.'

Hester lay where she was for a minute or two, pinched herself to make sure she hadn't been dreaming, and went into the bathroom for a shower which she took, not without regret, on her own. As she dried herself she studied herself in the steamy mirror, trying to be objective about it. Whatever his motives for asking her to marry him, Connah had proved beyond all doubt that physically he found her desirable. He also said he liked her, respected her and enjoyed her company. She pointed an imperious finger at her reflection. Now, she told it, you just need him to fall madly in love with you.

When Lowri arrived home she was in a bubbling mood as she described the treasure hunt. 'Andrea was quite sad when I said goodbye,' she said over supper on the loggia. 'He asked me to come back again. Can we come back some time, Daddy?' she asked.

'Quite possibly, if the Andersons will let us. We can't stay longer right now because they're coming here themselves next week.' Connah smiled. 'It is their house, *cariad*.'

'Andrea said we could stay at the *Castello* next time.'

'Would you like that?' asked Hester.

Lowri thought about it. 'I'm not sure. It's so *old!* It's great to play in but it might be a bit creepy at night. I'd rather stay here. Besides, we've got a pool here and there's only that crumbly old fountain with Neptune and the mermaids at the *Castello*.'

She chattered all through the meal and her favourite *panacotta* which followed it, then looked at her father in question as he reached out a hand to take hers.

'Lowri, we have some very special news for you.'

She eyed him with deep misgiving. 'Bad news?'

Connah smiled at her lovingly. 'No, *cariad*. It's very good news. While you were out this afternoon I asked Hester to marry me and she said yes.'

Lowri's mouth opened almost as wide as her blue eyes. She looked wildly from her father to Hester. 'You really, really mean it?'

'Would I joke about a thing like that?' said Connah lovingly.

Lowri jumped to her feet and hurled herself at Hester, tears pouring down her face. 'You're going to live with us forever and ever?'

'Yes, darling,' said Hester huskily and held the child close. 'Are you pleased?'

The child nodded vehemently, burrowing her face into Hester's shoulder. She looked up, her eyes shining like stars in her wet face. 'Does that mean I'll get a baby sister as well?'

Hester's face burned as a pair of amused black eyes met hers over Lowri's head. 'Maybe, one day.'

Lowri whirled round to face her father. 'Hester must come with us to see Grandma when we go back, then I can take her to meet Owen and Alice.'

'How do you feel about that, Hester?' asked Connah.

'I think you and Lowri should go to Bryn Derwen on your own first, while I visit my mother and Robert,' said Hester and smiled wryly. 'You can break the news to your mother gently, Connah, and I'll come with you next time.'

'Don't worry, Hester, Grandma will be pleased,' Lowri assured her. 'She's always telling Daddy he should get a wife.'

'And, being a dutiful son,' Connah said, smiling smugly, 'I've done my best to please her. I assume,' he added, hugging his daughter, 'that you're pleased, too.'

Lowri hugged him back as hard as she could. 'I never thought I'd be so lucky.'

'Neither did I,' he told her, meeting Hester's eyes over the shining dark head.

CHAPTER ELEVEN

DURING the flight home Lowri talked non-stop about the wedding, her face glowing with excitement.

'Can I be bridesmaid?' she asked at one stage.

'Yes, of course, but I'd like a very simple wedding,' said Hester quickly. There had probably been a grand affair first time round, with all the usual attendant fuss, and Connah would naturally want something very different for a second marriage. 'My mother and Robert had a private ceremony with just a few friends. I'd like the same.'

'But you can still be bridesmaid, *cariad*,' said Connah, as Lowri's face fell.

'With a puffy dress too,' added Hester.

'Perfect!' Lowri said, relieved, then smiled rapturously. 'Can I tell Sam?'

Since he was waiting for them at Heathrow, Lowri was able to tell him soon after they landed.

'And just as well,' murmured Connah as his daughter flew towards Sam. 'Otherwise she might have exploded.'

'Will you break the news to your mother first, before driving to see her?'

'No. I'll make sure she's feeling well before I spring any surprises. Lowri will just have to contain herself until I say the word.'

Connah smiled as Lowri came skipping back with Sam as he hurried to welcome them home. 'How are things in Albany Square?'

'No problems, Boss.' Sam grinned from ear to ear. 'Lowri's just told me the news. My sincere congratulations to you both.'

'Thank you.' Connah shook his proffered hand. 'It took some persuasion, but Hester finally said yes.'

Sam smiled at her warmly. 'I hope you'll both be very happy. Best news I've had in a long time.'

'Thank you, Sam.'

'Sam, Hester's going to be my stepmother,' Lowri broke in, beaming. 'And maybe one day—'

'Time we were on our way,' said Hester quickly, avoiding Connah's eye.

They had barely left the airport for the motorway before the combined effect of Lowri's excitement and a restless night sent her to sleep. Connah smiled over his shoulder at Hester. 'Out for the count?' he asked softly.

She nodded, shifting the child more comfortably against her shoulder. She hadn't slept much herself. After a brief doze towards dawn, she'd sat up suddenly, wondering if she'd dreamt it all. And had felt a great glow of happiness when she'd realised it was all true. But the glow dimmed slightly when Connah told Sam to drive Hester to her parents' house next morning.

'I'm taking off with Lowri to Bryn Derwen first thing, so I'll leave it to you to see Hester's delivered safely.'

'Right you are, Boss.'

Reluctant to wake Lowri, Hester postponed her protests until Lowri was in bed that night.

'I can walk home tomorrow,' she told Connah when she joined him in the study. 'I'll leave in the morning soon after you do, and I'll be back the same time the next day.'

'Indulge me, Hester,' said Connah, 'I'll feel a damn sight happier if Sam drives you there.' He drew her down beside him.

'Now, let's talk. Where would you like to go for our honeymoon? Paris? Bali? Blackpool?'

Hester chuckled, diverted, and gave it some thought. 'I suppose we couldn't go back to the Casa Girasole?'

'I can ask Jay. Is that what you want?'

'It's what I'd like.'

'Then I shall enquire.' He gave her a look that clenched certain inner muscles in response. 'But Flavia would have to come in a lot later in the mornings.'

'Would she have to come in at all?'

'I suppose I can always pay her the same money and tell her to take a holiday. For my part, I don't much mind where we go. Privacy is my priority.'

Hester looked at him steadily. 'Mine is a different place from your first honeymoon.'

Connah's eyes shuttered. 'When I come back from Bryn Derwen I'll tell you everything,' he promised. 'But right now I refuse to let the past encroach on the happier present. Talking of which, I must buy you a ring.'

Hester shook her head. 'A wedding ring at the appropriate time will do, Connah.'

He pulled her on to his lap so abruptly that she stared at him, startled. Back here in the formality of Albany Square, the sudden intimacy was unexpected. 'We'll go shopping when I come back,' he said with emphasis. 'Just in case you need reminding, Hester, this is to be a normal marriage in every way, including a short—very short—preceding engagement. Complete with ring.' He kissed her very thoroughly by way of emphasis.

Startled, thrilled, her veins humming with the response Connah's slightest touch aroused in her since he'd made love to her, Hester thanked him, her voice not quite steady. 'It's just that I'd hate you to think I was in any way mercenary.'

Connah gave her the smile which always turned her into a not-quite-set jelly. 'You mean you're not marrying me for my money? Why, then?'

Other than getting her heart's desire? Hester thought about it. 'Various reasons,' she said at last.

'One of them, I assume, is my daughter.'

'Since I wouldn't be working for you without her, yes.'

Connah nodded. 'And the other reasons?'

'The same as yours, more or less.'

'You mean rapport, respect and mind-blowing sex?'

Hester gave an involuntary crow of laughter which Connah smothered with a kiss.

'I suppose there's no hope of the last part tonight?' he whispered against her lips.

'Absolutely not!'

'When, then?'

Hester gave him a long look. 'I'd rather wait to actually sleep with you until we're married. Or at least until Lowri goes back to school.'

Connah's heavy eyelids lowered over a calculating gleam. 'Who said anything about sleep?' He eyed her in silence for a moment, then sighed heavily. 'You mean it.'

'Yes. Not because I don't want to.' She gave him a swift kiss so passionate that his grip on her waist tightened painfully. 'But Lowri might find it odd if I suddenly changed bedrooms.'

Connah smiled wryly. 'And God knows I want my daughter to be happy. But I'm going to do my damnedest to make sure you're happy too, Hester.'

'I hope to do the same for you, Connah,' she said soberly. 'I'll certainly try.'

'You don't have to try.' He tilted her face up to his. 'But if you won't sleep with me, a few more kisses like that one would make me happy for the time being. The very first kiss you've given me of your own accord, incidentally.'

'I don't go round kissing my employers,' she said severely.

'Not even the baby-faced actor?'

'Keir wasn't my employer.'

Next morning Hester kissed an excited, bubbling Lowri goodbye, then lifted her face for the kiss Connah took his time over, to his daughter's deep satisfaction.

'Give my regards to your mother and Robert,' he said as he got in the car. 'We'll have them over for dinner as soon as I get back. And let Sam drive you. Please,' he added, with an intense black look of something so much more entreaty than command that Hester gave in.

'I will, Connah.'

'I'll ring you tonight,' called Lowri as the car began to move. 'I expect Daddy will too.'

'Count on it,' said Connah.

Hester stayed where she was for a moment, feeling oddly forlorn as she watched the car glide away down the access road. She shook herself impatiently and went up into the house to see Sam. 'I'd like to leave in about ten minutes, if that's all right with you. Though I'd much rather walk.'

Sam nodded. 'I know you would. But Connah wants me to drive you there, so that's what I'll do.'

'You too, Sam?' she demanded. 'Is there something I'm not being told?'

'Connah doesn't confide in me, Hester.'

She sighed, defeated. 'OK. I'll be down shortly.'

Sam drove her to Hill Cottage, but tactfully turned down Moira's offer of coffee and promised to return the next morning to take Hester back to Albany Square. Moira and Robert hurried Hester through the house into the garden, demanding every detail of the holiday.

'Lowri was sweet, sending us so many postcards,' said Moira. 'She obviously had a wonderful time.'

'I think you did too, Hester,' said Robert, eyeing her glowing face.

She nodded happily. 'The best.'

They lingered over coffee in the garden, taking advantage of the weather, which was forecast to change later in the day. Hester handed over their presents, then sat back smiling as her mother exclaimed over the glove soft leather handbag bought in Florence, Robert equally delighted with his wallet from the same source.

'You were so extravagant, darling,' said Moira, 'but it's a gorgeous bag—I just love it.'

'Right,' said Hester, bracing herself. 'Now you're sitting comfortably, I have some news to give you. Some bad, some good.'

Moira braced herself. 'The bad news first then, please.'

'Mr Rutherford rang me while I was in Italy. His wife had a fall and lost the baby.'

'Oh poor *girl*! How is she?'

'Still desperately upset when I rang last night. I feel so sorry for her.'

'That means you don't have another job lined up yet,' said Robert, cutting straight to the chase.

'No. But here's the good news.' Hester took in a deep breath and smiled shakily. 'Connah's asked me to marry him. And I've said yes.'

Moira stared at her daughter in blank astonishment. 'I can't believe it!'

'I can, easily,' said Robert, surprising his wife even more. 'I had a feeling the wind was blowing that way when Connah drove here to collect Hester.'

'Well, I didn't. My maternal radar failed on that one.' Moira got up to clasp her daughter in a rib-cracking embrace. 'Are you really, truly happy about this, darling?'

'Really, truly,' Hester assured her. 'And Lowri is ecstatic.'

'More to the point, is Connah ecstatic too?' said Robert.

Hester smiled demurely. 'He seems to be.'

'So you're not just a mother for Lowri?' said Moira anxiously.

'No. Connah wants to marry me for the usual reasons.'

'You mean he's in love with you?'

'Not yet.' Hester gave her the details of Connah's recipe for a successful marriage.

'That's all very well,' said Moira, frowning, as she sat down again. 'But to make a marriage work you need rather more than liking and respect, rapport or not.'

Hester coloured slightly. 'The "rather more" isn't missing, Mother.'

'You mean he's physically attracted to you,' said Robert, nodding sagely.

'But do you feel the same about him?' demanded Moira.

Hester gave her mother a wry little smile. 'You know perfectly well that I fell head over heels the first time I saw him. But he belonged to somebody else then—'

'And you were very young!'

'Old enough to dream about him for ages. I just couldn't get him out of my head,' admitted Hester ruefully. 'When he walked into his study the day of my interview and I was actually face to face with my dream lover at last, I realised why no other man in my life had ever measured up to him. And if I didn't feel like that, liking and rapport or not, I wouldn't marry him.'

'Thank God for that,' said Moira, relieved. 'Has he talked about Lowri's mother yet?'

'No. Connah's leaving that until he gets back from Bryn Derwen.'

'But you think he still loves her?'

'I know he does.' Hester looked her mother in the eye. 'But I can live with that.'

* * *

Lowri rang after lunch to say they'd arrived safely, and Grandma was looking a little better. 'Daddy's taking me to the farm to see Owen so I can't talk for long. But I wish you'd come with us, Hester.'

'I will next time.'

'Give my love to your Mummy and Robert. Daddy says he'll ring you tonight about ten.'

Soon after the celebration dinner Moira had insisted on cooking, Hester pleaded weariness and went outside to climb the steps to her own room to wait, knowing, or at least hoping, that Connah would be punctual.

'Where are you?' he asked on the stroke of ten.

'Alone in my retreat. Where are you?'

'In the garden. Next time, I want you here with me, Hester. My mother's anxious to meet you. She's very pleased, by the way.'

'I'm glad. How is she?'

'Better, though still fragile. But the news that I'm getting married at last cheered her enormously. I think a big part of her problem in getting well was her worry over Lowri.'

'I do hope she'll like me.' But I want *you* to love me desperately, thought Hester and bit her lip, half afraid she'd spoken aloud, but, since Connah assured her that his mother would very definitely like her, assumed she had not.

'Lowri missed you today. So did I,' he added, his voice a tone lower.

Not sure how to respond to that, Hester asked about the visit to the farm. 'Did Owen like his belt?'

'Surprisingly, he was delighted—as much by Lowri buying him a present, I think, as the actual belt.'

'And how's Alice?'

'Blooming, very round, and very happy. Owen, by the way, is tickled pink at the prospect of a baby, so is Mal. But Lowri is so full of herself over having you for a stepmother, she wasn't as envious as she might have been. *Did* you miss me, Hester?' he added.

'Yes.' After four sun-drenched weeks spent almost constantly in Connah's company, Hester had missed him badly. 'I wish you could have been there to share the special dinner Mother whipped up. Robert produced some vintage champagne to mark the occasion.'

'Sorry I missed it. They were happy with your news?'

'Yes, once they were sure that I'm happy too.'

'I'll make an official visit as soon as I get back. With Lowri, of course. You can keep her occupied while I ask your parents' blessing.'

'No problem there. Do we have your mother's blessing too?'

'Very much so. With one reservation. She thinks I should have told you everything about Lowri's mother before asking you to marry me.'

'Why?'

'Once Lowri's in bed tomorrow night I'll explain, I promise. Now, tell me again that you miss me,' he added softly.

'I do. Desperately. I wish you were here with me right now.'

'I'll remind you of that tomorrow night, Hester!' he said, a note in his voice which curled her bare toes.

Sam arrived promptly at eleven the next morning. This time he accepted the offer of coffee and stayed chatting for a while with the Marshalls before driving Hester back to Albany Square.

'Your parents are obviously pleased for you,' he commented as they set off.

'They were—once they got over the surprise.'

'They're giving you into safe hands. Connah's a good man.' Sam shot her a sidelong grin. 'And damn lucky too, to get a wife like you at last.'

'Thank you.' Since meeting him again, it had astonished

Hester that a man like Connah was still single, but she had no intention of asking Sam if he knew why.

'Should I be doing some food shopping?' she asked as Sam turned into the garage.

'Not today. I've ordered enough in for the time being.'

As Hester got out she gave a smothered screech as a man rushed towards her from the open garage doorway.

'Please,' he said urgently. 'I need to talk to you—'

'Like hell you do!' Sam blocked his way, glaring at him.

A pair of angry blue eyes glared back. 'I wasn't talking to you. I just wanted a word with this lady.'

'Only after you deal with me,' snapped Sam. 'Name, please, or we call the police.'

The man stood his ground. 'That won't be necessary,' he said coldly. 'My name is Peter Lang, I'm a university lecturer and I'm here in town on a visit to my sister.'

'But why do you want to speak to me?' asked Hester as her heart resumed its normal beat.

He turned to her in appeal, pointedly ignoring Sam. 'I hoped you might give me some information.'

'What kind of information?' she asked, frowning.

'About the little girl in the park.'

Sam's face shut like a steel trap. 'Get the police, Hester.'

'For God's sake,' said the man, incensed. 'I'm not interested in her that way! I spoke to her because the child reminded me of someone I once knew. She told me that this lady isn't her mother, but—'

'For your information, Mr Lang, Miss Ward is the fiancée of the owner of this property,' said Sam brusquely.

'I see.' He reached into his breast pocket and handed his wallet to Sam. 'To confirm my ID,' he said, and looked at Hester. 'If I frightened the child, I apologise sincerely. I meant no harm.'

'As it happens, you didn't frighten her,' Hester informed him coldly. 'She'd been forewarned in school about men like you.'

His pallor deepened. 'I am not a paedophile,' he said through his teeth. 'I just want to contact her mother before I fly back.'

'If you want any information, I suggest you apply to my fiancé,' said Hester.

Their visitor nodded numbly. 'When would be a good time?'

Sam glanced at his watch. 'He'll be here soon. You'd better come up to my place and wait.'

When they reached his quarters, Sam glanced at one of the monitors. 'My boss has just arrived. Wait here, Mr Lang, while I talk to him.'

Sam ushered Hester out swiftly and shut his door a split second before Lowri came running up to throw herself into Hester's arms.

'Daddy said you'd be here.'

'Of course I am.' Hester hugged her close. 'Where else would I be?' She smiled up at Connah as he reached the head of the stairs. 'You're early.'

'Some of us were impatient to get away,' he said wryly. 'My intention was to stop for a snack on the way, but madam here wouldn't go for that. She wanted to get back to you.'

'Right,' said Hester, exchanging a look with Sam. 'I'll take Lowri up to her room to put her things away.'

'Could I have a private word, Boss?' said Sam.

Connah shot a searching look at him, then raised an eyebrow at Hester, but she touched a surreptitious finger to her lip and took Lowri off to ask about the visit to Grandma and the farm. Lowri was only too happy to oblige. Hester had been given every last detail when, after what seemed like hours, Connah finally rang her.

'Come down to the study, please, Hester,' said Connah in a tone which made her shiver. 'Sam will stay with Lowri for a while.'

'Daddy wants me downstairs,' Hester told Lowri. 'So Sam will come up here in a minute to keep you company. You can show him all your photographs again.'

'Why can't I come down too?'

'Daddy has a visitor he wants me to meet. I'll be back as soon as I can.'

Hester ran downstairs to find Sam waiting for her outside the study. 'Is Mr Lang still here?'

'No, he just left. The boss is waiting for you,' he said, and started upstairs. 'I'll go and see Lowri.'

Connah was standing in front of the empty fireplace and one look at his face filled Hester with dread.

'What's wrong?' she asked fearfully. 'Did you speak to this Mr Lang?'

'Yes. Come and sit down.'

She sat on the edge of one of the sofas, eyeing him with deep misgiving. 'Are you going to sit beside me?'

'No. I'll do better on my feet,' he said tersely, and ran a hand through his hair. 'My mother was right, as usual. I should have told you this before I asked you to marry me.'

'Is it something to do with Mr Lang?'

'Yes.' He paused, as though searching for the words to say next. 'There's no easy way to put this. Peter Lang is Lowri's father.'

Hester stared at him in total shock. 'I don't understand,' she said at last. 'If he was your wife's lover—'

'Laura was my twin sister, not my wife.' His face contorted suddenly. 'God knows how I managed to stop myself from strangling that man just now.'

'So Lowri's your niece,' Hester said slowly.

'Not to me. In every way other than biologically she's my daughter,' he said flatly. 'After Laura died giving birth to her, I adopted Lowri legally.'

'Welsh for Laura,' murmured Hester in sudden comprehension. 'So that's why you're so careful about Lowri's safety. You're afraid Peter Lang will take her away from you.'

'Just let him try!' said Connah fiercely, then shrugged. 'But he won't because he doesn't know he's her father. He never knew that Laura was pregnant.'

'So what did you tell Mr Lang?'

'That Laura was dead.'

'Nothing else?'

'Nothing.' Connah's eyes glittered coldly. 'He met Laura when he first started lecturing at Brown and she was at the British Embassy in Boston. They became lovers almost from the first and the inevitable happened.' His mouth twisted. 'But, before she could give her lover the glad news that she was pregnant, she discovered, due to a guest list she was compiling for some embassy function, that Peter Lang had a wife he'd forgotten to mention. Utterly heartbroken, she told her boss she was needed at home and caught the first flight available to Heathrow. I met her at the airport the night I knocked on your mother's door.' The bleak look in his eyes cut Hester to the heart.

'She was in the other room. I never saw her,' she said softly.

'She hadn't eaten or slept in days, so she was in such bad shape by the time we got to your house that I put her straight to bed. And, as you know, your wonderful mother let us stay until Laura was able to travel home with me to Norfolk.'

'Did Peter Lang try to contact her?'

'Yes, he was a nuisance. He bombarded Laura with telephone calls for a while. When she refused to speak to him, he flew over and went to the house, but Laura refused to see him either, because her condition was obvious by then. To give him his due, Lang made several more attempts to see her before he finally gave up and flew back to the States. After that he resorted to letters, telling her he was getting a divorce so they could marry. After the first one she returned the rest unopened. Laura saw things in black and white. The love of her life had deliberately deceived her and she couldn't forgive that. Laura was in a pretty low state physically as well as mentally and caught every bug going the rounds during the pregnancy. The final straw was pneumonia. The baby arrived a month early and, tiny though she was, survived. Laura did not.' Connah's face contorted with pain at the memory.

'I'm so deeply sorry,' said Hester, her heart wrung. 'When did your mother move to Bryn Derwen?'

'She'd always wanted to return to the part of Wales she came from, so I bought the house months before the baby was due. My intention was to move all three of them there after the birth, to give Laura a fresh start. But in the end my mother took the baby there on her own, engaged a nice, kind girl from the local village to help look after the child officially known as my daughter, and you know the rest.' He shrugged. 'Due to my success in the financial world, I've always been security conscious. But when I heard that some man was sniffing round Lowri alarm bells rang.'

'Why was Peter Lang here in town?'

'By some ironic twist of fate, he is working over here at the moment. But he flies back to America next week, ready for the start of the autumn term.'

'Unaware that he has a beautiful daughter,' said Hester thoughtfully.

Connah gave her a searing look. 'Are you implying that I should tell him?'

'That's entirely your decision. But I wish you'd told me.'

'Would you have turned me down if you'd known?'

'No—'

'Then I don't see what difference it makes.'

'The difference is that you didn't trust me with the truth,' said Hester bleakly. 'You left trust out of your blueprint for a successful marriage.'

'Of course I trust you,' he said impatiently. 'Enough to know that Lowri's happiness means a damn sight more to you than Lang's.'

'Are you going to tell her the truth one day?'

'I suppose I must.' Connah rubbed his eyes wearily. 'Probably when she first needs a birth certificate, which states that her mother was Laura Carey Jones, father unknown. But by that time she should be old enough to cope with the truth.' He opened his eyes to look at Hester. 'You're not happy with this.'

'No.' She got up. 'But don't worry, I'll do my best to put on an act. Lowri is so happy that I just can't let her think something is wrong.'

Connah caught her hand with sudden urgency. 'Has this changed your mind about marrying me?'

Hester shook her head silently.

'Because of my daughter?' he demanded.

'Partly,' she said honestly. 'If it wasn't for Lowry, I'd suggest we slowed down, backtracked a little. But—'

'But, because of Lowri, you'll keep your word.'

'I always keep my word,' she retorted. 'I was going to say that if it wasn't for Lowri, the entire question wouldn't have arisen. You're marrying me to get a mother for her—'

'And to provide a wife for myself, Hester. Don't forget that,' he said harshly.

'No,' she said wearily. 'I won't.'

'Good.' Connah released her hand, eyeing her in a way which put her on guard. 'But, before we leave the subject, I need your word that you'll never contact Lang to tell him the truth.'

She gave him a hostile stare, feeling as though a lump of ice had lodged in her chest. 'You really had to ask me that?' She flung up her right hand. 'All right. I swear I will never contact Peter Lang for any reason whatsoever, so help me God.'

'Hester.' Connah started towards her, but she turned her back on him and went from the room.

* * *

The period that followed the life-altering discovery was a hugely testing time for Hester as she and Connah, by unspoken mutual consent, kept up the fiction that all was well in the Carey Jones household. All three of them went to lunch at Hill Cottage the next day, at Moira's insistence, rather than the formal restaurant lunch Connah had suggested. Fortunately Lowri was so blazingly happy that any constraint between the newly engaged couple went more or less unnoticed during the meal as she gave Moira and Robert a blow-by-blow description of everything she'd done in Tuscany, including a great deal about Andrea.

'But, best of all,' she said with great satisfaction, 'was when I came back from the *Castello* on the last day and Daddy told me he'd asked Hester to marry him. I was so happy I cried like a big baby.' She beamed on the company at large. 'I can't wait to tell Chloe when I get back to school.'

'I hope you don't mind the short notice, Moira,' said Connah, 'but we're aiming for the day before Lowri goes back to school. Hester wants a small party here with you, but please allow me to arrange a caterer.'

Moira's eyes widened as she looked at her daughter. 'You didn't say it would be so soon, Hester.'

'We hadn't sorted the details when I gave you the breaking news.' Hester smiled at Robert. 'Will you mind having people tramping over your garden again?'

'Not in the least, dear.' He patted her hand. 'I'm flattered that you want the reception here. But won't it limit the guest list?'

'My share won't be long,' said Connah.

'My list won't be long either,' Hester assured him. 'The garden is too steep for a marquee, so the numbers will depend on how many can cram into the house if it rains.'

Lowri nodded in a very grown up way. 'But you want the party at home with your Mummy. When I get married I'll want you to do my party too, Hester.'

'Hey—let's sort this wedding first,' said Connah, smiling at her.

The next hurdle was a trip to rural mid-Wales for the formal visit to Bryn Derwen.

Marion Carey Jones came out to meet them as the car moved up a winding drive towards the pillared portico of a solid, four-square house built in the first decade of Victoria's reign. Her silver-streaked hair, cut short to frame her face, had obviously once been as dark as Connah's and, though her finely chiselled features bore traces of her recent ordeal, the likeness to her son was unmistakable. She held out her arms, smiling, as Lowri shot from the car.

'Grandma,' said the child, hugging her, 'we've brought her. This is Hester.'

'How do you do, Mrs Carey Jones?' said Hester, holding out her hand.

The other woman took it, but only to draw Hester nearer so she could kiss her cheek. 'That's such a mouthful, just call me Marion. Welcome, my dear. Connah, take Hester's things up to the guest room. Lowri, run and ask Mrs Powell to bring some tea to the conservatory.'

Having neatly arranged to get Hester to herself for a moment, Marion led the way through to the conservatory at the back of the house.

'No point in beating about the bush—has Connah told you everything now?' she asked without preamble.

Hester nodded. 'In the end he was forced into it, but I'll leave it to him to tell you about that.'

'Has it changed your mind?' asked Marion.

'No. But I wish he'd trusted me with the truth beforehand,' said Hester frankly, then looked round with a smile as Lowri came in with a plate of cakes.

'These are Welsh cakes, Hester. Mrs Powell made them specially.'

'How lovely. They look delicious.'

'Ah, good, Connah,' said his mother as he came in carrying a tea tray. 'You saved Mrs Powell a trip.'

'I don't think she was best pleased,' he said wryly. 'I think she wanted a look at Hester.'

'I'm sure she did. But you can introduce Hester to her later.'

Connah left any mention of Peter Lang until Lowri was in bed that evening after an excellent dinner served early by Mrs Powell who, far from being the ogre Hester had expected, was a trim, neat woman very obviously fond of her employer.

'Her only fault,' said Marion ruefully, once they were sitting in the conservatory later, 'is her fanatical tidiness. She doesn't like trespassers in her kitchen, including Lowri.'

'It's your kitchen, Mother,' Connah reminded her.

'It's a long time since I cooked anything there.' She smiled gently at Hester. 'Lowri is obviously delighted at the prospect of having you for a stepmother, my dear, but do I sense some reservations on your part?'

'Hester has doubts about a decision I've made,' said Connah bluntly. 'Please don't get upset, Mother, but you have to know. Peter Lang turned up at the house yesterday, asking for information about Laura.'

'Good heavens!' Marion's eyes widened, but she took the news calmly, to Hester's relief.

'Unfortunately,' Connah continued grimly, 'he arrived before I had time to tell Hester the truth about Laura.'

'Which, of course,' his mother informed him, 'you should have done before asking her to marry you.'

'I know,' he said bitterly.

'How on earth did Peter Lang find you?'

Connah explained, but she frowned as he mentioned the incident in the park. 'I made Lowri promise not to tell you.'

Marion Carey Jones gave her son a disapproving look. 'Making a child complicit in deceit is not a good thing, Connah.'

'I'm well aware of that. But at the time I was afraid to jeopardise your recovery.'

Her eyes softened. 'So what happened when you finally met Peter Lang yesterday? How did he take the news that he has a daughter?'

Hester tensed and at any other time would have felt amused by the look of guilt on Connah's face.

'I didn't tell him, Mother,' he said brusquely.

Marion Carey Jones looked long and hard at her son. 'So when are you seeing him again?'

'I have no plans to do that.'

She stiffened. 'Are you telling me that you intend to leave him in ignorance?'

'Yes—as Laura wished,' he said flatly.

His mother looked at him searchingly. 'Laura's wishes or yours, Connah?'

'Both. That's my decision, Mother, and it's not open to discussion. Now, if you'll both excuse me, I'm going to check on Lowri.' Connah gave both women a slight formal bow and strode out of the room.

'Are you all right, Marion?' said Hester anxiously.

'Yes. Don't worry. My heart's doing fine, other than feeling heavy right now.' Marion Carey Jones sighed deeply. 'Tell me how you feel about all this, Hester.'

'I don't feel entitled to have a say in it, but personally I think Connah's wrong.'

'I could see that. Does it make you want to back out of the marriage?'

Hester shook her head. 'Has Connah told you how we first met?'

'When your home provided shelter from the storm for my children?' Marion smiled. 'Yes. When he finally brought Laura home to me, Connah was full of gratitude to your mother, though, to be truthful, he didn't mention you at the time.'

Hester smiled ruefully. 'To Connah I was just the teenager who fetched and carried trays. But I fell madly in love with him the moment I set eyes on him, convinced that the lady with him must be his lover and they were running away together. I thought it was wildly romantic.'

'Whereas the truth was anything but.' Marion frowned. 'I want you to know that I strongly disapprove of my son's keeping it from you until after you'd agreed to marry him. Would you have refused if you'd known beforehand?'

'No,' said Hester honestly. 'When I met Connah again I realised why none of the relationships I'd had with men had ever come to anything. Though,' she added hastily, 'I never thought of marrying Connah. Especially after he told me that part of him had died along with Lowri's mother. But when he proposed I accepted, because I love him.'

'A powerful reason for saying yes—my son's a lucky man,' said Marion with warm approval. 'But you disapprove of keeping Peter Lang in the dark.'

'Yes.'

'But not enough to keep you from marrying Connah?'

'Of course not,' said Connah as he rejoined them. 'She won't back out, Mother, because of Lowri. Hester cares a great deal more for my daughter than she does for me.'

'Is that true, Hester?' asked Marion.

'No, it's not.' Hester gave Connah a sidelong look. 'We are both going into this marriage with our priorities firmly in place. As Connah told me right from the start, his requirements are respect and liking—'

'And a third element I shall leave out to save your blushes, Mother,' he said sardonically.

'Talk of sex doesn't make me blush,' she retorted. 'It would all seem rather cold and businesslike otherwise.'

Connah shook his head. 'My future wife is blonde, beautiful, intelligent and loves my daughter. She can even cook. What more can a man ask?'

His mother eyed him thoughtfully. 'And are you what Hester asks for in a husband?'

'I'm not a bad prospect,' said Connah, looking directly at Hester. 'I have my own teeth, reasonable looks and I can support a wife very comfortably. Hester says she likes and respects me—'

'Do you, Hester?' Marion cut in.

'Yes, very much.' Hester looked Connah in the eye. 'But if you have any more secrets I want you to tell me now, not after we're married.'

'Nothing else, I promise. What you see is what you get.' His eyes narrowed. 'So is the wedding still on?'

'Of course,' she said, surprised. 'Why? Are you having second thoughts?'

'Connah is probably afraid that the trouble with Mr Lang has given *you* second thoughts, Hester,' said his mother, and got up. 'I shall take myself to bed. Put the time alone to good use.' She kissed them both and smiled lovingly at Connah as he held the door open for her.

'Let me see you upstairs, Mother,' he urged.

'No need. I do very well if I take my time. You stay with Hester. Goodnight.'

Connah watched her go for a moment, then closed the door and turned to look at Hester. 'What do you suppose my mother meant by putting the time to good use? Rather than fall on each other with ravening lust, I suppose she means we should talk—about Lang, of course. Did she ask you to use persuasion to change my mind?'

Hester held his eyes steadily. 'No, she did not.'

'But that's what she wants. I know my mother only too well.' Connah shrugged. 'I need a Scotch. What would you like? Unless Mrs Powell is a secret drinker, there should be some wine left from dinner.'

'Perfect. Thank you.'

How civilised they were, thought Hester later, as they sat, uneasily silent, with their drinks.

'Look,' said Connah at last, 'you can back out if you want. Lowri would get over it in time.'

Hester put her drink down, startled. 'Is that what *you* want?'

'Of course it's not,' he said explosively, jumping to his feet. 'I'll show you what I want, Hester.' He pulled her up into his arms to kiss her until her head reeled. When he raised his head at last, his eyes blazed into hers. 'I think the ravening lust is a very good idea.'

Hester gave him a smile so radiant that he blinked. 'So do I.'

With a groan of thanksgiving, Connah picked her up and sat down with her in his lap, kissing her with mounting heat that she responded to helplessly, giddy with relief as they drew back from the abyss which had suddenly yawned between them.

He tore his mouth from hers at last and buried his face in her hair. 'This is torture,' he gasped as she clutched him closer. He raised his head to look down into her dazed eyes and smiled in pure male triumph. 'You want me!'

'Yes,' she simply. 'But not here on your mother's sofa.'

'My room's on the top floor, well away from the rest. Share it with me!'

Hester sighed as she slid off his lap to sit beside him. 'I will one day. But not tonight.'

'I didn't think so,' he said with regret, and put his arm round her. 'Now you see why I'm in such a hurry to tie the knot.'

Hester understood his physical needs only too well. Nevertheless, she couldn't help wondering if part of his urgency was the need to form a stable family unit in case Peter Lang found out about Lowri one day and demanded his rights as her biological father. But she kept that thought to herself, reluctant to disrupt the new-found harmony between them. Right now it was enough to be close to Connah in every way, physical and mental. No one, Peter Lang included, could be allowed to spoil the dream that had come true for her when Connah asked her to marry him.

CHAPTER TWELVE

AFTER the return to Albany Square the days passed in a hectic round of shopping for wedding finery and less exciting items like school shoes. To leave himself free for the honeymoon, Connah went down to London to work with John Austin, but immediately after he got back he asked Moira if she would take care of Lowri the next day while he took Hester to buy an engagement ring.

Once Lowri was safely delivered by Sam to spend the day at Hill Cottage, Connah took Hester first to a jeweller and then to lunch at the best restaurant in town.

'Champagne at this time of day?' said Hester.

'To celebrate the occasion. I won't be buying another engagement ring in this life,' he said, filling her glass.

Though the meal was superb, Hester felt too excited to eat much as she gazed down at the cluster of sapphires and diamonds on her finger.

'Not hungry?' asked Connah.

'Not really. Perhaps you'll bring me to this lovely place another time when I'm not so wired.' She smiled at him wryly. 'It's all a bit hard to believe. Not so long ago, my life was other people's babies—'

'Whereas now you're going to marry me and have some of your own,' he said matter-of-factly.

Hester smiled crookedly. 'We hadn't discussed that side of things.'

'No,' he agreed. 'But now the subject's come up, you do realise that Lowri will never stop nagging us until we provide her with a sibling. Or two.'

She nodded, resigned. 'I do, only too well.'

'And your main aim in life is to make Lowri happy!'

'I'd like to make you happy too.'

'In that case, let's go home.'

'But you've hardly touched your champagne,' she protested.

'With reason, so I could drive you home. Right now,' he added, his eyes smouldering into hers.

'You planned this in advance?' Hester asked when they were on their way back to Albany Square.

'No. Once Sam rang me to say that Moira had asked him to stay on to lunch at Hill Cottage it was a case of *carpe diem*. I seized the rare opportunity of the house to ourselves for an hour.'

'So you plied me with champagne,' she accused, laughing.

'Only enough to relax you, my darling.'

The endearment did far more to further his cause than the champagne. Hester's excitement mounted unbearably once they were inside the silent house. Connah took her hand to hurry her up past the study to his bedroom on the next floor, then picked her up and carried her over to the bed.

'I want you so much, Hester,' he said, looking down at her with heat which melted her bones. 'And not just for love in the afternoon, though God knows at this moment I want to throw you on that bed and keep you there until tomorrow.'

'Not tomorrow,' she said with regret. 'Lowri will be back at four.'

Connah gave a shout of laughter and collapsed with her on the bed, and suddenly they were in a tearing, laughing hurry, kissing wildly as they undressed each other with impatient hands. But once they were naked in each other's arms Connah took in

a deep, relishing breath of pure satisfaction as his eyes roved over
the curves gilded by the sunlight slanting through the blinds.
When looking was no longer enough he began to touch, his lips
following his inciting hands until, at last, her senses heightened
to fever pitch Hester could bear no more.

'Now,' she ordered gruffly, so imperious that Connah obeyed
with a smooth, impaling thrust and caught his breath as her inner
muscles tightened round him, her smoky blue eyes gleaming
almost black with satisfaction. His kiss devoured her as he moved
inside her and Hester moved with him, her response so heated
that, for the first time in his life, Connah Carey Jones lost control,
and all too soon they were gasping in each other's arms, joined
in the hot, throbbing rapture of orgasm.

Hester stayed utterly still, happy for a while just to lie there
with Connah's body pinning her down, but at last he heaved
himself over on his side and she drew in a deep, reviving breath.

'We have another hour,' he informed her, his eyes possessive.

She gave him a sleepy smile. 'Excellent. Because I've lost the
will to move.'

'Then we should stay exactly where we are.'

She stretched luxuriously. 'This is a very comfortable bed.'

'Since you'll be sharing it with me in future, I'm glad you
like it. I have a comfortable bed in London too,' he added. 'When
we stay at the flat on our way back from Italy you can give me
your opinion.'

Hester shivered as his lips moved down the curve of her neck
to her shoulder. 'I look forward to sleeping on it.'

'Don't bank on too much sleeping. I made my requirements
about that side of our marriage very plain, if you remember.'

'I do.' She rolled over to face him. 'How about mine?'

He smoothed a hand down her face. 'Tell me what they are
and I'll do my best to fulfil them.'

'I like this part of it a lot,' she said with candour. 'But I want more from our marriage than just sharing a bed or a dinner table, or even providing Lowri with a stepmother, much as I love her. I want to be part of your other life too, Connah. Or don't you think I'm up for that?'

He drew back, frowning. 'What do you mean?'

She smiled crookedly. 'Because I'm blonde and not bad-looking and make my living by caring for children, some men tend to take the package at face value and ignore the brain inside it.'

'Then they're fools,' he said flatly. 'While I was waiting for Laura to recover all those years ago your mother talked a lot about you—how hard you'd worked to help make the guest house a success. Also about your headmistress's disappointment over your choice of career,' he added.

Hester stared at him in surprise. 'She didn't tell me that.' Her mother had never talked much about the mysterious Mr Jones at all. But that, Hester knew, was because Moira had been fully aware that her child was languishing over a man who was not only right out of her league in years and sophistication, but belonged to someone else.

'So, quite apart from my bed, *cariad*, I'm only too happy to have you share every aspect of my life.' His eyes shadowed. 'I won't pretend I've lived like a monk since I took responsibility for Lowri, but I've steered clear of anything remotely like a close relationship. I sublimated myself in work instead. But these past weeks with you in Italy showed me what life could be with a companion like you to share it, and maybe even give me the child of my own I'd never realised I wanted until I met you again.' He pulled her close, a wry look in his eyes. 'Something just struck me.'

'I suppose you mean it's time to get up,' she said, sighing.

'No.' He kissed the hand which wore his ring. 'The moment I put that on your finger, I rushed you home to bed. I swear I wasn't demanding thanks, Hester.'

She grinned. 'Just as well, because I haven't actually said thank you yet.'

'Yes, you have—without words,' he whispered, his breath hot against her skin. 'So thank me again—in exactly the same way!'

The remaining days of Lowri's summer vacation flew by in preparations for the wedding. Connah went back to London for a while to his new restoration project, and this time Lowri made no objection because most of her time was spent at Hill Cottage, helping to get the garden ready for the wedding. She worked so hard that Robert soon presented her with her own fork, trowel and gloves.

'Brilliant! I really enjoy gardening,' she told him, delighted, as she thanked him.

'But you must wear the gloves, darling,' said Moira. 'Otherwise you'll have grimy hands with that lovely blue dress at the wedding.'

'Right then, everybody,' said Hester. 'Since you're all so busy here, I'd like to pop down into town for half an hour for a spot of personal shopping.'

Lowri looked up, frowning. 'But Sam's taken the car back to Albany Square.'

'I'll go in my own, darling. I won't be long.'

'Good, because we'll have lunch out here when you get back,' said Moira. 'If you'd like a break from gardening, Lowri, you can help me make sandwiches.'

Lowri eyed the flower bed she was weeding, obviously torn between her choices. 'I'll finish this bed after lunch then, Robert, if that's all right.'

'Absolutely,' he said affectionately. 'Go inside and have a cold drink, pet. You look hot.'

Hester was glad to be alone for once as she went into town. The particular shopping she had in mind was a secret she had no intention of sharing with anyone. To have something to show for her trip when she got back, Hester treated herself to some shamefully expensive cosmetics, then called in at Albany Square to hide her secret purchases. To her surprise, Connah opened the door when she announced herself.

'You're back!' she exclaimed, delighted, but her smile faded abruptly when he pulled her inside and refused to let her say a word until they were upstairs in the study with the door slammed shut behind them.

'I had a visitor today,' he announced in a tone which made her blood run cold.

No kiss, not even a hello? Hester made herself look at him in polite enquiry. 'Someone I know?'

'She certainly knows you. Her name is Caroline Vernon.' His eyes stabbed hers. 'But her maiden name was Lang. She's Peter Lang's sister.'

Hester frowned. 'And she came *here*? Why?'

His eyes stabbed into hers. 'Because you had a cosy little chat with her about Lowri while you were buying wedding finery.'

Hester stared at him blankly, too surprised at first to be furious. 'I most certainly did not!'

Connah looked sceptical. 'Then how else does the lady know that Lowri is Welsh for Laura, also that you were going to be Lowri's stepmother?'

Were? Past tense?

Hester stared at him angrily. 'Look, Connah, I don't know any Caroline Vernon. Nor do I know how she heard about Lowri. But it certainly wasn't from me. Or from my mother either, in case you're about to accuse her as well.'

'Which just leaves Lowri.' Connah eyed her with distaste. 'Surely you can take the blame for this yourself, Hester, rather than accuse a child?'

'You're doing the accusing, not me,' she said hotly, determined not to cry. 'I don't know this Vernon woman. If she says I told her she's lying. But if you prefer to believe her rather than me, that is, of course, your privilege. And now, if you'll let the prisoner out of the dock, I'm due back at Hill Cottage for lunch.'

'Lunch can wait,' he retorted. 'Perhaps you'd like to know the rest of the conversation.'

'Not really, but you're obviously going to tell me,' said Hester bitterly.

'She told me that her brother was utterly devastated when I told him Laura was dead. So when she rang him to say she'd seen Lowri, he sent her here to plead his cause. Next time he's in this country he craves the privilege of meeting my daughter, who is— I quote—a living reminder of the love of his life,' finished Connah with furious distaste. 'Do you think the man actually had the gall to say that, or was his sister trying to butter me up?'

'So are you going to let him see Lowri, Connah?' asked Hester.

'Like hell I am. For God's sake, Hester, he was married to someone else when he made my sister pregnant!'

Hester held her ground. 'I know that. But he obviously loved Laura very deeply. You said yourself that he kept on try-ing to see her.'

'But she wouldn't let him near her, remember. Lang not only made her pregnant, he broke Laura's heart. As far as I'm con-cerned, he as good as killed her.' Connah's eyes hardened. 'I'm not going to let him near her child.'

'Even though she's his child too?'

'No. Because, in every way that matters, she's mine.' Connah seized her by the shoulders. 'You swore you'd never tell Lang about Lowri, but obviously you didn't think that bound you when it came to his sister. What the hell possessed you to confide in the woman, Hester?'

'I did nothing of the kind. I don't *know* his sister.' She freed herself angrily, glaring at him to hide her desperate hurt. 'I didn't talk to anyone other than Lowri, my mother and the shop assistant while I tried on the dress—my wedding gown, incidentally. Perhaps I can get my money back,' she added bitterly and turned her back on him to run down the stairs to the front door, but Connah caught up with her before she reached it and held her by the wrist.

'What the hell do you mean by that?'

'Take an educated guess!'

Connah paled, refusing to let go when she tried to shrug his hand off.

'Lowri will be worried. I've got to go,' she snapped, without looking at him.

'We'll talk later, when she's in bed,' he said grimly.

Which was so much more a threat than a promise, that Hester arrived at Hill Cottage later with very little memory of having driven there.

Hester spent the rest of the afternoon giving the performance of her life, and where Robert and Lowri were concerned she was successful. Not so with her mother.

'What's up?' Moira murmured, keeping her daughter back for a minute when Sam arrived.

'Bridal nerves,' lied Hester.

'Anything to do with Connah's unexpected return today?'

'It was a surprise, certainly.'

'Not what I asked!' Moira gave her a hug. 'All right. I won't nag. But please ring me tomorrow.'

Because Sam sent a text to say they were on the way as they set off, Connah was waiting for them in the garage when they arrived. Lowri rushed to hug him, chattering like a magpie as they went upstairs.

'I didn't know you were coming back today. I've been helping Robert do the garden, Daddy, and it's going to look so beautiful for the wedding.' She beamed up at him. 'Only a week to go now. Are you excited?'

He smiled at her indulgently. 'Of course I am, even more than you.'

'Not possible,' she said, laughing, and turned to Hester. 'Are you excited too?'

'You bet. Now, off to the bath, Miss Jones. You need a good scrub, and don't forget your hands and nails.' Hester smiled coolly at Connah. 'I didn't expect you, so there's only salad and so on for supper.'

'Fine by me.' He took Lowri by the hand. 'Run up and have your bath, then come back down to me in the study. We'll play chess while Hester gets supper ready.'

Feeling she'd had a stay of execution, Hester prepared the meal as much as she could beforehand, then went up to have a shower. She took her time over her hair, which had gained a few highlights courtesy of the Italian sun, and, feeling in need of war paint for the encounter later, she made-up her face and eyes with more drama than usual.

Conversation over the meal was no problem, since Lowri talked non-stop about the wedding throughout. Connah exchanged a wary glance with Hester now and then and looked, to her intense pleasure, increasingly baffled by the pleasant smiles she gave him in return.

'Chloe rang me today as soon as she got home,' Lowri announced. 'She's been in Cornwall all summer. They've got a house down there. I told her all about the wedding and my bridesmaid dress. She was going to ring Olivia and Daisy right away to tell them, and told me to take loads of wedding pictures back to school with me.'

'I'll inform the photographer of your requirements,' said Connah, lips twitching.

Lowri giggled happily, but Hester eyed him in surprise.

'You've organised a photographer?'

'Of course.' His eyes held hers. 'No wedding is complete without a record of the happy day.'

She gave him one of her brightest smiles. 'I thought you avoided that kind of thing.'

'Ah, but the reason for my reticence no longer applies,' he informed her suavely, and turned to his daughter. 'We'll go back to our chess for half an hour before you go to bed, then you need an early night,' said Connah, and looked at Hester. 'Then later you and I can have some time to ourselves.'

'I expect you want to kiss Hester a lot after being away lately,' said Lowri, nodding sagely. 'Chloe says her dad still kisses her mother all the time. And they've been married for *ages*.' She rushed over to Hester suddenly and threw her arms round her. 'I'm so glad you're going to marry Daddy. I keep pinching myself to make sure I'm not dreaming.'

Later, when Lowri was settled for the night, Hester went back down to the kitchen to make coffee, then took the tray up to the study. Connah got up to stand in front of the empty fireplace, his tanned face tense as he watched her fill the cups. She handed one to him, then sat down with her own and waited in obdurate silence.

When he finally spoke, he said the last thing she expected.

'Hester, I owe you an apology. I asked Lowri tonight if she'd talked to a pretty dark lady when you were choosing dresses, and apparently she did, during a visit to the ladies' room. The woman asked her name, then commented on the lovely blue dress she'd seen Lowri trying on, so of course the child told her all about the wedding. Then Moira arrived to check on Lowri, and the lady vanished.'

'I see,' said Hester evenly. 'Mystery solved.'

Connah put his cup down untouched and sat beside her. 'I'm sorry—desperately sorry—for doubting you, Hester. I expected you to say the wedding was off when you got back tonight.'

'I fully intended to at one point,' she agreed, and felt an ignoble gush of satisfaction when his jaw clenched. 'But it lasted only as far as Hill Cottage, by which time I'd remembered that Lowri would be utterly heartbroken if I changed my mind.'

He winced. 'You mean you'll go through with the wedding just to keep my daughter happy?'

She shrugged. 'There are other reasons.'

He eyed her with uncharacteristic humility. 'Respect and liking?'

'Both of those were in short supply when you accused me of breaking my word,' she informed him tartly, then finished her coffee and stood up to put their cups on the tray.

'Where are you going?' he demanded.

'To bed. It's been a tiring day.'

'Stay for a while—please,' he said, a note of entreaty in his voice which almost soothed her bruised heart. But not quite enough.

She shook her head. 'I need an early night. There's a lot to do between now and Tuesday.'

He strode across the room and took her in his arms. 'At least kiss me goodnight to show you've forgiven me.'

Hester held up her face obediently and Connah crushed her close, kissing her with a passion which left her dizzy and breathless when he raised his head at last.

'Have you?' he said roughly.

'Have I what?'

'Forgiven me.'

She smiled crookedly. 'Not yet. But I'll work on it during my stay at Hill Cottage. I'm going home in the morning, until the wedding. Mother was all for Lowri doing the same, but I thought you'd prefer Sam to bring her over each day to me and fetch her back every evening so you can put her to bed. All this is subject to your approval, of course.'

Connah's eyes burned into hers. 'Retaliation, Hester?'

'Certainly not. I always intended to spend the last few days of single life with my mother.' She shrugged. 'I would have told you that this afternoon as soon as I saw you, but your accusation rather got in the way.'

'I've apologised for that,' he said harshly.

'And I've accepted. Goodnight, Connah.'

Hester sat watching the Chiantigiana unfold before her through Tuscan hills gilded by the setting sun. The views were as breathtaking as before, but this time there was no sleepy little head on her shoulder. She cast a glance at her husband, who drove as he did most things—with skill and concentration. The past few days had passed so quickly in some ways that it was hard to believe that here they were at last, Mr and Mrs Connah Carey Jones, bride and groom, but not husband and wife as yet in the true sense of the word, since the bride had spent part of her wedding night in the bathroom of the master suite, parting with her wedding breakfast.

Connah had been a tower of strength. Ignoring her impassioned pleas to go away and leave her alone, he'd held Hester's head, mopped her clammy face and fed her sips of mineral water until her stomach had finally decided to behave.

'It must have been the prawn canapés,' she said wanly as he tucked her into bed. 'I hope no one else is affected.'

'I'm not concerned with anyone else right now. My mother will see to Lowri if necessary,' Connah said firmly. 'And if you feel no better in the morning she can come with me when I deliver Lowri to the school.'

'No!' Hester struggled upright. 'I'll be better by then. I can have a break at Bryn Derwen when we drop Marion off on the way, but I shall go on to the school with you, no matter how I feel,' she assured him. 'Lowri's got her heart set on showing off her new stepmother. I can sleep on the drive to Heathrow afterwards.'

And it had been worth the effort, thought Hester as Connah negotiated the winding road with due care for his passenger's digestive system. Lowri's delight had been a joy to see as she'd introduced Hester to her friends.

'Almost there,' said Connah, as the familiar village came into sight. 'How do you feel?'

'Tired, but the meal we had at that sweet little trattoria seems to be staying put, thank goodness. ' Hester cast a rueful glance at his profile. 'You were so good last night, Connah. I never even managed to say thank you at the time.'

'What else are husbands for?' he said, smiling crookedly, and turned up the road which led to Casa Girasole.

Flavia had not been required to wait to let them in because Jay Anderson had handed over the key at the wedding. Connah got out of the car to unlock the door, then helped Hester out, eyeing her closely.

'Pale, but very interesting,' he commented, and surprised her by picking her up. 'Standard procedure for brides,' he said casually as he carried her into the house. He set her down with great care, then went back out to bring in the luggage. Hester looked around with a sigh of pleasure. Flavia might not have waited for them but her presence was evident in the vases of flowers everywhere, also in the note on the kitchen table.

'I assume this is about the food she's left for us,' said Hester as Connah joined her. 'My Italian isn't up to it.'

'I don't think mine is either, but you're right about the general message,' he agreed, studying it. 'I'll take the bags upstairs. But I suggest we leave unpacking until the morning. You still look fragile.'

'Not too fragile to carry my overnight bag,' said Hester. 'I'll just check to see what's on offer for breakfast in the morning, though it probably won't be a full English.'

'I'll settle for anything you care to give me,' he told her, meeting her eyes, and went out.

Which was clear enough, thought Hester as she inspected the contents of the refrigerator. Suddenly desperate for a shower, she went upstairs to the room she'd slept in last time and found all their luggage stacked neatly at the foot of the bed. This time her bridegroom was making it clear that he meant to share it with her. She smiled a little. She always knew where she stood with Connah.

He strolled out of the bathroom, looking as good to her as always in a thin shirt and linen trousers only slightly rumpled from the journey. He smiled as he put his wallet and keys down on the dressing table. 'I've left a message for Lowri at the school to let her know we got here. I've put my bath stuff in there, by the way, but you take first turn in the shower while I take a stroll in the garden.'

'Thank you.' She smiled, feeling absurdly shy. 'I'll make some coffee later while you take your turn.'

Connah could have showered in either of the other two bathrooms, but his intention was obviously to share everything from the start. She smiled ruefully. After the enforced intimacies of their unromantic wedding night, there was little left to be shy about.

Hester rang home to tell her mother they'd arrived and afterwards took everything needed for a shower from her overnight bag and got to work. In no mood to spend time styling wet hair, she pulled on a shower cap and stood under the spray only long enough to perk her up a bit. She dried herself rapidly, slapped new, expensive moisturiser all over her body and tugged an almond-pink shift over some of her trousseau underwear. She brushed out her hair, did the bare minimum to her face, then thrust her feet into flat silver sandals and went downstairs in search of her husband, the very word giving her such a buzz that she paused to savour it before going out on to the loggia.

Connah turned with a smile. 'You were quick.'

'I thought you might be as desperate for a shower as I was, so I put a move on.'

He put a finger under her chin. 'You look much better, Hester.'

'I feel much better.' Even with his touch sending shivers down her spine.

'Are you cold?' he demanded.

'Of course not. It's a beautiful evening. Shall we have coffee out here?'

'I've got a better idea. I put a bottle of very expensive champagne on ice—one of a dozen sent over by *Il Conte* as a wedding gift. I found them when I was looking through Jay's wine selection.'

She smiled, surprised. 'How very sweet of Luigi. Is he here at the *Castello*?'

'If he is, I trust he'll have too much tact to come visiting.' Connah raised her hand to his lips and kissed it. 'It is our honeymoon, remember.'

As if she were likely to forget! Hester sighed as she breathed in the night-time scents of the garden when she was alone. The honeymoon had got off to a spectacularly bad start, but from now on she would do her best to see it improved, if only by not throwing up any more.

A moon was silvering the water in the pool when Connah joined her to pour champagne. His hair was wet and slicked back from his face, which looked dark against his white shirt in the light from the shaded lamp on the table.

'A toast, Mrs Carey Jones,' he said, handing her a glass.

She raised it in toast. 'To us.'

'I'll drink to that! To us.' He drank deeply, then moved his chair closer to hers, the lamplight glinting on his wedding ring as he took her hand. 'My ring was a surprise, Hester. I was deeply touched.'

'I wasn't sure you'd care for one, but I bought it anyway.' She smiled a little. 'It was my reason for shopping on my own that afternoon without Lowri. I sneaked back to Albany Square to hide the ring. The last thing I expected was to find you there.'

'Or the accusations I hurled at you.' He raked his hand through his damp hair. 'After the things I said I'm amazed you turned up at the church, though I hoped—prayed—you would, if only for Lowri's sake.'

'Of course I turned up,' she said matter-of-factly. 'When I make a promise I keep it.'

'Twisting the knife?' Connah's fingers linked with hers. 'God knows you have the right. I was a swine to you that day, Hester. But I thought you'd deliberately gone against my wishes on something of such huge importance to me. As well as angry, I was desperately hurt—'

'So was I,' she said with feeling. 'I felt as though my heart was breaking on the drive back to Hill Cottage.'

Connah's grasp tightened painfully. 'Is it back in one piece now?' he said huskily.

'Not yet. You still have some repairing to do!' She smiled at him so cheerfully that he laughed and suddenly they were completely at ease together as they talked over the wedding.

'You were a very beautiful bride,' said Connah.

'I was all for wearing blue like Lowri, but Mother was so adamant you'd want me in something more traditionally bridal I went for ivory chiffon in the end.'

'Moira was absolutely right. Incidentally, it was very good of her—and Robert—to organise everything in their own home, rather than a hotel. The garden at Hill Cottage made the perfect setting for the party afterwards. Lowri was so happy,' said Connah fondly. 'So was I,' he added, 'at least I was once I saw you and Robert walk down the aisle, Hester. Jay couldn't understand why I was so stressed, but right up to the last moment I wasn't sure you'd be there.'

'Well, I was, and here we are,' said Hester and yawned suddenly. 'Sorry!'

Connah got up and drew her to her feet. 'You're tired. Let's lock up and go to bed.'

But at the foot of the stairs he paused to look down at Hester in question. 'Do you want me to take a turn round the garden and give you half an hour to yourself first?'

She grinned. 'Of course not. After last night, Connah, how could I possibly be shy about sharing a room with you?'

'God, I was worried,' he said with feeling as they reached the cool, airy bedroom. 'I was all for calling a doctor.'

'Which caused the first quarrel of our marriage,' she said, rolling her eyes. 'What a night you had.'

'I'm hoping,' he said, straight-faced, 'that tonight will be an improvement.'

'Me too,' she said candidly and gave him a smile of such shameless invitation that Connah scooped her up into his arms and held her so tightly she felt his heart hammering against her.

'Thank God for that,' he said hoarsely, 'though be warned; I want you so much I don't think I can be gentle.'

She shook her head impatiently. 'I don't want gentle. Just love me, Connah.'

'I do. I will!' He sat down with her on his lap, his mouth hot and possessive on hers for a long, breathless interval. At last he stood her on her feet to let her dress fall to the floor, then, without so much as a glance at the underwear she'd chosen so carefully for just this moment, he relieved her of it, then rid himself of his own clothes without letting her go.

'That was clever,' gasped Hester as their naked bodies fell in a tangle together on the bed.

'Desperate, not clever,' he said against her mouth, and kissed her with uncontrolled hunger that thrilled her so much more than any polished, practised caresses could have done that she responded to every touch and caress with a joyous abandon which soon robbed Connah of any last remnants of restraint. He gasped her name against her parted mouth and surrendered to her clamouring hands, thrusting home into hot, tight warmth as their bodies united in a wild careering race to a glorious place they reached almost in unison, straining each other so close they stayed locked together long after the tide of passion had receded to leave them quiet in each other's arms.

Connah raised his dishevelled head at last and looked deep into her dazed eyes. 'Tell me the truth, Hester.'

'I'll try,' she said warily.

He turned on his side, taking her with him so they lay face to face. 'Did you turn up at the church purely for Lowri's sake?'

Relieved, she smoothed the hair back from his forehead and gave him a sleepy smile. 'Of course not. I love Lowri dearly, but I'm not as noble as that. If you want the truth, Connah, wild horses wouldn't have kept me away for the simple reason that I fell madly in love with you the very first time I ever saw you.'

He tensed, staring at her incredulously. 'At the first interview?'

She shook her head. 'Long before that. On a January night ten years ago you smiled at me when I handed over your supper tray, and that was that.'

'But my darling, you were just a child!'

'I was seventeen, Connah, with a full set of female hormones, and you were the archetypal answer to a maiden's prayer.' Hester smiled lovingly. 'The fact that you were unattainable only made it all the more romantic. You were the dream lover who haunted my dreams for years. Then fate took a hand and I answered your advertisement. When you walked into your study that day in Albany Square, I found nothing had changed. I still felt the same about you. So did my hormones, the minute you shook my hand,' she added, eyes glinting. 'So that, Mr Carey Jones, was my reason for marrying you—nothing to do with liking and respect and so on.'

'Thank God for that,' said Connah gruffly, then pulled her close and kissed her, his hand possessive on the curve of her bare hip. 'Tell me again that you love me.'

'You first!'

'Of course I love you,' he growled. 'Why else do you think

the days before the wedding were such hell for me? I was sure, right up to the last minute, that you'd back out.'

'I love you too much to do that.' She kissed him and wriggled closer. 'So was tonight that improvement you wanted?'

'There's room for a lot more improvement yet,' he said, rolling over to capture her beneath him. 'It's a long time until morning.'

On the last night of the honeymoon, when the packing was done and everything was ready for departure in the morning, Hester lay close to her husband, unable to sleep.

'What's wrong?' he said into the quiet darkness.

'I've got a confession to make,' she said reluctantly. 'I should have made it as soon as we arrived, but I was afraid it would spoil our honeymoon.'

Connah reached over to switch on the light, then sat up and drew her up to sit propped beside him. He leaned over to kiss her swiftly, then gave her the bone-melting smile rarely bestowed on anyone other than his wife and child. 'Confess, then,' he said tenderly and brushed a gleaming gold lock of hair back from her forehead. 'Whatever you've done, I forgive you.'

Hester tried to think of some way to lead up to it, but in the end she blurted, 'It wasn't the prawns. I'm pregnant.'

Connah's eyes widened, a look of such delight dawning in them that Hester's filled with tears of pure relief. 'We're having a baby?' he asked incredulously.

She nodded and sniffed inelegantly. 'When I went shopping for your ring that day I also bought a pregnancy testing kit. I'd had my suspicions ever since the holiday here, so I went to the cloakroom in a coffee shop and found I was right.'

'Oh, my darling!' Connah hugged her to him, rubbing his cheek over her hair. 'And you couldn't tell me because I gave you hell the moment I saw you.'

She nodded and burrowed her face into his bare shoulder.

'I meant to tell you before the wedding, but then it occurred to me that you'd think it was my only reason for turning up. So I decided to leave it until I'd proved to you exactly why I married you.'

He turned her face up to his. 'Because you love me!'

'Always,' she said shakily, then gave him a crooked little smile. 'And it occurred to me that if you knew you might be wary of making love to me very much.'

'God, yes,' he said with feeling, thinking of the passionate hours they'd spent together in this very bed. He slid down to press his lips against her flat stomach. 'I hope all's well in there.'

'Of course it is!' Hester yawned suddenly. 'Sorry. Will you cuddle me to sleep?'

Connah moved back up the bed to hold her close. 'Tonight and every night,' he assured her, then chuckled. 'Let's make the most of it while we can.' He kissed her tenderly. 'Goodnight, wife.'

'Goodnight, husband.' Hester settled down happily to sleep, but after a while Connah whispered her name.

'What's the matter?' she asked sleepily.

'You were right.'

'I'm always right,' she assured him, 'but what about in this particular instance?'

'Now I'm going to have a child of my own, I feel a pang of sympathy for Lang. Not a huge one, admittedly, but enough to contact him when we get back, and tell him he can meet Lowri next time he's in the country.'

Hester clutched his hand tightly, her eyes filling with tears. 'Darling! What a lovely idea.'

'I thought you'd be pleased. But I'll say he's an old friend of her mother's,' he said, thinking it over. 'Then maybe, some time in the future, when she's seen him from time to time and she's old enough to cope, she can be told the truth—Darling, don't cry!'

'Sorry,' said Hester thickly. 'Expectant mothers tend to get emotional.'

'Expectant fathers too,' he said huskily, and kissed her tears away as he held her close. 'I know the perfect way to cheer you up,' he added after a time.

Hester wriggled closer, sniffing inelegantly. 'What is it?'

'Just picture Lowri's face when we tell her about the baby!'

THE MILLIONAIRE'S PROPOSAL

BY
TRISH WYLIE

Dear Reader,

A good friend of mine reminded me of something important this year—to be grateful for the good stuff when it's here. How many of us dedicate the same amount of time to appreciating the good things as we do focussing on the bad? Maybe it's because the bad can be so very overwhelming, and over the years life simply wears us down. Yet it's the good stuff that makes the difference, don't you think?

We need to laugh as often as possible, take a deep breath of air to remind us we're alive, look around us and see the beauty in things, spend time doing what makes us happy. Most of all we need never to get so old or so jaded that we stop dreaming or believing in moments of magic.

One of the things I love the absolute most about writing and reading romance is the fact it shows we all still believe in love in the twenty-first century. We may have busier lives, might be more cynical, but people still reach out for love in all its forms: in friends, in family, in a man and a woman who can make it through the rough times because life is richer together than it is apart. That's a little bit of magic right there.

So if there's one thing you bring with you out of Ronan and Kerry's story I hope it's a little reminder to make the most of the good stuff and any moment of magic that comes your way. Grab hold of it, celebrate it, savour it, and that way even in times of darkness you'll still be able to see the light. Just like Ronan will with Kerry by his side.

Hs & Ks,

Trish

Trish Wylie tried various careers before eventually fulfilling her dream of writing. Years spent working in the music industry, in promotions, and teaching little kids about ponies gave her plenty of opportunity to study life and the people around her. Which, in Trish's opinion, is a pretty good study course for writing! Living in Ireland, Trish balances her time between writing and horses. If you get to spend your days doing things you love, then she thinks that's not doing too badly. You can contact Trish at www.trishwylie.com.

CHAPTER ONE

KERRY DOYLE liked to consider herself a fairly patient woman. After all, she'd waited years to make her dream trip; researched, planned, scheduled everything to the nth degree. But if the man in the seat next to her poked her with his elbow one more time she thought she just might scream. She'd specifically allowed extra money for better seats on the longer flights for the added personal space that came with them. And it was a seven-hour flight from Dublin to New York—including the change at Shannon—one that was going to feel like twice that in the longer leg they were currently on if he didn't quit it soon.

And he'd shown so much promise in the 'scenery' department before he sat down too…

He poked her again, causing Kerry to let a sigh escape. It wasn't much of a poke—none of them had been—but even so…

'Sorry.'

It was a step in the right direction. 'Maybe if you sat a little more to the left?'

He turned in his seat, smiling at her with the kind of smile that probably worked wonders with the majority of women no matter how much he irritated them first. 'The stewardess already got me twice with the trolley. I'm not exactly built for these wee seats.'

All right, he had a point there. She hadn't been able to help noticing him when he got on the plane, especially when towering over her to place his bag in the overhead compartment. And he wasn't just scenic, he was tall—very tall. Not that she'd be able to guess accurately until she stood up and compared him to her own five seven, but if she had to hazard a guess she'd say he was well and truly over six feet tall. Add that to broad shoulders, a wide chest and muscled upper arms and even the fact that the rest of him seemed fairly lean wasn't going to help him fit into the space the airline had allocated, was it?

So she'd allow him that. She'd even sympathize a little, inwardly. 'No, you're not—but I'm just getting a little concerned about attempting to take a drink later in the flight if you bump me at the wrong time.'

It might also affect her choice of what she asked the stewardess for—after all, coffee and tea left stains. And the wardrobe she had with her had to last a long time. As always with Kerry it came down to practicalities—it was just the way her mind worked.

She accompanied her words with a polite smile in an attempt not to make an adversary for the rest of the flight, and then found herself suddenly distracted from further coherent thought by the way he examined her face before he replied.

Nice eyes. In fact he had *great* eyes. A pale blue made even paler when framed with thick dark lashes, which in turn highlighted the dark pools of his irises. Then there were shards of darker blue and white threaded through the paler blue—as if an artist's watercolour brush had been dipped into a glass of water and the colour hadn't quite mixed in yet. It was an unusual combination, and most definitely the kind of eyes a girl wouldn't forget in a hurry...

Kerry almost sighed again. For different reasons…

'Maybe we should set up some kind of a code?'

She dragged her gaze from his eyes long enough to note the hint of a smile on his devilishly sensual mouth. Well, having a sense of humour could only help with their predicament, so she allowed herself to smile a larger smile as she replied.

'Like me saying "Danger Will Robinson: drink approaching"?' And if he got that obscure reference to her childhood interest in truly bad nineteen sixties' science fiction she might have to love him a little.

'*Lost In Space*, right?'

Wow, he got it. She nodded, smiling a little brighter.

'Well, that would do it, all right. Or you could just dig me in the ribs every time I do it to you so I get a reminder about space of the personal variety.'

'That's certainly tempting.' Kerry's eyes narrowed as she pondered the 'temptation' involved in flirting with a complete stranger while travelling on the first leg of her grand adventure. Mind you, he was temptation personified—so who could really blame her? And even if he was dressed casually in jeans and a T-shirt just a shade or two darker than his sensational eyes, he *had* managed to afford to pay for better seating. That had to be a good sign.

Serial killers didn't travel in the good seats, she reckoned. Now kidnappers, well, *possibly*—the money was probably better…

His chin dropped and he leaned a little closer, employing a large hand to lift one side of her open book so he could read the cover, a hint of a smile hovering on the corners of his mesmerizing mouth.

'Enjoying the guidebook?'

Kerry turned it over on her tray table, grateful for the distraction, and nodding as she answered. 'So far—there's probably more detail in here than I need, though. I've read tonnes of them these last few months and this was one of the better ones.'

His dark brows quirked a minuscule amount when she glanced at him from the corner of her eye. 'More detail in what way?'

'Well, there's about a gazillion places listed in the back to begin with. And having never been there it's tough to decide what to see and what not when you're on a timescale, y'know?' Her gaze had locked fully with his again while she answered and a weird quiver of what almost felt like cold ran up her spine, goose-bumps appearing on her arms.

And when she felt like that it was normally an indication that she was clueing in on something—so what was it this time? Apart from the obvious feminine awareness of an incredibly good-looking male, that was.

She searched his face to see if she could figure it out. And even that was disconcerting. It was the proximity, she supposed. There was a certain intimacy to being seated beside someone on a plane. So the fact she was so aware of his breathing, the musky male undertone of his scent, the dark hint of stubble on his jaw, and each flicker of his thick lashes, was a completely natural reaction.

When she studied him a little longer than was probably considered polite, he turned his upper body in the seat and folded his arms across his broad chest.

'So how would you change it to make it more useful to you, then?'

What? Oh, yes, they'd been making polite conversation about the book, hadn't they? Kerry took a deep breath and looked back down at it, shaking her head a little at her uncharacteristic lack of being able to think straight. 'I dunno. Graded the chapters, maybe?'

'What way?'

'Length of stay? If you have two days you shouldn't miss this and that, a week you should try and see—that kind of thing.'

When she didn't get a reply she looked back up at him to discover a view of his profile, dark brows creased downwards in thought. He really was fascinating to look at, wasn't he? Not shaving-commercial good-looking, but certainly rugged enough to advertise outdoor wear or heavy duty Jeeps or maybe even activity holidays. He looked like a man's man and that meant he was automatically a woman's man too, didn't it? After all, there was something about a very male man that tugged at something deep inside a woman.

She was studying the short cropped dark chocolate of his hair when he snapped her out of her reverie…

'A list of things to pack for each length of trip might be useful too. Maybe a small section at the end of each chapter for whether you're a classical sightseer type or an adventurer or a party-goer or if you have kids along…that kind of thing…'

Kerry smiled indulgently as he mumbled to the back of the seat in front of him. 'Planning on rewriting the book now, are we?'

When he turned to look at her a smile danced in his eyes and she found herself mesmerized all over again before he hummed beneath his breath and answered with a softly spoken, 'Maybe.'

Unfolding his arms, he extended a large hand towards her. 'Ronan O'Keefe. And whatever you want to drink should really be on me to say thanks for buying a copy of my book. But as drinks are included I'll just have to promise not to make you spill anything.'

Kerry gaped, swiftly checked the name on the cover of the book, and then, rolling her eyes before shaking his hand, 'Just as well I didn't say anything too insulting about it, really, isn't it?'

And it explained the something she'd felt too. It'd been a forewarning of sorts, hadn't it?

Her hand enfolded firmly in the warmth of his long fingers, he held on just a little too long while fixing her gaze with his as he answered with a rumbling, 'Yes, it is.'

The warmth transferred to her smaller hand. He had the kind of firm handshake her father would have approved of and respected. But it wasn't quite respect Kerry was feeling. She even had to clear her throat before speaking.

'Would you have let on who you were if I had?'

'After a while.'

And the continuing sparkle in his eyes told her he'd have had fun with it too. 'Happened before, I take it?'

'Occupational hazard when travelling.' He inclined his head, 'I'm also incredibly good at recommending them to people in airport bookstores when I see them pick one up.'

When he added a lazy wink, Kerry couldn't help but laugh. Oh, he was a bit of a charmer, this one, wasn't he? Full of good old-fashioned Blarney, her nana would say with a throaty chuckle. He probably spent half his life chatting up women on planes, she wasn't anything special, which reminded her—it really was time she let go of his hand.

Gently extricating it, and immediately feeling the loss of warmth in contrast to the cool air from the plane's air-conditioning, she lifted her chin and challenged him with an upward arch of one brow,

'And how do I know you are who you say you are?'

'You could take my word for it?'

She turned her hand palm up and waggled her fingers, 'I might need to see your passport to be sure.'

'I might have a pen name.'

'Do you?'

'No.'

Her fingers waggled again.

'Not very trusting, are you?' He shook his head, working hard at keeping the smile twitching his mouth in check. 'Lesson one, by the way, would be: never give up your passport to a stranger when travelling alone.'

Her eyes narrowed. 'How do you know I'm travelling alone?'

'In my experience, people who travel together tend to sit together on planes.'

Good point. 'Well, it's not like I can grab your passport, climb over you and escape with it at twenty-seven thousand feet up, is it?'

'True—' he leaned a little closer and lowered his voice to a deliciously deep rumble '—though the climbing-over-me part might be fun to watch. No one's ever tried that before—brings a whole new meaning to the term "in-flight entertainment".'

When she heard the click of his seat belt and he leaned closer still, she automatically leaned back towards the window to make room for him. Not that it wasn't tempting to just stay where she was and 'sit' her ground, but this kind of dalliance was obviously something he was well practised at—and, Kerry being Kerry, she called him on it.

'Do you flirt with every woman you meet on a plane?'

Shooting her a challenging quirk of his brows as he reached behind him, he replied with, 'Would make for lots of short relationships, don't you think?'

'Another occupational hazard, perchance?'

'Possibly.'

The contortions eventually wielded a well-worn passport he waved back in front of her face as he got comfy again. 'I need this back. So be warned—I'll wrestle you for it if I have to.'

'Duly noted.' She reached for it, but Ronan moved it just out of her reach.

'Let's make a fair exchange.'

'Oh-h-h,' Kerry laughed throatily, 'I don't think so.'

'Picture that bad?'

'Are you suggesting I don't photograph well?'

He examined her face for a moment, the same low intimacy returning to his voice. 'I doubt it.'

Kerry felt warmth building on her cheeks, which she'd always thought for a woman her age was just plain old sad. That very thought then bringing her in a straight line to her excuse.

'Didn't anyone tell you not to ask a lady her age?'

He frowned in amused confusion, tapping his passport off the knuckles of his hand. 'And when did I do that?'

'My date of birth is in my passport.'

'Ah…'

'And anyway, you have an aisle seat—you could make a faster getaway. Someone told me recently that giving your passport to a stranger is a bad idea when travelling alone.'

There was a low chuckle of very male laughter, the sound making her smile at him again. Should she have to hazard a guess, Kerry would say that the 'flirting with women on planes' thing was pretty successful for him. Maybe the short relationships suited his lifestyle?

'Do I get a name?'

She spoke slowly, 'You already *have* a name, Ronan.'

'*Your* name.'

'We'll see…' She waggled her fingers again.

His stunning eyes narrowed briefly, the passport still tapping against his large hand. 'I'll swap you a look at my passport for your name.'

'Once I've confirmed you are who you say you are, I'll reveal my secret identity—how does that sound?'

'*That*—' he smiled again, forcing another smile from her in response before he added '—is a deal.'

When her fingers closed around the end of the proffered

passport he held on, waiting for her lashes to lift before adding, 'And I'm not the only one capable of a little flirting on a plane, am I?'

Tugging it free, she informed him with a haughty lift of her nose, 'You obviously bring out my dark side.'

'Not sure I'd agree with that.'

Kerry shook her head, dropping her chin to flip through the passport and discovering page after page of stamps from varying countries around the globe. 'Have you really been to all these places?'

'Nah, I make my own stamps—it's a hobby of mine.' He chuckled again when she glared at him. 'It's easier to write a travel guide for a country if you've been there, I find. I tried it from home but no one ever came to visit my kitchen after I wrote the guide for there—which is a shame really, 'cos I had some great package deals going.'

Kerry continued reading all the country names, trying to imagine what it must have been like to have visited so many places and seen so many things. It had to have made for an exciting life; he'd make one heck of a dinner guest. And it was yet another thing she could find attractive about him, because even if their 'relationship' was only going to last for the duration of the flight, she had to admit he was pretty irresistible on many levels—full of charm, in possession of a fully working sense of humour, capable of giving as good as he got, sexy as sin…a walking fountain of knowledge when it came to travelling…

Be silly not to take advantage of the latter, really.

When she found the photograph page she laughed softly. 'Oh, dear—now that's bad.'

Ronan leaned in to look over her shoulder, his upper arm pressed against her shoulder. 'Just needs a row of numbers across the bottom, doesn't it? And a couple of shots from either side to make up the set.'

Kerry turned her face towards his, her gaze searching his eyes back and forth while she breathed in deep breaths of his scent. 'Voice of experience?'

His smile was slow and oozing with blatantly male sexuality, the brush of thick lashes against tanned skin deliberately slow, she was certain. And when he spoke it was with that deep, rumbling, intimate tone again, the air between them seeming to vibrate and—well—sizzle a little, frankly.

'Not in that area, no,' he stage-whispered, 'but I did get detention after school on a pretty regular basis. Just don't tell anyone in case it affects my ability to get into some countries, okay?'

'Your secret's safe with me.'

When she answered in an equally low stage whisper, her gaze tangled with his again, a shiver of something running up her spine, radiating outwards, leaving her skin tingling and a strange tightness in her chest.

What was that? She'd never been so very aware of a man on such a cellular level before and it was—a little unsettling, actually.

'Could I ask you to put your tray down, please, sir?'

The voice of a stewardess broke the charged silence, forcing Ronan back into his allocated space before he lowered his tray, a smile aimed up at the pretty blonde as she served him his meal. He wasn't the least bit tempted to flirt with her, he noticed, not the way he had with the woman beside him. It was something unusual for him—not that he hadn't been known to make small talk with someone on a long-haul flight if they hadn't handed out the usual 'leave me alone' signals of burying their nose in a paperback or plugging in headphones.

But she was—intriguing, he supposed was the right word. What was someone like her doing travelling alone? No rings anywhere, he'd noted, so it would be a boyfriend rather than husband meeting her in New York if there was one. But something told him there wasn't either one or she wouldn't be flirting back with him the way she was. Women who blushed as prettily as she had weren't players in that league, were they?

Business trip, then—visiting friends maybe.

Only one way to find out, so once they had their meals in front of them he turned his head to look at her again. 'What takes you to the Big Apple?'

She handed him his passport, which he tucked between his thighs without removing his gaze from her face. She should be well used to men looking at her, as pretty as she was with gleaming chestnut hair waving around her fine features and the full mouth with a constant upward curve suggesting she smiled more often than not.

'It's on my fantasy list.'

It took considerable effort to keep a strangled edge out of his voice. 'Your *what?*'

Because his furtive imagination had just gone straight to Sinville with that one.

'Kind of like fantasy football only with destinations instead of players.' She nodded, tucking a strand of richly coloured hair behind her ear so he could see a small earring dangling against the skin of her neck as she leaned forward to examine what was on her tray—the simple sight intensely sensual. 'I've spent so long burying myself in work that this trip is made up entirely of places off the top of the list.'

Ronan watched as she flashed him a sideways glance and a small smile that warmed the hints of russet in her large brown eyes.

'I'm going round the world.'

And the husky sense of satisfaction in her voice was a pleasure to his ears. 'Alone?'

'Now, if you were me would you answer that question when a stranger asked it?'

'No.'

She nodded again, ripping the plastic off her utensils. 'There you go, then.'

'So are you?'

She turned her shoulders and fixed him with a steady 'straight in the eye' gaze. 'Now, Mr O'Keefe—'

'Oh, no, you don't.' He leaned a little closer—something he'd been doing a lot the last few minutes. 'I was Ronan five minutes ago—and *you* owe *me* a name.'

'That was before you threatened me with a knife.'

When she dipped her chin in the direction of his hand he looked down, then back. 'It's a three-inch plastic knife—I'd say you're safe from any lasting harm, wouldn't you?'

When she continued to challenge him with her steady gaze and a minuscule quirk of her perfectly arched brows he took a deep breath and set the utensils down, replacing them with a spoon and the dessert tub, which he automatically ripped the cover off.

Her eyes widened. 'You're eating dessert first?'

'Yup,' he answered with his mouth full of a surprisingly good lemon cheesecake, mentally making a note of it in association with the airline. 'Why wait for the good stuff? Life's too short.'

'That's profound. But I think you'll find it has more to do with the savoury-before-sweet rule.'

There was a brief pause while Ronan studied her, cheesecake dissolving on his tongue. 'There's a rule?'

'Yes, and for good reason.'

'Never was one for following rules.'

'I can believe that.'

Ronan sat a little taller, because he was quite proud of his reputation as a rule-breaker, as it happened. He'd never been one for accepting the going odds either. And he wasn't that easily distracted.

'*Name.*'

She laughed, the sound amazingly sexy in the intimate space between them, and Ronan had been on more planes than he could count on his fingers and toes combined and never once had he found himself wishing the flight could be a few hours longer than it actually was.

'Does it matter? Not like you'll ever see me again after this flight touches down.'

'We made a deal.' And as a rule-follower she wasn't likely to go back on a deal, was she?

She ran the rosy tip of her tongue over her full lips, bringing Ronan's gaze to her mouth as she formed the words.

'It's Kerry, Kerry Doyle.'

It suited her, was—*right* somehow. 'Nice to meet you, Kerry, Kerry Doyle.'

And her mouth curled into an answering wide smile that showed straight teeth and mischievous dimples—oh, she was really something.

'Funny guy.'

Trailing his gaze from her mouth to the warmth of her eyes, and then somewhat reluctantly for the first time in his life to focus on his dessert, he silently cleared his throat before digging a little deeper to satisfy his raging curiosity.

'Tell me more about this fantasy list.'

'Is it a good idea for a woman travelling alone to give her itinerary to a stranger on a plane?'

Actually he wasn't entirely convinced that was the kind of fantasies he'd meant, his mouth curling into a lazy smile at the thought as he loaded his spoon. 'We've just been introduced so technically we're not strangers any more—just as well, too, seeing you've just confirmed you're travelling alone.'

When a quick turn of his head afforded him a glimpse of a recriminating frown he grinned inwardly. 'Don't look a gift horse and all that. You have a bonafide destination expert lit-erally at your fingertips—feel free to take advantage of me.'

He threw in another wink for good measure.

'Oh, you just don't quit, do you?'

'Being helpful? Can't say women list that as my most memorable quality, no.'

'Flirting.'

'Ah.' It took considerable effort to hold the full-blown smile he could feel in his chest from making its way up onto his face. 'Well, you do know they say it's all about the individual's interpretation.'

Kerry laughed a low, husky laugh. 'You're incorrigible.'

'I've been told. Tell me about your trip, then.'

She did, over 'dinner', through coffee that didn't get spilt thanks to the code they had in place, and she even produced a colour-coded itinerary Ronan found highly amusing as she explained it to him while they ignored the movie. It was as they began their descent into JFK that he explained to her the treasures that could be found if she didn't limit herself to the usual sights that would swallow up great chunks of her time when she was stuck in huge lines of tourists all wanting to see the same things—Kerry scribbling notes into the margins of her neatly typed sheets of paper.

Her enthusiasm was palpable, watching the thoughts crossing her expressive eyes was addictive—and Ronan found himself regretting again the fact he hadn't met her in Dublin on the first leg of the flight.

'It must be amazing to spend your life seeing all the places you see.'

An innocuous statement, but the words twisted like a knife in his chest. 'Yeah, it's been great.'

Placing her itinerary with its brand new scribbled notes into a Ziploc bag, she leaned back against her seat and sighed, a small, contented smile on her mouth and a faraway look in her eyes as she turned her face towards his watchful gaze, her voice low.

'I can't imagine half the things you've seen—you're incredibly lucky.'

Lucky was far from the mark, as it happened. But Ronan's imagination was too busy deciding that, with both their heads against the headrests and their faces turned towards each other, it was too much as if they were lying side by side in a bed for him to descend into bitterness—his voice husky as a result of where his brain then took that mental image.

'Have you got everything on your fantasy list covered or is there anything else I can help you with?'

She chuckled, letting the innuendo slide. 'This trip is just the beginning. I've got almost three months to pack in as much as I can, so it's a taster, if you like. Then if there's anywhere I really enjoy I'll try and spend more time there next time round.'

She had dozens more adventures to look forward to. And enthusiasm danced in her eyes, highlighting the hinted shades of russet and gold in amongst the brown—though his imagination was probably filling that in…

She really couldn't be any more different from him if she tried, could she? But he managed to keep the envy out of his voice, just. 'I can recommend some great guidebooks to help you catch up with me, if you like.'

Kerry laughed the soft laugh he found so enthralling. 'I'll just bet you can. Do you have one for the first-time traveller? You know—with all those tips about never confessing you're travelling alone, or why not to give your name to strangers on planes and that one about the passport? They're all very useful.'

'And you ignored every single one of them—' he couldn't help smiling when she did '—though I'm glad you did 'cos, between you and me, this has been the shortest Atlantic crossing I've ever had.'

After only a moment's hesitation she leaned a little closer to whisper, 'You're welcome.'

He couldn't stop looking into her eyes. Searching each of them closely, with the sense of intimacy rising as he felt the soft wisp of her warm breath against his face. And the urge to kiss her was so strong when the cabin lights dimmed and his vision blurred that it was as physical a need to him as the one for oxygen.

He'd only have to lean just a little bit closer...

There was a jolt as the large plane touched down, a ripple of applause working its way through the cabin and making Kerry laugh again as she moved back and arched up to look over the seat in front of her.

'Okay—is it unusual for a pilot to actually land the plane safely here?'

When the cabin lights flickered back on Ronan eventually dragged his gaze upwards from where he'd been attempting to fill his eyes with the sight of her lithe body arched against her seat belt.

'It was a smooth landing.' He shrugged. 'Sometimes folks just think that merits a thank-you.'

'I'll remember that for next time.'

She had dozens of next times ahead of her, didn't she? With an unaccustomed wave of angry bitterness, Ronan thought he should make sure and clap whenever he touched down in Dublin again—a kind of 'thanks for the memories' to all the pilots who'd got him from one place to the other in the last decade.

Kerry settled back in her seat, took a deep breath and asked, 'How long are you in New York for?'

'Why?'

The words came out in a rush. 'I don't suppose I can persuade you to play tour guide for a day?'

It wasn't going to take much persuasion.

CHAPTER TWO

KAREN had to be losing her tiny mind.

Since when did she run around asking men she'd only just met to spend a day with her? Since never—that was when. It wasn't that she was stuck in some old-fashioned notion that a woman didn't have as much a right to ask a man out as the other way round, but it wasn't something she made a habit of. And what did she really know about this guy beyond the fact he was disgustingly good-looking, great company and more than a little fascinating to her?

She swiped her clammy palms along the sides of her crisp white shorts and pushed her sunglasses up onto her head, squinting as she looked around the crowded street. If he stood her up that would be one way of getting out of it, she supposed. But the truth was she didn't want him to stand her up—the idea of another day in his company having been sending a flutter of anticipation through her stomach since before she'd gone to sleep the night before. And she couldn't remember the last time she'd felt that before seeing a man. Not that it was a date, because it wasn't—she'd even offered to pay him for acting as her tour guide.

He'd laughed, mind you.

But it still wasn't a date. It was a stolen day, a one-off, a way of marking her newfound freedom by doing something completely out of character…

Lord, but it was hot. She really hadn't been prepared for how hot it was, or how heavy the air was, or how sticky and dishevelled she felt or how noisy and overwhelming New York was with the constant sound of car horns and the wail of sirens echoing from streets away or the number of people or—

Her breath catching when she saw him.

He was standing in the midst of all the people milling around in front of the Empire State Building and it was just plain daft that in that moment he was the only thing Kerry could see. It was simply that he was the only familiar face, was all. And, as much as she'd told herself she was fine with making such a large trip alone, the truth was some of the joy of her first night in New York had been tempered by the fact she had no one with her to turn to and share it with. Like the excitement of the first moment she saw the Manhattan skyline laid out in front of her, and it finally hit her that she was *in New York*!

She continued staring at Ronan, reasoning again that no one could really blame her—he was incredibly easy on the eyes. Standing with his feet spread, as if claiming the small piece of sidewalk underneath him, he had his hands on his lean hips while he slowly turned a circle, searching the crowd with a frown of concentration on his face. The bright sunlight made his short, spiking hair look lighter—a milk chocolate as opposed to the dark she'd thought it was on the plane—and he just looked so, so, well, he *did*.

Kerry raised a hand and waved it above her head.

But Ronan continued circling, so, feeling a little silly for waving like an idiot, she walked forwards, swiping her hands down her sides again as she got closer. 'Hi there—do you by any chance know how to get to the Empire State Building?'

The lazy smile that slid onto his mouth brought an immediate answering smile to her lips. How pathetic was it she was glad to see him? And it didn't bode too well for her conviction she could take her trip alone and still enjoy it just as much, did it?

'You're close, if it helps any.'

Stopping a foot away from him, she watched as his gaze travelled down her body all the way to her feet before rising faster than it had lowered. And she was surprised by how the simple glance suddenly made her feel warmer than she already was, every nerve ending tingling with awareness.

'So are we starting the grand tour here?'

Ronan casually pushed his large hands into his jeans pockets, adopting the pose of a man extremely comfortable in his own skin. 'Is there a queue all the way round the block?'

Kerry turned on her heel and surveyed the long line of people, sometimes three or four deep, stretching from the entrance until they disappeared around the corner; the thought of joining the end of a line that length in the sweltering heat was enough to draw a small groan from her lips.

'Yes.'

'Then no.' He shot a glance at the bag resting on her hip, the strap slung diagonally across her body between her breasts. 'I suppose you have the obligatory camera in there for pictures of all the sights?'

Kerry patted it with one hand, her chin rising with confidence. 'And sun cream and a mini-fan and a bottle of water and a map and energy bars and a mobile phone and—'

Ronan smiled wryly, long fingers wrapping around her elbow to turn her before he started walking into the crowd. 'Well at least if we get stranded in the desert we'll survive.'

'Are you making fun of the fact I like to be prepared for every eventuality, Mr O'Keefe?'

'Possibly. But if I achieve nothing else today it's my aim to sway you towards the merits of travelling light—I saw how much luggage you took off that carousel yesterday. And unless

I'm very much mistaken, this is supposed to be a fun experience for you—not an endurance test.'

Kerry felt the skin on her elbow tingling beneath his hand, warmth travelling like an electric current up her arm, over her shoulder and downwards towards her breasts, disconcerting enough for her to feel the need to gently twist free of his touch before it worked its way anywhere else. Then she felt the need to lessen the small rejection with a sidewards glance and a pout of her lower lip.

'I *need* all those clothes. It's a trip through two seasons and half a dozen countries—and that involves a varied wardrobe. And anyway, I only have the absolute necessities with me.'

Ronan sounded unconvinced. 'Your idea of bare necessities and mine aren't the same, I'd guess.'

'That's because you're a man and I'm a woman.'

'No—it's because I'm a seasoned traveller and you're a virgin.'

Kerry couldn't help making a small derisive snort.

And it was enough to make Ronan turn his head to look down at her face, his voice threaded with the cheek of the devil. 'In travelling terms anyway. Because obviously by your age and looking the way you do…'

Her jaw dropped.

But he merely chuckled and reclaimed her elbow to steer her closer to the kerb. 'Okay, Kerry, Kerry Doyle, I'm prepared to give a little on the traditional tourist stuff for the first hour or so to give you some quick photo op's seeing you're on a tight schedule—plus this is an easy way to get your bearings, so—'

'What is?'

He quirked his brows at her in barely disguised amusement, then jerked a thumb over his shoulder and added the words slowly as if he were talking to a complete idiot. *'That is.'*

Kerry was a tad bemused, folding her arms across her

breasts and blinking up at him before she asked, 'Mr Great Adventurer is putting me on an open-top bus with the rest of the tourists? My, my, aren't you the daring one? I'm so glad I have travel insurance.'

'We can take the subway and boil to death if you prefer. You won't see as much, mind you…'

Hard as it was to believe that anywhere barring the face of the sun could be any hotter than where she already was, and with him looking at her the way he was, Kerry wasn't prepared to find out. But she was a little disappointed—she could have found one of the many bus tours on her own. Somehow she'd expected more from Ronan. Had maybe secretly hoped for more? And that some of that sense of adventure might rub off on her?

He stepped closer and bent his knees until he was looking her directly in the eye, his proximity doing things to her pulse rate and breathing that she hadn't experienced since, well, since the plane, actually…

'Trust me.' His voice dropped seductively, the vibration of the deep tone reaching out to interrupt the usual rhythm of her heart. 'I promise you won't forget today.'

Kerry swallowed. She believed him—but somehow she knew, deep to the pit of her soul, it wouldn't just be the sight-seeing she'd remember. And that was a strangely scary thought. Especially when she'd spent so long waiting for a time in her life when she finally had her independence; she'd fought long and hard, worked more hours than she cared to think about, had constantly put the needs of others first. Not that she wanted to change that—but the last thing she needed was to get even temporarily attached to someone who was probably as reliable as an Irish summer.

'Can I ask you a question?'

He stood tall again, towering over her by a good six inches. 'Depends.'

'How many women you meet on planes end up asking you to play tour guide for them?'

'Regretting asking?'

'Curious.'

He folded his arms across his chest, mirroring her stance, the simple action accenting the muscles in his forearms and biceps. 'About how often I do this or why you asked me in the first place?'

'Yes.'

And why he'd agreed, she supposed. Not that she needed her ego stroked, but she was curious as to why he'd said yes as quickly as he had. He had to be in New York for a reason, didn't he? Meeting with a publisher? More research for a new book maybe? Someone who'd travelled as much as he had didn't make a trip just for the sake of it, did they? And if that was the case had he dropped whatever he was doing in favour of spending the day with her?

Because she really wouldn't want him to think that she'd repay him at the end of it with—or that he was onto some kind of a sure thing or—

'First up, let's remember you asked me and not the other way round—though I'd have offered if you'd given me five minutes. Or at the very least pointed you in the general direction of some of my favourite places.'

Kerry opened her mouth.

But Ronan wasn't done. 'Secondly, I don't tend to talk to people on planes much—and any I've bothered with have never been a beautiful woman travelling alone, more's the pity. So, yes—you're the first one for a guided tour. I'm only human.'

Of all the very many things in there she could have picked to ask questions on, Kerry's brain could only seem to focus on the one thing: he thought she was beautiful. Really? Not pretty or cute but honest-to-goodness beautiful?

It made her positively glow—a guy like *him* thinking that. So much for not needing her ego stroked.

'Thirdly—' he took a measured breath that expanded his wide chest before continuing with an almost reluctant tone in his voice, as if he wasn't completely comfortable saying the words '—I guess the idea of seeing things through your eyes appealed to me. It'll do me good to see it from a new perspective—who knows? I might even get a chapter of a book out of it. I'll even promise to give you an acknowledgement if I do.'

He recovered with a wink. 'You can *thank me later…*'

'Ronan—' But before she could find anything coherent to say there was a loud greeting from the upper floor of the bus.

'Ro—my man! C'mon up.'

Ronan grinned, tilting his head right back to throw an answer back. 'Hey, Johnnie boy—you save us the good seats?'

'Uh-huh. That your friend?'

'Yup.'

The younger man whistled. 'She's way too good-lookin' for you, old man—bring her up here so I can steal her away.'

Kerry laughed when the words were accompanied with an exaggerated wink and a beckoning index finger. 'And *that* is?'

Ronan cupped her elbow again, guiding her onto the bus as he leaned his head down, lowering his voice to a conspiratorial whisper.

'Best tour guide in New York City—just don't go telling him I said so or he'll be unbearable.' He stood taller, voice rising a little. 'These tours are all about the guides; get a local like John and you'll get more insight about the city and the best places to go than you ever would from a book.'

Kerry lowered her voice to the same conspiratorial level he'd used. 'Don't you know someone who could maybe *put it* in a book?'

'Ah-h-h, but these stories aren't mine to tell—they're his. And no two tours are ever the same with John. There's always something new to add or a different joke or something that happened the day before. And that's what travelling is all about—the people as much as the places. Some places you might forget, but you won't forget the people you met along the way. Memories Kerry, Kerry Doyle—yours, the people you meet's—that's what you'll have at the end of every trip you take. Moments; snapshots in time, if you like.'

They paused at the bottom of narrow metal stairs leading to the upper deck, where Ronan released her arm and Kerry felt the rush of air-conditioned coolness wash over the heated brand of his touch, creating goose-bumps on her skin. But even though she was aware of it, it was the wistfulness in his voice as he painted the romantic picture that captured her attention most, echoing a need inside her for the kind of moments he'd just described.

'You really love what you do, don't you?'

The sigh was silent, but she caught it. What was it that suddenly made him frown? Why did he turn away from her and look up the stairs as if he didn't want to look her in the eye? And why did she suddenly feel so ridiculously—*sad* somehow? She really wished she could place a mental finger on whatever it was.

He was quite the mystery.

'I did.'

Kerry wasn't completely sure she'd heard him say it, but before she could check a pair of feet appeared on the stairs and an upturned palm was offered her way.

'Come on up, sweet thing. I have a seat saved specially for *you*—Ro can just stay down there.'

'And leave her with you? Don't think so, pal.'

'Ro?' Picking on the nickname she'd previously ignored, she shot an amused glance at Ronan.

'Don't even think about adopting it. I can leave you stranded somewhere. Or with Johnnie—he's famous with the ladies, so if you prefer…'

Placing her hand into John's, she leaned back a little while walking up the steps. 'I think I'll stick with the devil I know.'

She'd always been a sucker for a mystery.

Ronan had spent half a day with her and he still didn't get her. Not that he'd ever felt the need to place people in boxes so he knew where he stood in the world, but normally he was a good judge—he was worldly-wise, after all. But her he just didn't get.

For starters he found it hard to believe someone like her didn't have a load of friends who could've gone on holiday with her. Not that everyone could take three months off work to travel round the world, but still. That thought process then led him to wonder what she did that allowed *her* to take three months off work. She was a little mature for a student taking a gap. He put her early thirties maybe—though she could have passed for younger—but she had a maturity and intelligence to the way she spoke and acted that made him believe she had some life experience under her belt. People over the age of thirty were—calmer, he supposed. They knew what they wanted, were less worried about what people thought, more 'together'.

And as the day progressed he couldn't help wondering something else: how she'd managed to stay single when she looked the way she did. Because he wasn't the only one looking at her as if she were the last female left on the planet, was he?

John flirted outrageously with her during the tour and although Kerry didn't overly play up to it she hadn't exactly discouraged him either; laughing that husky laugh of hers, her lips parting to draw in the odd gasp at his audacity when he made innuendos over the tannoy and then blushing adoringly straight after, eyes shining. And it had bugged Ronan, frankly. He didn't want Johnnie-boy to be the one getting all those reactions.

Almost as if somewhere in his mind Ronan had claimed her as his for the day.

She made a small moaning sound beside him and stretched long, slender legs directly into his line of vision, so he turned his head to watch as she stretched the rest of her body. And had to stifle a groan when his body reacted in a very swift, very male way to what he saw—the woman should wear a warning!

She'd clasped the fingers of one hand around the wrist of the other before lifting her arms above her head and had her head tilted back, eyes closed as she let the sun warm her face. And the combined stretching of legs and arms had arched her spine off the bench, her breasts straining against the snug fit of her azure-blue vest-top.

'I am *so* hot.'

Ronan couldn't help but silently agree.

'Is it normally this hot here this time of year?'

When she resumed a normal sitting position he just about managed to look at her face before she opened her eyes. 'They're having a heatwave. But it's probably the humidity you're feeling. We Irish aren't used to it. You'll adjust in a couple of days.'

'A couple of days before I move on then—don't s'pose you know what the weather is like in Canada?'

He cocked a brow and she smiled.

'Okay—yes, you do.' She rolled her eyes while reaching out for the iced water they'd bought from one of the street vendors who'd happily tossed it to the upper floor of the bus in exchange for a scrunched-up dollar bill thrown down at them. Something that had entertained her immensely at the time.

'I keep forgetting this is all old hat for you. I must look like a little kid on Christmas morning.'

Yeah, she did. But he liked that about her. He'd soaked up some of her enthusiasm as she took in everything on the tour, and the number of times she'd gently set her fine-boned hand on his arm to get his attention before pointing at something or leaned across him to get a better photograph of the Flat Iron

Building or the Courthouse or the Woolworth Building or City Hall had only added to his overall enjoyment.

Somewhere along the way he'd forgotten what it was like to feel so excited about everything. But, as good as it was to be reminded not to take things for granted just because he'd seen them a thousand times, it was also a little like poking an open wound with a stick; reminding him of the dark thoughts he'd been putting to the back of his mind the last few months—which had been a bit tough to take, and left him pensive.

What he needed was a way to lighten his mood, and to stop him obsessing about Kerry's 'hot' body.

He turned his head and focussed on the kids playing in front of them. At the bottom end of the island of Manhattan, Battery Park was packed the way it always was, hundreds of tourists milling around filling in time while they took turns patiently waiting in the mile-long queue weaving its way along the concrete paths to the ferries for Ellis and Liberty Islands.

The kids between them and the incoming ferries had the right idea in the heat, Ronan reckoned—in fact…

He grinned, taking Kerry's hand before standing up and tugging to get her off the bench. 'C'mon.'

'Where are—?'

'You said you were hot, right?'

She resisted, dragging her feet while trying to open her bag and stow away her water, a curtain of hair hiding their destination until it was too late, 'I did and I am but—'

She squeaked when the narrow fountain of water appeared directly in front of her feet, shooting high enough above her head to sprinkle her face on the downward journey. And Ronan chuckled at the look of surprise on her face, deliberately stepping back so another jet appeared beside them.

Kerry's eyes narrowed.

He shrugged. 'Cooler now, aren't you?'

For a moment she simply glared at him. And then she

caught him off guard by moving neatly to one side and tugging on his hand so he was stood pretty much directly over the next jet of water when it appeared.

Closing his eyes, he pursed his lips and shook his head hard to get the water off his hair. Then he opened his eyes, looked down to locate another of the metal rings, and when she tried to tug her hand free he closed his fingers tighter, hauling her forwards and smiling at her gasp as her breasts hit the wall of his chest.

She shook her hair out of her eyes, looked up at him with wide eyes and then laughed as he smirked and spun her—once, twice, in and out of several jets of cold water before releasing her without warning and swinging her out to arm's length where she was promptly soaked from head to toe by fountains either side of her. Only then did he allow her fingers to slip free from his, deliberately slow so they touched fingertip to fingertip for a few seconds before both their arms dropped.

He prepared himself for outrage.

But before his captivated gaze she simply tilted her head to one side, quirked an arched brow, and deliberately skipped sideways underneath another jet.

Ronan laughed, feeling an inner lightness returning to his chest that'd been missing for longer than he cared to admit. So he made a sideways slide in the opposite direction to her skip—and got wet.

Kerry checked the ground, made a skip back and to her left and got wetter still, lifting her arms from her sides and leaning her head back to welcome the cooling spray. Then she turned round and round in slow circles getting wetter and wetter as each plume of water appeared, her effervescent laughter drawing answering, somewhat lower laughter from Ronan as he watched.

She was amazing. He wondered if she knew that. Somehow he doubted *he'd* forget it. And, having talked to her briefly about 'moments', he knew he was experiencing one of them right there and then…

Kerry laughed at the sheer ridiculousness of what she was doing. What was it they said about people shedding their inhibitions when away from home ground? But it wasn't just that. She was having fun. Honest-to-goodness *fun*—joy bubbling up inside her like bubbles in a flute of champagne.

She was in New York, on the first leg of a dream of a lifetime and to top it off she was messing around with an incredibly sexy guy under a set of fountains in the bright sunshine in Battery Park. Life didn't get much better than that, she reckoned.

They managed to get wet another couple of times on their way out, both still grinning from the shared experience as they walked through the crowd and Kerry fully aware, but not the least bit bothered, by the amused looks aimed their way.

She shook droplets of moisture off her arms and lifted her hands to her hair—ruffling it in the vain hope the hot midday sun would dry it into something resembling curls rather than a frizzy mess. She then stole a sideways glance at Ronan, who was flapping the end of his white T-shirt back and forth, no doubt to try and dry it some—not that Kerry actually had a problem with it plastered against his well-defined chest.

And when he turned his head to look at her she felt her breath catch again, the way it had when she'd spotted him in the crowd. He really did do incredible things to her pulse rate, didn't he? She'd never met anyone who could do that—and so effortlessly too. He had only to breathe in and out and she found it completely fascinating.

They laughed.

'Well, you're cooler now, aren't you?' He nudged his upper arm off her shoulder.

So she nudged him back a little harder, laughing all the more when he made an exaggerated stagger to the side. 'You're a big kid, you know that, don't you?'

A large hand was slapped against his chest. 'Me? I'll have you know I'm the responsible one—I just made sure the chances of you getting heatstroke were lessened. You're the one who turned it into a game.'

Still smiling, but with her gaze now fixed forwards on the poignant sight of the mounted globe salvaged from Ground Zero, Kerry admitted in a soft voice, 'It was fun.'

She dropped her chin to study the painted toenails visible in her sandalled feet for a moment before giving in to the need to look back at Ronan, who was looking at her with a strangely intense expression on his face.

'You make it sound like it's something you don't normally make time for.'

She scrunched up her nose.

'How come?'

Spoken by the man who was as free as a bird to the woman who'd been trapped by responsibility for over a decade. 'I have fun. I just don't—'

'Have fun the way you just did?'

Normally the lack of smart suits and forcefully tamed hair was enough to fool the world into thinking she was more carefree than she actually was. And he hadn't seen her in work clothes, so, 'Do I look boring?'

'No, that's why I'm surprised—and now curious.'

Kerry liked that she could make him curious. In the short time she'd known him Lord alone knew there'd been plenty of things that had her curious about *him*, so it was a good feeling to be able to return the favour.

When she didn't speak he asked the obvious. 'So what holds you back?'

'Is therapy a complimentary part of the tour?'

'Ooh—*defensive*.'

How had he done that? Having used the gentle tone he just had, he'd made her feel guilty for not spilling her guts. And

Kerry never did, well, not unless she'd known someone a really long time, which technically made it a moot point because anyone who'd known her that long already *knew*.

But she wasn't going to ruin such an amazing day with a conversation examining the psychology of why she was the way she was in normal everyday life. So she brushed it over by nudging her shoulder against his arm again, lifting her other hand to push her fingers into the hair on top of her head and ruffling it before letting it fall.

'What's next? I assume from your previous disdain for people with patience that we're not joining the longest queue in the history of mankind so we can make some kind of Irish pilgrimage to Ellis…'

The low rumble of laughter reassured her she'd managed to brush over what could have been an awkward moment. 'You'd be correct in that assumption. But I do need to know how you feel about boats.'

Kerry stopped and turned to face him, considering a random point above his left ear while she answered. 'Kinda depends if we're talking rowboat or cruise ship here. Though I should warn you I hadn't planned on the cruise portion of my fantasy list for another twenty years or so. And I was thinking more along the lines of the Caribbean for that one.'

'I'm sure you'll enjoy that. But I'm thinking more along the lines of the Staten Island ferry. You can see Ellis and take some pictures of Liberty while I fill you in on the associated history free of charge—I'm helpful that way.'

Her gaze shifted to lock with his, the smile immediate and reciprocated just as fast. 'Lead on Macduff.'

He stared at her for a long moment, searching her eyes while a dozen thoughts crossed through the varying shades of blue in his. But just when she thought he might say something else, he laced his fingers with hers and tugged.

'C'mon then, Kerry, Kerry Doyle.'

The invisible angelic midget on one shoulder said she really shouldn't allow him to keep touching her the way he did; as if he had a right to do it and had been doing it for ever. But the equally small invisible siren in high heels on her other promptly reminded her she'd been just as keen to touch *him* on the bus tour. And fair was fair.

So she decided for just one day of her life she wasn't going to over-think. She was simply going to do things because she wanted to and because they felt right. Not because she was expected to behave a certain way or because she was concerned what other people thought—the trip was the first thing she'd specifically done for herself in a long, long time, after all. And she'd earned it; she didn't have to feel guilty about *anything*.

If karma was going to punish her for grabbing hold of one perfect day, then let it try—they'd be having a long talk about time served.

So she tangled her fingers a little firmer around Ronan's—softening any subliminal meaning he might get from it by then swinging their arms as they walked down the path out of the park.

He grumbled out a warning. 'You even think about doing any skipping to go with that arm-swinging and I'm tossing you under the first yellow cab I can find.'

'You're no fun.'

The look he gave her was so heated it practically melted her knees, his voice a low, deliciously sensual rumble. 'Oh, I can be fun. *Believe me.* And now I know how much fun *you* can be, my new aim is to make sure you have as much of it as humanly possible. So consider yourself warned, young lady.'

Kerry grinned the whole way out of the park. She could quite happily have the day never end...

CHAPTER THREE

LITTLE did she know it but Kerry Doyle had managed a bit of a miracle in the twelve hours Ronan had spent with her. She was a ray of sunshine. And, caught in her reflected warmth, he'd miraculously forgotten his reason for being in New York this time round.

It wasn't until the end of the night tour on another open-topped bus that he was faced with a very visible reminder of why he would never be able to forget, because when the light dimmed his world went dark, and he had to force his other senses into overdrive to keep from showing his weakness in front of her.

Thankfully Kerry had been distracted by all the varying photo opportunities afforded to her by the stunning sight of Manhattan lit up against the night sky Ronan didn't have to look at to know—so indelibly was it imprinted onto his mind after dozens of trips. And by the time they'd returned to Times Square he had enough light to work with to leave her with his pride intact.

He frowned as he stepped off the bus, jostling a couple of people in the crowd before he focussed hard on Kerry. He then allowed himself the luxury of studying her face one more time—watching as the newly familiar soft smile formed on her full lips.

Resentment built inside him like a tidal wave. In another

life he wouldn't have been letting her go. He'd have suggested sushi or lobster or cocktails in one of the bars overlooking the free floorshow that was Times Square at night. He'd have taken her back to the Empire State before it closed so she could see the panoramic view of the city from eighty-odd floors up and he'd have walked her back to her hotel—no matter how far it was—and kissed her long and slow before persuading her to spend another day with him.

Though being gentlemanly enough to leave after the kiss might have taken some effort—he had a sneaking suspicion kissing her might be something he didn't want to stop doing in any great hurry.

'Are you hungry?'

Not in the way she probably meant. Looking at her all day had brought on the kind of hunger he hadn't experienced in a long time, if ever. As if she'd uncovered something his body was desperately lacking and now that it knew it craved it as badly as the air he breathed.

He saw the open warmth in her face as the question hung between them and felt momentarily angry at the universe for having to turn her down. 'I've gotta go. I have an early appointment.'

At least he wasn't telling her a lie.

She nodded, turning her face away, then leaning her head back a little to smile up at him one last time, one hand resting on the bag at her hip, the other waving out to her side as she raised her voice enough to be heard over the hundreds upon hundreds of people and honking car horns and the yelled voices of vendors selling everything from fake designer label handbags to T-shirts to hotdogs to—

'I had an amazing day—thank you.'

And there was that word 'amazing' again. Somehow he knew he'd always associate it with her, 'You're welcome. I haven't been on one of those buses for years. But they're a good way to get your bearings the first time. Stick to them and crowds and you won't go too far wrong. No more flirting with strangers, mind.'

She laughed when he added the last part with an edge of mock severity to his voice. 'I'll keep it in mind. And I might take your advice on the helicopter ride before I leave too.'

'You should.'

'Another moment to remember…'

'Exactly.'

He stayed focussed on her and only her for as long as he could manage it without inviting the usual ache behind his eyes, but when it was getting too uncomfortable and he opened his mouth to say the words to let him walk away she distracted him again by moving in to place a warm kiss on his cheek.

It was *her* fault.

Because if she hadn't done it he wouldn't have had the opportunity he now had. He might have resisted the temptation to take one last memory with him, but now he couldn't, turning his head and pressing his mouth to hers before she had time to react. His hand lifted to cradle the back of her head, he took a step in so his body was close enough to hers to feel the added heat in the humid air, and only then did he close his eyes and let his lips drag over hers the way he'd been thinking about doing since he'd met her.

Every hair on his body immediately tingled with awareness; she tasted of the iced coffee they'd stopped for, a hint of raspberry flavouring lingering on her lips and practically begging him to sample more with the tip of his tongue.

So he did. He had to.

For a second Kerry froze, hands floundering on either side of her body while she was caught in the indecision of reaching for him or simply waiting until the world stopped tilting beneath her feet. Oh, heavens above, but the man had sinfully magic lips! And even while alarm bells rang in her head, they were already being drowned out by the sound of her own blood roaring in her ears.

When he ran the tip of his tongue over the parting in her lips, she opened up and met him in the middle, feeling his low hum of approval all the way to the tips of her toes.

When someone bumped her arm, Ronan's arm circled her waist—drawing her in against the protective hard planes of his body as he spread his feet wider. And Kerry's wavering arms automatically lifted in response, her hands settling on his shoulders while she instinctively stood on the balls of her feet to get closer still.

She wasn't even aware of the fact there were other people around them after that. All there was was him and the kissing. *Oh, my, the kissing.* Kerry had honestly thought she'd been kissed before—had she been able to think in a straight line she'd probably have had a look back in her memory to check. But after this—

She sighed contently. It was bliss.

Ronan tilted her back a little so he could kiss her deeper still. And it wasn't a hard kiss, or a kiss that said they were seconds away from being horizontal; in fact it was the very controlled softness and warmth of it, as if he was holding back from her, that wrapped tight around her heart and made it ache for more.

It was a kiss goodbye, wasn't it? He was ending the amazing day with an even more amazing kiss goodbye. And knowing that made Kerry ache as she'd never ached.

His hand slid forwards so that his thumb was brushing against her cheek when he lifted his head, a small frown deepening the crease between his dark brows as he blinked hard to focus on her. While Kerry in turn looked back at him with drowsy, heavy-lidded eyes and somehow eventually managed the energy to smile.

Ronan smiled back a split second before he removed his

hand, loosened his arm and stepped away from her, his voice just husky enough for her to know she wasn't the only one affected by the kiss.

'Enjoy your trip, Kerry, Kerry Doyle.'

She swallowed, smile wavering. 'I'll try.'

There really didn't seem to be much more to say. And she didn't want to ruin the perfect ending to a perfect day by trying to force out words that currently didn't exist in her scrambled brain. So she stepped back, turning her head to get her bearings before deciding to simply flag down a cab and head back to her hotel. After all, anything she did alone would only make her miss his company after everything they'd done together. She missed him already.

When she looked back he was gone and it took a few minutes for her to see his head in the crowd. He obviously wasn't one for long goodbyes, then. What man ever was?

And if she was honest, Kerry didn't think she'd have been able to say it either. So instead she stood still until she couldn't see him any more, only then turning in a circle to look at all the wondrous sights around her. It was a different universe. One city with a larger population than the entire island she lived on.

And she'd just been kissed senseless in the middle of Times Square by a good-looking guy she'd met on a plane less than twenty-four hours ago. How incredible was that?

She laughed, shaking her head at the sheer unexpectedness of it. Kerry Doyle. Kissing what amounted to a stranger in a strange land.

It was the stuff of dreams.

Ronan fiddled with the straw in his glass, rattling ice cubes against the edges while he looked out the large windows beside him and did his best to focus on the odd passer-by in the crowd.

The odd *specific* passer-by, that was…

At first he refused to admit everyone he focussed on was female, with brown hair and so much as the vaguest hint of Kerry to them. But after the sixth or seventh one he eventually told himself it was a natural reaction—an offshoot from numerous daily forays into wondering what she was doing and seeing.

Another brown-haired female walked into his line of vision and he turned his head to follow her, Al's voice sounding from across the table.

'I'm assuming from the fact we're avoiding talking about it that your appointment didn't go so well.'

'We're still not talking about it.'

'Right.'

Frowning when he confirmed it wasn't Kerry and promising himself he wasn't searching for her again, he turned his head to look at his old friend, making sure he was looking him straight in the eye before he spoke with enough of an edge in his voice to hint heavily that he wasn't about to be drawn out.

'Looking to help me drown my sorrows? 'Cos I should warn you I have a curfew these days—so if we're heading out on a pub crawl we need to get started sooner rather than later.'

The last thing he needed was a post-mortem on his appointment with the specialist. It had been a shot in the dark at best—no pun intended. But that didn't mean he wasn't going to try. What it *should* have meant was he wasn't surprised by the negative results.

He supposed he must still have hoped, though…

Al frowned. 'How can you make with the funnies?'

Ronan shrugged. 'How can I not? I'm Irish, Al—you take away my sense of humour, you may as well put me in a box and dig a hole.'

'You're barely thirty-two, Ronan.'

'And I've had my whole life to prepare for this so it's not like it's that big a shock. My uncle has lived with it since he was a kid—so I'm the lucky one.'

With a shake of his head Ronan knew signalled resignation, Al leaned back in his seat and glanced around the sports bar. 'You can't take this trip on your own—not this time.'

'Watch me try.'

'One more book will make that big a difference in the greater scheme of things, will it?'

Ronan shrugged again, leaning forwards and resting his forearms on the table as he watched the ice continue circling in the glass long after he'd finished moving it. 'Will to me.'

'Not like you need the money.'

'Not doing it for the money.'

There was a brief silence and then a low, 'I know.'

Slapping his palms on the wooden surface, Ronan sat upright again. 'Right, then—if you're gonna go all morbid on me I think I prefer you drunk. Let's go.'

'Last time I got drunk with you—'

'I swear—not over the state line this time.'

'Better not be.' Producing his wallet, he checked the bill on the table. 'My wife wasn't happy with a call from Boston that early in the morning.'

'Still came and got us, though.'

'Yeah, and still gives me hell for it. In this country we're s'posed to quit that kinda stupidity once we leave college.'

They pushed their chairs back at the same time, and Ronan stepped over and slapped a hand on Al's back, forcing himself to grin broadly. 'See, you needed me to keep you young. You'll have to find another partner in crime after this—I'll be relying on hearing about your adventures to keep *me* young.'

'Lauren says you'll be eighteen your whole life.'

'From her lips to God's ears, my friend…'

They were almost at the door when for some unknown reason Ronan looked up at the large screen on the wall. It was normally filled with the usual sights of football or baseball or basketball—dependent on the time of year—so he was surprised to catch sight of a news report. And for a second his heart actually stopped.

'What?'

He frowned in concentration, ignoring Al's curious voice as he attempted to read the bulletins across the bottom of the screen—his frustration rising.

'Can someone turn it up?' When it didn't happen immediately, he turned his attention to the people around him, his voice rising. '*Hey!* Turn it up!'

'…to recap…a sightseeing chopper crashed into the Hudson an hour ago…four tourists and the pilot were picked up by—'

Damn it.

Kerry felt she'd been remarkably restrained in the few souvenirs she'd picked up. With the current exchange rate and an array of shops to leave any sane woman drooling, it had taken a gargantuan effort not to shop as if the end of the world were nigh. But she had several thousand miles to go yet and, in fairness, Ronan had been right about her luggage. But then so had she—she *needed* all that stuff.

Could hardly leave New York empty-handed, though…

Smiling brightly at the doorman who'd been her best friend since she checked in, she dropped her chin to look in her bag for her key-card, knowing her way to the elevators well enough not to have to look up again until she had it in her hand.

'Not floating at the bottom of the Hudson, then,' a deep voice rumbled from over her right shoulder.

And Kerry's eyes widened before she swung round, her voice a little breathless in response to the sight of him calmly folding a newspaper and setting it on a coffee-table before he pushed to his feet. '*Ronan.*'

She gulped down a breath, 'How did you—?'

'I have my ways; took a couple of hours and a friend on a second phone, mind you. I take it you skipped my advice about a helicopter ride on your last day.'

She blinked at him. 'I was going to take one but—'

'You heard one fell in the river?'

'Yeah, well, that kinda thing can be a little off-putting even when nobody got hurt so—' It suddenly hit her why he might be there, her mouth curling into a smile in response. 'You were worried about me?'

His stunning eyes narrowed a little as he got closer, large hands casually pushing back the edges of his tan linen jacket so he could shove them down into the pockets of his light-coloured chinos.

'Thought I'd check—that's all.'

It was quite possibly the sweetest thing any man had ever done for her. But when how she felt must have shown in her eyes he frowned, shaking his head and drawing his mouth into a thin line before he got to her. 'Having advised you to go I might have felt guilty if you'd ended up getting wet again so—'

'Thank you.'

She smiled all the more when he looked irritated. Well, he'd just have to learn to accept the consequences of being sweet if he took it on himself to be that way. Though somehow she doubted he was the kind of man who'd appreciate being *told* he was sweet in the first place.

There were other things she could tell him she thought he was, mind you...

He dropped his chin and looked down at her bags, sinfully gorgeous lips twitching when he looked back into her eyes.

'You didn't seriously go out and buy more stuff to cart around on your trip?'

Kerry lifted her chin. 'A couple of souvenirs.'

'Uh-huh—and they needed that many bags, did they?'

'And a couple of things for friends...'

'Which you're *posting* home, I assume?'

Actually that wasn't a half-bad idea. If she'd thought of that she could have bought more. Maybe if she went back she could—

A hand appeared to wave a forefinger at her. 'Oh, no, you don't. You buy this much stuff at every destination, you're going to need a packhorse before long. Remember we talked about *downsizing*?'

'Have I just been adopted?'

The smile he gave her was disgustingly sensual, and mesmerizing as all hell. He even dropped his voice an octave so the air between them vibrated. 'Maybe.'

Kerry blinked at him again, lost for words, and, as she had spent almost half her life talking to people from all walks of life, it was quite an event.

He nodded once at the bags. 'Do you need to leave those up to your room?'

'Why? Where am I going?'

'You're bound to be hungry after all that shopping.'

'Maybe I already ate.'

'Did you?'

'No.' And yes, she could have lied about that, but she'd never been much good at lying. Do unto others and all that, she'd always reckoned. 'But maybe I don't want to eat *with you* now you're exhibiting these new stalker-like tendencies.'

'Yes, you do.' He rocked forwards onto the balls of his feet and quirked dark brows at her, light dancing in his eyes. 'And now I've adopted you it's my responsibility to make sure you're fed and watered.'

Kerry's eye's narrowed.

And Ronan chuckled as he rocked back onto his heels. 'And, anyway, I've been doing some thinking while I sat here waiting to make sure you hadn't drowned and I might have a proposition to put to you…'

The words dangled in the air between them like a flipping carrot, just enough of a mystery to pique her interest all over again. 'What kind of "proposition"?'

'Come to dinner and I'll consider telling you.'

'What does it say in your handbook about women travelling alone accepting random dinner invitations from men seeking to proposition them?'

'That might just be part of it.'

If it turned out Ronan was indeed a serial killer Kerry vowed she was haunting her nana in retaliation for all the Hardy Boys and Nancy Drew books she'd been given as a child, feeding her a love of mystery from an impressionable age. And she silently prayed she hadn't chosen this particular moment to be completely wrong about someone.

'Do I need to get changed?'

The question gave him an open invitation to look down over her body, which he did—at length—doing that weird skipping thing to her pulse rate he was so very good at.

When his gaze eventually tangled with hers again the darker blue was distinctly more prominent than any of the other shades. 'You'll do.'

Kerry damped her lips, waving a handful of shopping bags in the direction of the front doors. 'Well, go on, then. I'll leave my bags with the doorman. But my flight's tomorrow so we can't be out too late.'

Warm fingers wrapped around her elbow as he guided her to the door. 'We'll be back well before either of us turn into pumpkins.'

Dinner, naturally, had to be yet another experience she'd

remember. And leaning back in her seat, a large bowled glass of rich Cabernet Shiraz in hand and her stomach ridiculously full of the kind of pasta that had simply melted in her mouth, Kerry couldn't help but smile at her surroundings. Trust Ronan.

Little Italy was packed—the one narrow street made even narrower by all the tables full of diners spilling out from a cornucopia of small restaurants. And then there were all the people milling around trying to decide where to eat, and the sound of laughter and voices yelling out greeting and music spilling out to compete with music from further down the street. It was gloriously insane. Kerry *loved* it.

The world was a wonderful place with a little of his perspective.

Ronan leaned forwards, frowning the way he always did when he was studying her intently. 'Dessert?'

Kerry laughed. 'Are you kidding me? Those portions were big enough for three people—though I appreciate your restraint at eating the courses in the right order for a change.'

'So you should. And there's always room for dessert—trust me.'

She watched as he absent-mindedly rolled the sleeves of his crisp white shirt a little higher up his forearms, her gaze captivated by the movement of his long fingers. Then she looked up and watched as he turned his head to look into the crowd, thick lashes brushing against his skin as he blinked.

Somehow she doubted watching him would ever get boring—he was constantly studying his surroundings, taking everything in and most likely making mental notes, his obvious intelligence just adding to his attractiveness and making her burn to know how his mind worked. The suspense was killing her.

'Okay, now I'm fed and watered—out with it.'

She saw him shake his head before he turned to face her, tutting. '*Before* coffee?'

Kerry giggled, her eyes widening in surprise at the sound before she set her glass firmly away from her. That was quite enough of that stuff, then.

'The suspense is killing me. So spill it.'

'Three days in the States and she's already picking up the lingo.'

When she threw a warning glare his way he smiled lazily, leaning forward to rest his elbows on the table, long fingers playing with the cutlery he hadn't used while he studied her face. And under the influence of the sense-numbing wine it took a moment for her brain to kick in with a possible motive for his stalling.

'Whatever it is you're not entirely convinced it's that good an idea, are you?'

Ronan's brows jerked. 'And how exactly would you know that?'

Kerry waved a limp hand back and forth in front of her. 'Female intuition. We're born with it.'

He nodded at the table. 'How many glasses of that have we had, young lady?'

'Not enough to lose my ability to think. So if you don't think it's that good an idea why are you about to suggest it?'

His chest rose and fell. 'Good question.'

'Well, don't suggest it, then, if you're so unconvinced.' She reached for her glass, hiding her nose in it and her eyes from his intense gaze while she swallowed her sudden sense of disappointment with another mouthful of rich liquid.

'I want to suggest it even more now you've said that—if it was a go at reverse psychology then *bravo*…'

Kerry pursed her lips at the tinge of sarcasm, nodding firmly while focussing her attention on swirling what was left in her glass round and round in circles. 'It wasn't. But if that's how you feel then you definitely *should* suggest it. Go with your gut, shoot from the hip, live life without regrets, fortune favours the—'

She had dozens of these. But Ronan caught her attention by waving his arm at a waiter, smiling while he raised his voice to be heard above the background noise.

'Tiramisu and two coffees, please—the lady will have hers black.'

Kerry scowled at him.

And he chuckled throatily in reply, eyes still twinkling with amusement when he then leaned over the table, lifting a hand to beckon her with the same forefinger he'd waggled earlier.

'Come here, crazy girl.'

With a very deep breath Kerry fought the urge to be petulant and leaned forwards, setting her glass down on the white tablecloth and resting her elbows the same way Ronan had. Then she simply quirked her brows in silent question, and waited.

He examined her eyes for the longest time, as if sizing her up before he made his decision. 'What age are you Kerry, Kerry Doyle?'

What did that have to do with anything?

'Why? Do you want to add old to drunk and crazy?'

'No—and I don't think you're drunk; just slightly sozzled. You're obviously not much of a drinker—' he smiled a smile that warmed her inside more than the wine had, his voice dropping seductively '—but I'm sticking with the crazy.'

Actually she was nearly as okay with that as she'd been with him thinking she was beautiful. Crazy was much more interesting than the sensible or practical or reliable tags normally associated with her name.

'Why do you need to know what age I am?'

His eyes narrowed an almost imperceptible amount, the gaze so intense she could feel her toes curling. 'You're currently a bit of a conundrum, that's why.'

Her eyes widened in surprise. 'I am?'

'Answer the question.'

Kerry sighed dramatical[...]
'Thirty-six.'

'Didn't quite catch that.'

So she reluctantly raised her v[...]
tell me why you needed to know[...]
"never ask a lady her age" rule.'

'Right up there with the dessert ru[...]

'*Higher.*'

Amusement shone in his eyes, even [...]
head. 'You don't look thirty-six.'

'Thanks. I think. Now what does my age[...]
your proposition?' On top of the effects of half[...]
too many, her head was starting to ache attempt[...]
him out. So if blunt was what it was going to tak[...]

The nod was barely perceptible, but enough wh[...]
panied with another intense gaze for her to kn[...]
whatever doubt he'd had about what he was going to s[...]
was now gone.

'I've had an idea for a new book. And I want to hire [...]
to help me research it—with mutually beneficial per[...]
along the way.'

'Mutually beneficial *how*, exactly?'

'*That* we'll discuss over coffee…'

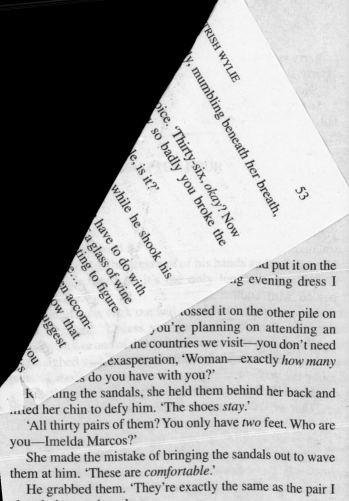

…, mumbling beneath her breath,
…ice. 'Thirty-six, okay? Now
… so badly you broke the
…, is it?'

while he shook his

…have to do with
…a glass of wine
…ing to figure
…e…
…en accom-
…uggest

…d put it on the
…g evening dress I
…ossed it on the other pile on
…you're planning on attending an
…ne countries we visit—you don't need
…exasperation, 'Woman—exactly *how many*
…s do you have with you?'

…ing the sandals, she held them behind her back and
…ted her chin to defy him. 'The shoes *stay*.'

'All thirty pairs of them? You only have *two* feet. Who are you—Imelda Marcos?'

She made the mistake of bringing the sandals out to wave them at him. 'These are *comfortable*.'

He grabbed them. 'They're exactly the same as the pair I already let you have.'

'No, they're not—these are *white*.' She held onto them as if her life depended on it.

He smiled lazily and she hated him for it. Hadn't she already compromised enough by letting him take over every-thing to begin with—changing her schedule left, right and centre so he could take her to what he considered to be the best places to see? Not that she hadn't enjoyed every single second of the nine-day Whistler Mountaineer tour they'd taken through the Canadian Rockies, something she'd probably never have thought of doing—mainly because she hadn't actually known about it, but still…

What the time had done was demonstrate the change in their relationship—they had moved from personal to almost professional. Yes, his proposition to act as travel guide while recording her reactions along the way had done that to begin with—but the first leg of their trip had highlighted it in spades. And, honestly, she kinda missed the ease they'd had with each other in New York. Her luggage was almost the last straw.

He tugged. 'Which just makes them more of a candidate for the reject pile. White isn't practical.'

Kerry, the queen of practicality under normal circumstances, tugged right on back.

'White goes with everything.'

'That's what you said about the same pair in the pale beige colour.'

'*Nude.*' When his eyes sparkled dangerously she felt an unwanted wave of heat building on her neck, gritting her teeth to add, 'The *colour* is called "nude".'

Humming under his breath, Ronan leaned his face a little closer to hers. 'For a second there I thought you were making a suggestion.'

He'd said it on such a low, flat tone that she wasn't sure if he was flirting or not.

'You should be so lucky.' Having mumbled back her reply, she decided the best way out of her current predicament might be to negotiate, especially since his proximity was distracting her so badly from her goal. Even after ten days in each other's company practically 24/7 he still had that effect on her.

And they hadn't kissed again or come anywhere close to it, but it certainly hadn't stopped her from thinking about it every single time she looked at him.

'I'll trade you.'

Letting go of the shoes, he held both hands up in surrender. 'Shoes for a little nudity? You're on.'

Kerry rolled her eyes. 'You're still completely incorrigible.'

Lowering his arms, he folded them across his broad chest and came back with, 'Yes, but you know that after this long. I have to say, though—you must really love those shoes.'

'I wasn't actually offering any nudity.'

'Spoilsport. So what is it you're offering in exchange? 'Cos everything in this pile is going; dragging around all that luggage is tiring me out.'

'You aren't the one dragging it round!'

'True, but watching you struggle with it is tiring.'

'You could have offered to help.'

'And how exactly would I prove my point that way?'

Kerry growled at him and Ronan had to use every ounce of his self-control not to laugh out loud. In fairness, she'd been a good sport about everything so far—for the most part. Though when he'd ripped up her colour-coded schedule in front of her she had gone a little pale. And that was after her jaw had dropped when he'd decided to shake up the majority of her flights and cancel all her hotel reservations.

But if this 'spur of the moment' idea of his was going to work all the way round the planet, then she had to trust him. And she'd loved the train trip, hadn't she? Every single day greeted with the kind of enthusiasm that had made him remember all over again how he'd felt when he'd first taken up travelling himself.

Which would have been a nice reminder if it hadn't stung a little—but, much as it galled him, Al had been right: there was no way realistically he could take a chance the whole way round the world on his own this time—Kerry was backup. He'd rot in hell before he was forced to tell her that, though, or why; most of all *why*.

He watched as she thought over her next move, smiling inwardly at the amount of effort she felt she had to put into negotiating with him. She over-thought things in his opinion—the caution at odds with the unfettered enthusiasm she'd displayed for everything they'd done so far. And he hadn't even got started yet...

'I'll trade three items for three questions.'

Her eyes narrowed. 'What kind of questions?'

'Questions like the kind you've been neatly sidestepping ever since you agreed to this.' He nodded when she avoided his gaze, 'Yes, I had noticed. I'm observant that way. It's starting to feel like I'm travelling with an international spy— well, one that's never been anywhere that is...'

'And this is part of your research for *The Virgin Traveller*, is it?'

'That's still a working title and, no, it's because I have a few things I still don't get about you.'

Kerry wrapped her arms around her midriff, shoes dangling off her thumbs. And Ronan recognized the move as a defensive one before she asked; 'Like what, for instance?'

He had a bit of a list, as it happened, but he figured it might be best to start with something simple. 'Like why you've waited this long to visit all the places you've dreamed of seeing, *for instance*—was money a problem?'

The frown was immediate, and she avoided his gaze again—so much for something simple. Except now he wanted to know all the more.

'If I know you better I can tailor the trip better.'

'You were doing fine until the luggage issue.'

The fact she mumbled her reply again had him fighting off yet another smile. She had an uncanny knack for doing that, as if she could reach an invisible hand inside his chest and tug the smile out of him. 'You'll thank me later.'

'You'll see I'm right to complain when I have to make you go *shopping* later.'

Wasn't ever gonna happen—he'd made the mistake of shopping with a woman once in his adult life and had taken a solemn vow it would never happen again. They made it into some weird test of a man's patience.

'I'll even let shoes be one item when technically they're two.'

'That's big of you.'

It was going to take a little more persuasion, wasn't it? He could be persuasive if that was what it took. And at least when he stepped closer it got her to look up into his eyes again—so he unfolded his arms to make more room in case he needed to get closer still. It didn't take a lot of encouragement, as it happened, not when he'd been fighting the idea of getting closer for ten days solid. He knew it was a *bad idea* though...

'You can't keep lugging those cases everywhere.' He let a slow smile loose on her, watching as her gaze dropped briefly to his mouth and then back up, the simple action intensely provocative, if unintentionally. 'You have to trust me.'

The tip of her tongue swept across her lips, drawing his gaze down the same way she'd just done with him. 'I do trust you. I wouldn't be here if I didn't.'

It happened on its own; almost instinctively his hands lifted to her upper arms, fingertips sliding up and down her baby-soft skin to soothe her. Having her stuff with her was a kind of security blanket; he got that. Especially knowing how much she liked itineraries and organization and being prepared for every eventuality. And the fact she trusted him meant something to him, his voice lowering in reaction.

'Your female intuition says I'm a good guy, does it?'

Kerry smiled a small smile, goose-bumps appearing on her

skin beneath his fingers, her voice equally as low as his. 'Don't think I don't know what you're doing…'

A part of his subconscious mind turned his hands over so he was running the backs of his fingers over her skin, searing heat tingling over his knuckles, up his wrists and into his forearms while he breathed deep breaths of her fresh flower scent and took a step closer until his toes were touching hers, 'What am I doing?'

She damped her lips again and Ronan couldn't help but wonder if she had any idea how big an invitation it was. She was a grown woman, after all, so how could she not know? But he'd promised himself he wouldn't take advantage of her on this trip. It was pointless after all and it'd been the only thing to persuade him it might work—for both of them.

The husky edge to her voice didn't help any. 'You're doing that thing you do when you know you need to up the ante to bend me to your will. You don't travel with other people much, do you? You're used to taking charge and doing things your own way.'

He quirked his brows. *Bend you to my will?*

She shrugged, frowning at a point at the base of his throat. 'Get your own way, then—win—whatever phraseology you want to use.'

'Yes, because you make winning so easy for me.'

Her gaze rose. 'It's the very fact I don't that makes you use this tactic, though, isn't it? You think it's your trump card. I voice a doubt or dig my heels in or ask about your plans and you turn on the charm to distract me.'

'Not working this time, I take it?'

A burst of almost nervous laughter brought the smile back to his face, and Kerry's chin came up another notch in return. 'I'm immune to this tactic now.'

Oh, was she indeed?

If something didn't stop him soon there was a very good

chance that promise of his was about to get broken—or at least adjusted some to suit the situation.

'I need to up my game, then, do I?'

'You can't kiss me into submission, Ronan.'

'And now she's challenging me…'

She started backing away, her eyes wide with surprise and glittering with awareness. 'When you sold this trip to me you didn't mention anything about random kissing being part of the deal.'

'You didn't complain in Times Square.'

'That was different.'

'Different how?'

Her mouth opened, then closed, then opened again. A dangling shoe was waved at him. And she was still backing away. 'That was a spur-of-the-moment kiss—a "perfect end to a perfect day kiss"—a "we know we'll never see each other again so it doesn't really matter" kiss. Whereas this, this— well, this is—'

'Different?'

'It's you attempting to kiss me to the point where I won't be able to think—like last time—only this time—' Her cheeks turned the most endearing shade of pink at the confession and Ronan found himself smiling all the more as he stalked her across the room.

He liked when she blushed.

She damped her lips one more time before continuing, the shoe waving in warning. 'You're playing dirty.'

And yet the sparkling in her eyes and the smile twitching at the corners of her mouth indicated she was quite enjoying that he was playing dirty. Even without the confession that he could kiss her to the point of not being able to think.

He liked that he'd been able to do that.

'I did say I'd trade questions for shoes, but you turned that down.'

'You said items—not shoes specifically.'

'Yes, but you've fought more over shoes than anything else.'

She backed herself into an armchair—literally. Because when the backs of her knees hit it, she flopped downwards, losing a shoe over one edge in the process. And when she immediately twisted round, scrambling to get it before he could, he took one long stride forwards, bent over at the waist and dropped his hands onto the rolled arms so she was trapped.

The triumphant smile she'd worn as she twisted back up with the shoe safely in hand faded when she realized her mistake. But she didn't lean back into the deep upholstery; instead she tilted her head back and her wide-eyed gaze tangled with his.

Man, but she was beautiful.

He spread his feet wide, bending at the knees so he could lean his upper body lower still, his voice dropping to the intimate level they'd got so good at using when they talked on a plane.

'And just think…'

A shrill ringing sounded from near the open suitcases, forcing Ronan to look over his shoulder to try and locate where it was coming from.

'It's my mobile.' Kerry poked him in the chest with her shoes. 'I've got to answer it—it'll be from home. I promised I'd check in at regular intervals.'

Saved by the bell. Probably just as well too.

'Very sensible—we can put that in the book.'

Kerry held her breath for the brief amount of time it took for him to make the decision to push upright and walk to the phone, only letting it out when she allowed herself to admit she was disappointed he had.

She'd *wanted* him to kiss her again *darn it*! What did a girl have to do—throw herself at him? And he had no one to blame but himself. If that first kiss hadn't been so—*memorable*, she mightn't feel the need to find out if she'd built it up out of all proportion in her head…

But it wasn't as if he'd shown any inclination to repeat it, was it? Not 'til now, anyway. And it probably wasn't a good idea—not while they were travelling together. If it fell apart, then that would be the end of the trip, and if it got serious it wasn't as if he were the kind of man who would settle down in a nine-to-five.

Didn't stop her from aching for the loss of a kiss that never happened, though, did it? Oh, no.

When he tossed her phone across the room she dropped her shoes, cupping her hands to neatly catch it before smirking triumphantly at him because she had and hitting the answer key.

'Hello?'

'Where in hell are you?'

'Yes, lovely to hear from you too—I'm in San Francisco.' She bent over at the waist to retrieve a shoe that had slid off her lap onto the floor between her feet, effectively hiding the frown on her face caused by her cousin's tone. 'I emailed you about the change of plans, remember?'

'You're travelling with a complete stranger you met on a plane? Have you lost your mind?'

'He's not a professional kidnapper, Ellie.'

Ronan's deep voice grumbled from across the room, 'If I was I'd have got rid of this luggage sooner.'

Kerry glared at him when he lifted his chin to look at her, her eyes narrowing when she heard a zipper being pulled and she realized what he was doing. 'You go anywhere near my underwear and you're a dead man.'

The thought of him lifting out the frivolous items one by one and deciding what she should and shouldn't wear was enough to form the suggestion of a low moan in the base of her throat. One that was accompanied with a sudden rush of warmth all over her body—

'*What?*'

The shriek in her ear made her grimace. 'Nothing. I wasn't talking to you.'

'He's there now?'

'Yes, he's persuading me to downsize my luggage.'

'In your *room*?'

Kerry couldn't help but smile at the Victorian sense of outrage. With her younger cousin's chequered history in the affair department it wasn't as if she really had the right to throw any stones, was it?

'Yes, in my room. He's attempting to get a sneak peak at my underwear while you're distracting me.'

There was a distinct silence on the other end of the line while Ronan's mouth quirked, at least three items she was going to debate later being tossed on the rapidly growing 'discarded' pile. And that very hint of amusement told her the thought of the underwear had indeed crossed his mind. He really was a bit of a devil.

But it was part of his attraction. That and the way he looked and that incorrigible streak of his. Was it any wonder she was so obsessed with the idea of more kissing?

'You're sharing a room with this guy?'

She rolled her eyes at the recriminating tone. 'No, he has his own room—not that it would be any of your business if he didn't.'

'*Kerry!*'

'Ellie, don't, c'mon, have you ever known me to do anything spectacularly stupid?'

There was only a brief pause this time. 'No. That's why this is worrying everyone so much. You know the family was never happy with the idea of you taking this trip on your own.'

'I'm not on my own any more, am I?'

'But we don't know anything about this guy.'

'I'm getting a little too long in the tooth for you lot to decide who I can and can't spend time with, don't you think? You were all going to fight me on this trip regardless.' She frowned a little when Ronan's dark brows lifted.

He'd just got a little insight on her life with his eaves-dropping, hadn't he?

'So we're not supposed to care now?'

Oh, for crying out loud!

She sighed heavily, 'I didn't say that.'

'What would happen to the hotel if something happened to you?'

Yes, because everything in the Doyle family life revolved around the hotel, didn't it? But, having already given up so much for it, Kerry really didn't feel three months was that much to ask for.

'Did something happen at the hotel?'

'No. Not yet anyway. But Doyle's isn't—'

'Doyle's without a Doyle at the helm—yes, I know the mantra, thanks.' She pushed to her feet and began pacing the way she normally did at home. 'But if it can't survive three months without me after fifteen years of making sure it runs like a well-oiled machine, then I haven't done much of a job, have I? Did Dad make you call me?'

'Well, when I told him about the email—'

'I thought so. Well, I'm not coming home early and you can just tell him that. If he wants a Doyle at Doyle's he can come out of retirement and do it himself.' And if she'd thought for a single second he would she'd have been on the first plane home. But he knew what she'd do if he tried to change what she'd done to the place. Complete autonomy was the one thing she'd insisted on when she'd given up every dream of her own.

Kerry swore silently as the all-too-familiar headache

rolled in over her temples, glancing at Ronan from the corner of her eye to see what he was doing. She didn't doubt for a second he was still listening—but what she wasn't prepared for was the sight of him holding up a nightdress he'd found, dangling the item in front of him from shoestring straps hooked off his thumbs.

His gaze rose and tangled with hers. And Kerry had to swallow hard when it felt as if a bolt of pure electricity shot across the room. Suddenly she couldn't seem to breathe, and her stomach did a weird kind of flip-flop thing.

She damped her lips. He blinked slowly a few times. And then it went on the 'keeper' pile before he dropped his chin and went back to work...

Oh, my.

Her cousin brought her back to earth with a bump. 'I don't think it'll come to that, Kerry, but he *is* worried about you. And Nana—'

'Oh-h-h—' Kerry laughed sarcastically, '—don't you dare tell me Nana told you to check up on me. Nana would be more interested in what Ronan looks like than she would about him being a possible kidnapper. In fact she'd find that an interesting facet to his personality. She's the only one who was behind me on this trip to begin with—it's the trip she'd have taken herself if—'

She *really* needed to get her cousin off the phone before her entire family history was hauled unceremoniously out of the closet, albeit across the Atlantic via mobile phone. She should just have agreed to the stupid questions-for-items deal—because if he'd wanted personal information, then by now she'd have at least half her stuff back.

She breathed deep, forcing the soothing tone into her voice that always worked best on her highly strung cousin. 'Ellie, I'm *fine*. And I'll be back when I said I'd be back. I promise.'

'At least tell me where you're going to be for the next check-in.' The pout was positively audible.

And it was a good question. One that involved Kerry stopping pacing long enough to look at Ronan again. Where he was merrily tossing item after item onto the discarded pile…

He was frowning and shaking his head at her ceramic straighteners when she asked the question, 'Where are we going to be this time next week?'

His chin lifted, straighteners pointing at his wide chest. 'You asking me?'

'Yes, I'm asking you—you're the one with the itinerary now.'

When he shrugged she dearly wanted to strangle him—because her cousin would be relaying every second of their conversation to Kerry's father within milliseconds of hanging up the phone. And she'd embellish the fact Kerry hadn't a clue where she was going to the extent where it would seem to the entire Doyle clan that she genuinely *had* been kidnapped.

'Fiji.'

'*Really?*' She couldn't help the bubble of excitement that leapt up into her chest and burst into a full-blown smile on her face.

Another shrug. 'Probably.'

'Ellie, we'll be in—'

'Might still be in Hawaii, though—depends on the flights from Honolulu to Nadi.'

Either one sounded pretty good to her, even with his blasé way of delivering the information as if they were about to run down the street to the corner shop. Yes, Hawaii had been on her original itinerary, but Fiji had been left out. And for the life of her, feeling as excited as she suddenly did at the prospect of going there, she had absolutely no idea why it had.

'Either Hawaii or Fiji—dependent on available flights. So I'll find a way of emailing or calling, even if it's just from the airport.'

'Fiji—seriously?' The jealous tone to Ellie's voice only added to Kerry's change of mood.

'*I know!*' If she'd been fifteen years younger she'd have jumped up and down.

There was a heartfelt sigh. 'Damn it. He's good-looking too, isn't he?'

'*You have no idea.*'

CHAPTER FIVE

CHAPTER FIVE

'SO KERRY, Kerry Doyle...'

Kerry was still smiling as she looked out of the windows of the restaurant to the city below, mentally cataloguing all her collected 'moments' from the last two days. From the second they'd made an atmospheric trip across the Golden Gate Bridge, plunging in and out of sunshine and rolling fog, she'd known San Francisco was definitely going on her list of places to come back to. The sun that never seemed to stop shining, the buildings oh-so-white in the bright light, the streets that ran in effortless roller-coasters across the city's many crests and bluffs, sparkling water and monumental bridges more or less permanently in view.

It was wonderful. And that was before she added in the people, who always seemed to end every answer to a question with the word 'enjoy'—which she definitely had. She wasn't quite doing what the song said, but she was leaving *some* of her heart behind.

Ronan was leaning back in his chair when she looked at him, a quiet certainty written across his face. 'You're a Doyle as in "Doyle's of Dublin", aren't you?'

Yep, there it was—though in fairness he'd done well to let it be for as long as he had. But there'd been just enough questions scattered throughout the last forty-eight hours for her to know it was coming, so she wasn't overly surprised.

She took a deep breath, focussing her attention on adding cream to her coffee. *Cream*. Not milk. She'd learnt that from her time in the States—though what that meant they called actual cream, she wasn't quite sure of just yet. They should maybe add some kind of dictionary for the basic necessities in each country to the back of Ronan's new book. She should suggest that—after all, that was why he was playing tour guide for her…

'I hope you're not about to tell me you gave the hotel a bad write-up at some point. I thought we'd been getting on pretty well 'til now—barring the luggage incident that is…'

'Never been.'

'That's almost as bad, coming from a travel expert.'

His sinful mouth quirked. 'It's probably got more to do with the fact I've only ever done an "off the wall" perspective on Dublin. Doyle's is as much of an icon as The Waldorf or The Ritz.'

Kerry inclined her head as she lifted her coffee. 'We like to think so.'

'And you run it.'

'Yes.' She took another deep breath before sipping some of the deliciously bitter blend, a sense of disappointment rising inside her at having to fess up to who she was. It would be a downward slide after that, wouldn't it? The new and improved Kerry she liked so much would once again be placed back into her Doyle wrapping and she'd have to stop pretending she was someone she wasn't.

And she hated letting her go.

When she glanced up from beneath her lashes he had his head to one side, elbows resting on the arms of his chair and his long fingers forming a tent.

'Now I'm even more curious about why you've never taken this trip before—not a money issue, was it?'

Her cup placed carefully back on its saucer without so much as a rattle, she lifted her chin to reply with a calm, 'I'd have thought it was more obvious why. Running Doyle's is a big responsibility.'

Ronan nodded his head just the once as he leaned forwards, lifting his elbows to the table the way he always did and lowering his tented fingers to the crisp white tablecloth before continuing with a gentle voice that crept in round the edges of her heart, 'Don't get defensive on me—there's no need.'

It took a giant effort not to groan, because there was *every* need. She wanted to be carefree Kerry, she wanted to be adventurous Kerry, she wanted to be the have-fun Kerry she'd been with him in New York and during their time in San Francisco. She wanted to be able to flirt back with him when he flirted with her—because sometimes he forgot himself, didn't he? And if they delved into her life she'd have to lose several of those things. Not least of all because she'd be reminded once again that getting involved with someone like him was pointless. Flirting was *bad*.

Stalling the inevitable, she looked back out the window, shrugging. 'I'm not.'

'Yes, you are.' Warm fingers captured hers on the cloth, lifting and tangling before squeezing to get her attention. 'And you were different on the phone to home too—your tone changed, you paced. Bit of a danger of executive stress in your life, is there?'

Kerry focussed her attention on their joined hands, the golden glow her skin was acquiring still a great contrast to the deeper tan on his skin. And then there were the other differences in their hands: his fingers longer and broader with neatly cut square nails—hers finer boned with the rounded fingernails painted a pale pink. His hand distinctly male with a faint smattering of hair bleached almost invisible by the sun running up onto his forearms from his wrists—her hand small against his, distinctly feminine…

'You haven't met my cousin—she can *be* stressful.'

'No, I haven't, but Nana sounds like fun.'

Kerry smiled, her gaze flickering over to meet his. 'She is. And she'd love every single second of this trip. In a different age she'd have been one of those intrepid women explorers who tramped across the desert or flew single-handed across oceans.'

The smile she got in reply was so warm she could practically feel her bones softening.

'Well, then, we know where you get your sense of adventure from, don't we?'

Which made her laugh ruefully. 'Oh, you really don't know me at all, do you?'

'Maybe not.' He squeezed her fingers again, waiting for her to look into his eyes before he continued in the low, rumbling tone that always did things for her. 'But you set out to travel around the globe on your own and you agreed to a magical mystery tour with a handsome stranger—that sounds pretty adventurous to me.'

'And yet I still looked so helpless when you met me you felt the need to take me under your wing…'

'Nah.' His stunning eyes sparkled across at her. 'I'm just using you for research purposes.'

When he let his fingers slide free Kerry curled hers into her palm, almost as if she subliminally felt the need to hold onto his warmth. But she smiled in reply.

'At least I know where I stand.'

Ronan's attention turned to his coffee and for no reason Kerry's mind returned to earlier in the day; they'd stopped for more Italian food in the North Beach area of the city, where apparently every Saturday afternoon the restaurant owner and his family would sing opera amongst tile-topped tables like the one they'd been sitting at beneath pictures of 'Papa' posing with Pavarotti.

Both Kerry and Ronan had smiled through the performance of the man who'd told them, 'This place is my life, my music.

I am tenor. My wife is soprano. Is beautiful here. People say: "Papa, don' change." I say: "Don' worry. I won' change."'

But in the middle of the magical singing, Kerry had looked across at Ronan and watched him 'zone out', his thoughts a thousand miles away. He'd frowned, his jaw had clenched, and Kerry had suddenly wondered what it was that was wrong. But then he'd looked at her and smiled one of his slow, disgustingly sexy smiles and she'd found herself smiling back—still burning with the need to know what he'd been thinking.

Looking back, she wondered if it had been that building frustration or the sheer emotion of the singing that made her well up…

Over linguini and clams he'd teased her about being carried away by the romance of the music—typical woman. And she'd parried back that he had no sense of what romance was—typical man.

It had brushed it over, but she still burned to know what he was thinking—even now while he was staring pensively into his coffee—which was probably why she'd remembered what had happened earlier.

But before she could make an attempt at turning the topic of conversation onto him, he lifted the cup and calmly continued with his own line of questioning.

'You've been running the hotel for sixteen years?'

'Fifteen. I was "in training" for the first three until my father had to retire after a heart attack—didn't have a clue what I was doing at the start.'

Ronan's brows lifted in interest. 'Not being groomed from the minute you stepped out of nappies?'

She smiled, despite being forced to look back. 'No—I was never aiming for the family business. It was my brother who spent every spare hour learning the ropes. He even took time doing everyone's job so he could understand what they all did. I thought he was insane.'

'What did you want to do?'

'Ah-h-h...' She grinned. 'I was going to be an artist and live a *very* bohemian lifestyle. The thought of it made my father want to tear his hair out and that only made me want it ten times more in my rebellious teens.'

Ronan's eyes glowed at her, his mouth curling upwards again—most likely in amusement at the idea of her being anywhere vaguely in the region of 'bohemian'. His voice was tinged with a seductive gruffness that sent her pulse fluttering as he asked, 'What kind of artist?'

'A painter—watercolour mostly. I used to be reasonably all right at it too, or so my tutors told me at art college,' She shrugged her shoulders, glancing down as she turned her coffee-cup in circles on the saucer. 'We all have dreams when we're young. But then we grow up and we do what we have to do.'

'What happened?'

She didn't look up as she said the words on a flat tone. 'My brother died.'

When Ronan didn't say anything she made the mistake of looking up, only to find him frowning at her before he asked in the same gruff tone, 'Were you close?'

Kerry smiled wistfully. 'About as close as you can get, I guess. We were twins—a ten-minute gap made me the baby of the family. They run in the family.'

'I'm sorry.'

'Don't be.' She smiled a larger smile to let him know it was okay. 'It was a long time ago. You weren't driving the lorry that hit them. And even if you were I wouldn't for a single second think you killed them on purpose.'

'Them?'

'He was bringing Mum home from the hotel.'

He visibly flinched and, although Kerry appreciated that he understood it had been rough for the family and for her, she'd had time to adjust to it. 'So I stepped into Jamie's shoes, not that I stood much of a chance of filling them when we were so very different. But Doyle's isn't Doyle's without—'

'A Doyle at the helm. Yeah, I heard that part.' He leaned forward in his chair again. 'Different what way?'

'You want my entire life story at one sitting?'

'Well, it's not like you've been willing to share voluntarily up 'til now, is it?'

'I could toss that one right back at you.' Had it possibly been part of the awkwardness she'd felt between them since New York? Two people spending practically 24/7 together could hardly go the guts of three months without getting to know each other better.

'I got here first.' His fingertips toyed with hers on the table-cloth again, thick lashes lowering and a small frown reappearing on his face, as if he hadn't even realized he'd reached for her until he felt her skin. 'Different how?'

'Nope, your turn—you always want to be a travel writer? You have brothers or sisters? Mum and Dad still around? Come on—fair's fair.'

'Always wanted to travel.' He shrugged. 'Writing about it was a natural progression. Two sisters—both married and I'm an uncle three and half times…'

She laughed, enchanted by the deep affection in his voice. 'How can you be half an uncle, you idiot?'

Leaning even further forwards, he brought his other hand into play, turning hers over and cradling it while he traced her palm with his forefinger. 'It's not due 'til Christmas.'

'Ah.' It was the only response she could manage while he was doing what he was doing to her hand.

'I've put in my request for another girl—I'm three for three so far.' Another small frown accompanied his words.

'Girls tend to hero-worship their Indiana-Jones-type uncles, do they?'

'Something like that.' He looked up from her hand long

enough to flash a devilish sparkle-eyed smile. 'I should get the hat, really, shouldn't I?'

'We can look out for one on our travels.'

'Wouldn't that involve shopping?'

'I've been really good so far.'

'You have. But don't think I'm not watching you every second. Just 'cos we posted home that parcel of unnecessary accoutrements doesn't mean you get to race out and replace them all.'

Kerry rolled her eyes. 'This is going to be the longest trip in the history of circumnavigation if I can't shop so much as once. You're stomping on my fantasy list a little, you know.'

His fingertip kept tracing lazy circles on her overly sensitive palm, the touch more erotic than anything she'd ever experienced. Oh, Lord, would he take so much time touching everywhere? Would he look at her the way he was right that second while he did? All heat and intensity and radiating toe-curling sensuality…

Never before had she wanted so badly to find the answers to those kinds of questions—with any man. She wondered if he could see it in her. Could he read her mind when he looked in her eyes?

Can you see how badly I want you to kiss me again?

Because she was rapidly becoming obsessed by it.

If he kissed her again he was in big trouble. Any number of the varying versions of silent oaths he'd made not to take advantage of their proximity would go right out the window. And little may she know, but the way she was looking at him was encouraging him to do just that. Forget every last one of them.

Every passing day with her it was becoming more and more of a physical need, but she was too amazing to be treated like a holiday fling. And it wasn't as if there could be any kind of a future in it. Not as if she'd be taking on the man she thought she was. In a scant few years he'd be someone drastically different from the man he was now. What right had he to take something that big from her when, from what he could tell, she'd already given up so much?

Ronan was many things, stupid wasn't one of them. All it had taken after his bout of uncharacteristic eavesdropping was a few carefully placed questions dropped in at seemingly random places in their daily conversations and he'd painted what he considered to be a fairly accurate picture of the kind of person Kerry Doyle was. And what it came down to was she was a giver.

Simple things would have indicated it. If someone was struggling with a door, she held it open for them with a smile. If someone looked as if they needed a seat more than she did, she gave it up with a smile. If a kid dropped something she would run after them for miles to kneel down and place it back in their little hands—*with a smile*.

She was constantly observant and on alert for those things and yet never complained when someone was rude or jumped a place in a line or let a door swing shut before she got to it. Though the smile wouldn't be quite so bright, he'd noticed…

Yes, Ronan had noticed all those things even before he'd started learning anything about her family and they'd made him like her even more than he already had.

And that was before he took into consideration the openness he'd liked from the beginning—not just in the way she would let excitement or pleasure or joy light up her face when they went somewhere new. Oh, no, she wasn't afraid to show deeper emotions either. Like in the Italian place he'd taken them to for lunch—when she'd listened to the owner sing opera and been so touched her eyes had filled with tears.

It had yanked him straight out of the morbidity he'd felt

himself sliding into only seconds before he'd looked at her. And he might have teased her about it, but he'd been completely charmed by the fact she was so emotive. Everything was on the surface with Kerry. Too many women played games in his experience; hiding who they really were in an attempt to make whatever they considered the 'right impression' on the man they were spending time with. But not Kerry.

Kerry was who Kerry was and she wasn't pretending to be anything else. Well, barring the fact she came from the wealthy background she did. Not that he could throw stones in that department.

And when he'd figured out who she was, he'd been stunned by the irony. She had no way of knowing how many times their paths must have crossed at home. He'd even bet his father had known her father at some point. Probably still did. It was a small country, after all.

Yet Ronan had never met Kerry. Mind you, he could probably put that down to the number of times he'd been home in the last decade. And when he had he'd had a scant couple of months to play 'catch up' so he could clear the decks to get away again—to pack as much travelling in while he was still able—so there hadn't been a whole heap of time for meeting new people.

He'd have remembered meeting Kerry.

With his gaze still tangled with hers, he couldn't help but feel exactly the way he had when he'd met her on the plane during the second leg of the flight to New York: wishing there were more time.

How many amazing places could he have shown her? How many things could he have seen with the same sense of magic he had the very first time simply because he was seeing them through *her eyes*? How many nights would there have been for long, languid sessions of—?

Well, suffice to say if he were the kind of man to let himself wallow in bitterness he'd have been doing it for not having those chances with someone like her.

But the specialist in New York had put paid to any glimmer of hope he had left so this trip with her was his last chance to escape facing up to reality.

Cowardly? *Probably.*

He could hear the husky edge in his voice when he spoke, echoing his intense desire to accept the silent invitation she was unconsciously issuing to be kissed.

'I'll make it up to you.' He silently cleared his throat and spoke in a steadier, intimately low tone. 'You tell me what fantasies didn't make it off that list of yours this time round and I'll see what I can do about fulfilling them. How does that sound?'

Kerry looked him straight in the eye—and the smouldering heat he saw in hers hit him so hard it was like being kicked in the chest.

Heaven help him—had she added being with him to her list? Because if she had—he wasn't so sure he had the strength to deny her. Not when he wanted her as badly as he did while she looked at him like that.

'You're gonna try and fulfil all my fantasies inside three months, are you?'

Even her voice did him in. He'd bet in decades to come that if he heard a voice remotely like hers, even in darkness, he'd feel drawn towards the sound.

Why did he have to meet someone like her now? What kind of sick cosmic joke was that? Ronan dearly wanted to hit something—*hard*.

Her head tilted to one side, finely arched brows then lifted a minuscule amount as she searched his eyes, as if she could see inside him and knew something was wrong.

He sincerely hoped she couldn't. And just to be sure, he smiled a slow smile at her, his fingertip tracing the answer to her question on her palm.

'Y—E—S—'

Kerry's moist lips parted in surprise, her gaze dropping to her hand as he finished tracing the 'S' and then rising as he smiled a larger smile at her.

She laughed huskily—the sound doing all kinds of amazing things to his libido.

Amazing. He thought it about her more and more with each passing day. And he wanted to be the man to fulfil at least some of those fantasies. Who could blame him?

'Tell me *all* of them.'

'My fantasies?' She waited long enough for him to nod—just the once. 'And then where would my sense of feminine mystique be, hmm?'

She quirked her brows, this time in challenge, a teasing light diluting some of the heat that'd been so palpable in the air between them. 'I gotta have something to work with to keep me interesting for the next couple of months, don't I?'

'You're interesting enough already.'

'You might not think so if you knew me better.'

He shook his head, reluctantly freeing her hand and leaning back in his seat as he mumbled his reply beneath his breath. 'I doubt it.'

Lifting his napkin from his knees, he nodded at her cup. 'Do you want to finish that? We have a way to go tomorrow and an early start, so—'

'Yes, an early night sounds good.' When her words translated into an innuendo regarding the activities people could get up to on 'early nights', his gaze locked with hers again, and he was rewarded with a dimpled, mischievous smile in return. 'I'm done.'

Good, because so was he—fighting the constant daily battle against his attraction to her was hard work. The sooner she was tucked safely away in her room, the better.

He made it all the way to the doors of their rooms, only

briefly checking up and down the wide hallway before he made the mistake of looking in her eyes again.

Bad move.

Because when her long lashes rose and she looked at him with the same silent invitation she'd issued over the table he could feel himself weakening, the memory of the one kiss they'd shared slamming into the front of his brain, his gaze dropping to her lips just as she damped them with the tip of her tongue.

Give him strength. Wanting her was *selfish*.

Her voice was breathless. 'If you aren't going to kiss me, then you have to leave—right now—before I do something I'll be embarrassed about in the morning.'

He looked back into her eyes. 'Not a modern-thinking, take-the-initiative-yourself kinda gal, then, I take it?'

'That's why you'd have to leave.'

'Before *you* kiss *me*?'

Her throat convulsed, her perfect teeth chewing on her lower lip as she nodded. 'If you want us to just stay friends on this trip, then I'm okay with that, but I need to know so I don't—'

'It's not that I don't want to—'

She stepped forwards and Ronan frowned hard, lifting his hands to her bare arms to physically set her away from him, his voice gruff. 'But it's probably better we don't. We have half a planet to get round yet and this would complicate things.'

The brief flash of agony in her eyes before she lowered her lashes almost did him in. She must be mortified. She'd just made it plain she wanted him to kiss her and he'd turned her down.

Her throat convulsed and she took a deep breath that lifted her breasts before her lashes rose. Then she smiled a smile that didn't quite make it all the way up into her eyes. 'You're right.'

Unfurling his fingers so he was brushing them over the soft

skin of her arms was hardly helping him make his case. 'I'm not the man for you, Kerry, Kerry Doyle. Trust me.'

Smaller hands appeared, wrapping around his fingers and lowering his hands all the way back down to his sides before letting go. 'Travel light—I know. Goodnight, Ronan.'

Stepping back, he watched as she turned to slide her card into the slot on her door, his eyes studying the smooth curtain of her hair while he fought to breathe evenly. He should turn away, he should go into his own room and forget this had happened, he should remind himself of all the reasons why he couldn't let her get involved with him, he should—

He stood still and watched her walk through the door. He watched it close in his face. And for a long while he just stood there listening to the thud of his heart as it beat hard against the wall of his chest until he finally found the strength to walk away.

But it cost him.

CHAPTER SIX

AFTER two more overheard conversations Ronan thought her family sounded as if they were a right pain in the—well, suffice to say if they kept interrupting the great effort he'd been making to keep Kerry smiling the way he'd finally managed to after the 'almost kiss' in San Francisco, then her phone was in great danger of being tossed in the next available body of water…

He glanced down at the top of her head, smiling at the fact she'd fallen asleep on his shoulder. It was a first for him on any kind of a plane—but then, somewhat miraculously, he was experiencing a lot of firsts with her around.

She made a small sigh in her sleep, nestling closer, and Ronan allowed himself to tuck her head beneath his chin even though she wouldn't get to doze for long, his gaze fixing on the few wisps of curling white clouds peppering the clear blue sky and the glimpses of azure blue sea beyond the tempered glass.

The irony was, if he'd managed to put all the pieces together correctly, they hadn't had that different an upbringing. Not really. Even with the common Irish bond removed…

The differences would only really appear at the point where she'd given up a lot of her own dreams to take on a role she might never have wanted if it hadn't been for the dramatic loss of half her family in one fell swoop. Whereas Ronan had arranged straight off that he'd always have the freedom to do the things he wanted to do—regardless of the responsibilities he held as heir apparent or the restrictions he would have to learn to live with in due enough course. Restrictions he was reminded of even as he looked out the window, the clear blue surrounded by a circle of black nothingness.

Kerry was living his life in reverse.

It was another reminder of why he shouldn't allow himself to get involved with her. Only trouble was he had a sneaking suspicion it was too late for him not to. The damage was already done, and was getting worse by the day. In fact, if he was honest with himself, he was now well into the region of *damage control*. She was already under his skin.

Kerry moved beneath his chin again, so he ducked back to try and see if she was waking up. And he was glad he'd decided to make the next leg of their journey a complete break for both of them—she needed the rest after their hectic country-hopping schedule so far, and it gave Ronan a chance to tick another person off his list while they were on this side of the globe.

Then there was the added bonus of yet another week full of golden opportunities to see Kerry in the bikini she'd worn in Hawaii. As far as Ronan was concerned she could live in it and he'd be more than okay with that. She was sensational. Luxury sports cars all over the planet could be sold in their millions if she lay across the bonnet in that bikini…

Even if seeing her in it tested his resolve to its absolute breaking-point. The first day she'd appeared in it he'd even groaned aloud—thankfully far enough away from her that she hadn't heard it. And he'd had to head straight for the water to hide the visible evidence of what the sight had done to him.

The pilot glanced down at the island beneath their wings,

jerking his thumb twice to say they were arriving, so Ronan gently nudged Kerry.

'Wake up, sleepyhead, or you'll miss it.'

He watched mesmerized as she came to life—her eyelids heavy the way they'd been after he'd kissed her that one time and the varying shades of russet and gold still endearingly soft with the sleep he could hear in her voice.

'Already?'

'Already.' He lifted his hand, curling his fingers under her chin to direct her gaze to the windows. 'Look.'

Kerry leaned forwards as she forced her eyes to focus. And when they did her breath caught at the beauty of it. Through the struts of the four-seat aircraft she saw something she'd doubted she'd ever see: a genuine South Sea island complete with fringe of white coral sand and a blue lagoon. It was the most beautiful thing she'd ever seen—a fantasy come true—and her voice was husky with more than sleep when she spoke, her hand unconsciously reaching for Ronan's to squeeze his fingers.

'Oh, you did *good* with this one. It's amazing!'

'I take it you like, it then?'

'No—I *love* it!'

'Can tick off another fantasy, can I?'

She laughed. 'You most definitely can.'

Tucked neatly into what Ronan had told her was the Yasawa chain of islands, the small resort had seemed like an impossible dream of a place when he'd finally got round to telling her about where they were going next. But the truth was he could have told her they were headed to the worst place in the universe and she probably wouldn't have complained. She'd already had such a good time destination-wise she almost had to pinch herself just to make sure she wasn't dreaming, even if it had taken several days for her to get over the toe-curling embarrassment of his rejection in the hallway.

But this trip was the first chance for her to grab hold of life with both hands and enjoy what the world had to offer and she couldn't let the fact she felt like a teenage girl with a crush around him get in the way.

She looked over her shoulder and felt her breath catch in her lungs at the sight of his face so close to hers. Then she glanced down and realized she still had his hand. Oh, she just didn't know when to stop. Wasn't one rejection enough for her?

So she let go and flashed a smile before looking back out the window—because she needed the distraction and because it was pointless dwelling on how very attracted she still was to him. She couldn't make him want her.

They splashed down, turning in one gliding motion from aircraft to boat, and then the pilot cut the engine.

'You'll need to carry your shoes or they'll get ruined wading in.'

Kerry aimed a sideways look at him as he moved away from her, blinking innocently. 'Yes, and it's not like I have that many shoes to sacrifice these days, is it?'

'And look how much faster we get on and off planes as a result of that. You're welcome, by the way.'

'I didn't say thank you.'

He smiled lazily. 'Yeah, but I know you meant to—so you're welcome.'

He took the shoes from her as she left the small plane, and with the other hand held hers as they waded side by side towards a cluster of Fijians waving a large welcome banner. Kerry giggled like an excited schoolgirl as their feet sank into the perfect white sand and the reception committee crowded round, grinning and forcing Ronan to free her hand as they pressed green coconuts towards them—complete with straw, hibiscus flower and slice of orange.

'*Bula!* Welcome!'

It was off the fantasy Richter-scale as far as Kerry was concerned. There was no way Ronan could top this one. He couldn't possibly.

A tall, ridiculously tanned man stepped out of the crowd and greeted Ronan with a manly hug before holding him at arm's length and announcing in an Aussie accent, ''Bout time too! Been too long.'

'It has.' Ronan lifted his hands to the man's shoulders, genuine affection written all over his face as he shook him. 'Good to see you, Frank.'

The older man's expression looked anguished for a brief second before being covered by a broad smile. 'You too, mate. I'm glad you can see the place one more time—me and Abbie been saying it would mean the world to us if you got to before—'

'This is Kerry,' Ronan interrupted him, dropping his hands to step back and draw Kerry forwards. 'I told you about her on the phone.'

Frank swiftly hauled her forwards to enfold her in a tight hug that stole her breath away, rocking her from side to side before he let go and placed her at arm's length to examine her face. 'Well, now—aren't you a pretty one?'

He cocked an eyebrow at Ronan, 'Didn't mention *that* on the phone…'

'Bad line from Nadi…' He carefully removed Kerry from Frank's hands and drew her back towards him. 'And you're a happily married man, so behave. Now do you have a spare bure for us or are we sleeping on the beach?'

Kerry tensed when he slung an almost possessive arm across her shoulders. Not that she actually had a problem with the subtle act of territorialism, but it was somewhat baffling—what was he doing? And why was he doing it? He'd already stated his friend was a happily married man so it wasn't as if he had to worry any—not that he would have even if the man had been single and a bit of a charmer—but hadn't he already made it plain as day they weren't anything more than friends? She didn't get it.

Actually, in fairness, for a man who claimed he wasn't the man for her he had a bit of a problem with not flirting with her too—that hadn't stopped. But he hadn't felt the need to touch her let alone tuck her in against the length of his lean body, until now. Was he simply demonstrating that they were friends?

Kerry's head was starting to ache.

Maybe she wasn't the first woman he'd brought to the island and this was him living up to his reputation?

Kerry was happier with the first option. But she had a deep and burning need to know just what exactly *had* been said on the phone now…

Frank led them across the perfect shoreline towards a chalet tucked into trees on one side and overlooking impossibly clear water on the other, chattering away to Ronan about the changes they'd made to the resort since his last visit. Meanwhile Kerry, while still listening with one ear, couldn't help but be mesmerized by her surroundings at the same time—and to think, they had an entire week in this place!

'She always this quiet?'

Ronan chuckled deep in his chest. 'I wish.'

Kerry nudged him hard in the ribs before smiling at Frank. 'This place is amazing, Frank.'

He beamed. 'I'm glad you approve.' Then he winked at her. 'And you must be somethin' for this bloke to be hauling you all the way out here to meet us. We always had to endure him alone before this.'

Well, that answered one question, then.

'Thanks for that, my friend.' Ronan shook his head. 'Though if you recall I visit for Abbie's cooking and the great view—not for your sparkling repartee…'

Kerry had another wink aimed her way. 'I save that for the ladies; it's wasted on him.'

She laughed.

So Ronan used the arm around her shoulders to pull her closer and stage-whisper in her ear, 'You'll have to forgive him—he doesn't get out much.'

'And if Abbie thought I'd get to meet women like you on a plane then I'd never get to leave the island again.' He scowled at Ronan, 'You're a lucky dog.'

Astonishingly Ronan didn't correct him.

Inside the bure Kerry stepped out of his hold to look around, turning in slow circles and moving in and out of open doorways as she took in everything from the high vaulted thatched-roof ceiling, separate sitting room and sunken Jacuzzi to the verandah with its day bed and private fish pond. Eventually stopping to stare at the hand-carved four-poster bed— her mouth suddenly dry as a world of possibilities opened up to her furtive imagination.

One bedroom.

'I'll take the day bed—you can have the fantasy bed and I'll tick that one off my list too.'

'Don't forget to leave a small light on at night,' Frank added without so much as a reaction to Ronan's clear announcement they weren't 'together', 'or you might fall in the Jacuzzi. *Again.* Not that it had anything to do with the lack of a light last time…'

Kerry lifted her brows in question as she looked at Ronan. 'You *didn't*—one cocktail too many, perchance?'

He didn't look the least little bit embarrassed about it either, jerking his head in the direction of the doorway. *'His fault.'*

Wandering casually in his direction, Kerry leaned her head towards his shoulder to inform him, 'Your halo's crooked.'

A loud burst of male laughter greeted her as she got to the doorway. 'Oh, *I like her.* Bring her back any time.'

When Ronan shot her a look that said she was in trouble, Frank took the opportunity to depart. 'Wander over when you're settled in—cocktail hour at the usual time—nice to meet you, Kerry.'

'You too, Frank.' She smiled as he left, aware of the very second Ronan stood beside her, her pulse dancing a salsa in reaction the way it always did.

There was a very brief moment of silence. And then a low, gruffly rumbled, 'Crooked, huh?'

Kerry laughed, the laughter turning to a shriek of surprise when Ronan suddenly wrapped his arms round her waist and lifted her off her feet. 'Put me down, you idiot—where are we going? You better not—*Ronan*—don't you *dare!*'

He bent over and unceremoniously dumped her into the Jacuzzi, water sloshing up over the edges and into her face so she was blinking furiously and still laughing loudly when the water splashed again as he joined her.

Kerry laughed all the more, if somewhat nervously, now he had them both in a Jacuzzi—fully clothed—as if it were something people everywhere did every day of the week. And her pulse rate went off the chart with him so close, her mouth suddenly dry.

He splashed water in her face. 'Welcome to paradise.'

Kerry blinked the water away, impulsively lifting her hands to ruffle his wet hair until it settled into dozens of opposing damp spikes. 'You're clinically insane—you know that, don't you?'

He studied her eyes for the longest while with arms outstretched, his fingers playing on the surface of the water. And it was torture, really it was. Didn't he have any idea what he did to her? Couldn't he hear how loudly her heart was beating? It certainly sounded loud to her.

'What do you want to do first?'

Now *there* was a question.

She swallowed hard. 'What are my options?'

His gaze dropped to her mouth and Kerry had to stifle a groan. *He was killing her!* And when he looked back up into her eyes she could see how the deeper blue had darkened in amongst the varying shades of his—realization hitting her like a blow to the chest.

He'd just thought about kissing her, hadn't he?

In the hall he'd said it wasn't that he didn't want to, but he'd been so *determined*—

She couldn't do it again. Once had been humiliating enough. So she wasn't going to open her mouth and take another chance, but that didn't mean she couldn't push him a little—just to see what happened. Maybe not the best plan in the greater scheme of things—but the brand-new, adventurous version of Kerry wanted to know…

She let herself float towards him. 'I guess I could dig my bikini out and go lie on the beach…'

Ronan floated back from her. 'We could go snorkelling— the sea-life here is pretty spectacular.'

'We could.' She had a sudden mental image of his lean, muscular body in his wet suit when he tried, unsuccessfully it should be said, to teach her to surf in Hawaii…Dear lord, but it had been hard not to gape at him…

He nodded firmly. 'Frank can teach you to dive if you like.'

She smiled impishly 'Are you looking to get rid of me?'

He made a sudden move, hauling himself up onto the edge of the tub. 'I'm going to go find where our stuff is.'

Kerry felt a bubble of joy rise inside her when he swiftly bounced to his feet. Oh, he wasn't as immune to her as he was letting on, was he? And even though she knew he'd been right about not wanting to complicate things she chose to ignore the fact that getting any further involved with him was pointless as she scrambled ungracefully out of the water to follow him.

'You know by now that I trust you, right?'

'I promise not to let you drown snorkelling.'

'Do you trust *me*?'

'Why, are you the first Irish female serial killer?'

'No—'

'Married?'

'No.' She scowled at his back. 'Would I be traipsing around the world with you if I was?'

'I'd certainly hope not.' A few feet away from her he turned, water dripping off his clothes and onto the wooden floor as he frowned at her. 'Where exactly are we going with this?'

Kerry took a deep breath, planting her hands on her hips. 'I'm curious.'

'About what?'

'About why it is you think I couldn't handle a holiday fling with you.'

He growled beneath his breath. 'Kerry—'

'No, come on—explain it to me. You said in San Francisco it wasn't that you didn't want to kiss me—'

'I explained why it wasn't a good idea,' And he said the words through clenched teeth so she knew she was touching a nerve. 'And it's still not.'

'You think I'd automatically expect a long-term commitment from you, don't you?' Her brows lifted with the question.

Ronan's hands bunched into fists at his sides. 'Woman—don't push me.'

She pushed. 'Are you gay?'

It was the most ridiculous question on the face of the earth—but she knew it would get a reaction. And did it ever, Ronan stepping towards her with anger rippling off every muscle,

'Did it *seem like I was* when I was kissing you in Times Square?'

Kerry shrugged her shoulders, her heart beating fast enough to have run a marathon. 'Are *you* married, then?'

A question that could really have done with being asked a lot sooner if she'd had a single doubt in her mind, which she hadn't—but it too had the desired effect, Ronan now looking as if he might genuinely strangle her.

His voice rose. 'Would I be traipsing around the world with *you* if I was?'

'I'd certainly hope not.'

He stopped in front of her, his jaw clenching, hands still in fists by his sides and Kerry almost baulked—almost. But she'd had weeks' worth of pent-up frustration building inside her and maybe she'd have coped with that eventually if he'd seemed completely uninterested—but he hadn't.

Not completely. While he was standing towering over her with heat radiating off his large body she thought about every single intense look, the number of times he'd looked at her mouth—both of which she'd put down to wishful thinking, particularly since his rejection. And she began to wonder if it *had* been wishful thinking.

She searched his eyes, her voice lowering. 'But you think I can't handle this, right?'

He stayed silent.

She kept her voice calm. 'You think this is easy to do after you rejected me last time? I'm risking humiliation on a scale hitherto unknown to womankind here. But I need to know—'

'Need to know *what?*'

Her chin rose. 'If I'm the only one fighting this!'

'You think I'm not fighting this every damn day?'

The words were thrown at her with such force that she knew they'd been dragged up from deep inside him. And it tore her up inside to know she wasn't the only one suffering, her vision blurring in response.

'Then why are we fighting?' When her voice wavered on the words she swallowed hard and took a deep breath before continuing, 'We're both adults, Ronan.'

Ronan lifted both hands and rubbed them down over his face, muffling a groan before he dropped them and looked her in the eye, his deep voice rough. 'Kerry, if I kiss you there's a very good chance I won't be able to stop. It's not you I don't trust—it's me.'

Her lips trembled, forming a smile. 'What makes you think I'd want you to stop, you idiot?'

'Kerry—' her name sounded like a plea, his large hands lifting to frame her face as he leaned forwards to look into her eyes more closely '—there's no happily ever after with me.'

Kerry lifted her hands and placed them on his, holding his intense gaze. 'Did I ask you for one?'

'You deserve one.'

Her heart filled her chest. 'I'd settle for happy in the here and now. Most people would these days.'

Ronan shook his head, and she could see the control he was exerting over himself—it was written all over him. 'You deserve *more.*'

'How about you let *me* decide?'

'Kerry—'

'You can use my name as many times as you like, but now I know you feel the same way—'

He silenced her the way she'd been aching for him to all along—the kiss anything but gentle—and Kerry practically fell into him, her knees giving way under the onslaught of so much released frustration. His lips were hard and bruising, but she didn't care, her hands moving to grip hold of his shoulders while she released her own frustration and responded with all the need she'd been holding inside.

When he rocked forwards, his hands dropped, arms wrapping around her and holding her tighter against the hard length of his body while he pillaged her mouth. And Lord alone knew how much further they'd have gone if one of the staff hadn't appeared with their bags—clearing his throat loudly from the doorway.

Ronan wrenched his mouth from hers, setting her firmly

away from him and turning to shelter her from prying eyes before he cleared his throat.

'Thanks.'

Kerry fought to control her breathing until he turned again, her heart still running a marathon and her pulse skittering through her veins while he looked down at her face. If he even thought about trying to reject her now she might have to kill him.

His hands rose to her face again, thumbs smoothing over her cheeks. 'Are you okay?'

She laughed softly. 'Little shaky on my feet, if I'm honest. But yes.'

'Good.' He smiled a deliciously slow smile. 'What am I going to do with you woman?'

Kerry bit her lip to stop laughing again and Ronan shook his head in reply.

'That's not what I meant.'

The laughter escaped.

And he shook his head again, thumbs still smoothing against her cheeks. 'I think we should go find some nice colourful fish to look at before we go rushing into anything, don't you?'

'Probably.'

The smile grew. 'Don't pout.'

He leaned in and brushed his mouth over hers, a mere whisper of a kiss when compared to the onslaught from moments before, his voice then rumbling against her swollen lips. 'Go get changed.'

Kerry followed him when he tried to lean back, brushing her mouth over his the same way he just had, her eyes wide open and staring into his. 'No more fighting, okay? What happens happens…'

'One step at a time.'

It was exactly what she'd meant. And she'd already pushed more than enough. She just had to pray she hadn't got herself in over her head…

* * *

'She doesn't know, does she?'

Ronan took a deep breath before dropping another carrot into the pan of salted water. 'No, and it's staying that way.'

'Ronan—'

The warning edge to Abbie's soft voice drew his gaze up to lock with hers before she could go any further. 'There's no point in her knowing.'

'You like her—a lot.'

He smiled ruefully. And Abbie nodded before turning her attention back to the artistic endeavors required for the kind of dessert Ronan would merrily sell a limb for. Abbie's famous desserts had been one of the things that firmly placed the island into Ronan's idea of heaven on earth from his first visit. It was why he never flew over their side of the planet without dropping in, even if it was only for twenty-four hours and an extra helping of dessert he could take with him to Nadi—to eat in the airport while he waited for another flight to wherever he was going.

Well, that on top of the fact they were some of the first friends he'd made when he took up travelling. And had remained two of the best ever since.

'She like *you* as much?'

'Now, Abbie…'

'Oh, don't bother pulling out that patented charm of yours for me, young man. I'm the one woman on the planet it doesn't work on and you know it.'

'Well, if you're the only one then that kinda answers your question for you, doesn't it?'

She threw a scowl at him, the twitch of her lips and the glow of affection in her eyes diluting it enough for him to know he wasn't in any real trouble, so he went back to the mountain of carrots she'd handed him.

But Abbie wasn't done, her voice filled with false nonchalance. 'Interesting that she's the first woman you've brought here, don't you think?'

'I thought she'd enjoy it.'

'Everyone enjoys it here—that's not why you brought her. You brought her 'cos this place has a special place in your heart and you wanted to share that with her. You *like* her.'

'You already told me I do—' he wasn't playing and she should know better '—so it must be true.'

The end of a wooden spoon was waved above the carrots, immediately catching his attention and lifting his gaze to follow the chocolate-coated implement as it was waved back and forth in warning.

'You don't fool me for a single second so you can just stop that. If you like her then why don't you take a chance and let her in?'

'You done with that spoon?'

It was held up so the chocolate began a temptingly slow downward path. 'You can have the spoon when you answer the question.'

'Fine, then.' He frowned as he let the words slip free on a flat tone he knew rightly wouldn't fool her. 'I don't need a nursemaid just yet, that's why.'

When he reached for the spoon she lifted it higher, a look of disbelief on her face. 'You think she'd stay with you because she felt sorry for you? What kind of woman did you bring to my island?'

'That chocolate is gonna drip all over the place in a minute—seems like an awful waste to me.'

'*Ronan!*'

With a deeply heartfelt sigh, he dragged his gaze from the chocolate to a random point at his left, digging deep to keep his patience and not howl at the sky the way he felt like doing. 'It's my choice not to tell her, Abs. I don't have to explain why. Leave her out of it—she's—well, she's—'

'I got that after ten minutes with her.'

He nodded. He'd always considered his friends fairly good judges of character. They were *his* friends after all, he always told them—that showed how good at judging they were...

'How are you managing to hide it?'

Actually it had taken some pretty intensive forward planning, which could only be a good thing in the long run, he felt—a practice run of sorts. He'd learned how to use his vast knowledge of their destinations to avoid dimly lit places at night, how to make sure he always gave her plenty to look at so she wouldn't focus too much on him—and so far so good. All he had to do was maintain the deception all the way back to the Emerald Isle and he'd be grand. She'd never have to know and he'd never have to see pity in her eyes.

He opened his mouth to voice the one concern he'd had about bringing her here. 'I might need you and Frank to help me some later. You still eat in the dark by hurricane lamp, right?'

He knew she knew what he was aiming at when her hand reached across and squeezed his, her voice threaded thick with emotion. 'Already?'

'Just don't go letting me make a fool of myself.'

'We won't.' She handed him the spoon.

'See—now that's why I love you, though in fairness you get extra points over Frank for the desserts.'

'You're incorrigible.'

'Yeah, someone else tells me that these days too.'

CHAPTER SEVEN

KERRY felt her idea of heaven on earth now came down to a few basics.

Having every whim indulged, whether it be a horseback ride along white sands just before sunset or being taken to a desert island by boat where they could wade ashore and spend a full day completely alone; picnicking on the selection of lobster, buttered rolls, salad, pineapple, pawpaw and a jug of watermelon juice beaded with moisture Abbie packed for them—even though Ronan complained bitterly about the lack of desserts.

And then there were the hours whiled away floating across acres of yellow coral waving with the surge of the sea, with shoals of black and white damselfish looking very much like mint humbugs to Kerry as they swam by, and bright red and white clownfish poking their faces out of sea anemones while a yellow and black angelfish picked a fight with a blue-striped wrasse. Ronan informed her of all their names when they would surface for air and she would describe them amidst bursts of bubbling laughter when he laughed at how breathless she was from trying to stay under as long as possible without drowning.

Then there was the hammock specifically tailored for two Ronan decided they should adopt for after Abbie's delicious lunches. They would lie gently swaying together, the sea breeze wafting over them as they shared the most embarrassing stories from their childhoods or the worst dates they'd ever been on or he'd wheedle more off her fantasy destinations list and tell her about them if he'd been there—the majority of which he of course had—and sometimes they'd even get round to discussing things he could put in the book they both seemed to have so conveniently forgotten since they'd got there. All of it interspersed by soft, exploratory kisses that went on for ever…

Heaven on earth.

But even with all those wonderful experiences and memories it was only truly heaven on earth for Kerry because Ronan was there—it was sharing everything with him that made the experiences into *moments* she would remember for the rest of her life.

She was falling hard for him.

It was the atmosphere, she told herself. It was the romance of the island, she reasoned. It was sharing so many magical experiences she could only have dreamed of—she'd tried using every one of them as an explanation for the way her heart would positively glow with warmth every time she looked at him.

But it was him.

And she couldn't seem to stop it from creeping up on her, which only served to make the aching inside her grow—especially in the darkness of their bure at night, when she would listen for any sound of him moving on the day bed while she lay alone in the huge four-poster bed meant for two.

They had two full days and three nights left in heaven. And she really didn't want the something to keep them apart any more—even if she had to let him go in the end.

'*If you care about him as much as I think you do don't give up on him just yet. Be patient.*' Abbie's words still whispered in the back of her mind, long after the walk back from dinner…

The dinner get-together had rapidly become another favourite memory for Kerry to keep. With Frank presiding over the long table set out under a banyan tree, lit by hurricane lamps and decorated with pots of orchids, she'd felt welcomed into their tight-knit group from the very first night as they filled the balmy night air with laughter and the warmth of the open love Ronan obviously shared with his friends. And Ronan hadn't been the least bit behind the door about touching her in front of them, tangling her fingers with his, wrapping an arm around her waist to draw her closer after he'd abandoned all pretence at conversation with the arrival of Abbie's chocolate truffle cake, which to Kerry's secret inner chocoholic's glee turned out to be a milk chocolate pudding and white chocolate ice cream drizzled with dark chocolate sauce—*bliss!*

Though she'd soon learned the arm-around-her-waist trick was a way for Ronan to sneak some of her portion as well as his own by tickling her ribs.

But he'd been more than happy for his friends to accept her as being 'his'. And she'd felt her confidence grow because of it.

By the third night he'd taken to leaning in close to say something in a deliciously intimate rumbling voice that tickled the sensitive skin on her neck. Or he'd tuck her hair behind her ear. Or press his lips to her temple—sometimes simply aiming the kind of intense heated look at her that had her glancing around the table to see if anyone else had noticed what he'd done to every single one of her nerve endings…

By the fourth night it was Abbie she found watching them nearly every single time she checked. Sometimes with a look of open curiosity, sometimes with a small frown, sometimes with an affectionate smile that gave Kerry the hope she approved of what she saw.

A hope she had confirmed on their nightly stroll across the starlit beach to Ronan and Kerry's shared bure. With Ronan and Frank several feet ahead of them Abbie had linked their arms and smiled at the backs of the two men while she spoke.

'I'm glad he brought you to visit.'

'Me too—I can't tell you how much I've loved it. You're incredibly lucky living here together.'

'We think so too.' She squeezed Kerry's arm, 'You'll have to come back and see us again.'

'I will.' And she meant it, even if the very thought of visiting without Ronan was so painful it almost doubled her over. She really was going to have to get a better handle on her emotions.

'You're good together.'

Heat rose on her cheeks. 'Well, we're not actually—'

She didn't want Abbie to think there was more to it than there actually was. Or worse still for Abbie to say to *Ronan* that she thought there was. Because that wasn't the 'agreement', was it?

'Yes, you are—whether you choose to admit it or not.' She studied Kerry's face for a few steps, looking forward to check how close they were to the men before lowering her voice to add, 'If you care about him as much as I think you do don't give up on him just yet. Be patient.'

A light came on inside the bure.

Abbie turned to hug her as Frank reappeared, whispering above her ear, 'He can be hard work, I know—but he's worth it.'

Swallowing down a lump of emotion, Kerry managed a nod and a choked, 'I know he is.'

And she meant it. Even if she didn't see how a rolling stone like him could ever be happy with someone who could only wangle one trip a year at best.

Then Frank was there, kissing her on the cheek and wishing her goodnight before swinging his wife into his arms and waltzing her up the beach—the sound of their laughter echoing in the distance long after Kerry went into the chalet.

But she could still hear Abbie's voice in her head hours later when she heard Ronan moving on the day bed and she held her breath, straining to hear his breathing above the sound of the surf outside. Four nights she'd tried and she'd yet to hear it, but it didn't stop her trying.

'You're still awake, aren't you?'

He said it just softly enough that if she hadn't been he wouldn't have woken her. 'How did you know?'

'You weren't snoring.'

'I do *not* snore.' She turned onto her side and hauled the light cover up to her chin in indignation. 'And even if I did you shouldn't tell me I do.'

'There's another rule, is there?'

Her mouth curled into a smile. 'Yes, there is. And if there isn't there should be. Ladies aren't supposed to snore.'

'Betcha Nana snores like a trooper and doesn't care who knows it.'

The subject of Kerry's beloved nana had proved one of his greatest sources of amusement when they shared stories on the hammock…

'Nana is of an age where she says she's earned the right to do whatever she wants, no matter what people think or say. Or what they tell her she can't possibly do any more…'

There was only the briefest heartbeat of a pause before he answered, 'I think I'm a little in love with Nana. Think I'd stand a chance with her?'

She'd probably love him too. Didn't everyone?

'So why are you awake?'

'Why are you?'

'I asked first.'

'Can't sleep.'

Kerry rolled her eyes in the darkness, 'Well, duh.'

She was immediately rewarded with a deep chuckle of laughter. 'Now that's mature.'

'I've obviously been spending too much time with you.'

'I'd have come up with something more mature than that. I'll have you know I have an extensive vocabulary—and not just in the one language. I speak three types of *foreign* fluently.'

'Go on, then. Say something in *foreign* to me.'

'Okay.' She heard him moving around again, his voice a little closer when he eventually spoke—as if he'd turned so his head was now at the bottom end of the bed. '*Je n'ai avant jamais rencontré quelqu'un comme vous. Mais je suis très heureux que je vous ai rencontré.*'

How could his voice possibly manage to sound even sexier in French? It really wasn't fair.

'And what does that mean?'

'It means I promise not to tell you if you snore in the future…'

'That's good of you. *Je suis heureux je vous ai rencontré aussi. Même si vous dites le le mensonge impair d'éviter de dire réellement quelque chose de gentil à moi.*'

'Damn.' The smile came through in his voice. 'How's your Italian?'

'Well, you could tell me in Italian that you've never met anyone like me and you're glad you did—if you like. But I'll still answer that I'm glad I met you too—though maybe not as smoothly as in French.' She smiled into the darkness, her heart still swelling in her chest from his confession. 'We hoteliers tend to pick up the basics of popular modern-day "foreign".'

'And I s'pose you'll still tag on the fact you feel that way even when I lie to avoid admitting I said something nice?'

'You could be nice more often.'

'If you're not careful I'll come over there and show you just how nice *I can be.*'

'Promises, promises…'

The words were out before she could stop them. And when the bure went quiet she fought the instinctive need to curl into a partial foetal position to try and hold the groan of embarrassment inside. She couldn't believe she'd just said it—not that she hadn't meant it, but—

But what did he expect after all the kissing and touching and playing about in the sand and the hammock he loved so much? And that was before she took into account what he was doing to her poor heart on an almost daily basis. No wonder she—ached—the way she did most nights when she lay alone in a huge bed designed for honeymooners.

'If I come over there all the effort I've put into being as close to a gentleman as I get will leave this bure at great speed. I've seen that nightdress you're only just wearing.'

Kerry had to take a moment to swallow, lick her dry lips and control her breathing before she responded to the husky edge in his voice. 'You put this nightdress on the keeper pile—remember?'

He made a noise that sounded distinctly like a growl of warning. 'Catching glimpses of you wearing it is something altogether different—trust me.'

'You see me in a bikini every day.'

'I know. And that's exactly why I've had to put so much effort into being gentlemanly.'

'Not that you find me repulsive, then.'

'No.' He sighed impatiently into the darkness. 'If you were repulsive I wouldn't be having problems getting to sleep over here knowing you're over there wearing what you're wearing.'

The new-version Kerry couldn't help but push a little. 'I could take it off if that'd help.'

There was a distinct sound of movement swiftly followed by a muffled groan, which made Kerry smile ridiculously on her side of the room, her heart taking on an erratic rhythm at the thought of him struggling to stay where he was.

'Are you hiding under your pillow?'

'Woman!' His raised voice told her he'd come out of hiding, the frustrated edge telling her she was pushing him a step too far. 'I'm still trying not to make this thing between us any more complicated than it already is. *Help me out here.*'

'You're right.'

'I know I am.'

'It's already complicated.'

'Yes, it is.'

'And we have very different lives.'

'We do.'

'Once this trip is over there's absolutely no reason why our paths would cross. They didn't before.'

'*Exactly.*'

'We might never see each other again.'

'I know.' His voice dropped.

And she might have seen sense at that point if it hadn't held the edge of fatalistic resignation it had. But in the darkness she could feel it magnified tenfold—the *answering need* in him. She could feel it tugging at her soul from clean across the room.

Her voice shook on the words. 'Every fantasy on my list. That's what you wanted to give me, right?'

'Don't—' He sounded strangled.

'Thing is, somewhere along the way I think I've maybe added you to that list—' her breath hitched, her voice barely above a whisper as she tried to force the rest out while she still had the courage '—and every day we spend touching—and kissing—just, it just—well, it makes everything *more*—I guess…'

Oh, she was making a real mess of this, wasn't she?

'*Kerry—*'

'You see, I can't sleep over here on my own either, because—' She took a deep breath and tried again, the words tumbling out in a rush '—I guess I miss you beside me now

I've got so used to it. 'Cos when we're in the hammock in the afternoon I have no problem dozing off, do I? But in here I just spend all my time thinking about you all the way over there and I guess that means I must *need you* beside me and this aching—'

There was a loud thud followed by a muffled curse and a, 'Don't move. And don't *dare* take anything off—I *mean* it. I'm coming over there.'

Kerry held her breath, her heart thundering so loudly in her ears she could barely hear him until the bed dipped behind her and an arm snaked around her waist to bring her back against the hard length of his body where he lay above the covers. And for a long moment after he'd curled his knees into the backs of hers and rested his chin on the top of her head, she just lay there—waiting—until he took a deep, shuddering breath; as if it had cost him dearly to come to her when he'd been trying so hard not to.

It tipped her over the edge.

The aching in her chest finally broke free to form silent tears as with all her heart and soul she willed him to trust her—to believe in her and let her into his heart the way he'd wormed his way into hers...

'Don't cry.'

Kerry took a hiccuping breath, because she'd thought she'd done a pretty good job of not letting on she was.

He turned her in his arms so his breath whispered over her damp cheeks while he traced her face with impossibly tender fingertips. 'Don't cry—not because of me—you hear?'

The incredible softness in his husky voice reached out and wrapped around her aching heart. 'I hear.'

'And I can see you—even in the dark—did you know that?' His fingertips traced up to her hairline, over her temple, taking time with each arch of her brows while he continued in a low rumble that sneaked in around the edges of her soul. 'Right now I can see your face with the sun on it—the way you look when I see you every day; smiling the way you do. I can see all those things right this minute Kerry, Kerry Doyle. Just like I can lie in the dark every night and see you in this nightdress. Or half not in it, I should say. I can see *that* best of all…'

Her hiccupped breath was released on a soft burst of laughter. 'Still incorrigible.'

'Always.' His smile came through in his voice, his fingertips tracing each closed eye—lingering on the edges of her lashes for a while before tracing her nose, as if committing her face to memory by touch. 'So don't cry because of me.'

'I'm sorry.' She reached for him as she said it, turning her body into his, because she *was* sorry—sorry she'd ruined things a little by being so emotional in front of him. Everything had been so—right—since they'd come to the island. And now she'd taken a little of the magic away by not being able to leave things be.

'Don't do that either.' His fingertips had moved from her nose to her cheek, smoothing away any lingering moisture at the same time as he added the shape to whatever mental picture he was drawing. 'Don't ever apologize for being who you are. You feel things and you're never afraid to show you do. Most women don't do that second part, you know.'

Old-version Kerry hadn't either.

Even if she'd had the courage to tell him that, she wouldn't have been able to form the words, because by then his wandering fingertips had begun to trace her mouth—starting at the outer edges and following the shape until she parted her lips to draw in a breath. And then he traced the plumpness of her lower lip, taking a hint of moisture from inside the upper edge to dampen it before she felt the air displace above her face.

'Don't change. Just don't cry.'

The first kiss was so heartbreakingly gentle she sighed

against his mouth, breathing in when he breathed out—her hand settling palm-down on the heated skin of his bare chest, moving until she had it directly above the firm thudding beat of his heart below his breastbone.

She tilted her head back into the soft pillows to allow him better access—he then angled his head and hesitated for the briefest second before repeating the sliding touch of firm lips over soft. And they kissed like that for the longest time, the ocean beyond the walls of the bure the only sound beyond the joint breathing that changed by increments from deep and slow to shallower and quicker when soft kisses weren't enough any more—for either of them.

Ronan's large hand moved over the soft skin of her shoulders while the other toyed with the hair spread out on her pillow and Kerry's one hand remained constantly on the beat of his heart while she let the other trace each muscle in his arm from the wrist up—revelling in the sensuality of his distinct maleness and the delicious sense of femininity she felt magnified by the sheer size of his body laid out next to hers.

'Mmm,' he groaned against her now swollen lips.

'Mmm-hmm.' She smiled mid-kiss, unable to break the contact long enough to form coherent words.

Ronan groaned again, the sound deeper in his chest this time, vibrating beneath her palm. 'We…need to…'

'Mmm.'

'Kerry—'

Her hand had reached his wide shoulder, so she used it for leverage and rolled onto him, scrambling ungraciously through the light sheets as she stretched her body along the length of his, breasts squashed against his chest, her legs lined up with his—the only thing between them now a bundled lump of cotton and the sliding silk of her nightdress.

Ronan used both hands to frame her face, lifting her head back so he could break the kiss long enough to speak, his chest heaving beneath her. 'Kerry, we should stop. I promised myself I wouldn't let it go this far.'

She smiled into the darkness. 'Didn't want to take advantage of me, huh?'

He exhaled his answer. 'Exactly that.'

'Didn't talk to *me* about it tho', did you?'

'Not really a conversation starter.'

'Might possibly have come across a tad arrogant…'

His chest shook with silent laughter. 'Might.'

One large hand moved from her face to smooth down over her hair, past the bare skin of her shoulder to the smooth silk against the small of her back. And Kerry smiled all the more at the fact he couldn't stop touching her while he was trying to stop what they were doing. What was it they said about actions speaking louder?

It was gloriously empowering.

'Don't I get a say in it now?'

'Probably best not.'

She wriggled to get more comfortable and wanted to laugh aloud when he tensed underneath her—she could win this battle quite easily if she set her mind to it, couldn't she? And she'd never seduced a man before.

'Am I too heavy for you?'

'No.'

It sounded distinctly as if he was gritting his teeth. So she wriggled again, just to see…

Ronan growled. 'But you could *quit that*.'

'Wanna know what I think?' She rested her forearms on his bare chest.

'Not sure it's safe to find out—so, no.'

'What *I* think—' she stifled laughter when he made a deep sound of exasperation '—is that this partnership needs a little more equality.'

'Really.'

'Yes, you see so far I've tiptoed around you—'

That got her a burst of disbelieving laughter. 'Oh, have you indeed? God help me.'

She nudged both arms down a little. 'Yes—*I have*. But this is supposed to be *my* trip, isn't it?'

'It is.'

'Except that you've made the decision to call all the shots and have a go at fulfilling my fantasies along the way, haven't you?' She didn't give him a chance to interrupt. 'And I kinda love that, don't get me wrong—'

'But?'

'*But*—I don't need you to make every decision for me. I'm a big girl. What happens—happens, remember?' She took a huge breath of warm air and laid it on the line just in case he hadn't got it already. 'And I don't think you'd be over here if you weren't finding it equally tough as me to stop it from happening.'

'I think we've established that.'

'So why are we fighting it again, then?'

'Because I already care about you too much to hurt you— that's why.'

Kerry knew that. She'd probably have suspected it for a while if she were surer of herself, but the way he'd just been with her—with so much gentleness in his voice and his touch, and using words that would have broken through the most hardened of hearts…

She knew he cared.

'Know what Nana would say if she was here?'

'After she'd kicked me from here to next week for being in your bed, you mean?'

'Actually having met you she'd probably pretend she didn't know where you were while she imparted her words of wisdom. In fact—now I think about it—you said something similar to what she'd say on the plane that first time, about desserts.'

She could hear him shaking his head. 'Okay, crazy girl—I'll bite. What did I say?'

'Life's too short.'

He tensed underneath her again, the hand on her back stilling. So she lowered her voice and kept going, staying patient the way someone who knew Ronan better than she did had advised.

'And Nana would add that you should grab hold of happiness when you find it—no matter how short or long an amount of time it lasts.'

Ronan didn't speak, but tension rolled off him in waves and his heart was thundering beneath her arms. He was still fighting, wasn't he? She could feel it in him. And it was one hell of a battle. Kerry could sense that instinctively too. What she didn't get was why. She'd made it plain as the day was long that she wanted him—he obviously wanted her—and the kissing they'd been doing had been leading them to where they were for days.

'He can be hard work...but he's worth it.'

And he hadn't moved away. So Kerry took that as a positive sign and moved her arms to rest her head on his chest, her hands on his shoulders. Then she stayed there, simply because it was where she wanted to be—and because she wasn't giving up on him.

Ronan could take as long as he needed to think about what she'd said. She'd be patient. She'd wait. And she'd keep on letting him know she wanted him.

Because she felt he was worth it—and she loved him. She'd been falling since the first time she'd looked in those sensational eyes.

She was in well and truly over her head.

CHAPTER EIGHT

IT WAS time to leave the island. And, having spent forty-eight hours battling his needs, Ronan was uncharacteristically silent, and all too aware of the fact. As aware as he was of the fact Kerry had noticed too. Not that she'd pulled him on it. She seemed to know not to push him further than she already had and he was glad of it.

Fighting his own needs was one thing—fighting hers was something else entirely.

He also knew how much Frank and particularly Abbie were struggling to keep smiles on their faces. It was exactly the kind of thing he'd been trying to avoid since he'd decided to see as many of his friends as possible, the need to see them yet another reminder of his own selfishness? he wondered.

But it was *precisely* the kind of reminder he needed not to let Kerry any closer than she already was, even when every bone in his body desperately wanted him to. And reminders like that could never be thrown at him enough, because when it came to Kerry he was a weak man—a *very* weak man.

The Fijian staff draped garlands of hibiscus flowers around their necks and Frank and Abbie walked them all the way into the water. Ronan then watched with a constricting tightness in his chest as each of them hugged and kissed Kerry, Abbie whispering to her with tears glistening in her eyes—while

Ronan silently prayed she wasn't saying anything that might make it more difficult for him later on. Then, with Kerry safely in the seaplane, he waded back to say his own goodbyes, his mouth drawn into a narrow line when Abbie held him just a little too tight for just a little too long.

He managed a smile when he held her at arm's length, scowling at her with mock severity. 'Stop that. Just think of it this way—how you look now is how I'll always see you. You'll never age.'

When tears welled up in her eyes and splashed over her lashes he hugged her tight again, pressing a kiss to her temple as he forced his throat to work. 'Gorgeous for ever, Abs, even when I can't see your face any more.'

She sobbed, and Frank took her under one arm as Ronan turned away. He'd suffered through the worst of their goodbyes the night before and there really wasn't anything else to say.

One of the staff then made the last wading steps even tougher for him by strumming a guitar—all of them singing 'Ise Lei'—a sad farewell to Fiji.

Someone, somewhere really had it in for him.

On the plane, Kerry said nothing, she simply set her smaller hand in his, tangled their fingers and squeezed before the engine roared and they lifted off over the blue lagoon he knew he'd probably never see again.

'Open the window and throw your garland into the water— if it drifts ashore you'll return,' their pilot kindly threw back over his shoulder.

Making Ronan dearly want to beat him to death with a string of bright scented flowers...

Instead he let go of Kerry's hand to open the window while she lifted the garland over her head. Once it was dropped, she turned to him.

'Now you.' She waggled her fingers, making him think about the first time she'd asked to see his passport.

Not this time. He shook his head, lifting his to replace hers. 'Mine looks better on you. Let's just see if yours makes it back.'

Even if he did make it back, he wouldn't be the same man, would he? It wouldn't be the same experience.

The plane took its time rising, giving them just enough time to watch Kerry's garland float towards the beach, the sight bitter-sweet. But good, he told himself. He liked the idea of the people that mattered to him together on the island again some time in the future.

Now all he had to do was get through the next few weeks without Kerry cottoning onto why he was fighting. Somehow, knowing her as well as he did now, he doubted she'd see it the way he did. And there was no way she was changing his mind.

In the meantime he had plans for more fantasy fulfilment. Because if he was going to hurt her at the end of their three months together, then he was going to make sure every preceding second was a gateway to every adventure she ever took...

It was the best gift he could give her.

Kerry got suspicious when, off his own bat and without any persuasion, he suggested she went shopping in Sydney. 'What kind of things?'

He shrugged. 'A long dress, couple of smart casual outfits, pair of posh shoes if you really have to—which, knowing you, you will.'

'I *had* a long dress in San Francisco. But *someone* wouldn't let me keep it.'

He chose to ignore the fact he might actually have been wrong about something.

'You can stop somewhere and get your hair done too if you like. I have a few people to see while I'm here anyway so I'll be busy.' He set his hands on her shoulders, turned her round and then used the knuckles of one hand in the small of her back to nudge her towards the hotel-room door. 'Do you need money?'

'No—I have money—and I doubt your publisher's will swallow dresses and a hairdo as research expenses.'

'You'd be surprised what I can get away with.'

She stopped in the open doorway to frown at him. 'What's wrong with my hair?'

Ronan shook his head, smiling indulgently. 'There's nothing wrong with your hair. But you might want to swap the sexy beach look for something a tad more sophisticated for where we're going next. Or I'll pay the price for not warning you before we got there.'

'Where are we going?'

'It's a surprise.'

'I hate surprises.' It was a fib he'd most likely call her on but she *would* hate surprises if she wasn't at least marginally prepared for them—this was a new, and somewhat worrying development, especially if it involved her being pushed forcibly out the door to shop for clothes for a mystery destination. It was a woman's worst nightmare—didn't he know that? And it wasn't as if she could phone a friend to ask what everyone else would be wearing…

'You've loved every surprise I've come up with so far and you'll love this one too. Though frankly I can't believe it's taking this much effort to get you to go shopping.'

'It's been so long I'm worried I've forgotten how to do it.'

'I'm sure it'll come back to you.' He leaned in and kissed her, the woeful expression on her face apparently too much to resist. 'Now shoo. The sooner you go, the sooner you'll be back.'

She brightened. 'Meaning you'll miss me?'

'How can I miss you when you won't go away?'

He was entirely too clever for his own good. 'In that case I won't be back for ages. That way you can get an opportunity to miss me *bad.*'

His chin dropped and he sighed, making Kerry smile at the top of his head. Still fighting it—yes, showing signs of weakening though—she hoped. She just had to keep going and pray he got half as attached to her as she was to him. And if by some miracle he did, then they could maybe talk about the possibility of seeing each other any time he was home from one of his trips or—better still—about taking another trip together. She didn't want to clip his wings, but it didn't mean she didn't want more time.

Time more than anything. Because it was running out. They had ten days to 'do' some of Australia, three days in Hong Kong, a couple of days in Dubai on the way back and then Paris, because she'd promised Nana she'd be there on a certain date and it was the only thing she'd insisted Ronan couldn't change.

He'd told her on the flight from Fiji that he'd left any other short stops in Europe off his mental list because it was easy for her to get to on her own some time in the future. And it had hurt hearing it—especially when he'd said it so calmly; as if it didn't matter she'd be doing it without him.

'Be back before four or we'll be late.'

'*Bully.*'

'I'll revoke the shopping privileges if you're not careful. And you'll regret it when we get to the surprise…' He shot her a look that said 'on your own head be it, young lady'.

So Kerry silently admitted defeat before she lifted a hand—her thumb and forefinger creating a small space for her to squint through. '*Little clue* to help with my shopping decisions…?'

'Nope.' But an answering pout earned her another kiss. 'I'm helping you learn to roll with the punches and be spur-of-the-moment. You'll thank me later.'

The new Kerry could learn to be spur-of-the-moment; she felt she'd done very well with it so far…

But she got suspicious again when they reached his secret destination that evening—complete with all the purchases she was eternally grateful for when she walked onto the platform. What he'd allowed her in San Francisco during the 'travel light' lesson would never in a million years have seen her through a trip on Australia's version of the Orient Express. And she'd never have forgiven him for that.

She'd thought he'd have trouble topping the island experience but the Great South Pacific Express was close—completely different, but close when it came to the fantasy fulfilment he was so hell-bent on. The carriage interiors were rich and polished, a dazzling mixture of craftsmanship and comfort and old-fashioned—*opulence*—quite frankly. Which was why, when she discovered he'd booked them, not one, but *two* top-end cabins, she wasn't just suspicious about the fact he'd separated them at night again but about how exactly the huge expense was being dealt with. Something wasn't right, and she just couldn't quite put her finger on what it was…

After he'd made polite conversation about the area and the train all the way through a sensational dinner in one of the restaurant cars, Kerry mentally gritting her teeth to stop herself from starting an argument in front of such an elegant audience, they'd moved on to a lounge complete with baby grand piano. Then she calmly waited while tapping her toe on the carpeted floor, until they both had sparkling crystal glasses of a crisp Pinot in hand, before launching into the line of questioning she'd formulated.

'Tell me about this publisher of yours.'

Ronan shot her a narrow-eyed stare. 'Why?'

'You must make a fortune for them with your books.'

'They do okay.'

Judging by the dangerously flat-toned edge to his voice, she was onto something. So she calmly crossed her legs beneath the deep russet satin skirt of her new halter-necked evening dress, plucking an imaginary strand of hair off it while she continued.

'Well, they must think so to fork out this amount of money so you can indulge a virgin traveller…'

Apparently she wasn't fooling him with her calm exterior.

'Is this a glimpse of Kerry Doyle from Doyle's of Dublin I'm getting right now?' He jerked his chin at her. 'Because if that's who I'm talking to I'm not sure I like her all that much.'

It stung. But she recognized it for what it was and called him on it. *'Defensive.'*

'You've been weird ever since we got here.'

'Pot. Meet kettle.'

He shrugged his wide shoulders beneath the dinner jacket that had magically appeared out of nowhere. And Kerry was no fool when it came to clothes—she'd recognized it for what it was the second she'd stopped drooling at the sight of him in it. And what it was was expensive. It was as if he'd transformed from her lovably incorrigible rogue to the kind of man who frequented her family's hotel on a regular basis in the blink of an eye. And, added to the lavish surroundings and his ease within them, it had left her wondering who exactly it was she'd fallen for.

When he turned his head and focussed on the pianist she took a deep breath. 'So what does something like this go down as on your expenses sheet?'

'Travel.'

'And that suit you look so gorgeous in?'

'Clothing, funnily enough—glad you approve.'

It was how someone who was dating a secret agent probably felt. 'If you're paying for this entire trip out of your own pocket, then I want to know. And I want to split it with you. It's not like I hadn't already budgeted for it.'

'You're helping me with research for a book.'

It hadn't felt as if she was helping him all that much with a book, actually. Not really. Yes, they'd discussed it, and, yes, he'd spent the very odd occasion on his laptop, but even so…

And now she had a sneaking suspicion there was more to it. *'Ronan—'*

'Kerry—' he looked her straight in the eye, a muscle in his jaw clenching, '—leave it alone. The expenses are taken care of in exchange for the insight I've got from you on travelling for the first time. That was the deal, remember? And I've got more from this trip than you might think I have.'

Oh, he was hard work all right.

She damped her lips, took a sip of her wine and tried a different approach. 'We've never talked much about your family.'

'We've talked plenty about my family.'

Then why was he so defensive about them all of a sudden too? It was as if she were talking to someone she'd never met before!

'I'd like to know more.'

'Why?'

'Possibly because I'm sitting over here feeling like I don't know you as well as I thought I did?'

'Why do you need to know more than you already do?'

Because I'm in love with you and I want to know everything about you. But she couldn't say that, could she? Especially not when he was making her feel as if she'd fallen in love with a fantasy—ironically, when he'd wanted to fulfil all of those...

'What's changed between Fiji and here?'

'Nothing.'

And now he was lying to her? She shook her head, suddenly tired beyond belief—and she couldn't be patient with him when she was tired.

'Do you want out?'

Ronan looked stunned by the question. 'Out?'

She waved a hand back and forth between them. 'Of this. Part of the deal was if either one of us wanted out at any stage we'd go our separate ways, remember?'

'I don't want out.' And he said it with enough controlled anger in his voice for her to know he meant it. 'Do *you*?'

'No. I don't want to argue with you either.'

'Then don't.'

It was tough not to when he was being the way he was. 'You're shutting me out—but you know that, don't you?'

The muscle in his jaw clenched again. He knew. But he wasn't going to stop doing it any time soon, was he? So she might have to give up, temporarily, because this wasn't getting them anywhere—was doing more harm than good to her vulnerable heart.

So she set her glass to one side and, with another deep breath, pushed to her feet. 'I'm going to turn in.'

Ronan frowned up at her as she stepped over, bending down to kiss his cleanly shaven cheek before lowering her voice to add, 'Maybe tomorrow the Ronan I know will come back. I miss him.'

THERE WERE no words to describe how he'd felt when she'd asked him if he wanted 'out'. Angry didn't begin to describe it. Furious wasn't anywhere near *angry* enough. Livid was closer, he supposed. Livid that she'd thought he could just up and walk away from her when they'd only just left the island and all that had happened there. Didn't she have any idea what it was going to take to walk in a few weeks' time—what it was going to take getting through the lead in to it? Why would he try to speed up the process?

But none of that mattered when compared to the moment of panic he'd felt when he'd thought *she* wanted 'out'. And the fact he'd felt it so strongly just went to prove how weak he was when it came to her.

He should have hated her for that.

But instead he was on his way to find her for more damage control. Because any steps he'd tried to introduce it had just blown up in his face. So now he had to try and fix it. And then think up another way of gently backing off so he didn't hurt her any more than he had to.

The narrow corridors of the train weren't as well lit as he'd expected, disorienting him for a moment and forcing him— *godamn it*—to ask for help from a steward, which didn't improve his mood even if it did make him thankful she'd left when she had. And between that and his sudden sense of urgency to get to her it ended up taking longer than he'd planned. Especially when he had to stand outside her door and breathe deeply before he faced her again.

She radiated surprise when she opened the door. He could feel it in the air.

'I *am* the publisher.' He frowned hard when no amount of concentrating would bring her face into focus. Not that he needed to see it to know what she looked like. She was indelibly imprinted onto his brain now—both visually and by touch. But not seeing her—*hurt*—and he didn't want it to.

'Okay.'

He clenched his jaw, shoving his hands deep into his pockets so he wouldn't be tempted to just reach forward, haul her into his arms and kiss it better. 'That's why there's never a problem with expenses.'

'I see.'

He clenched his jaw harder at the words she'd chosen. But he deserved the coolness he was getting, didn't he? If he'd been her he'd probably have slammed the door in his face. 'We own newspapers, magazines and radio stations up and down the country as well.'

'Anything else?'

'Bought into a TV station—that's why I was home.'

'Name?'

'TV station or the company?'

'Actually I was checking yours is still the same but the company name might be interesting too.' She stepped back, letting a little light in. 'Are you coming in?'

No, coming in was a bad idea. It had been tough enough

looking at her in the dress she'd bought. He'd even wondered if she'd bought it specifically to make him crazy. It highlighted the russet in her brown eyes, baring, not just her shoulders, but the most tempting expanse of smooth-skinned back he'd ever set eyes on—and as to how it hugged her curves and dipped between her breasts…

The woman was hotter than Hades.

The door clicked shut behind him and he frowned all the harder, focussing his annoyance at having stepped inside on his other frustration. 'Don't the lights work in here?'

'The little one by the bed is fine.'

The hell it was. Everything was still shadowed and it left him floundering—which he hated to the pit of his stomach. In better light he'd feel as if he was on surer ground. He wanted to be able to see her face while he talked to her so he could gauge her reactions, watch the thoughts as they crossed her expressive eyes.

He wanted to be able to look at her. It was like having his gut put through a mangle.

Kerry's sultry scent surrounded him as she walked past and sat on the edge of what he assumed was the aforementioned bed, the material of her dress rustling, her voice as soft as silk. 'So you're disgustingly rich, then, I take it?'

'Indecently rich—less attractive to you now, am I?'

She ignored the bitterness in his voice. 'So you being some kind of millionaire—it's a secret, is it?'

'Not at home, it's not.'

'But you don't make that big a deal of it when you're away. You like to be accepted as yourself and not because of how much money you have.'

Sometimes he could swear she saw inside him. It was more than a little unnerving—and she didn't wait for him to speak, which meant she already knew the answer.

'What did you say the company was called again?'

He hadn't. 'The Millennium Group.'

'You're *that* O'Keefe?' She laughed huskily. 'Well, now, that *is* interesting.'

The laugh dragged him physically across the room where he exhaled with relief as the lamp shone enough soft light on her face for him to see her, his voice dropping to a calmer tone. 'Interesting how?'

'Because if your father is Brian O'Keefe, then I think he plays golf with my father from time to time.'

Ronan sat down on the deep bed beside her. 'I did wonder how we'd not met when I realized who you were.'

'Not so small a world after all, then.'

'Apparently not.' He took a hand out of his pocket and lifted one of hers from her lap, tangling fingers and resting their joined hands on his thigh, his gaze fixed on the sight. 'I'm not home much—probably explains it some.'

'How do you manage that with such a huge company?'

She sounded genuinely interested in the logistics, which made sense when Ronan thought about it. If she wanted to travel more then she'd need to know how to arrange her working life better. And that was something else he could pass on, wasn't it? He smiled.

'I'm a wizard when it comes to the art of delegation. Surround yourself with good people, reward them for good work and you get people you can trust.' It was just that simple, he'd found. 'Doesn't matter if it's a big company with dozens of divisions or an iconic hotel in the middle of Dublin—it's all about teamwork.'

'You make it sound easy.'

And the edge of wistfulness in her voice practically crucified him, his gaze shifting to hold hers. 'It is. You just have to be determined to make it work. And be prepared to weather the odd muck-up from time to time.'

She grimaced and Ronan smiled affectionately, his free

hand reaching to tuck a lock of soft hair behind her ear, fingertips tracing her long droplet earring on the way down so his knuckles grazed the sensitive skin on her neck. 'You can let go a little if you put your mind to it. If you want something badly enough you work towards it—and I'll bet you're great with goals.'

'Is that why you're in here making up with me after our first real argument?'

'We didn't argue.'

'We did—we just did it *very quietly* this time. It's the silent ones do the most damage,' And she lowered her voice to a stage whisper as if it were some kind of secret or maybe in case someone somewhere heard her and proved her wrong later on by making a loud argument do the most damage.

It would happen in some version at some point and Ronan knew that, his voice rough with the knowledge. 'You can do it, you know—delegate more so you can travel to all the places you want to. Think about it.'

Kerry smiled a smile that tipped the lid off his sanity. 'I will.'

She was beautiful. In sunlight she glowed, when she laughed she lit up from inside—but in soft lamplight that made the sparkling in her eyes look like stardust she was breathtakingly beautiful. And that was *exactly* what she was doing to him: stealing his breath—making his lungs ache for its loss—his heart thundering so hard in his chest he could barely hear the sound of the train running over the tracks below them.

He suddenly couldn't speak.

Kerry searched his eyes for the longest time, the backs of her fine-boned fingers still resting softly against his thigh and her free hand lifting to frame his face as she smiled the softest, most sensual smile he'd ever seen.

But she didn't say anything.

Instead she let her hand gently turn his face before sliding over his jaw and round to the nape of his neck where she added enough pressure to close the gap between them—her chin lifting so she could press her full, soft, warm lips to his.

Need flashed through him like a firework exploding in the sky—the point of detonation dead centre in his chest and radiating outwards in a shower of burning sprinkles until his skin tingled from the scalp on top of his head to the very soles of his feet.

Dear God, how was he supposed to leave this woman? Give him strength.

'*Stay.*' The word was said against his lips.

Ronan was a weak man.

CHAPTER NINE

THE woman who'd left Ireland wasn't the same one who'd return. Kerry smiled at the thought.

The train travelled north where they disembarked for a private visit to a Hunter Valley vineyard and cellar in Australia's wine-growing region—Kerry still drunk enough from the memories of a night with Ronan to not feel any great effects from the wine-tasting. Then they made their way towards Brisbane—spending a day and a half exploring the city and two nights exploring each other. And on the fifth day they stayed on the train while it passed through the scenery of rural Queensland—laughing over lunch, kissing on the observation deck of one of the carriages, retiring early to their cabin; *theirs* because the other one had become a tad redundant…

Day six was a wondrous adventure to discover the Great Barrier Reef—they were flown onto a private pontoon to swim, snorkel and discover yet more amazing marine life, Ronan then ordering fish for lunch just to tease out her sense of moral outrage at him eating something they'd spent all morning admiring.

'How could you?' She laughed. *'Murderer.'*

And before the trip ended they ascended the scenic MacAlister Range to Kuranda to take a breathtaking cable-car ride above the rainforest treetops where Kerry got so emotional about the beauty of it she almost wept.

'Oh, no, you don't.' Ronan drew her into his arms. 'We talked about this in Fiji…'

So she tried to explain 'happy tears' to him between the kisses he plied her with to 'make her feel better'. But he said he wasn't buying that—and continued making his point about feeling better with admirable displays of diligence and attention to detail in their cabin practically the whole way back to Sydney…

Kerry had left home with a starry-eyed dream of seeing the world and was approaching the homeward journey feeling a bit as if she'd had it handed to her.

It was just that simple.

But she still hadn't said the words. Thing was, even at her age, she'd never once been in a situation where her heart and soul were on the line—not to the same extent as they were now. She was so very, very happy but she knew the universe had an unerring habit of balancing the good things with equal measures of bad.

Loving Ronan the way she did, it therefore followed that the balance of life could very well break her into billions of irreparable pieces if she had to give him up. But she had spent too much of her life being cautious to hold anything back now.

When he would look at her with so much quiet intensity, touch her every chance he got, smile at her with so much warmth, it convinced her she was cared for in return. That if they could just find the courage to take a chance they might find a way to make it work.

'I hope whatever it is you went to get was worth the embarrassment of almost single-handedly demolishing that poor man's shop displays.' She smiled impishly at him from the bench she'd been ordered not to leave 'til he got back.

Ronan frowned. 'I thought we agreed no peeking?'

'The crashing sound followed by lots of shouting in Chinese kinda caught my attention.'

He plunked himself down on the bench beside her, tossing a bag onto her lap with a dramatic sigh. 'See, that's what I get for trying to do something nice. Did it ever occur to you, young lady, that part of the reason I don't do it more often is 'cos you're so un-flipping-appreciative of my efforts?'

Kerry spluttered. 'I think you'll find I've been nothing *but* appreciative of your *many* efforts for quite some time now. Do I need to up my game?'

Absent-mindedly scratching his chest, Ronan studied the orderly chaos of Hong Kong around them: clanging trams festooned with unfathomable Chinese advertisements, buses careering round corners and parting scurrying crowds. 'If you up your game any I think you might kill me.'

He flashed a devilishly sexy smile and Kerry grinned in return. Lord, but she had it bad.

A nod was aimed at the bag. 'Go on, then.'

Any notion she might have had about teasing him again died an immediate death when she looked in it; wide eyes blinking with surprise while a lump of emotion clogged her throat.

When she didn't speak he leaned forwards to study her face. 'Wrong type of stuff?'

Kerry shook her head, her lower lip trembling. 'No.'

He lifted his hand to tug on the end of her pony-tail, his deep voice threaded with the gentleness that always made her heart shift. 'Figured you could make some souvenirs of your own so you don't go mental with the shopping again.'

Oh, he could try and make jokes about this one. But what he'd done was the most amazingly considerate, thoughtful, caring, romantic—

He had *no* idea how deeply it touched her.

'Tell me you're not about to cry?' With a low chuckle he jerked his brows. 'Didn't we have this discussion above a rainforest? Don't make me use the same tactic all over again now.'

She almost choked letting a burst of laughter out, because

if that'd been meant as a threat it was hardly likely to be effective, was it?

'I love that you thought of this.'

He shrugged it off. 'Paint me something pretty to keep when we're done and we'll be even.'

'When we're done'. The flash of pain when he said the words so calmly was swift. He had a tendency to drop them into conversation at random. Never seeming to see the damage they did.

But, Kerry being Kerry, she did what she always did when he inadvertently reminded her they still hadn't talked about the possibility of seeing each other when the trip was over. She tried to get closer; it was a knee-jerk reaction.

Setting the bag of art material to one side, she climbed over onto his lap—his hands automatically rising to her waist and the sound of a familiar deep chuckle vibrating between them before she silenced him with a long, slow kiss. His large hands flexed tighter, he hummed against her lips and Kerry smiled inside, threading her fingers into his short hair.

Then she rained kisses all over his gorgeous face.

Ronan laughed throatily. 'Would you quit it, woman? You'll wear me out before we get to Dubai.'

But when she kissed him again he didn't protest, instead making a pretty good job of wearing *her* out by kissing her back until she saw stars behind her eyes. Only when she was breathless and languid and lying across his lap with her head on his shoulder and his arm for support did he reach for the bag again and drop it on her, planting a kiss on her forehead before hoisting her up and setting her on her feet.

'I think you should paint me a temple first.'

Kerry held the top edge of the bag in both hands, a small frown on her face. 'It's been a long time since—'

'You'll be rusty, that's all.' He stopped in the middle of the crowd, hands back on her waist to haul her in closer before he bent his knees and ducked down to look up into her eyes. 'You should never give up your dreams, Kerry, Kerry Doyle— you hear? Just because your life changes doesn't mean you give everything else up.'

For someone who didn't want her to cry, he always seemed to do a good job of saying things that choked her up. 'I couldn't paint.'

'You said your tutors said you weren't that bad.'

Kerry hit him in the chest with the bag. 'No, you idiot, not I couldn't as in I was no good—I *couldn't*.'

'Why?'

She shrugged one shoulder.

But that combined with the way she couldn't look him in the eye was enough for Ronan to want to know more, standing tall, his hands lifting from her waist to frame her face before he used the pads of his thumbs below her chin to tilt her head up so he could look her in the eye.

'Tell me.'

When he used the soft tone that always seemed to work best on her, she smiled the smile that always hit him dead centre in his chest. 'You're doing that thing you do again.'

'Which thing?' He puffed his chest out. 'I have a wide and varied repertoire.'

'Oh, I *know*.' She laid the bag against his chest and leaned on it, her eyes darkening and her voice huskily low so he knew her thoughts had just gone exactly where his had. 'You're wheedling information out of me by being sweet and gentle.'

Ronan snorted in disgust. 'Sweet and gentle? What are you trying to do to my reputation?'

Dropping her head towards her shoulder, her pony-tail swinging against his fingers, she quirked her brows. 'I know—the truth hurts.'

Damn but she was amazing. Even when insulting him.

He kissed her as a sweet rebuke, only stopping when she

was leaning into him as if her legs couldn't hold her up. And he loved that he could do that to her, so he smiled.

'Tell me.'

She took a deep breath, her chin dropping so that she was directing her words at the open collar of his shirt. 'I just couldn't. When I painted I was happy. And it just felt wrong, even for a moment, to feel that happy and—I don't know— content, I guess, when everyone else was so lost in grief.'

'So you put all your energy into helping them instead. And buried how you felt while doing it, right?'

She aimed a wry smile at his throat. 'Sometimes it astounds me that you can do that.'

'Do what?'

'Explain me so easily.'

It made him smile. Because he remembered how he'd felt his first day with her, a lifetime ago in New York, when he'd not 'got' her at all—and it had intrigued him. Getting to know Kerry was a gradual process—like peeling back the layers of an onion— and the more he learned and understood, the more he liked what he found. But that was a downward slide, wasn't it?

He just couldn't seem to stop himself from wanting to take that slide, though.

'You always put other people first.'

She frowned. 'You make it sound like a weakness.'

'It is. If you don't keep anything for yourself.' When a look of pain crossed her face—and, yes, he did notice, because she might think she hid them when they happened but she wasn't that good at it—he took a deep breath and tilted her chin back up. 'Which is why you should paint. Make time for it. If it makes you happy you shouldn't *not* do it—*promise me*.'

Kerry searched his eyes for the longest time. And when she did that it always frightened him because she was so very good at seeing inside him. She seemed to know the right moment to tease him, when to smile the soft smile that soothed his soul, when to crawl onto his lap and kiss him until he couldn't think about anything but the here and now…

But it made him fearful of her seeing the one thing he didn't want her to see. Actually, that was a lie—there was more than the one now.

Her voice was seduction personified. 'I promise.'

She looked at him with such intense warmth it was like looking directly into her heart—and that slayed him, tore him in half; half wanting to physically throw her away from him and deny what he saw there by roaring at her and saying things to make her hate him, and the other half wanting to haul her close and throw his head back so he could laugh manically at the sky with joy.

Swallowing down a tsunami of angry regret, he dropped his chin and sought her hand, tangling their fingers before tugging her through the crowd. 'C'mon—I'm sure I saw a temple somewhere.'

It wouldn't be that hard to find one. At every junction there was a different Hong Kong from the chaos they were currently standing in: tiny Taoist temples suffused with incense, plangent bells and beating gongs or an apron of grass where office workers were practising T'ai Chi. And frankly Ronan could do with finding that kind of peace somewhere else when the only time he seemed to truly feel it was when he looked into a pair of autumnal eyes…

He had to stop doing this—to both of them.

No amount of losing himself in the moment was going to change the future.

And if he hadn't felt that way in Hong Kong, then in Dubai he had a big enough reminder thrown straight at him to jerk him back into reality.

He should have known better. But it was what he got for allowing himself to feel so full of male pride at how Kerry reacted to everything he did and everywhere they went. And what was it they said about pride and falling over?

Purposefully he'd headed them for the Creek, the heart of 'old' Dubai. East of the major Jumeirah developments, it was a sea inlet where, between downtown high-rises, some of the area's more venerable traditions still survived—and Ronan had known instinctively Kerry would love it there. Because at the end of the day, the trip had long since been all about what Kerry would love best. He wanted to hand her the world on a silver platter and say, 'Here—it's yours—grab hold of it.'

As if he were handing on an imaginary baton…

And the way her face lit up with enthusiasm was reward enough. She could light up from inside the way she did for ever as far as he was concerned. It was how he planned on re-membering her when he let her go.

Along the wharves of the creek were multi-decked, wooden dhows that'd plied the Gulf for centuries—sailors' laundry flapping as the boats rocked gently at their moorings, the clothes tossed in the same breeze that waved Kerry's rich chestnut hair around her shoulders and into her eyes so that either she, or more often than not Ronan himself, was con-stantly reaching up and tucking it behind her ears.

Next up were walls of cargo they laid bets on the contents of—sacks of basmati rice, boxed electronic goods from Malaysia, fridges from China—while water taxis chugged past them to spirit workers across the water to where a mosque, a Hindu temple and a Sikh gurdwara stood side by side. And on both banks of the estuary, the sight of a grid of souks announcing Dubai's original *raison d'être* was enough of a reason for Kerry to laugh joyously at the combined sights, flinging her arms around his neck and kissing him until he finally admitted to himself she could very easily have been *his raison d'être*…in a different life…given the chance…

He did it again: got lost being with her, blocking out his reality.

The hint of what was to come should have been in the afternoon, when they wandered the narrow streets and covered walkways monopolized by gold, spices, saffron, heady perfume and countless textiles. Kerry marvelled—with the kind of blatant jealousy that made Ronan chuckle under his breath— as women veiled in black clutching expensive handbags peered into shop windows at enough varying wares to appeal to the professional shopper. So he in turn pointed out to her the men in white robes and classic checked headgear strolling, sitting and chatting without the least bit of interest in shopping...

'The world won't end if you don't shop,' he calmly informed her, stifling his need to laugh out loud at her expression.

To which she replied with an elbow in his ribs and a smirk, 'Economies will crash if I don't—trust me.'

But it was those narrow streets that proved his downfall. Because while wandering hand in hand with her he made the mistake of letting time get away from him. And even though at nightfall things came alive with neon signs vying with glittering jewels and the streets thronged with locals and foreigners from pretty much everywhere, the fact remained—*night fell*. So while, with a sickening jolt of realization, he'd known he'd made a serious mistake and had headed sharply back in the direction of the hotel—they'd already walked too far for him to do anything about it getting dark too fast.

He was pretty much stuffed after that.

At first he could have put the constant bumping into people down to the fact the streets were so crowded, but every now and again they would hit a spot that wasn't so well lit up and when they did he froze, turning to try and find something he could latch onto to get him out of trouble—out of the terrible darkness he'd one day all too soon have to live in.

Kerry caught on the second time it happened. 'Are we lost?'

'Hmm?' He frowned hard, narrowing his eyes to try and find a lifeline. Wasn't as if he could tell her if they were, was it? And he'd tell her what was really wrong and ask for her help over his cold, rotting corpse. The steward on the train had been bad enough. But to ask Kerry to be some kind of two-legged guide dog? No chance!

Stupid, stupid, STUPID mistake. He should have paid more attention; shouldn't have let himself get sucked into a bubble of make-believe with her. She'd *made* him forget. And now he was in danger of literally falling flat on his face and ending up looking like the biggest loser of all time.

She laughed and he felt her step closer to his side. 'We're lost, aren't we?'

Fighting down a wave of the kind of frustration he was still fairly new at trying to master, he turned his face to her voice, racking every inch of his brain for a solution. 'Have I ever got us lost, woman?'

'They say there's a first time for everything…'

Ronan's heart was now thundering in his chest and in his ears—which was a pain in the behind when he needed to be able to hear. *Don't panic, Ronan—deep breaths—keep smiling—find something to aim for.* That was the plan so far. And at least with her hand held in his he only had the one arm to keep from doing something really pathetic like wavering out in front of his body. God, how much he *hated this*.

And now she was chuckling.

Damping down the need to rage at her for something that wasn't her fault, he gritted his teeth and threw out an option. 'Okay, then—you're such a well-seasoned traveller now, you get us back to the hotel. I'll let you lead the way.'

'Oh, my—the *pressure*…'

'Yup—and I have that much faith in my training I'm even going to close my eyes 'til we get there.'

'So you're *completely* in my hands, are you?'

'Let's even that up some, shall we?' Using the hand he held, he tugged her towards him, moving the backs of his fingers until he got his bearings so he could place both hands on her waist. And the sound of her husky laughter while he closed his eyes and made a game out of running his hands over her body was enough to give him faith in the fact he was getting away with it—in more ways than one.

He turned her round, wrapped his arms around her waist and lowered his head to her hair—breathing a deep breath of her amazing scent before placing his cheek against her ear to grumble, 'Now—back to the hotel so I can be completely in your hands *properly*.'

Her hands lifted to lie on his at her waist as she started walking. 'Still incorrigible, you know.'

And a genius.

Because not only had he just got himself out of the danger zone, he had her in his arms and was able to nuzzle her neck and mumble in her ear at the same time.

'You love that I'm incorrigible.'

Kerry laughed again, guiding them through the crowd. 'I kinda do.'

'What can I say? I'm a lovable kinda guy.'

'You have your moments.'

'I'm the best travel guide you've ever had—*face it*.' He managed to get his thumbs under the edge of her cotton top, smoothing over warm, soft skin above the waistband of her linen trousers.

'You're the *only* travel guide I've ever had—and you *know that*.' She mirrored the movements of his thumbs on the backs of his hands, her voice full of a smile when she moved to one side and he stumbled. 'You still have your eyes closed, don't you, you idiot?'

'I do.' He took a deep breath of Kerry-scented air and opened his eyes. 'Can't see a thing.'

Nothing. Just blackness; that all-engulfing fall down a bottomless hole into nothingness—and he wasn't somewhere where he knew how many steps to count to get to somewhere, which meant it was tough to damp down the rising bubble of panic in his stomach that made him nauseous. And it was that natural need to panic that did his head in most, because it was a sign of fear. It led him to think about the awful sense of loneliness he'd felt the first time he'd ignored the deep-seated need to switch on every light he could find, instead forcing himself to sit in the dark, facing his fear—facing his future. Then he'd gone through the inevitable stage of chasing every option there might be in the known universe, no matter where or what the cost was or how experimental. And now he was at the end of the line.

He couldn't hide from it, couldn't outrun it. Couldn't play let's pretend with Kerry for ever…no matter how much he wanted to…

'You're still insane…'

Breathing deep to ease the pain in his chest, he played along. 'Insanity is a large part of my charm. That's why dozens of women chat me up on planes and end up falling for the "let me give you the world" line…'

Her shoulders shook against his chest. 'If I *had* fallen for that line women all over the planet would be making feminist pilgrimages to my house to beat me to death. That's not what I fell for.'

The words were immediately followed by a tensing in her slight frame and Ronan felt it, frowning hard in response. He was officially an ass. Leading her down a path where he might trick her into saying the words he'd have wanted to hear more than anything else in another life was cruel. Hell, she might not even feel them. And if he hadn't been so selfish he wouldn't have wanted her to. But he did.

God, how much he wanted he wanted to hear them.

When his chest constricted enough to cause him actual physical pain, he tightened his arms around her waist—as if subliminally trying to hold on, frowning all the harder when he realized what he'd done. Enough was enough. And this little reminder had been sent to tell him that.

So he dug down deep inside for the words to start pushing her away. He'd managed a few before but they'd been half-hearted efforts. It was time to up his game.

'Well, then, I'd better think up a new line for the next woman who chats me up on a plane, hadn't I? Now that I know how much fun it can be playing tour guide it seems a shame not to do it again. I might try for a blonde next time, though—you know, for variety…'

He felt the sharp intake of breath through the arms around her waist, inwardly cursing the universe when he closed his eyes again.

'A girl on every continent, huh?'

Credit where credit was due—she managed to keep her voice light—and it wasn't as if he could see the flash of pain in her eyes or whispering over her face.

It was the first time he'd ever been thankful for that kind of blessing in disguise.

'Suits the lifestyle of a rolling stone, don't you think?' And if she even for one second thought about suggesting she fill the post of 'Irish-girl-for-every-continent' she'd give him the perfect opportunity to start a massive row. If any man *dared* treat Kerry like that Ronan would—

Would what? He couldn't have it both ways, could he? But it would be an icy day in hell when he'd let her sell herself short like that.

'No home and hearth for Ronan Indiana Jones O'Keefe in this lifetime, then, I take it?'

He hesitated on an answer, took time to swallow down the bitter burst of laughter generated by her cool words. For a moment he allowed himself to look down into the dark pit of his soul that was filled with raw emotion and self-pity.

Residual bitterness laced his voice as a result. 'May as well just put me in a box.'

Kerry Doyle was the right woman in the right place at the wrong time, he told himself. That was all. *And it killed him.*

He forced a smile onto his face. 'Are we there yet?'

'If you start asking me that every five minutes, Ronan, I swear—'

'Are we there yet?'

CHAPTER TEN

PARIS in the autumn. It was an amazing way to end their trip—would have been nigh on perfect if it hadn't included the word 'end'.

And the fact they hadn't even broached the subject of seeing each other ever again was making Kerry ache every single second of every day. Since Dubai it had mushroomed until it felt like a cloud constantly hanging over her head. And Ronan had been dropping more and more of his deeply hurtful, supposed-to-be-flippant statements out into the air since Dubai too, which didn't exactly give her the confidence to search for a possible solution.

Thing was, for every one of the things he said that she found painful, he did a half-dozen things that made her believe he cared for her more than he was letting on. When he'd talked about other women he'd held onto her so tightly it was as if he never wanted to let go. When he'd talk about any future trips she could take alone he'd spent a long time making quite sure she wouldn't visit anywhere she might be placed in harm's way—with ad-libbed warnings about talking to 'handsome strangers' on planes or anywhere else for that matter, as if the idea would bug him even when he wasn't there. And then there was the way he would make love to her…

Making her believe she was deeply loved, as if she was

the most precious woman in the world; one he would never, ever tire of.

How could he do that if he didn't care?

When she'd told him she had to be at the Jardin du Luxembourg on the fifth because she'd made a promise to Nana, he'd booked them into a hotel in the traditionally intellectual heart of the city. And, like everywhere he'd ever taken her, it was perfect. South of Île de la Cité—she could almost feel the ghosts of long-ago writers, philosophers and jazz legends haunting the cafés and nightspots all around them.

And then, to add to the list of positive signs Kerry was almost desperately forming, he took her straight to the Musée d'Orsay—reputedly one of the best spaces to enjoy art in the world. The building itself was enough to convince Kerry—it was a light-filled work of iron, glass and moulded plaster with windows fit for a cathedral, barring the lack of coloured glass. It was gorgeous, the bright light lifting her spirits and letting her dare to hope for a solution again.

And Kerry loved that he was so keen to make sure she renewed her interest in art. Heaven knew he'd sat over her shoulder enough times when she'd started painting again in Hong Kong, until she'd finally given up and admitted she couldn't concentrate with him being there—for *varying* reasons. But he'd always wanted to see what she'd done, had been impressed just the right amount for her to know he'd genuinely meant it and, after spending many an hour patiently tapping away on his laptop or reading while she'd sketched and painted, he'd taken a lot of time choosing which ones he wanted to keep.

Would he really have done that if he hadn't cared?

They spent the entire morning meandering through the galleries distributed on either side of the central nave, paying special attention to a collection of impressionist and post-impressionist paintings by the greats. Monet, Degas, Renoir,

Cézanne, Van Gogh, Gauguin, Seurat, Pissarro… The names were never-ending. It really couldn't get much better, except there was a 'something'—something just not quite *right*.

Then it hit her. It was how Ronan was studying things.

She didn't know what it was about the way he looked at everything but it was somehow—odd—to her after a while; a little *too* intense, maybe? Not that she didn't appreciate him trying to make the effort for her, but there was just… *something*…

Near the end of the impressionist paintings she caught him pinching then rubbing the bridge of his nose between his thumb and forefinger.

'Headache?' Well, that would make sense of it.

Ronan turned his head to look at her, blinking a couple of times as her question sank in. 'No, why?'

'You're pinching your nose the way people do when they have a headache.'

The smile took a split second to land on the sinful mouth she loved so much. 'I'm not used to staring at these things, is all. They're starting to blur together.'

Kerry would have bought that if there hadn't been that split second of hesitation before he smiled. She was a connoisseur of his smiles, after all. And of the varying sexy, slow, lazy, cheeky or even bemused smiles he had—not one of them had ever been hesitant about making an appearance.

She narrowed her eyes and studied him.

Ronan frowned, then stepped forwards and took her elbow. 'Well, I don't know about you but all this art appreciation has my stomach rumbling.'

When she resisted the gentle tug he looked down at her, his brows sliding up a quarter-inch in question. But when she tilted her head and studied each of his stunning eyes in turn he frowned harder.

'What?'

'Are you sure you're okay?' Her mind found another viable reason for what it might be. 'You really didn't have to spend all morning wandering round here if it's not your cup of tea, you know. I'd have been happy wherever we went. Aren't I always?'

'I thought you'd enjoy it.' He shrugged.

She smiled. 'I have.'

'Well, then.'

The second time he tugged she followed. But when he turned he practically knocked over a tourist with a video camera. Immediately releasing her elbow, he caught the small woman's arms to stop her from falling.

'Excusez moi, mademoiselle.'

One of his patented smiles was enough to earn forgiveness—and the immediate arrival of a man who proved the woman was a 'madame' rather than a 'mademoiselle'. And then Ronan stood tall, turning his head before a slow smile appeared as he reached for Kerry again.

'Low blood sugar. Need. Food. Now.'

Kerry smiled as she shook her head, but the whole way down the stairs with her hand grasped firmly in his she couldn't help but feel the oppressive weight of the 'something not quite right' sitting on her shoulders. And it made her stare all the harder at him, which in turn led her to notice things she hadn't noticed before.

Such as how he was constantly turning his head to look around him.

It had always been one of the things she loved about him—the way he would take everything in. She'd known from the beginning that he was highly intelligent and if his quick wit hadn't hinted at it then his vast stored knowledge of everywhere they went would. So she'd always put his quiet intensity down to intelligence. But something wasn't right.

What was it?

'Do you want anything from the gift shop?'

And now he was inviting her to shop? There was something very wrong.

'I might get some postcards of the paintings we saw.' She pursed her lips and pushed to see just how distracted he was by whatever it was. 'Maybe some T-shirts or a framed print or any history of art books they have that look any good…'

'Okay.' He turned his head and studied the shop for a second, releasing her elbow. 'I'm gonna get some fresh air—I'll meet you by the river.'

'Okay.' But she didn't move, her feet rooted to the floor while she watched his tall frame striding with familiar confident ease along the brightly lit arched thoroughfare and out the doors into bright sunshine.

And she still didn't move.

Lifting her hands to her jean-clad hips, she blinked hard as she focussed on a random spot in the middle of the glorious windows curving up into the ceiling, trying to force her brain to remember any other times when he'd done anything that might have been considered 'odd' if she hadn't been so distracted by other things. That was the problem, though—he'd been thoroughly distracting from the very beginning. And that, coupled with the many amazing places they'd been to and the cornucopia of emotions that battled and then blossomed as their journey progressed, had been more than enough to keep her mind occupied.

Maybe she was overreacting? So desperate to grab at straws that might indicate he cared anywhere near as much as she did, so aware of the sand slipping inexorably through the hourglass measuring their time together…

She shook her head, inwardly berating herself for being plain old daft. The man had a headache and was being a baby about it—full stop.

* * *

Ronan watched the water lapping against the banks of the Seine, then tipped his head back to look up at the bright blue sky above him, filling his lungs with crisp air to try and clear his head. He had the headache from hell. Though why he couldn't have just said that to Kerry he had no idea—male pride, no doubt—but had he really got that touchy about any sign of weakness? How pathetic did that make him?

And then he'd practically steamrollered over some poor unsuspecting tourist. *In front of Kerry.*

Maybe it was just as well they were almost done.

Even if every cell in his body felt as if it were shrivelling up and dying at the very thought of it.

Instead of standing feeling sorry for himself he should really have a think about how exactly he was going to distance himself from her over the next few days. Because so far any of the ideas he'd had had turned his stomach. Flirting with another woman under her nose would be plain low and he didn't think he could do it with any great level of conviction anyway. Picking a fight was an option, but then that meant he'd have to stand there looking into her eyes and seeing the very second he started hurting her. And he knew he'd have a difficult job not giving in to the need to make it better if that happened.

That left physically distancing himself some more. He could suggest splitting up for the afternoon—that would be a start. And there were a few people he could drop in on and tick off his list. He just needed to make sure there wasn't the tiniest sliver of a chance of Kerry talking about meeting up again in the future…

The sound of a boat engine got him to drop his chin long enough to watch as it went by—allowing himself to surrender to an overwhelming sense of emptiness as he did. And then he had a go at seeing how much he could see on the opposite river bank while he rehearsed what he'd say in his head—each word already tasting like acid on the back of his tongue.

Kerry smiled when she saw him. There was just something about the sight of a gorgeous male on an autumn day standing by the banks of the Seine with the wind catching the edge of his chocolate cord jacket and a frame of chestnuts, poplars and maples in hundreds of shades fit for the paintings they'd spent a morning looking at over his head, leaves billowing down and scattering at his feet...

She moved the box of headache tablets she'd found in the bottom of her bag end over end in her hand as she approached him. And was less than twenty yards away when she slowed down.

Random memories suddenly flashed into her head in such a jumble it took a second for her to try and sort through them. She was being daft again, wasn't she? So she shook her head yet again and stepped forwards—her gaze locked on Ronan's profile.

Lifting a hand, she waved at him.

A couple of steps closer and for no reason in the world she could feel a lump forming in her throat. He was still staring straight ahead, so she looked to see what it was that had his attention so fully he wasn't catching a glimpse of her from his peripheral vision. She had on a long bright red sweater, after all, so you'd have thought he'd have noticed...

A couple of feet away, steps faltering, she held her breath, waved again—and still got nothing. Completely out of the blue it made her think about the time she'd waved like an idiot at him in front of the Empire State Building and he hadn't noticed then either...

He turned his face towards her and smiled. 'Creeping up on me to go "boo", were we? I didn't see you.'

And just like that, instinctively, she knew. With a throw-away phrase millions of people all over the world probably used every day, Kerry's female intuition kicked in and she *knew*. Knew but didn't want to know—every part of her willing it not to be.

'You didn't see me.'

Ronan frowned at the monotone in her voice, stepping forwards when he saw what must have been written all over her face. 'What's wrong?'

Kerry stared back at him, her chin lifting as he closed the last of the gap. 'You couldn't see me. Because you have no peripheral vision, do you?'

From the very beginning he'd never once looked sideways at her, had he? He always turned his head or moved his upper body—and then there were all the times he'd bumped into things…

He let out a huff of air that made a feeble attempt at being laughter, and she could practically see the lies formulating. 'Where did that come from?'

Not lies, then—she'd been wrong about that. Not the truth or an answer—but *not a denial*. Damn her stupid intuition. And the 'something not quite right' was sitting so heavily on her chest she could barely breathe while her mind filled in some of the clues: elbowing her on the plane, jostling people in crowds in New York, the displays he'd knocked over in Hong Kong and the tiny woman he'd almost flattened not that long ago when he'd turned too fast.

Ronan was holding himself taller, was breathing a little faster, smiling a smile that didn't make it up into his eyes, his stunning, beautiful eyes—the eyes that had been the first thing she'd fallen for.

'You have no peripheral vision.' She said it again so he'd know she knew. And maybe because she needed to repeat things to make her heart believe them when it ached not to. 'How bad is it? How much can you—'

Oh, dear God. Her mouth went dry as she pieced together a little more, her breathing now a series of short, sharp breaths that put her about two minutes away from the very first panic attack of her life.

'*Dubai*—' She choked on the word and had to clear her throat before trying again, her eyes misting. 'In Dubai…you couldn't…that night…you couldn't…'

'Kerry—'

No, she had to keep going now she'd started; she had to know all of it. 'You c-couldn't see in the dark, could you? You made it…into a game…but—'

'*Stop.*'

His whole expression changed, his face literally darkening. He was angry she'd figured it out? He hadn't intended to tell her, had he? All that time he'd been fighting the need to kiss her, to want her—particularly in Fiji—it was because he didn't want to take a chance on her finding out. Whereas in New York that first time it hadn't mattered, because there was no chance of her figuring it out in one day…

It killed her.

'You couldn't *see*, could you?'

He shifted his weight from one foot to the other, frowning harder, a muscle in his jaw clenched and then finally she got a calm, completely monotone, 'No.'

How had she not known? Why hadn't she caught it? All those times they'd had dinner in well-lit streets and restaurants, all the times he'd arranged morning flights so they went to sleep early. But in Dubai he'd made a mistake, hadn't he? After being so careful to hide it for so long he must have lost track of time; darkness had crept in and he'd held her hand tighter and walked faster to try to get to somewhere he could hide it from her again. And when they'd walked out of any light—he'd stopped and turned round and—and she'd thought he was *lost*. She felt as if she'd been hit by a bus.

He'd been so *devious*. 'Night blindness.'

'Yes.'

'And in the daylight?'

'Tunnel vision.'

He was so deathly calm, so matter-of-fact, while Kerry couldn't breathe any more, she genuinely couldn't. And she was suddenly cold—the shivering starting deep inside and radiating out until she could feel it in her bones and her teeth threatened to chatter.

Ronan reached his hands up but she automatically stepped back—because if he held her she'd crumble.

His voice was full of barely suppressed anger at the small movement. 'Quit it, Kerry. I mean it—you're working yourself up into a state over—'

'Nothing?' She laughed a little hysterically. 'Don't you dare say it's nothing! How bad is it?'

'Kerry—'

'How bad?' Her voice cracked on the words one octave away from being yelled at him.

And the simple answer broke her.

'Progressive.'

She literally folded, bending a little at the waist to try and get her breathing under control as a low moan escaped her lips. *Not him.* Not Ronan. He spent his life seeing all those wondrous places—travelling the world and collecting a million moments he could store in his memory. *Seeing them was his life.* And he was losing that? *No!* She wanted to wail at the unfairness of it.

All the places he'd shown her; places so magical and wonderful and beautiful and he wouldn't be able to see them again? How could he stand it? How could he be so calm about it? How——

'Come on.' His large hands grasped hold of her arms to draw her forwards, voice back to a low monotone again. 'Let's sit you down. And you know how I feel about crying, so you need to stop.'

'Don't cry—not because of me—you hear?' Words said to her in the dark when he'd held her in his arms in the four-poster bed that first time she'd cried. *Not because of him* he'd said. He'd told her he could see her in the dark; had traced her face with his fingertips as if he was memorizing her.

She was dying inside.

And when she lifted her chin to look at him she didn't make any attempt to hide the tears streaming down her face. So many signs all along the way and she'd missed every single one of them.

Ronan took one look at her and swore viciously under his breath, his fingers tightening. 'This is *exactly* why I wasn't ever telling you. I won't have you looking at me like I'm a flipping injured puppy! And I sure won't have you doing this in front of me. You think I *need* this from you?'

'You can't tell me not to be upset about this, Ronan—how can I *not* be? It's *you*.' She tugged her arms free so she could swipe angrily at her cheeks. 'Your whole life revolves around seeing things. How can you—?'

She froze when another piece of the puzzle dropped into place, her gaze locking on a pulse beating in the tight line of his neck and then rising, slowly, until she was looking into the eyes she loved.

'You've been saying goodbye to everyone, haven't you? All those people you've met up with everywhere we've been—*dear God*.' She swallowed hard. 'Frank and Abbie. That's why they were so upset—they *know*. They walked us down the beach every night so I wouldn't know you couldn't see in the dark, didn't they? And you wouldn't throw your garland out the—you wouldn't because you *knew*—'

He knew he wasn't going back? And he'd let her throw hers out the window and they'd watched together as it floated back to shore. She felt so betrayed; as if she'd been the last one on the planet to know. They'd *all* kept it from her.

The moan building inside her made her wrap her arms around her waist to hold it in while the tears formed heated rivers on her cheeks.

'*And me.* This trip with me.' She flung a listless arm out to one side and returned it to her waist, her gaze dropping to the base of his throat again because it hurt too much to look in his eyes while she laid it all out. 'You're what? *Grooming me?* All those times we've talked about places you think I should see—all the places you took me to—to make me fall in love with travelling. And the travelling light lesson and the virgin traveller learning from the pro…'

A sob broke free. 'Talking to me…about *delegating*. So I could make more time to travel.'

When she'd thought at the time he might have been hinting if she made more time they might be able to travel together again…

'*Just because your life changes doesn't mean you give everything else up.*' That was what he'd said to her about her painting that day.

But all along he'd been handing some kind of imaginary baton on to her while he said goodbye to all the friends he'd made over the years, because he—

Because he was locking *everyone* out?

Her eyes rose. 'This is your last trip.'

After he'd said *that* to *her*? He was going to what, then? Relegate himself to half a life? Shut the world out and go home and never see any of the friends he'd made again? He thought because he wouldn't be able to see their faces it meant he should never visit them again? Didn't he know how much his friends loved him? She'd seen him with Frank and Abbie, for crying out loud! How could he think that they'd never want to see him again? How could he lock himself away?

'May as well just put me in a box.'

She sobbed again. Damn it—*he'd said that himself!* How could such an intelligent man be so incredibly dumb? How? And he'd said it with so much derision in his voice she'd believed he was telling her it was a fate worse than death to be at home in Ireland. She'd thought he was telling her that someone like him would never settle down—that she shouldn't think he might want to be tied down by her in any way. And he'd been dropping all those things into conversations ever since—pushing her away, little by little. She'd thought it was because he didn't care as much as she did.

No, that wasn't right. She'd made a complete fool of herself by making a pass at him only to be turned down, and then she'd thought he didn't want her the same way she wanted him, *and then* she'd thought he didn't care as much as she did! She'd even believed for a little while that he might be fighting his feelings…

She'd been *half right*, hadn't she? He'd been fighting, all right—fighting his way through all the lies he felt he had to tell her because he wasn't prepared to let her *choose* for herself.

How dared he?

Dragging a ragged breath into her aching lungs, she forced her blurred gaze to lock with his. 'You've lied to me every step of the way since the very day we met. How could y—?'

'What the hell was I supposed to do? Shake your hand and say, "Hi, I'm Ronan and in a few years I'll be blind"? Now there's a chat-up line! I should carry a tin for money and rattle it under people's noses, should I?'

Raising his voice wasn't one of his better moves, even if the bitterness in his words was like a blunt knife forced into her aching chest. 'Of course I'm not suggesting that! But you took the choice from me—how can you not know that? It's what you've done all along—with *everything*! Like I'm some weak, defenceless female who can't handle anything—is that how you *see me*?'

He roared down at her. 'Yes, because you're taking the news so well right now, aren't you?'

'I'm not taking it well right now because you've *hidden this from me*!' How could he be this stupid?

'Stop it!' The dangerous level of white-hot fury told her just how much he'd been holding inside. 'What did you expect me to do, Kerry? You're a giver—you've given everything up for other people your whole life! I'm not adding my name to the list—*full stop*. I'm no one's sympathy case!'

Her voice rose in reaction to his. 'And you've seen that as my weakness all along, haven't you? Well, let me tell you something, Ronan O'Keefe—you don't know me anywhere near as well as you think you do! Because I *am* the strong one in my family—I'm the one that holds it all together— I'm the one that's there when the rest of them need support or advice or someone to take the weight when they have problems elsewhere. And if you think some weak, pathetic female can do all that, then you're even more of an idiot than you are for thinking you can just go lock yourself in a room and stagnate. You'll go insane and you know fine well you will!'

'You don't know anything about the plans I've made.'

She laughed, but it was still laced with anger. 'I know whatever they are they involve you making some of the most universally stupid decisions ever made!'

'Like letting you be the strong one for me and making you give up even more of your own dreams to do it, you mean?' He stepped forwards, his eyes flashing. 'You may have been the strong one for your family, Kerry—but it came at a cost, didn't it? And now I'm supposed to roll over and play dead while you do the same thing for me?'

Kerry lifted her chin. 'It was my choice to make. And that's the one thing you've not given me: *a choice*. If you care even the least little bit about me, then you'd want me to have what I want.'

'Haven't I wanted to give you everything you want the whole way through this?'

'Including *you?*' Her eyes widened in amazement. 'You gave yourself to me *for me,* did you? The poor woman who needed a holiday affair to liven up her sad life?'

Ronan looked as if he were about to explode. 'I gave in because I couldn't stop myself from wanting you more than I've ever wanted anyone or anything my entire life!'

'But not enough to trust me.' She shook her head and looked back at the river, unable to believe what he was saying to her. Her heart still thundering, she looked way down deep inside for the strength to force calmness into her voice. 'I had no idea you had so low an opinion of me.'

She glanced at him from the corner of her eye, just in time to see him rock right back on his heels, swearing enough to turn the air blue around them before he glared at her. 'This has *nothing* to do with *you!* I make my own choices—no one else does it for me.'

Despite how badly she was shaking, she managed to smile cruelly at him. 'Oh, yes, you've made that more than clear—thank you. This had *nothing* to do with me.'

He'd had no intention of letting her in from the beginning, had he? He wasn't letting anyone in. His own private hell; no room for anyone else—least of all a woman incapable of loving him enough to see him as more than just his ability to see.

Did he honestly think she'd have reacted like this if she hadn't loved him as much as she did?

Ronan was fighting to get control of himself, sucking in deep breaths of air, his hands on his hips, head tilted back, and after a long while his chin dropped and his gaze collided with hers. 'I can't hold two of us together through this. I'll have enough to adjust to.'

'You selfish son of a—'

The flat tone tugged hard on the thread he was holding onto his anger with. 'I'm *selfish* for not wanting you to give up your life to nursemaid me? Tell me exactly how that one works.'

'So you did this for me 'cos I'm the kind of woman who's not strong enough to love you for better or worse? Or you did it for you, 'cos I'm the kind of woman who might force herself to love you because she feels sorry for you? Either way I fall woefully short, don't I? You've decided I'm incapable of loving you because you're you, haven't you? I'm not allowed to look you in the eye and decide for myself if I want to spend the rest of my life with you no matter what life throws our way? How dare you decide what I can and can't feel? *How dare you?*'

With every sentence the tears were flowing hotter and faster and thicker down her cheeks. How could he think that? He really didn't care about her one iota as much as she'd grown to care for him.

And that was that. There was no more. The journey was over.

He didn't love her.

When he clenched his jaw, his hands hanging in fists by his side the way they had when she'd pushed him on the island, she stepped back—because she wasn't pushing any more. There was no point.

He stepped forwards.

'Don't come near me, Ronan.' She reached up and used her sleeves to swipe her cheeks dry, blankly noticing that she still had the headache tablets in her hand. Just as well, really—she was going to need them.

She couldn't bear to look at him again; it just hurt too much. So she turned on her heel and walked away. Not even thinking about whether or not he was following until a last thought occurred to her and she turned round with her chin held high as she walked back.

Ronan was standing statue-still, fierce, blistering anger radiating from him as she cleared her throat.

'One more thing: if our places were switched—if it was me that was losing my sight and you were in love with me—would you stay with me out of pity? Or would me loving you back have been enough?' She felt herself welling up all over again. 'Would you hate me if I pulled the stunt you just have? As much as I hate you right now? Because if you'd have given me the choice I wouldn't necessarily have chosen you, Ronan—but I might have picked *us*. For a while it felt like together we ruled the world. That's how it felt when there was an "us". But there never was an "us" was there?'

She laughed what felt distinctly like her last laugh; it didn't even sound that genuine to her own ears.

'You decided that and now we'll never know what I would have chosen. I take it back; I'm not glad I met you.' She nodded to confirm it as she turned away for the last time. 'I wish I never had.'

CHAPTER ELEVEN

IT TOOK a long time for Ronan to get past his anger enough to believe with any degree of conviction Kerry mightn't have meant some of the things she'd thrown at him; many of them which, with hindsight, he knew he'd deserved.

'I'm not glad I met you. I wish I never had.'

He knew *he* didn't feel that way. There was no way he would trade his time with Kerry. She'd been the best thing to happen to him in a long while; ever since he'd first started to notice the change in his vision during the day and had to admit it was finally happening. Since then he'd felt as if he were walking around with a hammer hanging over his head; being with Kerry had made him forget, at least for a while. With her, he'd been more alive—had smiled more, laughed more, wanted to pack even more into his days. She'd been like the sun to him. And he'd naturally turned towards that brightness while darkness was creeping in everywhere else. No, he wasn't the least little bit sorry he'd met her. But he was sorry he'd hurt her so badly and that she'd got so many things wrong when she was yelling at him…

But that didn't mean he'd shake off such firmly held convictions without putting up a fight.

So he walked while he thought—at first to shake off the

boiling anger, and then, when that gradually subsided, to go through everything she'd said. It was what Paris was meant for, after all. Well, that and the most obvious other thing, of course—which just rubbed salt in the wound when he was constantly surrounded by couples all happily in love.

What would he have done if she'd been in his shoes?

It had never once occurred to him to look at it that way. Why? He'd been so damn busy doing what he thought was the right thing, that was why. And she'd figured out every single little clue in the last ten odd weeks in the space of about half an hour—known exactly what he'd been doing—which just proved he'd been right all those times when he'd thought she could see inside him.

It was reassuring to know he could be right about *something*—because she'd taken every other thing that had made perfect sense to him up until a couple of hours ago and thrown it in the flipping river. *Women.* Whose idea was it to make them so intuitive? Seemed like an unfair advantage in the battle of the sexes to him.

And, yes, she was right—he had had to be devious. But what did she expect him to do? It wasn't as if he ran all over the world advertising his problems. Who did that anyway?

But she had no idea what she'd be taking on with him. Not just that he'd be reliant on her for more things than he would want to be, but that he'd not exactly be the easiest guy to live with when it happened. *He knew him.* There were going to be days when he'd be a bear and days when he'd be better left to wallow—not that he planned on allowing himself too much of the latter, mind you.

As to the locking himself in a room to stagnate… Like hell. He'd had years to think about how he'd live his new life when the old one was taken from him. And he'd made plans to stay as busy and active and productive as humanly possible—not as if he'd not still be *him*, was it? He'd just be a toned-down version.

But the way he'd looked at it, he'd already packed more into ten years than many people did into a lifetime.

'Grooming her' to take his place was an accusation pretty close to the mark, though. He might have to give a little on that. But she'd loved so many of the places he'd loved that it had made sense to him to pass on some of what he knew. And she had a world full of adventures ahead of her. Why wouldn't he want to encourage her to take them? So it therefore followed he'd try and help any way he could.

Maybe he'd not have to give all that much on that one, after all…

Mind you—he hadn't expected to have her turn it round so all of his reasoning came down to her being lacking in something in his eyes. *And selfish?* Selfish for not letting her in? It made him laugh; selfish had been wanting her as much as he had. How could she not see that?

Venus and Mars.

But he'd not had a chance to make any of those points or say any of those things to Kerry. Or so many other things that needed to be said. He just prayed she wouldn't get as upset as she'd been again. *Ever again.* It had been the worst experience of his life seeing her like that: so anguished—for him. *Broken*—and he'd been the one to break her. He'd watched the bright, beautiful, spirited, strong-willed, intelligent woman he loved crumble before his eyes. And he'd done that to her. He didn't know if he could ever forgive himself for that.

The only thing he knew for certain was he couldn't leave it the way it had been left. She wanted the right to choose. Then that meant he'd have to lay it all on the line for her. *All of it.*

No more lying—to her or to himself.

So after three hours of wandering he went looking for her. With no initial idea of where he'd find her, which frankly had panicked him a bit, until he remembered why they were in Paris in the first place. If she wasn't there he'd try the hotel, search the whole city if he had to and lay siege at the airport as a last resort.

Trouble was, the Jardin du Luxembourg wasn't exactly the size of someone's back garden. So when he would look back on it in the future he'd have to put it down to luck that he found her sitting on a metal chair by the Fontaine de Médicis, surrounded by hundreds of shades of autumn leaves in russets and browns and golds above her head, under her feet and reflected in the mirrored surface of the water—all the shades he loved in her eyes—and bright sunshine shining on her face; Kerry Doyle in her natural habitat.

She lifted her chin as he approached and he watched her while she watched him—the air of tension lying between them palpable even from twenty feet away. And the fact that the light seemed to have died inside her slayed him—it really did. *He'd done that.*

Her breasts rose and fell with a deep breath when he was closer, her voice holding the soft husky, edge that had always got to him most.

'What do you want, Ronan?'

'You knew I'd come find you.'

'Why would I know that?'

He frowned. How could she think he wouldn't?

'And sitting here looking back on everything I've started to see things more clearly. I get it all now. There's nothing else you need to say to me.'

'What exactly do you see more clearly?' He stood with his back to the ornate fencing and huge mounted concrete jardinières, not ready to pull up a chair beside her while he had a suspicion he might not like the answer to his question.

He was right.

'I was thinking about all the times way back at the beginning when you would take my elbow or hold my hand—like you did in New York. At the time I thought you did it because you liked touching me, but now I'm wondering if you just did it—'

Ronan clenched his teeth when he realized where she was going. 'Because I needed to rather than because I wanted to?'

Kerry simply looked up at him, her gaze tangling with his and a deep, empty sadness filling her eyes.

Ronan folded his arms across his chest before glowering down at her. 'Thanks for that—but it had more to do with the fact I haven't been able to stop touching you since the day we met. It's something I've never had any control over no matter how hard I tried.'

'Well, that's what I hoped once, but the longer I had to think about this now I know everything, the more time there is for paranoia to set in.' She shrugged and looked away from his face, the very visible lack of fight in her enough to make him want to shake her back to life. Having her yell had been better than this.

He clenched his jaw and took a breath, unable to take his eyes off her in case she disappeared again and he didn't get a second chance.

'I didn't plan for any of this to happen.'

She cocked a brow and looked at him from the corner of her eye. 'Oh, that's not true, now, is it?'

'I meant us. I didn't plan for an "us".'

'There isn't an "us".'

Ronan took a deep breath. 'Yes, there is. If there wasn't, would I be here?'

The confession didn't get her to look at him and it was

enough to make Ronan fearful that he'd already done too much damage. Though the fact she sat back a little and wrapped her arms around her middle was enough for him to hope she was holding her emotions inside—probably because she'd let so much out already, and maybe partly because he'd given her such a hard time about not being strong last time. When, actually, a sign of some emotion might have helped around about now…

He couldn't keep changing his mind, though, could he? 'I've known since I was a kid that one day I'd lose my sight— it's hereditary, carried down the female side to the male. Once it happens in your family a couple of times they know to look for it. My kids would all be able to see but my daughter's son's might not. And sometimes the boys will be blind when they're little, sometimes it happens later—I'm one of the lucky ones. My sisters are all carriers but thankfully so far they've only had girls.'

Kerry didn't say anything, didn't move.

So with a heartfelt sigh, Ronan stepped to the side, grabbing hold of a chair and dragging it over to sit, he rested his forearms on his knees and focussed on her profile, his tone still low.

'I was in New York to see a specialist. Knew it was a long shot, but had to try. And I have made plans for when I can't see any more and none of them involve me locking myself away in a room somewhere—just so you know. I planned on using this trip to see as many people as I could while I still can, but not because I don't plan on ever hearing their voices again.' His chest tightened when he saw the first tear streak silently down her cheek, her eyes still focussed on some random point straight ahead of her. 'I've made lots of plans because I knew I had to. I was prepared.'

Kerry's throat convulsed.

full of life, ~~~~ ~~~~ ~~~~ ~~~~
your own good, ~~~~ ~~~~ ~~~~
You set off to travel arou~~~~ the wo~~~~
that would make your nana ver~~~~
then at some point I won't hav~~~~ ~~~~ ~~~~ ~~~~ put to hold you
back from some of the adventures yo~~~~ ~~~~ ~~~~. And I couldn't
live with that. Especially not when I'v~~~~ ~~~~ken most of those
adventures myself. I know what you'd be missing out on.'

'But that's not your choice to make.'

At least it got a reaction, 'Maybe not.'

And that earned him a sideways glare. 'No maybe in it. I'm
the only one who gets to choose where I go to and when and
how and with who. Just because I've let you lead me around
the world doesn't mean I wouldn't have managed a version
of it on my own. I went with you because I *chose* to go with
you. That doesn't mean you'd get to tell me where and when
in the future.'

The very mention of the word 'future' was enough to give
him a little more hope. 'Okay.'

The one-word reply got her to look at him. And when she
did she frowned, rapidly swiping the two lonely tears off her
cheeks as she continued—as if by backing down on one thing
he'd opened a floodgate.

'You don't know me well enough to know what I can and
can't cope with. And even when you do, don't for one second

took another breath. …you'd be taking on with me. I—' …and I have more of an idea than you think I … rose. 'And you *really* need to stop telling me … and can't do.'

… smiled a small smile at that, forcing it away to continue, …was going to say I'm hard work. And the way I've been on this trip with you isn't how I always am—there are days when I don't do so well with this and—'

'I'm not the least bit surprised. I'd be angry at the world if it was me. And I'd wallow. And I'd be scared—not that I think you're likely to ever confess to that one. Though I'm probably not as much work as you can be, even on this trip—'cos you weren't always that easy, as it happens.' She almost smiled.

And it dragged a rueful smile onto his mouth. 'I tried not to complicate things, if you remember.'

'Not lying would have been one way of helping with that, don't you think?'

'It was a lie of omission—it wasn't ever meant to hurt you. Like I said, I wasn't prepared for a you…'

Kerry's shoulders relaxed a little, her gaze dropping to the usual spot at the base of his neck as she drew in another deep breath, her voice softening. 'I wasn't exactly prepared for a you either. But you could have told me, Ronan. I wish you'd believed in me.'

He waited until her lashes rose. 'I thought I was doing the right thing—for both of us.'

'You were wrong.'

'Well, duh.' He tried a warmer smile on for size, holding his breath until she smiled back at him. 'I finally understood that when you asked me what I'd have done if it was you in my shoes.'

The suggestion of light in Kerry's eyes made his chest tighten. 'And what would you have done?'

'Probably been just as angry at you as you were at me when I realized you'd hidden it…'

She quirked her brows in a way that simply said, *see*, and it was enough to get him to continue.

'And I wouldn't have let you go. Not ever.'

It took a second, a half-dozen different emotions clouding her eyes. And then the light switched on inside her, lighting her face and softening her eyes to a warm glow. 'You could just take a shot at telling me you love me, you know.'

'It wasn't as simple as that, there were—'

'Yes, it was, you idiot. It's exactly that simple. It's the only thing that really matters.'

Breathing evenly became a bit of an effort for him, his chin dropping and a frown appearing on his face as he tried to find the right words to make her understand.

'You still don't get it. It's not you that's the weak one here, Kerry—it's me, and I *hate* that,' He pursed his lips into a flat line and forced his chin back up. 'I'll need you more than you need me.'

Her voice was filled with infinite patience, 'Listen up, genius—if you think I don't need you every bit as much as you need me, then you're sorely mistaken. I *do* need you.'

'I love that you're as open and giving as you are, Kerry, it's just—'

Her eyes sparkled. 'Careful—you almost said it.'

The sigh was one of exasperation this time. 'Is there any chance of me getting to complete a sentence? I'm trying to explain here.'

'If you'd just tell me you love me then I could say I love you too and we'd be done. Then we could get to the good stuff.'

There was a long moment of silence when he paused for breath, her words swirling in around him like a blanket, muffling out the rest of the world until she was all there was—which left him floundering for more words when she leaned forwards and rested her forearms on her knees, her face close to his.

'You done now?'

Pretty much, but, 'I can't see you go through what you went through today. It was hell to watch.'

'I only went through that today because it was such a shock—I didn't see it coming. I missed all the signs. And, loving you as much as I do, the thought that you've felt the need to hide so much from me *killed me*. That's all.' And she'd said all of it in a calm, sweetly soft tone with only the faintest shimmering in her eyes—she even shrugged her shoulders at the end.

It almost made him believe her. 'So you're fine with it now, are you?'

'No, I'm not fine with it. What kind of a stupid question is that?' She scowled at him. 'I hate that this is happening to you. *I hate it.* But I can't stop it, can I? I'm assuming, knowing you, that if there was a way to fix it then you'd have found it.'

'It wouldn't be for want of trying, no.'

She nodded. 'Then there's nothing we can do.'

We. How could such a tiny word completely cripple him emotionally? He swallowed hard, dropping his gaze to her fine-boned hands and fighting the need to reach for them. 'And that's that, then—you won't break down on me again like you did today? 'Cos, seriously—you might be strong enough to go through it again, but I'm not so sure I can take it on a regular basis.'

Her hands reached across and took his, fingers tangling and

squeezing. 'Happy tears only. That's the best I can promise you. Though for the record—it would help lots if you never held anything back from me ever again and if I ever get upset over anything else you could just hold me and I'd feel better. Or you could kiss it better for me.'

Ronan's mouth twitched. 'Worked before.'

'It did. Almost worth squeezing a few tears out for…'

He chuckled, lifting his chin to look into her dancing eyes. '*Woman*…don't you *dare* play me…'

'You'd catch me on it if I did.'

'I would.'

'Okay.' With an impish smile and her face lit up with the inner glow he loved best, she wriggled further forwards on her chair until her knees hit his. 'I'm gonna throw some stuff in here before you start to work through any of the other feeble excuses you have for attempting to stop me choosing to be with you.'

'You've got remarkably confident for someone who'd convinced themselves they were being used as a guide dog not that long ago.'

'Blind jokes. *Funny*.' She scowled at him. 'And paranoia like that only set in 'cos I'd convinced myself you didn't love me—because if you had you'd have trusted me. Now I understand your twisted logic came partly from the fact that you *do* love me. And do you want to know why I'm so sure you do—apart from the obvious fact that you came looking for me to talk this through, that is?'

'I'm pretty sure you're going to tell me.'

He got a firm nod. 'You have to, you see, because I couldn't love you to the pit of my soul the way I do if you weren't the right one for me. And if you're the right one for me then you have no choice but to feel the same way back. That's how it works. I'm your one in six billion—you're mine. But you should know that already when you've been all over the entire planet and never bumped into me before now.'

There was a very Kerry sense of logic in there that made complete sense to him. Even if it was proof positive of what he'd known for a long time. 'I'm still standing by the fact you're more than a little crazy.'

An arched brow quirked. 'Our fathers play golf together, for crying out loud. If we weren't meant to meet when we did, then don't you think we'd have at least *known* about each other before?'

Actually he didn't have an answer for that one.

'That's what I thought too. This was meant to happen. You just messed up the great scheme of things by not believing in it. Whereas I was the one racking her brain for weeks trying to find a way to make it work…'

He smiled affectionately. Getting told off by Kerry wasn't all that bad really. Not now he knew they were going to be all right. Because they were, weren't they?

'Now—let's just talk about the travelling thing, shall we? You have me all trained up so there's plenty of adventures to be had—*together*. You know all the best places to go and you can tell me where and how to get there, because you have this innate talent for retaining all kinds of details in your head—a veritable walking encyclopedia, in fact. And I know you're going to try and tell me there'll come a point when you can't do all the things you can do now but you can't say—'

'I didn't say I was giving it up. You assumed I was. When I met up with the friends I did it was only to let them know it might be a long time before I saw them again—and I wanted to *see* them while I still could, that's all.' He took another breath. 'But I wasn't about to have you jump up and volunteer to hold my hand when—'

'Ronan, I love holding your hand. I've been holding your hand since our first day together. I'm holding your hands now. I'm not going to stop doing it just because something else changes. I *love* you. And when you love someone you hold their hand. It's a sign of affection.'

'You are the bossiest woman I've ever met. Have you finished lecturing me yet?'

'After the stunt you tried pulling?' She laughed in disbelief. 'You have years of this coming, mister.'

Then she leaned in and pressed a swift kiss on his lips, 'You just hate that I'm making sense when you've spent so long telling yourself this could never work.'

If she'd shut up for five minutes he might get to tell her he'd had some changes of heart on that subject. Truth was, if he was honest, he would never have come looking for her if he hadn't wanted to find a way to make it work. But then he was a *weak man* when it came to Kerry; he always had been…

'That long list of things you said I was: confident, fun, adventurous—'

'Sassy…' he mumbled under his breath.

'Yes, those.' She smiled warmly at him, her heart in her eyes. 'You need to know it's you that brings all that out in me. It may always have been there but with you I'm—*more*—more of everything. Without you I'd be *less*. That's why I need you.'

'Less sassy is fine with me.'

'And you made me paint again.' This time her eyes shimmered suspiciously enough to make him frown again. 'Lord, but I loved you for that. I should never have let it slide. But now I have it back and, since I was sat here in this park with plenty of time to think, I have a theory on how we could use that too…'

His chin dropped to his chest with a groan. 'I'm never

leaving you on your own for this long ever again if it gives you this much time to prove a point you've already made.'

Soft musical laughter sounded above his head. 'I'm very glad to hear it. I'm never leaving you either.'

'Well, could we hurry up and get to the good stuff, then, do you think?' He smiled down at their hands.

She let go of his hands and framed his face, tilting his chin back up so she could look in his eyes the way she did that made him feel she could see inside him, her voice seductively low and filled with emotion.

'Close your eyes for me.'

'Why?'

'Do I have to blindfold you?'

'Blindfold for the guy who's losing his sight—that's considerate. I *feel* loved now.'

Kerry scowled fiercely. 'We need to talk about the blind jokes at some point.'

'Later.' He closed his eyes. 'Happy now?'

'Can you still see me?'

Oh, she knew how to take his heart and scrunch it up into a little tiny ball, didn't she?

He had to clear his throat to speak. 'I can always see you. I told you that once before.'

Since he'd met her she was all he could see—in the daylight when he couldn't stop looking at her, and when he was in the darkness, whether awake or on the fringes of sleep. She was all he saw.

He lifted one of her hands off his face and set it flat against his chest, covering it with his own. 'I see you with this. Your hair is a really deep chestnut and it does this sexy curly thing all around your face. Your eyes remind me of autumn. And you're smiling that way that makes it look like you're lit up from inside. I see you. And that's before I go into all the things I see inside you; you're amazing. I've thought that from the get go.'

He heard her take a shaky breath, her voice filled with emotion. 'Then you see me better than anyone else ever has.'

'They weren't looking properly. We going-blind types tend to pay more attention than most…'

Soft lips brushed across his, her sweet breath whispering over his face. 'You really need to learn that being nice doesn't need to be disguised under something flippant, you know. We'll work on that. Now tell me what you can hear.'

Ronan knew what she was doing—and there was barely enough room left in his chest for his lungs to work properly. 'Your voice—you breathing—my heart beating loud, if we're being honest.'

'We are from here on in and don't you forget it. What else?'

'Leaves rustling.' He tried to nail each sound down one by one. 'The fountain—birds—'

He smiled as he got more. 'Wind in the leaves still left on the trees—kids laughing somewhere. Damn, I'm good at this.'

'Keep going.'

He dropped both hands to her jean-clad thighs; up over her hips to her waist where he spread his fingers wide and squeezed tight. 'I can smell damp leaves on the ground and the water behind me and that scent that's always been Kerry, Kerry Doyle to me. Gotta love that scent, really…'

It earned him another kiss, words vibrating against his mouth. 'Still incorrigible. I love you, you idiot.'

Men didn't cry. But if they did he would have when his heart swelled to bursting point. Because he suddenly knew what she was going to say about the painting. 'Now you're going to fill in the rest for me, aren't you? With lots of references to impressionist paintings…'

There was only a heartbeat of a pause. 'The sky above us

is a light, bright pale blue. Think about looking from the window of a plane and how far it stretches out—then add clouds so thin you can see little pieces of the sky through them. And 'they're drifting so you know there's more of a breeze higher up than there is down here. Like that time we lay on the beach in Fiji and watched them go by for hours on end…'

Ronan's hands tightened as she continued in the richly warm, slightly husky voice he loved so very much. 'All around us there are trees, leaves turning all the colours of autumn—brown and russet and red and ochre and gold all mixed together. You can see the sky through them in places. Paris at the Fontaine de Médicis is your reference for autumn from today on…'

For the rest of his days when he thought of autumn he would think of finding Kerry surrounded by those trees. And he'd think of the colours in her eyes. She was clever, his woman—taking hints of the things they'd seen together to help paint the picture inside his mind. Showing him she could be his eyes when he couldn't see any more. How had he thought for one second he could live without her in his life?

'It reminds me more of a Van Gogh than a Monet, but we might need to see more paintings for you to get the references from art…'

Ronan had to clear his throat. 'You're doing fine.'

Her voice lowered again, soft and intimate like it was when they talked on a plane or after making love, when they would lie side by side in the darkness at night laughing and sharing the way only they did. 'You see—it's another sign that I was always meant for you, me loving art from when I was little. My mother taught me all the names of the colours so one day I could tell you what they are. I just had to get on the right plane at the right time to find you, that's all. And now it all makes sense. You brought bright, vibrant colour into my life—all I'll be doing is giving it back to you.'

A sound distinctly like a laughed sob made him open his eyes. And Kerry was so close he could see the tears forming in her beautiful eyes, his throat clogging up and his vision blurring, his voice rough.

'I love you. More than I could ever begin to tell you.'

She sobbed a husky chuckle of laughter. 'I know.'

When he swallowed hard she leaned in closer and searched his eyes. 'Are those happy tears?'

Ronan sat a little taller, frowning at her. 'Like hell. It's the wind here—it's sharp.'

Kerry pursed her lips and nodded. 'Mmm-hmm.'

He leaned in and kissed away the 'happy tears' he could see in her eyes before nudging the end of his nose on hers, gruffly informing her, 'You better marry me, then.'

Kerry nodded. 'I better had.'

'Honeymoon in Kenya do?'

Her face lit up with the excitement he loved to invoke in her, her nodding firm. 'Absolutely.'

The hands on her waist smoothed up her back to press her closer to his chest, his voice rumbling over her lips. 'Good—'cos I have a flight booked at the beginning of the month.'

Kerry jumped back a little. 'I can't organize a wedding in less than a month!'

'Yes, you can. We worked on spur-of-the-moment, remember?' He moved in for another kiss.

But Kerry leaned out of the way. 'A month isn't spur-of-the-moment! It's make-Kerry-crazy.'

'We got that one covered—' he pressed against her back more firmly and lifted his other hand to the back of her head to stop her getting away '—and I have a venue in mind that'll fulfil the fantasy for you—trust me. Then we can tick that one off the list too.'

'*You* tick all my fantasies.'

He didn't waste time on another word. Instead he showed her how much he loved her by kissing her until she went limp and languid against him. Only then did he lift his head, smiling contentedly down at her heavy-lidded eyes and answering drunken smile.

'And I get to meet Nana. Think I can get her to love me as much as you do?'

Kerry's lower lip trembled. 'Oh, she'll love you, all right. And she'll have plenty of helpful words of wisdom too—most likely with a lecture when I tell her what it took to get us to here. You wait and see…'

'I'm looking forward to it.'

'One more thing.'

'There always is with you.'

'I should tell you about the hereditary thing that runs in *my* side of the family.' When he stiffened she moved in to slide her mouth over his, stage-whispering the rest. 'Three generations of twins now, you know…'

'You have got to be ki—'

EPILOGUE

A WEDDING could indeed be planned in less than a month. Though Kerry would always wonder just how they managed it. But with determination, teamwork, Ronan's enthusiastic imagination and Kerry's organizational skills it all went off without a hitch.

Mind you—marrying a millionaire determined to make things happen no matter how much it cost to *make them happen* helped.

She married him wearing Nana's beautiful nineteen-twenties rose silk wedding dress complete with antique wax flower headpiece and floor-length veil and all the way through the ceremony Ronan's stunning eyes shone at her, making her glow from head to toe.

And he hadn't done too badly with their location either, not that Kerry would have expected anything less now she knew him so well…

Something certain members of her family doubted she could after a mere three months. But then, much to Ronan's deep chuckling amusement, she'd pointed out that they'd spent one thousand eight hundred and forty-eight hours together pretty much constantly one on one. And if that was split down into normal 'dating' hours then technically they'd been seeing each other about a year and a half. So if a couple were as much in love as they were after a year and a half and they decided to get married then the rest of the world wouldn't have a problem with it, *would they?*

'You forgot to stick your tongue out and say "so there",' he pointed out afterwards.

'Ooh, don't think for a second I wasn't tempted!'

They had pictures taken on lawns sprinkled with autumn leaves in the grounds of Kinnitty Castle; a gothic revival castle at the foothills of the Slieve Bloom Mountains near where Ronan had grown up. Because flowers and dresses and 'girl stuff' were all hers, he calmly informed her, but the role of 'fantasy fulfiller'—*'all mine and always will be'*.

And in the spirit of 'surprises' he'd even managed to keep the location from her up until the week before, something Kerry didn't have any complaints about with the faith she had in his ability to make her happy—especially when they were sitting in the Great Hall of the O'Carrolls for a banquet in spectacular fantasy setting: crisp white linen softly finished with luxurious green centre runners complemented by the green chair bands on champagne seat covers and the lilting music of an Irish harp weaving a spell over their families and friends.

It was the stuff of dreams.

Though they were probably the only wedding reception on the face of the earth with about ten choices of dessert—because Ronan didn't see why he had to choose *one* when they could have a little of *all of them*…

And Kerry made it through the entire day without crying—almost.

It was when they went to see Nana before the dancing began that did it. Because with both of them hunching down in front of her, one of each of her small crinkled hands on their faces and Ronan thanking her for sending Kerry out into the world to 'find him' when he needed her most, so much emotion welled up in Kerry's chest that it had to go *somewhere*…

But then when he found out Kerry had only been at the fountain in Paris because that was where her grandfather had proposed to Nana he said straight away it made even more sense to him they'd found their own happy ending there.

'Not ending, you idiot—*beginning*.' Kerry smiled before kissing him for saying it.

He squeezed the fingers tangled in his, the band of her wedding ring pressing between them. 'Oh, no, you don't— *stop that.*'

'What's she doing?' Nana turned her head.

'She's about to cry and ruin her make-up. You should speak to her—she never listens to me.'

Nana laughed throatily the way Kerry loved most. It had always been an indication of her wicked sense of humour, that dirty laugh of hers. 'Looks beautiful in my dress, though, doesn't she?'

Ronan's deep voice huskily rumbled the answer, his sensational eyes glowing with deeply felt emotion. 'She does. *Very beautiful.*'

'Tell me what she looks like, Ronan.'

So he did, describing every last detail in the same husky tone and making Kerry smile through her tears—*happy tears*—because she'd *never* been happier.

She mouthed the words at him. *I love you.*

And his fingers squeezed again, chin lifting before he smiled the most sinfully sexy slow smile and mouthed back, *Love you too. Woman.*

It was the only thing that really mattered.

* * * * *

TEXAS RANGER
TAKES A BRIDE

BY
PATRICIA THAYER

Dear Reader,

This is a first for me. I've written numerous western stories over the years, and several of the locations were in Texas, but I've never written a Texas Ranger as a hero.

I have to admit I was a little intimidated just by their reputation alone. And I wasn't quite sure what exactly their job entailed. Was it more of an honorary position? Did these men, and now women, just walk around wearing white hats and a silver badge?

Then I talked with Carol Mathis, Administrative Technician for Ranger Company E in Midland, Texas. She eagerly answered all my questions about this elite group of 116 lawmen and women. The Rangers have protected the people of Texas since 1823. Their jobs include anything from going after kidnappers and bank robbers to helping find missing people. No job is too small or too large for a Texas Ranger. And, when it's needed, they still climb on a horse to go after the bad guy.

In my story, *Texas Ranger Takes a Bride,* Chase Landon goes in search of a boy who's been kidnapped by escaped convicts. The stakes are raised when he learns the child is his own son. Mallory Hagan, the woman he once loved but walked away from to become a Ranger, never told him of the boy. Now they have to put the past behind them and work together.

Once again it's been my privilege to learn about the Rangers. They are truly heroes. Thanks, Carol, for all your help.

Any mistakes in this story are mine and mine alone.

Enjoy,

Patricia Thayer

Patricia Thayer has been writing for over twenty years, and has published thirty books with Mills & Boon. Her books have been twice nominated for various awards in the USA, including the National Readers' Choice Award, the Book Buyers' Best, and a prestigious RITA® Award. In 1997 *Nothing Short of a Miracle* won the Romantic Times BOOK Club Reviewers' Choice Award for Best Special Edition.

Thanks to the understanding men in her life—her husband of over thirty-five years, Steve, and her three grown sons and three grandsons—Pat has been able to fulfil her dream of writing. Besides writing romance, she loves to travel—especially in the west, where she researches her books first hand. You might find her on a ranch in Texas, or on a train to an old mining town in Colorado, and this year you'll find her on an adventure in Scotland. Just so long as she can share it all with her favourite hero, Steve. She loves to hear from readers. You can write to her at PO Box 6251, Anaheim, CA 92816-0251, USA, or check her website at www.patriciathayer.com for upcoming books.

To Helen,

I loved your fierce loyalty to your family and friends,
your joy for life, your bright smile and your
special way with words.

And I'll miss you, my friend.

Gentle Persuader, Helen Haddad,
June 13, 1933 – October 17, 2007

CHAPTER ONE

SHE HADN'T BEEN ABLE to shake the uneasy feeling.

Mallory Hagan looked out the kitchen window toward the barn and corral area. Still no sign of Buck and Ryan. She trusted her father to take care of her eight-year-old son, but that didn't stop her from worrying.

On the plus side, he was a good rider, and his grandpa had taken him out on the trail many times. Just not overnight.

And never had they been four hours overdue.

Mallory paced the large ranch kitchen and stopped at the wall phone. Unable to stop herself, she picked up the receiver and called her dad's cell phone. It went right to voice mail…again. They must be in a dead area.

She looked up when the housekeeper, Rosalie, walked into the kitchen. "Still no sign of them?"

Mallory shook her head. "I'm getting concerned."

"Do you think Buck is checking his watch? No. He has his grandson out there, teaching him the cowboy way of life."

Over the years the housekeeper's once rich brown

hair had turned salt and pepper. It was pulled back into a no-nonsense ponytail, revealing warm hazel eyes and defined cheekbones. Rosalie Dudley had been the only other female in the house since the death of Mallory's mother over fifteen years ago. Mallory loved her like a second mother.

"So you're saying I'm being overprotective."

Rosalie smiled. "No, I'm just saying Buck wouldn't let anything happen to the boy. You two are his life."

Buck Kendrick owned a lot of land in this part of West Texas. On his forty-three sections he ran a large cattle operation, along with numerous oil wells, dotting the mostly barren landscape of mesquite, ocotillo cactus and buffalo grass that survived the area's lack of rainfall.

Mallory knew her father would give it all up to have his wife by his side, and another half-dozen kids to inherit what he'd worked so hard to build. But she was his only child, and Ryan his only grandchild. And since her husband's death, there weren't going to be any more children. Sadness welled inside Mallory as she recalled her turbulent marriage to Alan. Toward the end she'd feared for her and her son's safety.

Living outside of Lubbock, Texas, she'd been able to play the part of the dutiful wife. And keep Buck from knowing the truth about her husband's drinking and incomprehensible actions.

She brushed aside the thought. "You know, Dad isn't as young as he used to be."

"You better not let Buck hear you say that."

Mallory smiled. "Well, he still does too much. And I'm afraid he's going to show off for Ryan."

"Probably, but he's got Joe and Mick with him," Rosalie assured her. "So let the ranch hands deal with Buck. And we better concentrate on the roundup. We'll have about three dozen hungry cowboys to feed this weekend, not to mention the other family members."

"That's why I'm here." Mallory let herself smile. This was the weekend she came home every year. Lazy K Ranch's late-spring roundup. With Mallory's busy horse broker's business in Levelland, they couldn't get back to Midland very often. Just about four times a year.

"Are you going to make fried chicken?"

Rosalie nodded. "Your dad has already put in his order. He knows it's the only time I let him indulge in fried foods. How about you making that potato casserole?"

"And some red beans and rice, of course." Mallory reached for a note pad when her attention was drawn to the kitchen window. Outside, a horse and rider were walking toward the barn. She looked closer. It was Joe. He was slumped over his mount.

"Rosalie, Joe's back, and something's wrong." She hurried out the door and kept the momentum going until she reached the horse just as two other hands arrived to help him down.

"Looks like he's been worked over," the ranch hand said.

Mallory knelt down beside him on the ground. "Oh, God, Joe, what happened? Where's Ryan and Buck?"

The foreman's face was etched with pain. "Two men ambushed us right before dawn. They shot Buck and worked over Mick and me pretty good."

She gasped. "What about Ryan?"

"That's why Buck sent me for help."

Mallory's heart pounded harder as she looked around for any sign of another horse. "Where's my son?"

"I'm sorry, Mallory." He grimaced. "I tried to stop them, but they took the boy with them."

He had to be overlooking something.

Chase Landon sat in his office at the Ranger Company in Midland, Texas. He'd gone over and over the same information for the past week. He'd prided himself on his ability to find clues that others had missed, but this old case still had him stumped.

Since joining the Texas Rangers nearly nine years ago, one of his goals had been to find his uncle's killer. He also knew he should leave it to the Rangers' Unsolved Crimes Investigation Team in San Antonio. But this was too important to Chase, and he refused to give up.

"Anything new show up?" fellow ranger Jesse Raines asked as he stuck his head though the doorway.

"No." Chase leaned back in his chair. "Ballistics still doesn't match. There had to be another gun there. Another shooter."

"We could go back and take another look." Just being recently commissioned, Jesse was eager to help out on any and all cases. "But after all this time, it's probably long gone."

"I don't think the shooter had enough time to get rid of it," Chase said more to himself than to his partner. He closed the manila folder and stood. "Anything more on the Sweetwater escapees?"

Jesse cocked his thumb toward the door. "The captain is talking with the state troopers now."

Although he'd been in the Midland Company for only the past year, Chase knew this area well. He'd grown up in the oil-rich Permian Basin of West Texas. His first job in law enforcement had been with the highway patrol there.

Suddenly the captain, Bob Robertson, walked in. "Landon. Raines. It looks like we've been called in," he told them. "The two escapees, now identified as Charles Jacobs and Berto Reyes, have shot a civilian and carjacked a vehicle. Now, they've taken an eight-year-old boy hostage. So I need you and your gear ready in thirty minutes."

The captain glanced at Chase. "Sorry, Landon, looks like your vacation is temporarily on hold. I need you on this."

"Not a problem," he said. "Where did they abduct the boy?"

"It was on the Lazy K Ranch. Southeast of Interstate 20."

Chase felt as if he'd been socked in the gut. Then dread washed over him. "Buck Kendrick's place?" He barely got the words out.

The captain nodded. "It's Kendrick's grandson, Ryan Hagan."

Chase stopped breathing. Mallory had a son?

"You know the man?"

Chase managed a nod. "A long time ago." He had trouble thinking of her with a child.

"So you know that even from Kendrick's hospital bed,

he's demanding that every law officer in the state join in the search for his grandson. Not that I blame him." He sighed. "We better get to it. The helicopter will take off in thirty minutes." The captain walked out with Jesse.

Chase sank down into the chair and rubbed his hands over his face. This was crazy.

Mallory Kendrick.

The pretty, ebony-haired girl with big green eyes. An incredible contrast to her olive skin from her mother's Spanish roots. Tall and slender, she had legs that men fantasized about. But Chase had had to quit seeing her. She was too young, and way out of his league.

She was the daughter of rich oilman and rancher, Buck Kendrick, and he was a kid from the poor side of town who would never fit into her lifestyle. But damn, even after all these years, thoughts still lingered of what might have been between them.

Mallory Kendrick…Hagan had made him crazy for years. From the time she'd turned eighteen clear through to their heated summer romance and their breakup when he went off to join the rangers.

Chase leaned back in his chair and closed his eyes. If there had been a woman who could have deterred him from his dream…Mallory was the one.

Funny thing was he'd returned to Midland to see if they could work things out between them, but he quickly learned he was too late. He'd remembered vividly how good old Buck persuaded him to back away when he'd showed up at the door and learned Mallory had gotten married to another man and was on her honeymoon.

Over the several months that followed, he'd tried to

convince himself it was all for the best. It didn't stop his misery. Even concentrating on his new career with the rangers, he managed to let Mallory interrupt his thoughts for a long time. She was the one reason he'd nearly refused the transfer here a year ago. He'd wondered if he might run into her. He hadn't so far.

And now, he was going to drive up to her door.

Her son was in danger. That had nothing to do with their past. It was the little boy he had to concentrate on…the boy he had to find. As a ranger, he couldn't walk away.

Mallory stayed in the kitchen, and there was no point looking outside to see anything. It was after dark, and in the country that meant black as pitch. Besides, there were dozens of law officers who had cordoned off the area and set up a base at the barn. She could go down there. And do what? What she wanted was to grab one of Buck's guns, climb on a horse and go search for her child. They weren't about to let her do that. Look where that had gotten Joe and Buck.

She had seen her father brought in hours ago. She didn't go with him in the ambulance, sending Rosalie instead. Luckily, his wound wasn't life threatening, and he only had to spend overnight in the hospital.

Afraid and anxious, Mallory resumed her pacing while her mind worked overtime thinking about how scared Ryan had to be. And she knew that the convicts were lifers and had nothing to lose if they killed her son.

No. No. A tear ran down her face as she began to tremble again. She had to get him back. Ryan was her life…. They'd gone through so much together.

Her thoughts turned to the man from her past, Chase Landon. Nine years since Mallory had seen him. Back then he'd been a state trooper, with dreams of being a Texas Ranger. And when that day finally came, their idyllic summer had come to an end…and he had walked away from her, breaking her young heart.

Now, that man was going to be the one to help rescue her son. A few years back she'd read the story about how Ranger Chase Landon had tracked a robbery suspect to the Mexican border and talked him into surrendering. She was hoping for the same outcome now.

Hearing the helicopter fly overhead, she felt her heart race in anticipation. More commotion outside, along with voices. She released a slow breath, went to the door and opened it.

Chase stood well over six feet tall. His dark brown eyes were piercing, and his chiseled jaw was rigid. Dressed in army fatigues and sporting a baseball cap, he looked more like a soldier than a Texas Ranger.

Mallory knew one thing. The man still affected her in the same way he always had. His dark brooding looks still demanded respect. She once knew the softer, gentler side of this man, too. Right now, that seemed like a lifetime ago.

"Mallory," he said with a nod.

"Chase. I've been expecting you." She stepped aside allowing him inside followed by another ranger. He was about the same age as Chase, but with lighter hair and coloring. He was nearly as tall.

Chase thought he could handle their meeting after all these years, but seeing Mallory again drove all logic

from his head. If anything, she was even more beautiful at almost thirty than at twenty-one. Her midnight-
black hair was still long and silky as the wavy strands
lay against her shoulders. Her wide green eyes were no
longer bright, but frightened, bringing him back to the
reason he was here. It didn't stop the strong urge to pull
her into his arms. He resisted it.

"Mallory, this is Sergeant Raines, Jesse. Jesse,
Mallory…Hagan."

She took his outstretched hand. "It's nice to meet
you, sergeant."

He nodded. "Wish it was under better circumstances."

She bit down on her trembling lip. "Just bring my son
back to me."

"We're going to try really hard to accomplish that,
ma'am." Jesse looked at Chase. "I'll head down to the
command post."

"I'll be there soon." Chase had given Jesse a brief
summery about his past relationship with Mallory on the
trip here. He knew Raines would keep the news private.

They both watched him walk out the door, then
Mallory turned to Chase. "You should go, too."

"I will, but first I need to talk with you. How is your
father doing?" he asked as he directed her to the kitchen
table and pulled out a chair for her to sit down.

"He's going to recover," she said. "He'll be home
tomorrow."

"Good. Now, maybe you can answer a few questions."

She looked up at him with those trusting green eyes.
He quickly glanced away as he pulled a paper out of his
pocket. It was a map of the ranch.

"Joe told us your father made camp here at this group of rocks." He circled the area with his finger. "Right before dawn, two men appeared, one with a gun, catching Buck, Joe and Mick by surprise still in their sleeping bags. Then the convicts took some extra clothes, and the horses. When they went to take your son…Ryan, Buck tried to fight them. He got shot, and Joe and Mick were beaten."

She nodded. "Dad said Ryan wasn't hurt when they took him. Joe's horse wandered back to camp—that's how he was able to come for help." She blinked at tears. "Please, you've got to get my son back before they do anything bad to him."

Chase wanted to promise her he could, but there weren't any guarantees when it came to finding prisoners who had nothing to lose. "We're going to do everything we can to find them, Mallory. They took your father's cell phone, so we're hoping to be able to make contact with them."

"Do you think they're heading to the border?"

"It's a possibility," he told her. "The convicts didn't plan this escape. From the second they'd carjacked the vehicle on the interstate until now being on horseback, I'm thinking that they're just making it up as they go along."

She shivered. "That's what scares me. They're desperate men, Chase. They could just decide there's no need for Ryan any more."

He reached for her hand, a natural reflex. It was cold and shaking as he cupped it in his. "No, Mallory, they *do* need the boy now. He's their bartering tool. So you have to stay positive." He worked up a smile. "I have a feeling Buck taught his grandson how to survive out there."

She nodded, and surprisingly returned with a hint of smile.

It immediately took his breath. Finding his voice, he asked, "Tell me what Ryan knows, Mal."

She released a long breath. "He's a good rider." Her brow wrinkled in concentration. "And can read animal tracks. Dad taught him to how find a direction by the sun and the stars."

"That's good…the boy knows how to handle himself." Chase didn't want to think about the other dangers out there…mostly human ones.

"So you think that could help him?"

He nodded. A strange feeling came over him as he studied Mallory. The woman he'd once cared about… she'd always wanted a husband and family. He couldn't give her that all those years ago. Hopefully he could at least bring her son home.

"He sounds like a great kid."

"He is, but he's still my baby."

He watched a tear fall and he reached out and brushed it away. He couldn't imagine how she felt, but he did feel for her. It was something that hadn't changed. "Mallory, I promise to do everything I can to bring him back."

Chase stood. He needed to put some space between him and her. "I'll be heading out to the camp. If the search dogs picked up their scent we'll follow." He looked around to see the room empty. "You shouldn't be alone. Is there someone to stay with you?"

She shook her head. "No. I sent Rosalie to bed."

"What about your…husband?" Why wasn't the man there with his wife?

She looked at him a long time, then said, "Alan died two years ago. It's just Ryan and me."

CHAPTER TWO

As THE SUN ROSE in the sky from the east, Chase knew that the twenty-four-hour mark had come and gone, and they hadn't found them.

He swung his leg over the back of the horse and climbed down, as the other rangers did the same. The bloodhounds were taking a break, too, from their long trek across the dry plains, crossing Interstate 10 into Reeves County. Their trainers had them drinking water beside one of the prison vehicles.

Chase concentrated on his job and knelt to examine the tracks in the sandy soil. There were two sets of hooves and they were headed south. Mexico.

It didn't take a rocket scientist to come up with that equation. Once they crossed the border the two men could get lost for a long time, especially when Jacobs and Reyes had been sent to prison under the "three strikes you're out" law. They had nothing to lose.

And that was what worried Chase the most.

The two weren't taking the easiest route. They were heading toward the Barrilla Mountains. There were fewer towns and traveled roads, but mostly because the rocky terrain provided better cover from the search helicopters.

Still, the escapees had to get across the Rio Grande. That was his job. To make sure they didn't make it to the border, or they might never find them…or the boy.

How could he go back and face Mallory with that kind of news? He recalled the devastated look on her face. It had affected him more than it should have, especially when he needed to keep this case on a professional level.

Hell, how was he supposed to do that when he knew if he'd hung around years ago, so many things might have turned out differently.

Chase took the small picture of the boy, Ryan, out of his pocket and studied it again. His chest tightened as the cute kid with his curly dark hair and big eyes grinned back at him. Envy and regret surged through him as if he were on a runaway horse.

He shook it away as Raines came up beside him. "Same tracks?"

"Looks like we're headed for the border." He slipped the photo back in his pocket, then reached for his cell phone and called headquarters.

Bob Robertson came on the line. "Tell me you located them, Landon."

"Sorry, not yet, Captain. We've picked up their tracks again." He gave their location. "And as we thought, they're headed for the mountains."

"Damn, I wish I wasn't right on that one. Maybe they aren't as dumb as we thought. Do you need more manpower?"

"No, we have enough to handle it." Chase hesitated, then asked, "How is Mrs. Hagan holding up?"

"She's scared, of course," the captain said. "I was hoping to give her some good news."

Chase had hoped that, too. Suddenly he heard Mallory's voice in the background.

"Hold on, Chase. Mrs. Hagan has something to tell you."

"Chase…" She said his name like a plea.

"Mallory, we haven't found them yet."

"I know. It's just that when you do, make sure you tell Ryan that Buck is okay." He heard the tears in her voice. It killed him. "Dad's worried because Ryan saw him get shot."

"I'll be sure to tell him."

There was a long pause, then she said, "Ryan will trust you because you're a ranger."

"Mallory, I'm going to do everything I can to bring him back to you. You got my word on that."

"I know you will. Thank you, Chase."

When the line went dead, he was glad. He needed to concentrate on finding the suspects and forget the past. He clipped the phone back on his belt as Jesse watched him.

"This job is harder when a kid's involved—and especially when it's someone you know."

Chase nodded. Although he'd given Jesse the brief rundown of his past with Mallory, Chase didn't want to delve any deeper. What he couldn't understand was why after all this time Mallory could still get to him.

"It's okay to admit you have feelings for her," Jesse said. "She's a beautiful woman."

Chase glared at him. "This isn't the time to notice a woman. We've got a little boy to find." He thought back to the choices he'd made in favor of his career. Being a Texas Ranger had been all he'd ever wanted. Mallory had been the only woman he'd even thought about sharing a life with. In the end, he chose the career over her. He tried to tell himself she'd been too young for him. Too late he realized that she was everything he'd wanted, but it was Mallory who didn't think he'd been worth waiting for.

She'd married another man.

Chase quickly wiped away that thought as he took a drink of water from his canteen. Too many years had passed to renew a relationship that had been doomed from the start.

"We need to get moving." He walked around his horse, then climbed on and adjusted his hat as Jesse followed suit.

He'd recalled earlier that day when he glanced toward the house and saw Mallory. She tried to look hopeful, brave, but he could see her pain…her misery. Who could blame her? Her child was out there.

He rode off, praying today was the last one they had to spend in this West Texas heat. More importantly, that a little boy would be found safe and could go home to his mother. And Chase could go back to business as usual.

Or could he?

"Stop smothering me, woman," Buck Kendrick growled at Rosalie. "I can walk just fine."

"You're supposed to take it easy so you won't open

the wound," the housekeeper told him as she followed him into the kitchen.

Mallory watched her father's slow gait. He suddenly looked old and he wasn't even sixty yet. He had thick, gray hair, and warm hazel eyes. He was tall and trim, but right now, his broad shoulders were a little slumped over. His expression was pained, and she knew it wasn't from the gunshot wound he'd received in his side.

"Any news?" he asked.

"No. I did talk to Chase Landon."

Her dad didn't look surprised at the mention of Chase's name. "We've got the rangers looking for the boy, we can't ask for anything more."

"You both need to eat," Rosalie interrupted the silence and began to put together the fixings for lunch.

Her father frowned. "Crazy woman. She thinks about food at a time like this."

"Rosalie is trying to stay busy the best she can."

Buck cursed. "I should be out there looking, too."

Mallory felt the same way. "No, Dad. Let the rangers do their job. Like you said, they're the best. And they're trained for this kind of thing."

"I know. I know." He sank into the kitchen chair. "I shouldn't have let them take Ryan…. He's so little. I begged them to take me instead."

Even though Buck wouldn't normally have begged any man, he would have for his family…his only grandson. He loved the boy more than his own life.

Mallory sat down beside him. "I know you did, Dad. None of this is your fault."

"Damn. What kind of world is it when you aren't even safe on your own land? They stole my grandson."

Mallory remained silent and let her father vent. This was a second time Buck Kendrick hadn't been able to protect his family from the cruelty of the world.

He finally looked at her. "Have you told Landon about Ryan?"

Although they'd never openly talked about it, her father knew about Ryan and she'd wondered when this day would come. She shook her head. "No. But he'll know soon enough."

Buck nodded in agreement. "Whether he figures it out himself or not, it's time he knows the truth. And Ryan, too."

Nearly three hours later, the search team finally lucked out.

A local rancher gave them the information they'd been hoping for. Two men and a boy on horseback rode along the back of his property, heading toward the foothills. The rancher also told them about a line shack at the base.

"If the rancher hadn't spotted them," Jesse began, "the shack could have made a perfect hideout."

Chase nodded. "And there's some supplies there. Even if they just stop for some food, we've gained some time."

"They still have about an hour on us."

Chase discussed the situation with the other men. They decided to keep the dogs at the ranch house. And Chase and Jesse would ride up alone, hoping to catch the escapees off-guard. After the rancher gave them directions for a back route to the cabin, Chase and Jesse headed through the rough terrain of the mountain range, using the thick trees for natural cover. The jeep, with backup men, waited about a mile way. Chase hoped the surprise element worked. They didn't need to put Ryan in any more danger. If they weren't careful, this operation could go bad real fast.

At a group of rocks behind the rough-hewn cabin, they climbed off their horses and tied them to a tree. Silently, they made their way toward the back of the structure, happy there weren't any windows. Once flattened against the structure, Chase crept along one side as Jesse moved along the other side toward the open front door. He listened to the voices inside.

"We can't stay the night," one of the escapees said. "We can't even stay another hour. I tell you they're on our trail."

"The kid's asleep in the saddle," the other man said. "And I'm tired of carrying him. Besides, the horses aren't going to last much longer."

"Then we'll take fresh ones from that rancher. There were several out in the pasture."

Suddenly one of the men came outside, wearing jeans that were too short, and an open shirt revealing a once-white T-shirt. Charlie Jacobs. As far as Chase could see he didn't have a weapon on him.

"I'm going to get us some fresh mounts," he called over his shoulder as he jumped down the step and walked to his horse.

Chase made his way to the back of the cabin as did Jesse. He motioned for Jesse to go after the man.

The ranger nodded, then hurried off toward his horse.

Chase went back to the side of the shack. He couldn't see inside to tell where the boy was. And he didn't want to take a chance on rushing in if one of the escapees had a gun pointed at the kid. He had to wait him out.

Ten minutes later, he got a text message from Jesse. *Got him.*

Chase knew Jesse would return as backup. Should he wait? Suddenly there was more commotion inside and the prisoner came to the door. "Stay where you are, *niño,* I need to pee, but I'll be close by."

Chase's heart rate accelerated as the man he recognized in the picture stepped off the stoop and started for the outhouse. He wouldn't get a better chance than this.

Chase took off running and tackled the guy to the ground with a thud. He knocked the air from his lungs, but the man was still able to put up a fight. Finally Chase landed a punch that connected with the man's jaw and threw him to the ground again. Enough time for Chase to pull his gun and aim it at the suspect.

"Go ahead. Give me a reason to shoot you...dead."

In answer Reyes cursed in Spanish, and raised his hands over his head. Chase instructed him to get into position, then he pulled his handcuffs off his belt and put them on him.

About that time, Jesse showed up. He grinned. "Sweet mercy. This is turning out to be a good day. Really good day."

Chase wasn't sure about anything until he saw the boy and knew he was safe. Once Jesse took charge of the prisoner, Chase holstered his gun and took off toward the shack. At the doorway he stopped, not wanting to frighten the boy.

"Ryan," he called out. "Ryan, it's okay. I'm a Texas Ranger."

He looked inside to find a small figure huddled in the corner of the bunk. His eyes were big and red from crying. Chase blinked in the dim light and studied the boy's dirty face, but he recognized him from the picture.

"Are you gonna take me home to my mom?"

Chase allowed himself to smile. "Yes, I am. She said to tell you that your grandpa is okay."

Ryan's eyes brightened. "Grandpa tried to fight them. I'm glad he's okay."

The kid had dark eyes and curly brown hair. His face was long and there was a small cleft in his chin. His features were so unlike Mallory's, but he looked familiar.

"Are you really a Texas Ranger?" Ryan said, interrupting his thoughts.

Chase nodded as he pointed to the silver badge on his camouflage shirt. "Yes, I am. We've been tracking you for miles. Boy, is your mom going to be happy to see you."

With a smile the boy climbed off the bed and came to Chase. "I bet she cried 'cause I got kidnapped."

Chase knelt down in front of the boy. "She's been pretty brave, too. You're very important to her and your grandpa."

Chase felt something tighten in his chest. What if they hadn't got here in time?

"Did they hurt you?" Chase asked.

Ryan shook his head. "Not much. They pulled me around some. But I didn't cry," he said as he pulled up his shirt to show off some bruises and red welts along the thin torso.

Chase examined him and was drawn to a strawberry-colored birthmark on his small chest. It was very similar to the one Chase had on his lower back. The same type that his Uncle Wade had on his shoulder.

Chase stood, but his gaze remained on the boy. His lungs didn't seem to work as he noticed so much more about the child. The similar chin with a small indentation. His dark eyes…

He shook his head. He couldn't think that Mallory would do this to him. Nothing this cruel.

"Are you taking me home?" Ryan asked.

"Yes, so we need to get going."

It surprised Chase when the boy slipped his small hand into his. "I'm ready." Together they walked out to the porch to see Jesse come toward them.

"Boyd and Grant have the prisoners secured…." A slow grin appeared as he studied the two of them. "If I didn't know better I'd say you two looked like—" He paused. "Sweet mercy," he breathed as his smile died away.

"Close your mouth, Raines. We need to get the boy back to his family."

Jesse nodded. "Right. Then you bring…Ryan down by horseback. And the helicopter is going to meet us at the ranch."

Chase nodded. He didn't want to speak right now. What could he say? Until he confronted Mallory, he wouldn't know for sure. He stole another glance at the boy.

That wasn't true. There was no doubt in his mind that Ryan Hagan was his son.

* * *

Hearing the helicopter overhead, Mallory hurried outside. It had been two hours since Chase's phone call and she'd heard Ryan's voice. Her son was back safe.

They landed about a hundred yards away in the pasture, but she didn't care. She took off running. She needed to hold her child in her arms, to see for herself he was safe.

The blades were slowing down as Chase stepped out, then reached back and lifted Ryan to the ground. Together they started toward her. Father and son.

She stumbled on seeing the two together. They were so much alike, everyone had to see they were related. As much as she dreaded this day, she was happy it was finally here. The only problem was how much Chase and Ryan would hate her for keeping this secret?

"Mom," Ryan called and shot off. He nearly jumped into her arms.

"Oh, Ryan," she cried. "You're safe." She hugged him tighter. Inhaled that wonderful familiar boy's smell of dirt and sweat. She loved it. She released him and did a quick examination. Although he'd been checked out in a small clinic near where he'd been found, she needed to see for herself. "You sure you're okay?"

His head bobbed up and down. "I'm okay. The doctor said I just got some bruises." He yanked up his shirt. "But they don't hurt anymore."

Just then Buck and Rosalie appeared and were calling to him. Before Mallory could stop her son, he shot off toward them. She was left alone with Chase. She finally was brave enough to look at him.

"Is he mine, Mallory? Is Ryan my son?"

Mallory swallowed and managed a nod.

His jaw worked. "We need to talk." He glanced toward Ryan. "I'll be back tonight."

"No, it's too soon."

He tipped his hat back, his gaze bore into hers. "Too soon? Hell, Mallory, I'd say it's years too late."

He turned and walked back to the helicopter. The pilot started it up and soon it was in the air.

What was she going to do now? How could she explain everything away?

Buck waited for her as Rosalie took Ryan on ahead into the house. "He's going to take a bath."

She shook her head. "Kids are so resilient, aren't they?"

"Oh, I think Ryan's going to have his share of nightmares for a while." He studied his daughter. "But we'll be here for him."

She felt the tears sting. "Chase knows, Dad. He knows Ryan is his son."

He nodded. "It's time. That boy needs a father…a real father, but only if Chase will be there for the boy."

Mallory didn't need to go into the reasons for their breakup. Buck Kendrick hadn't been happy about his young innocent daughter dating a man who never planned to make a commitment.

"I've made a lot of mistakes, Dad. To start with, I never should have married Alan…. I should have tried harder to contact Chase."

"Sweetheart, we can't stand here and try to atone for all the mistakes made in our lives. If so, I'd have to take some blame, too. I pushed you into that sham of a marriage…but you and Alan seemed to be a great match." He shook his head. "I had no idea that would turn out so badly."

"Dad, stop it. It was my choice."

Alan had been her boyfriend in high school, but knew his feelings for her were stronger than hers for him. When Mallory went off to college she ended their relationship, knowing she wanted to experience life. But they'd stayed friends. When she came home that summer from college and saw Chase, she fell hopelessly in love.

Chase didn't. When he got the call to join the rangers, he was packed and gone without so much as a backward glance. Alan had been the one who came back into her life and was willing to take on another man's baby. So she thought…

"But he hurt you and Ryan…and I can't forgive him or myself for that."

"Maybe if I'd tried harder to contact Chase all those years ago, it would have made a difference." She looked toward the house. "Now, my only concern is protecting my son."

He had a son…. He had a son….

The rest of the day those words had played in Chase's head, even during all the paperwork and debriefing on today's capture. He'd thought it would keep his mind off facing Mallory's betrayal. It didn't do any good. He was angry. How could she keep their son a secret?

Jesse stopped by his office right before the shift ended. "Hey, Chase. Wanted to let you know that Jacobs and Reyes are back in Sweetwater." He shook his head. "Man, I'm glad they're in lockdown now, especially

Jacobs. He's one mean son of a gun. The guy seemed to get pleasure out of telling me what his plans were for the boy. Reyes was pretty talkative, too. He was interested in your relationship to Wade Landon."

That wasn't uncommon. "How so?"

Jesse shrugged. "When I said Wade Landon was your uncle the guy just grinned. Think he'd know anything?"

"What's Reyes? Forty-two? He could have been around back then. I guess it wouldn't hurt to check his record.... Monday." Reyes wasn't going anywhere.

Jesse started to leave, then turned back. "You want to go for some food…maybe a beer?"

"Thanks, but I have plans," Chase told him as he cleared off his desk.

Jesse didn't move. "Well, if you want to talk, I'm around," he said and started to leave.

"I'm going to the ranch to talk with Mallory."

Jesse nodded. "I'd say that's a good place to start." He smiled. "Well, like I said, I'll be around if you want to…get a beer."

"Thanks."

Chase watched as Jesse walked out. Would he ever be ready to talk about this? If he were honest, he wasn't sure about his own feelings. How are you supposed to handle the news that you're a father? That you have a son? There were eight years he'd missed with his boy. How was he supposed to feel? The problem was he felt too many things, joy…fear…and a lot of anger…

Before seven that evening, Chase had showered and changed, then walked out of his town house and climbed into his dusty white truck to head to the Lazy K Ranch.

He knew one thing. Learning Ryan was his kid had affected him like nothing else had in his life. He'd spent less than two hours with the child, but already he felt a bond.

But an instant father? What if Ryan hated the idea?

Chase turned off the highway and drove down the road that led to the Lazy K Ranch. He'd traveled this route many times when he'd been dating Mallory. Mostly he'd come by when Buck wasn't home or out on the range. Her father hadn't been crazy about a—so-called—older man dating his college age daughter.

Chase made a snorting sound. He was all of twenty-eight back then.

His heart rate accelerated as he pulled into the circular drive of the Spanish-style home. The golden stucco-and-stone structure revealed Buck's wife, Pilar Kendrick's, Spanish heritage. The patio out front was made of hand-painted tiles with a large fountain in the center. He climbed out of his truck and went to the door and knocked.

It wasn't too long before he heard footsteps from inside. "I'll get it," called a child's voice. The door opened and a freshly bathed Ryan with his hair combed neatly stood smiling up at him.

"Hi, Chase."

"Hi…Ryan," he answered, suddenly feeling awkward.

"Mom said you were coming tonight. Will you have supper with us? Rosalie made enchiladas."

"That's pretty hard to pass up."

"It's my favorite." His dark eyes were bright. "That's why she made it. For me."

Chase stepped though the doorway into the terra-cotta tiled entry with rough-plastered, cream walls and dark wood trim that matched the rest of the house.

"You should get special treatment," he told him. "You were brave to handle everything."

"And I didn't cry…much," he said proudly, then leaned forward. "I got scared sometimes, but don't tell Mom 'cause she'll start crying again, and I don't like it when she's sad."

"It's our secret."

"What's your secret?"

Chase looked toward the archway that led into the living room to find Mallory. His chest constricted as if he couldn't draw air into his lungs. She had on a long, multicolored skirt and a rose-colored T-shirt. Her shiny ebony hair lay in soft waves against her shoulders. Although her green eyes were weary, she looked beautiful. That was something he didn't need to notice tonight…or any night.

"Nothing. Just some guy talk."

"Well, you can talk about it later. Rosalie says supper is ready." She looked at Chase. "I hope you're hungry."

He nodded as Ryan ran on ahead. "This isn't going to keep us from having our discussion."

"I know, but Ryan needs family right now." She straightened. "This doesn't just involve the two of us, there's a child to think about. And I'm going to do everything I can to protect him."

"Is that what you've been doing for these years, protecting him from me?"

"However you feel about me, Chase, don't take it out on Ryan. We'll settle things after my son goes to bed."

"I agree with you there, except he's *our* son, Mallory." He glared at her. "You need to remember that from now on."

Mallory sat on Ryan's bed watching him sleep. She silently thanked God over and over again for bringing her son home safely. When he'd been kidnapped she wasn't sure she'd ever get the chance to put him to bed again. Now that she had a second chance, she also had a second threat. Was Chase a threat to her family?

She saw the look on his face during supper, and knew he wasn't just going to walk away. And she wouldn't deny Ryan his father, either. Not again.

She placed a kiss on her son's forehead and watched as he curled up on his side and snuggled deep into the pillow. She walked out and closed the door behind her.

Whatever was going to happen with Chase, she still had to return home to Levelland in a few days. The success of her business depended on her being there. She couldn't expect her partner, Liz Mooney, to handle both the training and the broker business. She headed down the stairs to the great room where she had left Chase with her father.

Surprisingly, she found the two men leaning over the dining table going through one of Ryan's baby albums. She hadn't wanted to notice how devastatingly handsome Chase was. At nearly thirty-seven, he was toned and trim. She sighed as her gaze roamed over his long body. He wore jeans better than any man she ever knew. They rode low and fitted over his tight rear end and muscular thighs.

"That's the first time I got him on a horse," Buck said. "Mallory threw a fit."

She started into the room. "That's because Ryan was nine months old."

"I was holding him…firmly," her father said.

She frowned at him. "He was still too young to be on a horse."

"After that she wouldn't let me take him out of the house until he was three."

Mallory smiled, but Chase didn't. She didn't blame him. She'd been the one who'd caused him to miss all those years.

Buck closed the album. "Well, I think I better call it a night." He turned to Chase. "I can finally sleep now. Thanks for bringing Ryan home."

Chase nodded. "I'm glad it worked out."

Buck paused for a long time. "So am I." He placed a kiss on his daughter's cheek and walked out of the room.

Mallory suddenly felt nervous. For a lot of years she'd wondered about Chase. She'd known he'd become a Texas Ranger, but she never dreamed he'd be back here…in this house.

And after today everything would change…her life and Ryan's life would never be the same.

"Can I get you some coffee?"

"No," he said as he folded his arms over his chest. "All I want right now are some answers."

She nodded, directed him to a brown sofa, and took

the chair across from him, putting the glass-top coffee table between them. "Ask whatever you want."

"I'll start with the obvious. Why didn't you tell me you were pregnant?"

"At first, I couldn't believe it was true," she said weakly. "We used protection."

He didn't respond.

"And I *did* try to call you."

"Like hell you did," said growled. "I don't remember any phone calls from you saying you were pregnant with my child."

She took a breath and let it out. "I called…your mother. I asked her to get you a message…and that it was important that I talk to you."

She saw a glint in his eyes that told her he'd gotten the message. "You should have tried harder— Told her the reason."

"The day we broke up and you left, I was devastated."

"If I remember correctly, you were the one who told me to get out," he challenged.

Mallory remembered everything about that last night. They'd made love. She told him she loved him…and he told her he was leaving for Austin to join the rangers. "You chose to leave."

"I told you before we started dating, that our relationship couldn't go beyond the summer because I would be leaving for training. Besides, you were returning for college."

"That was my father's plan. I wanted to go with you, and you didn't want me. You let me know that being a Texas Ranger was all you wanted."

His jaw tightened. "So to punish me you didn't tell me about my baby and you married another man."

"It wasn't like that." She stood and went to the window. "I was so hurt. My world ended when you went off to Austin. I was convinced you'd find someone else…and forget all about the naïve college girl back home."

She took a breath, and continued. "About three weeks later, Alan came to the ranch with his father. I hadn't seen him since we graduated high school. We'd dated off and on, but mostly we used to be friends." She looked at Chase's stone-cold glare. "I had just learned I was pregnant… I was shocked and scared. And, yes, I told Alan. He listened to me, let me cry it out. He told me he'd always love me…that he'd take care of me and the baby. He asked me to marry him right then." She left out the part about Buck's trouble with the ranch, and Alan's father stepping in as a business partner.

Chase's fists clenched. "Nice to know you forgot me so quickly."

"I didn't!" she gasped. If he only knew how much she'd loved him. She also didn't tell him she was terrified to be a single mother. "I didn't decide to marry him until after I tried to call you several times, but you never returned those calls." She paused for his explanation. She got none. "You weren't coming back to me, were you?"

His gaze never broke with hers. "Doesn't seem to matter now. You didn't give me the chance."

"It seems answering my phone call would have given you a big chance." She felt tears well. Even after all these years, why did it still hurt so much? Pride was fighting with her emotions. "So when Alan asked me to marry him, I accepted."

"After all these years of your silence—when you've been living happily ever after with my child—you expect me to believe anything you say."

CHAPTER THREE

MALLORY WAS FUMING. How dare he?

"I didn't think you wanted us." She lowered her voice. "You didn't call me, or see if I was okay."

He glared at her for a long time. "So you just hopped into bed with another man to find a more favorable father for your baby."

"No, it wasn't like that. We—" She stopped. There was no reason to tell Chase about how long it took her to give herself to her husband.

"You what, Mallory?" he prodded. "Found it easy to give yourself to another man."

"No, it wasn't easy. You knew you were the first man…and how much I loved you." She took a breath. "It was you who didn't want me… And I was convinced you didn't want our baby, either."

He was silent as he glared at her. "If I'd known we created a child that night, I never would have left you."

She closed her eyes. "I didn't know that. I was young and scared, Chase. And so unsure that I could compete with your dream." She tried to stay calm. "And you had always made it clear that avenging your uncle's death, and being a ranger came first in your life."

Chase's gaze moved from hers, not before she saw a flash of his own guilt, too. So she'd hit a nerve. He wasn't so righteous now.

"Maybe I was wrong to turn to Alan, but he said he loved me…that he'd love Ryan." She hesitated and that caught his attention.

"What happened?" he repeated. "What did Hagan do? Did he change his mind about the boy?"

"Nothing at first, he was a good husband…and good to Ryan. But he wanted more children…."

"But what?" Chase coaxed.

"I agreed, but I never got pregnant and Alan learned he couldn't father a child. After that our marriage was never the same. And his relationship with his son was… strained."

"Stop calling him that," Chase said angrily. "Ryan is my son." His hands clenched. "What I want to know is was the boy punished for your husband's…inadequacy?"

"No! And stop interrogating me like a criminal. Alan never lifted a hand to Ryan." Her husband had saved that for his wife. "We separated not long after that." Her voice softened. "About two years ago Alan was killed in an accident."

"It still doesn't excuse what you did, Mallory. You kept my son from me."

She wasn't about to tell him her recent plans to find him. He wouldn't believe her. "And you ran out on me," she emphasized. "I was miserable and lonely, and I turned to another man who promised to love me. I never got any promises from you."

Chase opened his mouth to argue when a child's cries drew their attention.

"Ryan," Mallory gasped as she ran to the stairs and hurried up to his room. Chase was right on her heels.

She pushed open the door, rushed to the bed and eased down beside her son as he was thrashing around on the mattress. "Ryan, wake up, honey."

The boy gasped and sat up. "Mom!" he cried and hugged her. "They're coming after me again."

"No, honey." She held him close. "Those men are in jail. They can't hurt you anymore."

Chase stood at the door feeling awkward as he watched Mallory rock her son back and forth. This was all so new to him. How do you learn how to be a father? How do you make up all those lost years?

Maybe he should just walk away. Who would know? He saw the boy's tears in the dim light and something tightened around his heart. Ryan had stolen that same heart the second Chase walked into the shack to find the eight-year-old trying to be so brave.

No, he was staying put. "Ryan…" He walked inside and stood at the end of the bed.

"Chase…" Ryan quickly wiped his eyes. "You're still here."

He nodded. "Your mom and I were talking. I wanted to make sure you were okay. Sometimes after something bad happens, people get scared again."

"Grown-ups, too?"

"Yeah, I've seen grown men cry. How you acted the

last two days was very brave. And a lot of people get nightmares." He walked around to the side of the bed and sat down across from Mallory. "I've had a few myself."

"Really?"

"I wouldn't lie to you."

That got a smile from the boy and another funny feeling erupted inside Chase.

"Ryan, you still need to go back to sleep," his mother added. "There's the roundup tomorrow. And if you want to help—"

"I do," he told her, then glanced back at Chase. "Will you come, too? It's so much fun. Grandpa can't ride but I get to help 'cause I'm eight this year."

"Ryan, Chase probably has to work."

"No, as a matter of fact, I'm off for the weekend." He smiled at Ryan. "It's been a few years since I did any roping. Maybe you can show me some pointers."

"Sure. So you'll come?"

"Wouldn't miss it."

Mallory turned back to her son. "You will unless you get some sleep." She kissed him and placed a light-weight blanket over the boy. "Good night, Ryan."

"Good night, Mom. Good night, Chase."

"Good night, son," they both said in unison.

Mallory allowed Chase out first, then she flicked off the light and closed the door. Silently they walked downstairs.

"Are you angry because I said I'd come tomorrow?"

She shrugged. "I'm protective of my son."

"Our son."

She didn't hide her frustration. "Okay, let's discuss

our son. You really want to be in his life?" When he
started to speak, she raised her hand. "Before you
answer, Chase, be sure, because once you announce
you're his father you can't just walk away. I won't let it
happen to him, not again…and I don't care if you are a
ranger. I'll fight you or anyone to protect that boy."

An hour later, Chase found himself parking his truck in
front of Jesse Raines's house. Too keyed up to go home,
he decided to take him up on his offer.

He walked to the door, seeing the small tricycle and
toys scattered in the yard. Another pang of sadness
rushed through him as he knocked, then wondered if
he should have just gone for a drink by himself. He
wasn't the type of guy who shared much, especially not
his feelings.

All that changed when the door opened and Jesse
appeared. Dressed in nylon shorts and bare-chested, the
young ranger looked as if he'd just finished a five-mile run.

"Hey, what's up?"

"Is it too late to take you up on that offer for a beer?"

Jesse smiled. "Never. Just happen to have a couple
cold ones."

Chase stepped inside the neatly kept living room.
An overstuffed sofa and chair were placed in front of
the large television. Next to it was an overflowing toy
box. The sound of kids in the background was muffled
by a closed hall door.

Jesse slipped on a T-shirt and motioned for him to
follow him into the kitchen. He opened the refrigerator
and took out a couple of long neck bottles. When Chase

had transferred to Midland, Jesse had been the one who reached out to him. They had become friends.

He twisted off the caps and handed one to Chase. "How'd it go tonight?"

Chase took a long drink, then shrugged. "Ryan was happy to see me."

"That's a good start." Jesse walked to the sofa. "So you're the boy's father?"

Chase nodded and took the chair at the table. "Yet, I don't have any legal right to be with him. Hagan is listed as his father on the birth certificate."

Jesse took a drink. "You can go to court—that is, if you want to acknowledge Ryan."

"If you think I'm going to cut and run—"

"I didn't say that," Jesse interrupted. "But there's being a father, and there's being a father. You can write a check for child support, or you can take an active role in his life."

Chase got up. "Hell, this is all so new to me. It changes everything." He thought about his career plans. "I don't have family anymore. When Mom died a few years ago…" He paused, thinking about Sara Landon who had wanted nothing more than a few grandkids. "Damn, she had a grandson."

"Don't do this, Chase," Jesse warned. "You didn't know about the boy, either."

"And according to Mallory, she tried to contact me. Then this…Alan raced in to rescue her. Later on her marriage went sour…."

"You believe her?"

He paced, recalling years ago his mother calling him

about Mallory's message. He was still angry over the fight, and decided not to talk to her just then. "Yeah, and for Ryan's sake, we need to get along."

He looked toward the doorway and saw the petite woman with blond hair holding a baby in her arms. Jesse's wife, Beth.

"Hi, babe," Jesse said as he went to her. "Do you remember, Chase Landon. Chase, this is Beth, and this sweetie is Lilly." He squeezed the baby in his arms and was rewarded with a giggle and a pat on the cheek. "Our son, Jason, is sleeping."

"Hi, Beth. Sorry to intrude on your family time."

"Please, Chase, you're welcome here any time." She stood next to her husband and he wrapped an arm around her shoulders and pulled her close.

"Jessie told me about your rescue today…and finding your son. You have to be so happy."

Chase glanced at Jesse. There's no doubt he shared the news with his wife. Was that how loving couples did things? "Yeah, I'm very happy he's safe, but under the circumstances of how I learned about him, I'm still working on that."

She nodded. "I'm sure you are."

"Do you have any advice for me?"

"Just think about your son. Put him first."

Yeah, think about Ryan. Anything to keep his mind off beautiful Mallory and how much he'd once loved her. All he had to do was think about her keeping his child from him.

"I need to go." He set his bottle on the counter. "Nice to see you again, Beth. You, too, Lilly."

After the goodbyes, Jesse handed the baby to her mother. "I've been invited back to the Lazy K for their roundup tomorrow," Chase said. "You want to come along?"

"I think I'll pass," Jesse said, following after Chase. "The past two days in the saddle were enough for me." He smiled. "Besides, I wouldn't want to intrude on your father/son time."

Early the next morning, Mallory watched Chase's truck come up the road. Some things never change. When Chase Landon gave his word, he stuck by it. So she knew that if he decided to be in their son's life, he would be there.

And now, that was something she had to deal with from now on. She also had to take the blame for this. It had been a mistake not to tell him about his son.

She'd been a coward back then. She'd married in haste and realized not long after that it had been a mistake. Alan had seen her regret, too, but he wasn't about to let her go, and had used subtle threats to keep her under his thumb. She'd worried mostly about Ryan's safety. She'd stayed, but when Alan's drinking got worse and he started taking swings at her, Mallory found a way to leave.

So she couldn't blame Chase if he hated her. She had been weak back then, but no longer. And she couldn't let a war start up between them. Ryan would see it, too. Her son was loyal to her, so their feud wouldn't sit well with the child.

Chase climbed out of the truck. Well over six feet tall, his buckskin boots only added to his height. He was dressed the part of a cowboy in worn jeans and a chambray shirt. His straw Resistol hat sat low on his head, shielding his dark gaze.

Mallory struggled to take a breath into her starved lungs. Darn, he could still get to her.

Suddenly Ryan went running toward his father. He stopped just short of giving him a hug, but his excitement was obvious. Chase put a hand on his shoulder and together they walked toward the barn.

"They look good together," Rosalie said as she glanced away from her task of chopping vegetables.

"Yeah, they do, but will they get along as father and son?"

The housekeeper shrugged. "Not your choice to make. Although it already looks like Chase Landon is staking his claim." She smiled. "I always liked him."

Mallory blinked. "Since when? You hardly said two words to Chase when I brought him home."

"Wasn't my place," she admitted. "Besides, back then Chase was a lot more man than you could handle."

He was definitely that. "Well, as you've witnessed, it seems I'm lacking when it comes to men."

Rosalie shook her head. "No, Mallory, you had to put up with more than a person should ever have to. Look at you. You were a single mother who fought to protect her son, and build a new life. Now, you run a successful horse broker business."

Mallory smiled. "I guess I have done pretty well." She glanced out the window again. "But I've got a really big problem now."

Rosalie took another look outside. "Oh, I don't know. I wouldn't call that good-looking Texas Ranger a problem. Trouble maybe, but seems to me that's exactly what you need to get your blood going."

This time Mallory laughed. It felt good…at least for now.

Chase watched Mallory come out of the house. She was tall and graceful, not to mention beautiful. Even when he'd first met her years ago, she'd taken his breath away…and stirred his body. Dammit, nothing had changed.

"Good morning, Chase," she said in a soft voice.

"Morning," he replied.

"Mom, Chase is going to ride with me. Grandpa has a horse saddle for him. So we have to go."

Mallory nodded to her son. "Okay. Why don't you go and see if your horses are ready. I need to talk to Chase a minute."

The boy frowned, but he took off, leaving them alone.

"Are you going with us to see how I handle myself?" Chase said.

Mallory looked hurt. "Of course not. I trust you." She let out a tired breath. "Look, Chase, a lot has happened in the past few days. Can't we just try and get through this?"

God, he wanted to hate her. Then he thought back to the young girl who'd done everything to draw his attention. She had no idea she already had, the minute he looked into her green eyes. But that was long ago, and he wasn't the same man now.

"There's no getting through anything, Mallory. I'm going to be around from now on. Soon, Ryan will know that I'm his father."

Chase took off toward the corral, leaving her standing there. What did she expect? He wasn't going to be pushed aside any more. He wanted to be a part of his son's life.

Buck was waiting for him with a saddled mount. "I wanted to be able to ride today especially since Ryan is old enough to take part himself. But at least, you'll be with him."

Chase studied Buck. There'd been a time when the man had threatened to throw him off his property. Now he seemed to be welcoming him with open arms.

"I know Ryan is happy you're okay, Buck. This situation could have turned out badly."

The older man visibly shuddered. "I know. I owe you a lot, Chase."

Chase shook his head. "I was doing my job."

"Is it your job to be here today?"

"I'm here because I was invited by Ryan." He straightened. "If you have a problem with that—"

Buck raised his hand. "No, Chase. I'm being overly protective of my family. I guess I want to know what your intentions are."

"Not to be rude, Buck, but that's between Mallory and me."

The older man nodded. "I know it is. Just don't blame my daughter for everything that happened in the past. We both know I had a lot to do with how things turned out back then. I pushed her hard to marry Alan. If it's any consolation, I'll regret it until the day I die."

Chase recalled the heated discussion he'd had with Buck Kendrick. It took place right in this house, just a week after his daughter's wedding…to Alan Hagan.

Before Chase could say anything, Ryan called to him. He waved back and took the horse's reins from Buck. "Like I said, it's between Mallory and me." He walked off.

It wasn't going to be an easy day for anyone. But when he went toward the corral and saw the smile on Ryan's face, he realized it was all worth it.

The boy stood next to a small painted mare. "This is Mazy," he announced. "She's my horse when I come here. I have my own horse back home. First, I had a pony, Speckles, but last year Mom got me a chestnut gelding. His name is Rusty."

Chase linked his fingers together, Ryan placed his boot inside and Chase boosted the boy up into the saddle.

"Do you have your own horse?"

Chase climbed on his mount. "No, no yet. But I've been looking for a small place of my own where I could keep a few horses."

"Well, you get to ride all the time with the rangers."

Chase smiled. "I wish. Most of my work has me in a car. I do get to go out on training maneuvers so we can practice tracking lost boys."

Ryan grinned. "And you're really good, 'cause you found me."

"We had some help, several other men and a couple of bloodhounds."

Ryan pushed his hat down as they rode out to follow the others. "Well, you found me and you captured one of the bad men."

Guiding the horse through the gate, Chase watched the boy expertly handle his horse. "How did you find out all this?"

"Grandpa and I were reading the paper this morning. And he said you knew Mom when she was young."

"Yeah, I knew your mother long before you were born."

The boy looked thoughtful. "Grandpa also said you're a hero."

His chest puffed out a little when his son called him a hero. "No, I'm not a hero. I'm trained to catch bad guys."

The boy looked thoughtful as they rode through the gate. "Maybe I can be a Texas Ranger when I grow up."

"Sure, but it takes a lot of years of hard work."

Those dark eyes that mirrored his gazed solemnly at him. "Good, because I want to be like you."

Chase had to swallow back the sudden dryness in his throat. His son wanted to be like him.

Three hours later, Rosalie and the other women had worked to set up tables on the shaded patio, knowing once the herd was brought in to the holding pens the men would want food, and plenty of it. Well, lunch was ready.

Mallory had gotten a call from Mick saying the men and herd would arrive shortly. She stepped outside to see a dust cloud followed by the soft sounds of bawling calves. She smiled, realizing she hadn't been as worried about Ryan going out as she thought she would be.

Chase wouldn't let anything happen to him.

She grabbed her camera as she stepped off the wooden deck and walked out to the pens. The sounds grew louder and the dust cloud bigger as she climbed the fence railing to look toward the range of mesquite and patches of grass.

She searched the row of cowboys riding drag behind

the herd. It took awhile but she spotted Chase. Tall and broad, and looking comfortable in the saddle, he had his rope in a lasso ready to chase after any strays. Something churned inside her, as she recalled the first time she'd laid eyes on the man.

Chase had been a Texas state trooper then. He'd pulled her over in her new car and lectured her on her reckless driving. She hadn't remembered a word, only his piercing brown eyes and the way he looked in that uniform.

The rest of the summer, she'd continued to race up and down that section of highway just to have him stop her again. He did. Back then, she'd been the pursuer. Three weeks and two speeding tickets later, he'd agreed to go out with her. From the start it had been intense…so hot…and she'd thought…very real.

Mallory released a breath when she spotted Ryan riding next to Chase. It was so obvious to her that they were father and son.

Ryan looked toward the pens, searching for her. He grinned and waved when he found her. She took a picture. She also got several others of the two of them.

Over the next thirty minutes, Buck stood at the gates and supervised the separating of the mama cows from the calves. When the job was completed, they broke for lunch and the ranch hands and neighbors headed for the patio.

Ryan ran up to Mallory. "Did you see me, Mom?"

"I sure did," she told him. "Looks like you're getting pretty good at this. I guess Grandpa doesn't have anything to worry about when he retires and you take over the Lazy K."

He beamed and squinted up at Chase. "Grandpa is going to leave all this to me some day."

"That's a pretty good deal," Chase said as he pushed back his hat.

Ryan did the same. "Well, it won't be for a long time."

"Good," Chase began, "because you need to finish school first."

The boy wrinkled his nose. "That's what Mom says, and then I have to go to college. Why do I have to do that just for some cattle?"

"You have to learn math to know when someone's trying to cheat you…and how to invest all your money."

"Is that important?" Ryan asked.

"Sure is."

"Do I have to go to college to be a Texas Ranger?"

"Yes, you do. That's just part of it. I was a state trooper for eight years before I could even apply to be a ranger."

His eyes rounded. "Wow. That's a long time."

Chase exchanged a quick glance with Mallory. "You know what's great about being eight years old?"

Ryan shook his head.

"You've got time to think about what you want to be when you grow up. So why don't we get some food, I'm starved."

Ryan laughed. "So am I."

"Go wash up, I'm right behind you," he said and the boy shot off.

"Sounds like you had a productive morning with Ryan."

"Yes, we had a good time." He shook his head. "I had no idea how much a kid could talk. Is that normal?"

She smiled. "It's not usual for him, but he's excited. And not everyone is quiet and brooding like you."

"I don't brood. And I just don't talk unless I have something to say." His dark gaze met hers. "Besides, when we were together, we weren't too interested in talking."

Mallory glanced away, unable to stop the flood of memories. They'd been so hungry for each other, there hadn't been much reason for conversation, unless it was to let each other know their desires. "We never talked. Maybe that was the problem."

He studied her for a moment. "No, Mallory, you keeping Ryan a secret is the problem," he said, then stalked off.

Okay, so this wasn't going to be easy. She was willing to do more penance for her sin, but it was going to be on her terms.

She wasn't that young, naïve girl Chase once knew and left without a second glance. She'd survived far too much to let another man dictate to her.

Mallory walked to the deck and stationed herself behind the table and the group of people lined up for the meal. She put on a smile and took over scooping up rice and beans.

"Well, don't you look pretty today, Ms. Mallory," Lee Preston told her as he held his plate.

She'd known the local rancher all her life. "Why thank you, Lee. I'm glad you could join us today. Dad sure appreciates it."

"He had a rough couple of days. I'm just being neighborly. I don't doubt he'd do the same for me."

She served several other ranchers and Mallory came

to realize how lucky she'd been in her life. West Texas neighbors were the best. Her son and Chase were next in the line.

"Rice and beans?" she asked.

"Yes, please, ma'am," Chase said as he nodded his head.

"What about you, Ryan?"

"I'll have the same, Mom," he said as he mimicked Chase. She scooped up their helpings, feeling a little jealous that she'd been excluded.

They started to walk off, then Chase turned back to her. "Will you be able to join us?"

"Yeah, Mom. Come eat with us."

She nodded. "Okay, save me a place and I'll be there as soon as I can."

Chase walked away, knowing he didn't need the distraction of Mallory. But he had no choice. They all needed to get along for Ryan's sake. He sat down at the end of the table and Ryan took the chair beside him.

"It was fun today," Ryan said.

"Yes, it was. It's been a long time since I've herded cattle."

"You're gonna stay for the branding, aren't you, Chase?" Ryan asked.

"Sure," he told him. "I was hoping to team up with you."

The boy pumped his fist in the air. "All right!"

"Your grandpa asked if I wanted to be a heeler. Want to help?"

"That's cool."

"What's cool?"

Mallory arrived at the table and took the empty seat

across from them. Today, she was wearing a pair of worn jeans that hugged those mile-long legs of hers. Her hair was pulled back into a loose ponytail, and some strands had worked free. Her eyes locked with his and suddenly memories of their summer together came rushing back. How easily he'd gotten lost in their green depths, the husky sound of her voice….

He quickly pushed the memories aside and said, "Buck asked me to help with the branding."

"I'm going to help him, too," Ryan said. "Chase asked me." The boy took a big forkful of beans and ate them.

That got a raised eyebrow from Mallory. "I'm not sure if that's a good idea, Ryan."

"Aw, Mom. Grandpa said I could help him this year, but because he got hurt he can't do it." He put down his fork. "P-please, I want to help Chase."

"I'll watch him closely," Chase assured her. He wouldn't let anything happen to his child. "He'll be the third man on the team so that should make it safe enough." They both knew frightened calves could be unpredictable.

Still she hesitated. "Okay, but don't get too carried away." She turned to Ryan. "And you do exactly what you're told."

The boy bobbed his head up and down. "I will. Oh, boy." A big grin appeared. "Can I go tell Joe?"

His mother looked down at his nearly clean plate. "Finish eating first."

The boy gobbled down the last few bites, then stood up. "I'm done."

"That was fast. But haven't you forgotten something?"

His eyes widened. "Oh, Rosalie's pie. I can bring

you back some, Mom." He smiled sweetly. The kid could be a charmer. With her nod, he turned to Chase. "You want some pie?"

"I wouldn't turn a piece down. Any kind is fine."

The boy shot off, leaving the two alone at the table.

Chase could see Mallory was upset. "You think I should have consulted with you before I asked Ryan?"

"I am his mother. It would have been nice. You know the dangers of a roundup."

It made him angry Mallory thought he couldn't keep their son safe. "So it was okay that for two days I tracked down the boy, then rescued him from criminals, but you don't think I'm capable of keeping him safe during branding."

She blinked. "Of course, I know you will. It's just—"

"It's just that you don't want to share your son." He stood, then leaned down and lowered his voice. "You better get used to it, Mallory, because I'm here and I plan to be a part of Ryan's life. A big part.

"I have a lot of years to make up for."

CHAPTER FOUR

WOULD THE WEEKEND ever end?

Mallory walked toward the branding chute and pens just in time to see Chase and Ryan share a high five after they released the calf's hind legs and the animal scurried away. Another hand opened the gate and sent the steer back to its mama.

"Good job," Chase cheered his son. Ryan smiled, puffing out his chest.

This was the second day of the roundup, and the third day Ryan and Chase had spent together. It was easy to see how attached her son was getting to Chase. She didn't believe it was all hero worship, either. Mallory felt her stomach tighten with guilt. For eight years, she'd denied her son a real father and still all she could think about was keeping Ryan to herself. Old habits died hard. She was overly protective for a good reason.

Mallory shivered, recalling Alan's constant anger. The frequent fights...the rages that would eventually turn physical. Her own pride kept her from leaving for a long time, but then she had to survive…and most of all, she had to protect Ryan.

She recalled the last time Alan had taken his brutality out on her. Afterward, he'd left the house, and she'd taken her chance, maybe her last. She'd managed to gather her frightened son and together they'd hiked across their property to find safety at her neighbor Liz Mooney's place.

She'd called her father and he brought her back to Midland. Buck had wanted her stay at the Lazy K but she needed her independence, to make it on her own. In the end, she'd accepted Liz's invitation to become business partners. It still hadn't stopped Alan's threats on her and her son. Her ex-husband had even mentioned Chase.

One thing Mallory knew for sure, no other man would control her or her life ever again. She looked toward Chase. Not even a good-looking Texas Ranger.

She stepped closer to the edge of the pen. The amazing father-and-son team was tackling yet another calf. She smiled, feeling the years of regrets that she hadn't given Ryan this relationship sooner. Of course that posed another question she knew she had to face, telling Ryan of her secret.

"Hey, Mom, did you see us?"

She smiled. "Yes, I've been watching you. You're a great team."

Buck stood in the background, giving praise, too. Even Chase gave his son a rare grin. She studied the man she had tried to put out of her mind over the years. It never worked. Just seeing Ryan grow and look more like his father daily didn't help, either.

She had been so much in love with Chase back then. Now, he was back in her life, hating her for keeping Ryan from him. Would he ever forgive her for being young and foolish?

She put on a smile as the dynamic duo came out of the pen. Both were dressed in jeans, Western shirts, and white straw hats; their leather chaps flapped as they strolled toward her. Good heavens, they even walked alike.

"Grandpa said we should take a break 'cause we've been working so hard."

She held out two bottles of water. "I bet you can use these."

"Sure can. Thanks, Mom."

"Thanks, Mallory," Chase said as he took the chilled bottle. He didn't take his eyes off her as he twisted off the lid and placed the bottle against his mouth. Then he tossed his head back and drank half the bottle.

Mesmerized, she watched the sweat roll down his face and had to stop herself from wiping it away. She quickly glanced away. What was wrong with her? She didn't need any thoughts like that. It would only lead to trouble. She stole a glance at Chase. He was watching her with those dark eyes. A warm shiver slid down her spine. Definitely big trouble.

"Hey, Mom, can we go swimming?"

She turned her attention to her son. "Had enough branding?"

Ryan pushed his hat back off his face. "I'm kinda tired."

"Me, too," Chase admitted. "I'll probably have some mighty sore muscles tomorrow." He rotated those broad shoulders. "It's been awhile since I've branded a steer."

"You looked pretty good to me," she said, then realized how that sounded and quickly added, "but if you'd rather swim…"

Ryan looked up at Chase. "I want to swim, don't you? Grandpa's pool is really neat. It's got a slide and a diving board."

"Man, that's a hard choice. Do I want to wrestle smelly calves, or float around in cool water? What should I choose?"

Ryan started to giggle. "The pool. I'll go get my trunks on. Come on, Grandpa's got a lot of extra suits for people."

"Okay, I'll meet you there," Chase called, then looked at Mallory. "Are you going with us?"

She shook her head. "No, but I'll probably hang around to make sure you kids don't do anything stupid."

He smiled. "So you're going to spoil all the fun."

"It comes with the territory of being a parent. Someone has to act like an adult."

"Mallory…"

"Chase…" They both spoke at the same time.

"You go first," he prompted.

She sighed. "I was going to say that we haven't had much of a chance to talk. And since Ryan and I will be leaving tomorrow—"

He frowned. "Whoa…back up. You better change those plans," he insisted. "You're not taking my son anywhere, not until we have this straightened out."

Later that evening, Chase walked out to the Kendricks' backyard. The pool was empty now, and the wrought-iron gate locked for safety. In another section a large manicured lawn was trimmed with yard lights and colorful flowers. The crickets chirped, keeping him company as he waited for Mallory. She was putting Ryan to bed.

Chase paced the terra-cotta-tiled patio. He was anxious and a little angry. No, a lot angry. It happened every time he thought about the eight years he'd missed with his son. Now, Mallory said, "Here are your two days, sorry but I have to leave and take our son."

No, he wasn't going to let that happen. That meant he needed to do something to stop it…legally. He wanted a life with the boy. He knew what life was like without a father. There was no way he'd allow that to happen to his son. He wanted more. The boy was his only family.

Years ago he'd thought Mallory would be his family. As it turned out, she didn't love him, and he'd been quickly replaced by another man. Worse, she walked away with his son. No more. No matter how much she could still get to him, he wasn't going to let her have her way on this.

He'd contact a lawyer tomorrow.

The French doors opened and Mallory stepped outside. She'd changed out of her jeans before supper into a yellow sundress that exposed her delicate shoulders and the golden hue to her skin. Her hair was down, dancing around her face.

"Sorry it took so long," she said. "I helped Rosalie put some things away." She directed him to a grouping of teak chairs around a table.

He waited for her to sit first, then took the chair across from her. It seemed strange that they'd once been lovers, and had made a child together, yet this felt more like a formal business meeting. Maybe that was a good thing.

"I guess what you want is to discuss how we're going to tell Ryan you're his father."

"How generous of you," he growled, but immediately regretted his words.

"Look, Chase. I've already admitted I was wrong not to tell you. I can't change the past. At least believe me when I say I'm not going to stop you from being in your son's life."

"And you need to understand that I can't fully trust you, Mallory."

She looked hurt. "I accept that. But it's Ryan who's my big concern. I don't want him hurt."

Chase cursed, stood and began to pace. "You don't think he's going to be hurt when he learns you kept him from his father?"

Mallory rose, too. She knew she'd be paying for her mistakes the rest of her life. "Yes, he will be. Alan wasn't the father he should have been."

Chase raised a hand. "I don't want to hear about your dead husband. And don't compare me to him. Ryan is my son."

She sighed. "Yes, he is. But tell me, Chase, how active are you planning to be in his life?"

"Very active. I plan to go to court and get partial custody."

Mallory didn't like to be threatened, but she also

knew Chase had the right to do this. She didn't like that, either. "Please don't, Chase. Can't we work something out between us?"

He frowned. "It's a little late, don't you think? You've kept Ryan from me for so long."

She went to him. "If you want to hurt me, fine. But a court battle would hurt Ryan, too."

How different things would have been if Chase had been around to raise his son. It had been something she'd wished for every day in the last nearly nine years…every day she'd looked at Ryan, saw the likeness and remembered how much she'd loved his father.

Would Chase remember what it had been like, too? Although he'd never said the words to her, she always knew he cared for her.

Mallory studied his rigid jaw and knew how stubborn Chase could be. He wasn't going to give in easily, but she had to try. "You and I can work out visitation," she continued. "And I promise, I'll let you see him whenever you want."

He stared at her for a long time. "My, aren't we suddenly eager to cooperate."

"Yes, I am. I love my son. I'll do whatever it takes to keep him from getting caught in our battle."

His gaze bore into hers; then came the smirk. "If I remember, Mal, you enjoyed those battles between us. You had quite a temper when you didn't get your way. We used to get into some pretty heated…arguments."

She had been spoiled back then. She'd grown up fast after marrying Alan. "I've matured a lot since then. Things are different now."

He glanced over her body and she saw a flicker of awareness in his eyes. "Oh, I don't know, you seemed pretty grown up back then, too."

Mallory couldn't stop the blood from rushing to her face. "I was eager to please. I would have done anything for you."

His gaze lingered on her. "And I would have for you. You could turn me inside out with a look. You had a power over me…" He closed his eyes. "Damn. Why did it have to happen like this…" he said, his breath caressing her face. "I would have dropped everything for you…for my child…."

Move away, she warned herself, but couldn't seem to gather up the resolve.

He leaned forward and brushed his lips against hers. She sucked in air as he eased away. "Damn, you could turn me every way but loose."

She bit her lip to keep from begging him for more, told herself she was just curious, but knew it was more. It had always been more with Chase.

He didn't disappoint her and dipped his head toward her. His mouth captured hers. This time there was no doubt about his intentions as he quickly deepened the kiss. He wanted her. Drawing her to him, he moved his legs apart, fitting her intimately against his body. She was just as eager for him as his tongue slipped in and out of her mouth, tasting her, caressing her.

She whimpered, feeling his hands run over her back, searing her skin. He had her unable to think beyond that wonderful hunger he'd always caused deep inside her. Suddenly he released her. In the dim light she could see a mixture of raw desire and anger in his gaze.

"I guess we never had a problem in that department."

She stiffened. "Well, I'm happy you got to test your theory. But in the future please refrain."

"You're right." He walked away, then back again. "I want time with my son."

"I agree, but I live outside of Lubbock, over a hundred miles away from where you live. It's not like you can drive across town."

"Maybe one of us should relocate."

She stared at him for a long time. "I take it, you mean me."

He shrugged. "You were raised here in Midland and your father lives here."

"I've lived outside of Lubbock for years. Ryan was born there…my business is there. I can't leave."

Chase couldn't leave the rangers, either. A transfer was possible, but it could take years.

He caught a glimpse of the woman he'd kissed senseless. That wasn't wise. It also wasn't wise to learn that he was still drawn to her. Maybe it was good she lived in another town, except he wanted to be close to his son.

"I don't like the idea of being a weekend dad."

"I have room at the ranch. You could stay there when you visit…for Ryan, of course."

So she still wanted to have everything her way. "So that's your answer. We tell Ryan I'm his father, and then you leave here. I don't think the boy's going to be too crazy about that idea."

"No, that's the reason I think we should *wait* to tell Ryan who you are."

He just stared at her. "You don't think eight years is long enough?"

"Ryan's been through a lot. Let him get used to you. I can see you're building a friendship."

Chase hated that she was right. "So are you willing to stay here so I can spend time with him?"

"I can't, Chase. My business doesn't run itself. I have a scheduled horse auction. I've made a commitment, too. My clients depend on me."

"And I have my job here."

She closed her eyes. "Then we'll have to wait until one of us has some time off."

"I guess that would be me. It just so happens, I have two weeks vacation coming. So it looks like you're going to have a house guest for a while."

The next morning, Mallory finished loading the SUV and was ready to leave for Lubbock…and her home for the past three years. Chase had arrived just moments ago to help share the news with their son…that he was coming to the ranch. As much as Mallory wanted a father for Ryan, she knew however this turned out she would end up the bad guy.

At least she had a reprieve for a few weeks.

"I'm coming, Mom," Ryan called and she could hear his footsteps on the stairs. Her heart pounded harder… faster. She glanced at Chase who stood by the fireplace, eyeing a picture of a much younger Ryan. Another reminder of a time he'd missed with his son.

Ryan hurried into the room. He smiled at his mother, then spotted Chase. "Hey, Chase, what are you doing here?"

"I came to see your mother…and you."

The boy's smile dropped. "To say goodbye?"

"Not exactly," she said. "Last night Chase told me that he's been thinking about buying a horse."

"You know that small ranch property I talked about buying?" With the boy's nod, he continued his half-invented story. "Well, it's up for sale and I put in an offer. And I thought since I had some time off, I'd look at some horses." He glanced at Mallory. "Your mom is going to help me find just the right one."

"Cool. We have a lot of horses at our ranch."

Chase relaxed a little. "And that's where I plan to start my search. Your mom has invited me to come for a visit. Would you mind me hanging around for awhile?"

"No! I mean, I want you to come to the ranch."

Mallory had to turn away as another surge of guilt overtook her. She'd lain awake most of the night, trying to think of a way to explain to her son that she'd lied about his father. She hoped over the next two weeks she could find a way.

Ryan continued to cheer. "Oh, man, I can't wait to tell Bobbie Everett." He looked at Chase. "He's my best friend in the whole world. He's gonna flip when I tell him you're a Texas Ranger, and you rescued me."

Buck walked into the room. "Hey, what's all the racket in here?"

Ryan ran to his grandpa. "Grandpa, Chase is coming to stay with Mom and me for a while."

"That's good. Then you can spend some time together."

"He can meet all my friends."

Chase stood next to Mallory, both watching their excited son. Then he turned to her, his gaze moved over her again. "Are you ready for me as a house guest?"

No! "As long as you remember this arrangement is for Ryan's sake," she reminded him. "Let's not make this personal."

He nodded. "Not to worry, I learned my lesson a long time ago."

Before leaving on vacation, Chase needed to stop by the office and talk to his captain. Mallory asked if she and Ryan could follow so they could thank the men involved in the rescue. He didn't object, but was a little disappointed he couldn't introduce Ryan as his son. But that would happen soon enough.

Inside, the rangers gave Ryan a cheer and applause, deeming him a hero for acting so brave during the kidnapping. The captain awarded the boy with a ranger's baseball cap, then Carol, the administrative assistant, showed him and Mallory around the office.

Chase went into the captain's office to let him know he'd be out of town for awhile. "I'll be just outside of Lubbock. Here is the number I can be reached at if you can't get me on my cell."

"It would have to be quite an emergency before I'd call you back from vacation. You're long overdue, Landon." He eyed Ryan and Mallory outside the glass partition. "Just tell me you aren't looking for a new home with the ranger company in Lubbock."

Chase smiled, thinking about how he could put in for a transfer. "Hardly," he told him. But realistically it wasn't so far-fetched for Chase not to consider it. He'd do pretty much anything to be close to his son.

Robertson nodded. "Good. So go and enjoy your vacation."

"Plan to," Chase said as they walked out.

"One more thing," the captain began. "Have you done any follow-up on the escapees, Reyes and Jacobs?"

"What do you mean?" Chase asked, knowing he'd finished all the paperwork from the capture.

"I'll let Jesse fill you in," Robertson told him.

Chase walked out into the hall and met up with Ryan and Mallory. "I have some work to finish with Jesse."

Mallory nodded. "Then we'll take off. You have my directions?"

"You really are coming?" Ryan asked.

"I'm really coming." Chase tugged on Ryan's new hat, finding he was excited to spend time with his son. "Give me a few hours. I need to stop by my place."

Chase looked at Mallory, finding more confusing feelings. And how dangerous it would be to act on them. There couldn't be a repeat of last night's kiss. "I'll see you later, too."

He watched them both walk out the door, then headed down the hall and into Jesse's office. "Captain said you wanted to see me."

He stood. "Probably not important, but Reyes is making noise since he got out of solitary."

"Like what?"

"Just more of the same. He says he has information about Wade Landon's death. And he wants to make a deal."

"He's a three-time loser," Chase said, not wanting to get his hopes up. "There are no deals."

Jesse shrugged. "I know, but it wouldn't hurt to go talk to Reyes."

"What if it's a load of crap?"

"And what if it isn't?" Jesse countered. "What if Reyes knows what happened that day?"

"Then he's got to have more details than just mentioning Wade Landon's name to get me excited."

Chase was pretty sure of one thing; his uncle's death had been a gang-style killing. And Reyes was connected to the *Bandidos* gang, but so were a lot of other men in prison.

He moved toward the door. "Well, it's going to have to wait, because I'm off to the Mooney Ranch for two weeks."

Jesse grinned and sat down on the edge of his desk. "Ryan mentioned it several times." He lowered his voice. "So, you're going to play dad."

"We haven't told Ryan anything yet. I just want to spend some time with him, hoping he'll get used to me."

"From what I've seen of you together, I'd say you're a perfect match. What does his mother think of this arrangement?"

"I don't think she's crazy about me barging in…but she'd better get used to it. I'm going to be in Ryan's life, whether she likes it or not."

CHAPTER FIVE

LATER THAT DAY, Chase turned his truck onto a narrow road about ten miles outside the small town of Levelland, just west of Lubbock. The large tires dug into the loose gravel surface, kicking tiny rocks upward, causing a pinging sound against the belly of the truck.

He turned and drove under an archway that read, Mooney Ranch, headquarters for Mallory K Horse Broker. Chase saw ahead a compound with several whitewashed structures, along with two huge arenas. The house was a large, two-story clapboard, painted a sunny yellow with white trim.

Chase parked next to a mud-crusted truck imprinted with the ranch's name on the side. He climbed out and looked toward the corral where a woman sat astride a large stallion. He gathered she was Mallory's partner, Liz Mooney. He took a moment to admire the skilled rider as she worked the beautiful chestnut quarter horse through the Western Dressage pattern.

They were magnificent together.

Suddenly he heard a screen door slam and a kid's voice call, "Chase!"

He turned to see Ryan jump off the porch step and break into a run. A German Shepherd mix dog scurried behind him, barking. The boy was fast and a little awkward as he made his way across the yard. Chase resisted catching him in a big hug.

"Hey, kid, haven't seen you in a while," he joked.

"Yeah, like two hours," Ryan said, while the dog nudged at Chase for attention. "Max, sit," Ryan ordered, and the animal obeyed. "How long you going to stay, Chase? Will you go riding with me?"

"Ryan, let's give Chase a chance to catch his breath."

They both turned to see Mallory. She was dressed in her usual jeans and a fitted pink blouse. He had trouble pulling air into his lungs, recalling how much he liked that color on her.

He shook his head. *Don't go there.*

"Hi, Mallory."

"Chase," she returned. "You made it okay."

"You gave good directions."

"Hey, Mom," Ryan called, "Can I show Chase around?"

She raised an eyebrow. "Since Chase is interested in buying a horse, how about I show him around? And you can come along."

"Okay, but don't show him my…project. I want to." Boy and dog ran on ahead toward the barn, leaving his parents behind.

"Like I said before, he's got far too much energy."

"Well, you're about to get a big dose of it so you better get plenty of sleep," she warned. "And now that school's out, you'll have him all day long."

He sighed. "I'm looking forward to it."

She finally smiled. "So is Ryan."

His gut tightened as he watched her. If there was anything that hadn't changed over the years, it was that she could still stir him up. He glanced away. "What project was Ryan talking about?"

"I'll let him tell you."

They started walking toward the barn. "How does your partner feel about me…showing up?"

"Liz? If she doesn't like it, she'll tell you."

He glanced toward the corral and saw the woman in question climb down from the stallion. She handed the reins to a man, then walked out of the arena toward them.

She looked to be in her midfifties, but her trim body and long rust-colored braid made her seem more youthful. As she approached, Chase caught her fresh-scrubbed look, showing off a dusting of freckles across her face.

"So you're the famous Texas Ranger," she said, and looked him over. "I thought you were a giant or something the way the lad described you."

Chase laughed. "Sorry to disappoint you."

She gave him another exaggerated once-over. "Oh, no, I'm not disappointed at all. In fact, I'm grateful to you for bringing Ryan back." She stuck out her hand. "Hello, I'm Liz Mooney."

"Chase Landon." He shook her hand. "It's a pleasure to meet you, Mrs. Mooney. Thank you for letting me stay here."

"It's Liz, and it's not a problem. This is Mallory and Ryan's home, too."

Mallory decided it was time to join the conversation.

"We're partners," she added. "Liz is the breeder and expert trainer. I sell the horses and handle the business end of things."

Liz snorted. "Don't let her whitewash it. If it hadn't been for Mallory's skills, the ranch wouldn't have survived. She's built quite a successful business for both of us."

"We've made a good living," Mallory admitted. "And the arrangement has been perfect for both of us. The best part, I get to stay home with Ryan."

"That's good," Chase said, not giving her any attitude. That surprised her. Maybe they could do this.

A horse whinnied and Liz glanced over her shoulder. "Well, it seems a certain guy is getting impatient. I better go and show him who's in charge." She turned back to Chase. "I'll see you at supper."

"I look forward to it, Liz," he said.

The older woman hurried off toward the corral and Mallory and Chase continued on to the barn.

"She seems nice. How long have you been partners?"

"Officially about two years. We were neighbors first. Alan had inherited his grandparents' ranch—the land borders Liz's property." She stopped, not wanting to go into any detail of her marriage. "When I separated from Alan, Ryan and I came here to stay at first. It was only supposed to be temporary, but Liz had recently lost her husband…and lost her desire to train horses. You can say we kind of helped each other through a rough time." She faced him, not ready to explain how Liz's home had become her and her son's safe haven. "She adores Ryan."

"I'm sure your father would have liked you to come home to Midland."

"Of course, but I wanted to be independent. I wanted to teach the same to Ryan." She sighed as they walked on. "I began by helping list Liz's stock on the Internet, along with advertising her training expertise. She has the reigning champion, Sparks Will Fly, in stud here."

Chase whistled through his teeth.

She continued. "And, yes, I sell his stud services via the Internet, too."

He broke out into a grin. "You're quite the business-woman. I'm impressed."

For some strange reason, she cared what Chase thought. "Liz has been a big help, especially when I branched out and started brokering other horses in the area. It took some time, but we've made a name for ourselves."

"I'd say so. I'm impressed, and a little envious." He glanced around. "You have a nice place here."

"Thank you." That meant a lot to her.

"Growing up in an apartment in town, I always wanted a small ranch."

She didn't know that. "I thought you always wanted to be a ranger."

"That, too. But I plan to retire someday."

"I guess I never thought about you retiring, not until you found—" She paused. "I mean you were so anxious to find the answers to your uncle's shooting. Was his case ever solved?"

He shook his head. "No. There hasn't been any new evidence."

She felt his demeanor change. Even after all this time,

he hadn't seemed to let it go. "I'm sorry, Chase. I wish…"
She didn't know the right words to say. She never had.

He stopped at the barn doors, his dark gaze locked
with hers. "You wish I could find the person who
brutally shot Wade, and stripped him of his badge as if
it were a souvenir?" He paused as if composing himself.
"Yeah, me, too. Me, too. Maybe we'll catch a break
someday…and find the guy."

Before Mallory could say anything more, Ryan
called out and waved for him to come to a stall.

"You better go see what he wants."

Chase started down the aisle, but Mallory stayed
back. She'd already gotten too engrossed in his personal
life. It was hard not to react to the pain she still saw in
his eyes. When they'd met, Wade Landon's death had
been fairly recent, and Chase had been so determined
to find the killer. She hated that he hadn't gotten the
closure he needed.

She watched Chase and Ryan and smiled. She
wanted to give them time alone together, although she
wasn't sure what her son had planned for his father.
Maybe if Chase concentrated on just being Ryan's
father, he'd find what he'd been missing.

She knew he had no family left. There'd only been
his uncle and his mother to start with. And they were
both gone. His own father had bowed out of his life a
long time ago. Ryan was all the family Chase had now.
Hopefully, his son could help fill some of that emptiness. Regret rushed through her, recalling it was something she'd never been able to do.

"My, my, my. There's a man who'd be hard to pass up."

Mallory turned to see Liz. "I thought you had a stallion to work."

"Juan put on the wrong bridle." Her friend studied her. "And what are you going to do? Just stand in the background and watch them?"

Liz had been one of the lucky few; she'd been happily married for over thirty years. She knew everything from Mallory's past, including Chase.

"What do you expect me to do? Chase let me know a long time ago that he didn't want me in his life…especially after what I did."

"Well, looks like things have changed. You have something he wants…his son."

"I'm not starting up with him just because of Ryan." She couldn't handle that kind of hurt again, not for any man.

"It seems like a good place to start," Liz told her.

Mallory shook her head, knowing her friend's ability to play matchmaker. "No way. One bad marriage is my limit. I'm not letting any man dictate to me again."

"Did Chase show any signs of that before?"

"No, but neither did Alan."

"Are you kidding? Your ex-husband was selfish all of his life. Of course I put a lot of the blame on his daddy and mama who spoiled him rotten. And when he couldn't have you…he tried to control you."

Mallory allowed Liz to be the expert since his grandparents' ranch bordered her property. She'd known Alan Hagan all his life, the good and the bad.

"Just because they were rich doesn't mean they're better than anyone else."

"Well, Alan is dead now." She recalled the horrible car accident he hadn't survived. "He can't hurt Ryan or me anymore." She glanced toward her son. "And I won't let anyone else hurt us ever again."

"Okay, you handle it your way." Liz shook her head and sighed. "Those two sure look good together."

Mallory noticed it, too. She realized that having Chase here was the right thing to do for her son. She wasn't so sure about herself.

After Ryan went to bed for the night, Chase followed Mallory across the compound to his temporary living quarters. They stepped up onto a small porch of the cottage.

"It's not that large, but I'm sure it will meet your needs," Mallory said as she unlocked the door. "And you'll have more privacy here. Believe me, Ryan can be pretty trying. The kitchen has been stocked with essentials. But we want you to come up to the house for meals."

"I'll be fine, Mallory," Chase assured her.

She opened the door, reached in and flipped on the lights, illuminating the room.

Chase stepped inside behind her. He was impressed as he took in the large room that held a sofa, a chair and a kitchenette with a counter and two stools. Down the hall, he found a newly tiled bath and a small bedroom. He tossed his duffel bag on the bed and returned to the main room.

"At one time this was the foreman's house," she explained. "But we don't have one now. A foreman, I mean. And the ranch hands stay in the bunkhouse. We use this place sometimes for guests and clients."

"It's great," he assured her. "And you've been gracious enough to allow me to stay here."

"No, Chase, I owe you. I took away a lot of time you should have had with Ryan." She looked sad. "So any time you want to be with Ryan…you're welcome to stay here."

He wanted more than just to visit Ryan. He wanted his son to come stay with him in Midland, too. Would Mallory be willing to let him visit? "Do you have time to talk?"

Nodding, she sat in the chair while he took a seat on the sofa. "If this is about telling Ryan who you are—"

He raised a hand. "No. So much has happened to him that I think you're right, we should wait a little while. Of course our son isn't stupid. He'll probably figure it out pretty soon on his own. I'd like to be prepared." He paused a minute, trying to figure out how to approach the next question. "How did Alan really treat Ryan?"

Mallory didn't like to talk about her marriage with anyone, especially not Chase. "Alan was attentive to me during my pregnancy, but afterward, he couldn't seem to get by Ryan's different looks, especially after he found a picture of you." She glanced away. "He got angry, but it was directed at me." Mallory felt herself flinch just thinking about that time with her abusive husband. And more and more, Alan was jealous of the time she'd spend with Ryan.

"And I made sure I kept Ryan away. And I know for pride's sake, Alan wouldn't say anything to him." She'd never let the violence touch her son. "I came to realize that I'd made a mistake, and I took Ryan and we left."

Mallory felt the still raw emotions building. She shook her head trying to shut away the nightmare of her marriage. The months of living in fear. Alan's threats of retaliation after she'd left him. For a long time, she'd worried that he might go after Chase.

She sighed. "It was sad for Ryan because he didn't know why he'd never had his father's love. And I couldn't tell him about you."

Chase's fists clenched, wishing he had Hagan alone for just five minutes. He sure as hell wouldn't show the coward any mercy.

Chase also knew he had to take responsibility…take some of the blame. He should have been there for her…for his son. Instead, Mallory had paid the price.

He crossed to her, crouched in front of her chair. "How bad did things fall apart, Mallory?"

She wouldn't look at him. "It doesn't matter," she insisted. "It's over now. I admit the marriage was a mistake. And there's nothing I can do to change the past." Tears swam in her eyes. "Please, believe me, Chase, if I'd known what a disaster it would have been, I'd never have married Alan. If you would have called me…"

God, he hated seeing her tears, her pain. "I know, Mallory. I was angry, too….When I got the message that you called, I couldn't talk to you. What you wanted I couldn't give then," he lied. He had wanted her. He'd just realized it too late.

She nodded and brushed back her hair. "I'm glad you're going to be in Ryan's life. He needs you. I saw that the minute you two were together." A tear found its way down her cheek. She swiped it away. "Just love him."

He couldn't stand it any more. He reached for her and pulled her close. "I didn't think it would happen so fast, but I already do love him."

She finally broke down and sobbed. He scooped her up in his arms and carried her to the sofa, reveling in the fact she clung to him. Her sweet body pressed against his. Even after all these years, it felt so right.

"I'm sorry, Chase," she whispered. "I've made such a mess out of everything."

"Sssh," he breathed and held her. Damn, she was breaking his heart. "We've both made mistakes, Mal. I have to take some blame, too. If I hadn't left you back then—if I'd stayed—" He wasn't about to tell her that he'd returned only to find she was already married…so all he could do was walk away from her a second time.

It broke his heart.

Mallory raised her head and looked at him, her green eyes luminous. "No. I knew all along how much you wanted to be a ranger. And you are such a good one."

"I was wrong to leave you the way I did," he said. "I wish I could go back and change—"

She placed her finger against his lips to stop his words. "We can't do that, Chase." She gave him a sad smile that made his chest ache. "Please…no more regrets. Let's just look toward the future."

He swallowed and managed to nod. He still had a lot to make up to his son. So things were going to be different from now on. He was going to be in both their lives.

She touched his face and he about lost it. "You're a good man, Chase Landon."

What he was feeling and thinking right now was far from being good. "And you're a good mother." He couldn't resist her any longer and touched his mouth to hers.

"Chase…"

"Quiet, Mal. We've talked enough." He was at the end of his patience. His mouth closed over hers, and he forgot about everything else but the woman in his arms. A whimper escaped her as he deepened the kiss. He parted her lips, and delved inside to taste her. She was just as hungry as her arms went around his neck and she pressed against his chest.

He was quickly getting lost in her scent, her touch, her taste. He wanted more…. Pushing her back on the sofa, he started to stretch out beside her, but she resisted and broke off the kiss. There was fear in her eyes as she pushed him away and sat up. "I can't do this, Chase. I just can't." She stood and went to the door.

He sat there a moment trying to gather some composure. He hated that she still could get to him. "It's okay, Mallory. Although enjoyable, it's far too late for seduction."

She gasped. "You're the one who kissed me," she tossed at him. "I only stayed to talk about Ryan."

"It's hard to turn you down when you're so tempting," he said, trying to cover his own weakness. Her. He definitely hadn't been thinking of Ryan when he had Mallory in his arms. "You were a willing participant in the kiss, too."

She shook her head. "I'm not going to jump into bed with you."

He raised an eyebrow, trying to ignore the leftover feelings. "Seems to me we've always had that kind of reaction toward each other."

Her eyes were pleading. "Reactions or not, I'm not ready for this."

"Okay, but there's no reason to be afraid of me."

She squared her shoulders. "I'm not afraid of you or anyone," she insisted. "I just don't want to get involved with you. I think right now we should concentrate on being Ryan's parents."

"That's fine by me." He motioned for her to leave.

"Okay. Good night," she said and walked out.

Chase watched her hurry toward the house. His body still ached for her. Damn, he hadn't planned for this to happen. He didn't want to desire Mallory again. He'd vowed he wouldn't let her get to him again…. But it was too late. He cared about her, probably always would.

There was a lot more at stake this time. With their history, how were they supposed to keep away from each other?

The next morning brought sunshine and mild temperatures for an early June day. Liz was outside unloading the new mare.

Ryan was dancing around the breakfast table setting out the flatware waiting for Chase to appear. Mallory was anxious about the same thing, but for a different reason. She'd overreacted last night.

It was just a few kisses, though Chase's kisses were

anything but ordinary. She shivered. He might be a good guy, but she didn't trust herself, or any man at this point.

"Chase said he'd be here at seven," Ryan said. "He was going to help me on my project."

Mallory glanced at the kitchen clock. It was only ten after. "If Chase said he'd be here, he'll be here." She set down a plate of eggs and bacon. "Now eat."

"Okay," he groaned and had just picked up his fork when the back door opened and Liz came in, followed by Chase.

"Chase," Ryan called as he jumped up from the table and rushed to greet him.

"Sorry I'm late. I helped Liz unload the mare. She's real pretty. After breakfast we'll go see her."

"Are you going to buy her?" Ryan took him back to the long pine table.

"I wish, but she isn't for sale," he said. "She's here to make a foal."

"You mean Spark's going to cover her," her son said in a matter-of-fact tone.

Mallory bit her lip to keep from smiling. Most ranch kids learned about sex from watching it with the animals. Ryan was no exception.

Liz sat down and joined in. "Yep, I'd say Spark is going to be a daddy again."

"But we never get to keep any of them," Ryan complained.

"That's because your mom and Aunt Liz have to make a living," Chase told him.

"I know." The boy smiled again. "I'm lucky, too,

because I have my own horse, Rusty. What kind of horse do you want?"

Chase shrugged. "Not sure yet. I haven't had much time lately to look."

Mallory came to the table carrying two plates, setting one in front of Chase.

His dark eyes met hers. "Thank you," he said.

She swallowed. "You're welcome," she barely managed to say. She sank into the chair across from him.

He was freshly shaven and his hair was combed back from his high forehead. His brown eyes had golden flecks in them and were fringed with long, black lashes. He grinned and her heart leapt. Good Lord. Get a grip. She couldn't do this for two weeks.

She put on a smile, too, ignoring her pounding heart. "I have a few listings to show you," she began. "If you're interested in any, I'll take you to see them."

"Sounds good."

They ate for a while, and Ryan said, "Chase, are you still going to help me with my project?"

"Yes. But I don't know what that project is." He looked around the table, and both Liz and Mallory shrugged.

The boy glanced at Liz, then his mom. "You have to come with me to see it first."

Chase looked at Mallory. She knew her son had been gathering leftover wood from the repairs to the corral and the stalls over the last few months. She suspected that he wanted to build something.

Definitely a father-and-son project.

* * *

After breakfast, Liz went out to the mare's barn while Ryan disappeared upstairs to finish his chores. Chase sat at the table and looked around the big farm kitchen. There were knotty pine cabinets and cream-colored tile covered the counters. The hardwood floors were scarred, and a few of the boards squeaked. It was a great room.

Mallory stood at the sink finishing the rest of the breakfast dishes. She was ignoring him. He had gotten under her skin last night. She had done the same to him, stirring up memories of their time together. A time he didn't need to think about today, or any day.

He didn't want to think about what she'd gone through in her marriage to Hagan, either. It only made him angrier. She wasn't about to trust anyone right now, and after last night, especially not him. He needed to tread slowly, or keep out of her way.

His gaze moved over her slim figure. The nice curve of her bottom was outlined by her jeans. Suddenly his own jeans were uncomfortable and he shifted in his chair. This wasn't going to be easy.

Mallory came to the table with the coffeepot. Her dark hair was tied back into a ponytail, and a thin row of bangs brushed against her forehead. "Want more?"

His gut tightened again. Definitely. "Only if you join me and we talk."

"Unless it's about Ryan, we've already said everything, Chase."

She was right. He'd be foolish to start up anything with her. He had a job with the rangers to return to, and his home was over a hundred miles away. Then he recalled last night and how she'd felt in his arms, the way her lips felt under his…that had him forgetting all practicalities, and everything that had happened in the past.

He also saw her determined look. "Not a problem," he lied.

She looked relieved. "It's for the best. You're trying to build a relationship with your son."

Suddenly Chase realized that he wanted his son's mother included in some of those plans, too. But she was right. It wasn't possible. "You're right. Ryan has to be my main focus. Although, it would help if you would turn ugly and didn't distract me." When a rosy blush spread across her cheeks, he couldn't stop. "You are one hell of a beautiful woman, Mallory Hagan, but I'll try to control my urges."

"Oh, that makes me feel so much better," she said, trying to act irritated.

"Happy to oblige." Grinning, he leaned back in his chair as she sat down across from him.

"All I care about is that you oblige your son."

A warm feeling spread through him. "I like that."

"What?"

"That you called him my son." He leaned forward and grasped her hand on the table and squeezed it. "I might be angry for not knowing about him, Mallory, but never about the great kid you raised."

"Thank you, that means a lot."

There was a sudden commotion upstairs, then a sound on the stairs warned them Ryan was coming. Mallory pulled her hand away.

"Hey, Mom, I finished making my bed and cleaned

my room," he announced, then turned to his father. "Chase, you ready to go now?"

"Sure," he said and carried his mug to the sink. "We'll see you later."

"Yeah, Mom, later."

Together they went out the back door and walked past the barn about fifty yards to where there was a big tree. The thick trunk was split and two branches angled out about four feet from the ground.

"What do you think?" he asked Chase.

He had no idea what Ryan was talking about. "It's a great tree." He moved underneath and looked up into the oak. "You got plans for it?"

Ryan nodded and went to a bush where an old horse blanket covered a stack of wood. On second look they were wood scraps. "I want to build a tree house. Just for me. But I need help."

Chase pushed his hat back. "I'd say so. It's a big project for one guy."

"I know. Grandpa was supposed to help me but he got too busy, then he got shot." Squinting from the sun, Ryan looked up at him. "So I was wondering if you ever built anything before."

Chase eyed the branches, searching for a good base for the platform. "I've built a few things in my day. In fact, I had a tree house once. My uncle Wade helped me build it."

"Cool. So you know how?"

He wasn't an expert with power tools, but he could put something together. "Yeah, I could help you."

Ryan pumped his fist in the air. "All right. Wait until I tell Bobbie about this."

"Whoa, slow down, Ryan. This needs to be approved by your mother first."

His smile drooped. "Why? She won't let me. She'll just say it's too dangerous."

CHAPTER SIX

"OH, RYAN…it's too dangerous," Mallory said, looking up at the enormous oak tree.

Her son gave his best pout, then looked at Chase. "I told you she'd say that. She thinks I'm still a baby."

Mallory resisted the urge to argue with her son. She'd only end up the bad guy. "We've talked about this, Ryan. You could fall out of the tree and hurt yourself. I thought you were going to build something on the ground."

"Mom…" he whined. "That's no fun. It won't be cool unless it's up there and no one can see me. Like a secret hideout."

Great. How was she supposed to keep an eye on her child if she couldn't find him? "It's still pretty high up."

"Chase will build it real strong…and safe. Right?" Those pleading brown eyes turned to Chase.

"Well…sure," he began his pitch to her. "I'd put four-by-four posts in the ground for support, and build the base about six, seven feet high." He raised his hand over his head, giving her an estimate of the height. Then he had the nerve to smile at her. He was worse than Ryan. "I'll make sure it meets all your standards."

"What does that mean?" Ryan asked.

"Her rules on how we build it." He folded his arms over his chest and his gaze caught hers. "What do you say, Mal?"

"Yeah, Mom, what do you say?" Her son stood next to Chase and mimicked his father's words and actions. She was lost. She couldn't take this away from either one of them.

"Are you sure it will be safe?"

"I'll put in extra braces and a sturdy ladder."

"Okay…I guess you can build it."

Her son launched himself into her arms. "Oh, thanks Mom, I love you." Just as soon as he released her, he hugged Chase. "Thanks, Chase. I'm gonna call Bobbie and tell him." The boy tore off toward the house.

Mallory turned back to Chase. "I hope you know what you've gotten yourself into."

He grinned. "I doubt it, but I do know I'm going to love every minute of it."

"I'm sure you will," she said sternly. "But next time, will you come to me first so we can form a united front?"

"It seems a little unfair to gang up on an unsuspecting kid."

She couldn't think with Chase staring at her. "Oh, do you have a lot to learn."

He stepped closer and lowered his voice almost seductively. "Maybe you could teach me some of the secrets of parenting."

She laughed, hoping to break the mood. It didn't

work. "Foolish man, there are no secrets. You just hope you stay one step ahead of them."

He arched an eyebrow. "With Ryan, I doubt that's possible."

"Now you're getting it. Always expect the unexpected and never think or even mouth the words, *my child would never do that.*"

That caused Chase to grin as he raised his right hand. "I promise. But I want something from you now."

She sobered. "What's that?"

"Keep telling me whenever I do something wrong."

She smiled. "That's a guarantee. Just remember, you can't give Ryan everything he asks for."

"It's hard not to."

"I know. And the tree house is a good thing since you two will be working on it together. He needs the company of a man. I'm afraid with just Liz and me there isn't much testosterone around here."

"Well, I'll see what I can do. Now, if you'll direct me to the nearest lumberyard." He paused. "Wait, why don't you go with us and I'll treat you both to lunch?"

She blinked in surprise. "No. I mean this is for you two."

"I don't want to exclude you, Mallory. You're his mother. We need to show Ryan we all get along."

Mallory already knew she could get along with this man. Too well. She recalled their shared kisses just the night before. But any more involvement could be disastrous for all of them. She carried too many scars from her failed marriage. And she doubted he'd ever completely forgive her. But for Ryan's sake she was going to make this time together work.

"Okay, I'd love to go, but I'm paying for half the lumber."

"No way," he argued. "If you do, then you have to help us build it."

"Okay, you win, but I get to test it for sturdiness. If it doesn't meet my standards, it comes down."

He sobered. "That's one thing you don't have to worry about, Mallory. I'd never put our son in harm's way."

She sighed, seeing his heart-wrenching look. "I know you wouldn't, Chase. I guess I'm a little overprotective. It's just been Ryan and me for a long time."

He came to her. "I'm not trying to take him away from you, Mallory I just want to be a part of his life. I want to be his father."

An hour later, Chase, Mallory and Ryan were sitting in a booth at the local diner, eating hamburgers. Chase glanced out the window to see the bed of his truck loaded down with lumber.

"You sure you got enough supplies?" Mallory asked, fighting a smile.

So he'd gone a little overboard. "I think so. We're not sure how big we want it, yet."

"Yeah, Mom," Ryan said. "We're not sure."

Mallory played with the straw in her glass. "I can understand that. Is it going to be a one or two-bedroom? And you'll need to think about property values in the area."

Chase enjoyed her humor, even if it was at his expense. "Very funny. But you wanted it sturdy, I'm making sure it's sturdy."

"Just don't make it so nice he'll move out there permanently."

The boy stopped eating. "But I want to sleep out there," he said. "Chase said we could—" his voice faded, as he realized he was giving away the secret.

Chase was surprised that Mallory just smiled. "Seems you got talked into a lot." Her gaze met Chase's and she lowered her voice. "Eventually, you're going to have to say no to him."

He couldn't take his eyes off her mouth. "I know, but I'm just having too much fun."

They both looked at Ryan as he attacked his hamburger. "That's it, son. Eat up," Chase said. "You're going to need your strength when you swing that hammer."

"I know." The boy chewed another bite. "Can we start on the tree house when we get back?"

"We'll see, but there's rain predicted."

"If it doesn't rain, can we?"

So many questions. "We can start." Across the diner, Chase caught an older woman watching them. She looked to be in her sixties. She had dark hair streaked with gray and a stocky build. There was a frown on her lined face as her eyes riveted on Ryan.

"Oh, no, not now," Mallory whispered under her breath. "It's time to leave." She nudged at Chase.

When the woman started to walk toward them, Chase pulled his wallet from his pocket, took out a twenty-dollar bill, and put it with the check. "Ryan, why don't you go pay for lunch so we can get started back?"

Nodding, the boy slid out of the booth, grabbed the money and took off. The woman looked curiously at

Ryan, but continued to their table. "Well, so you have the gall to show your face in town."

Mallory sighed. "Becky, I have as much right to be here as you do."

The older woman's eyes narrowed. "My son had rights, too, but you took them away."

Mallory's body stiffened, but Chase saw her hands tremble as she clutched them in her lap. "Alan took a lot from me, too." She released a tired breath. "Can't we just let him rest in peace?"

"There's no peace," she said angrily. "I lost my son, but you still have yours. You even managed to take the child away from us."

"I didn't take anyone away," Mallory said in a quiet voice.

Becky turned her glare on Chase. He had no doubt the woman had figured out his part in all this. "I'd say you're the boy's real father."

He just remained silent…for now.

"Too bad you didn't show up sooner, then my son wouldn't have suffered with this woman." Before he could react, she turned and marched off.

Chase wasn't sure what to do. He shot a quick look at Mallory who was blinking away the threatening tears.

"I guess you need to get in line. Seems I messed up a lot of lives with my choices."

Before Chase had a chance to react, she slid out the other side of the booth and hurried to Ryan at the cash register.

Whether she deserved it or not, he didn't like seeing

her hurting. One thing he knew for sure, Mallory was the one who'd suffered the most from those choices.

That afternoon, Mallory sat in her office. The room had once been the study, but the space was big enough for both Liz and herself. She especially liked the location of her desk, right in front of the big window that overlooked the ranch. She could see Liz working in the arena, and off beside the barn, she found Chase and Ryan, digging holes for the posts.

It was hard to concentrate on her upcoming schedule since the man had stripped off his shirt, revealing a muscular chest and arms. His broad back wasn't bad, either. Of course, she knew he had to keep in shape for his job. She just didn't expect it to affect her so much.

Turning her attention to her son, Mallory noticed that he'd removed his shirt, too. Normally, she'd worry about sunscreen, but they were working in the shade of the tree.

Mallory stood and walked away from the window. "Stop it. Just let them do their thing. They don't need you to interfere in their fun."

If only she didn't feel like she was losing a part of Ryan. Was she jealous because the man she once loved and wanted to marry only wanted their son?

If she were honest, she'd admit how much she wanted them to be a family. Okay, maybe not in the traditional sense. She didn't know if she could ever trust herself with a man again. Even Chase.

Especially after the near disaster in the diner. She'd always known Becky Hagan had it in for her. Although Buck and Al Hagan had been friends and business associates, Alan's mother had been against the marriage. No one was good enough for her precious son. Things got worse after the separation.

The slam of the screen door alerted Mallory to Ryan's arrival. She closed her laptop and walked out into the hall, then through the dining room with the dark stained wainscoting and woodwork. There was a huge table that seated ten easily, along with a matching sideboard that had been in Liz's family for generations.

She heard laughter as she stepped into the kitchen, finding Chase and Ryan making sandwiches, peanut butter and jelly. The simple sight make her chest tighten. They smiled alike, with the same brown eyes.

Ryan looked up. "Oh, hi, Mom. Chase and me got hungry." He placed a slice of bread on top of his creation and took a big bite.

"Hope you don't mind," Chase said.

Her pulse raced and she couldn't slow it. "Of course not." She went to the refrigerator and pulled out some milk. "You've been working for hours." She got two glasses from the cupboard and filled them, then took their drinks to their place at the counter. "Get much done?"

"We dug the post holes and set them in cement," Chase said. "The cement needs to dry, then tomorrow, we can frame the base."

He bit into the bread and chewed. How could a man look so sexy eating peanut butter and jelly? Her gaze roamed over him. He leaned against the counter in low-riding jeans with his shirt unbuttoned, exposing just a hint of his muscular chest and rippled stomach.

"Mallory…"

She quickly redirected her attention to his face. "Did you say something?"

He tossed her one of those rare smiles. "I just asked about your afternoon."

"Oh, I stayed busy. I've got a client coming by in a few days to look at one of Liz's colts."

"Oh, no, not Sets Off Sparks," Ryan gasped.

Mallory nodded. "Mr. Paterson wants a good mount for Western Dressage."

Ryan hung his head. "I wanted to keep him."

"And I told you earlier we need to make money to keep the ranch going, or keep your stomach full."

She poked teasingly at her eight-year-old. "But I wouldn't be surprised if the new owner hires Liz to help with the training. So the colt will be around for a while."

"Good."

"And I think…" She wrinkled her nose at Ryan. "That you should take a bath before supper."

"Aw, Mom. Do I have to?"

She sniffed again. "Oh, yes, you have to."

"You know, that's not a bad idea," Chase began. "I'm pretty ripe myself. A shower would cool me off, too. And I may just rest for a little while."

Chase watched as Ryan reluctantly agreed, then finished off his milk, and headed up the stairs for the dreaded bath.

Mallory turned to him and those green eyes locked with his. "Thanks for the help," she said. "He's been going nonstop since the roundup. So have you. You've got to be tired, too."

"It's a good kind of tired," he said, recalling how he'd

been too restless last night after their shared kisses to get much sleep. Suddenly his body stirred at the memory at her tempting mouth…her body. "I wouldn't mind some quiet time." What he wanted was to share more time with Mallory.

Although she didn't seem to feel the same. She moved around the kitchen, cleaning up the mess, and avoiding him. Everything had been going fine between them until they'd gone to lunch. Until her past reared its ugly head.

"Tomorrow afternoon Ryan goes in to the therapist."

Chase knew it was a good idea to talk about the kidnapping. "Has he been having any more nightmares?"

She shook her head. "At least something is going good."

He knew she wasn't talking about Ryan. He carried his plate and glass to the sink where she was staying busy. "Mallory, I'm sorry about what happened at the diner."

She glanced at him, then finally shrugged. "You have nothing to be sorry about. It's my problem."

"Still, no one has a right to talk to you like that." He inhaled her soft scent and he had trouble concentrating. "So…I take it Becky was your mother-in-law."

She nodded and continued to wash. "Although my dad and Alan's dad were business partners at one time, Becky Hagan had never been happy about my marrying her precious son. She blames me for Alan's car accident."

"Were you driving the vehicle?"

"No. But he started drinking heavily after he learned he couldn't father a child."

"Once again, you didn't force your ex to drink, or to get into the car."

She set a washed glass on the counter and shut her

eyes. "I should have stopped him, but he was so angry—" She paused and took a breath. "We'd already separated and Ryan and I were living here, but he kept coming by…at all hours."

Chase tensed. How bad had the man terrorized her? He hated to think that Hagan had his hands on her. Damn, no one deserved to go through that. "Did he hurt you?"

She finally turned to him. "I got out, Chase. I got Ryan out." Her gaze was intense. "You have to know, I would never let anything happen to him."

This was killing him. "I know, darlin'." No matter what happened to her, she'd never let anything happen to their son. "But what about you, Mallory? Did you truly get out?"

She shook her head and started to leave, but he reached out to touch her arm.

"It's okay, you don't have to tell me. Just know that you aren't to blame for what happened."

He couldn't stop himself as he reached out and cupped her jaw. She was so soft. Bravely she bit down on her trembling lip.

He was losing it. The last thing he needed right now was to start up anything with her that didn't pertain to their child. What she needed in a man, he couldn't give her, but that didn't stop his desire for her. Some things hadn't changed.

With the last of his common sense, he dropped his hand. "I should go." But before he could get his feet moving, his cell phone rang. He pulled it off his belt, and saw that it was from the office.

"I need to take this." He walked to the back door.

"Landon," he said.

"Chase, it's Jesse."

"What's up?" He knew it had to be important for his partner to call him on vacation.

"Just a heads-up. I'm going to Sweetwater Friday to see Reyes." There was a long pause. "He'd rather talk with you."

Chase wasn't going to get excited. "Then he better come up with something worth hearing. I'll only give him what he wants, if he gives me something. At least a name, some kind of proof that he knows who shot Wade."

"I'll let you know if that happens. Later." Jesse ended the call.

Chase slipped his phone back in its holder and looked over his shoulder at Mallory. "Sorry."

"Why be sorry? You have a job, too."

Surprisingly, it was a job he hadn't been thinking about much. Not since he came here. He thought about the fun he had spending the day with Ryan. "Yeah. For a long time it was all I had."

"Is there a problem? Is that why they called you?"

He shrugged. "One of the prisoners who took Ryan says he knew my uncle. He wants to talk to me."

Her cat-green eyes widened. "Will you have to go back?"

"Trying to get rid of me?"

For a long time she just stared at him. "No. It's nice having you here…for Ryan."

He walked back to her. "Just for Ryan, Mallory?" He was crazy for doing this, but he couldn't seem to stop himself. "What do you feel about me being here?"

"I told you, Chase, you're welcome here any time," she hedged. "But that's all I can give you."

Two days later, Mallory was up with the sun. So was the father-and-son construction team. They were busy at work beside the barn. It was hard, but she tried not to be too nosey about the project. The platform had gone up yesterday. This morning they'd been working on the stairs.

She also tried to stay away for another reason. To protect herself. She wasn't ready to share any more of her past with Chase. She knew a lot of the problems in her marriage hadn't been her fault, but the emotional scars would take a long time to heal…if ever.

"Is this the best price?"

She shook away her thoughts, and turned back to Jerry Patterson, the buyer for Sets Off Sparks. "Not only is the price set, it's a great price for a horse with his bloodline." Jerry always had to feel he was getting a deal, especially if he was doing business with a woman. But eventually Mallory could bring him around to her way of thinking. And he could afford the colt at any price. "And…Liz is giving you a deal on the training. I'd say take it, because if you don't, she's had two other offers."

The forty-something, local rancher grinned. "You're good, Mallory. I hope Liz knows what a great salesperson you are."

"What Liz knows is top quality stock. I just sell them."

"Well, you can stamp *sold* on this animal." He pointed over his shoulder. "Hopefully he'll turn into an AQHA reigning champion."

"I don't doubt it." She started walking Jerry back to his truck. He usually wanted to hang around and chat. She didn't have the time, especially since he'd been trying to get her to go out on a date for the past six months. About the time his second divorce became final.

Jerry glanced toward the barn. "Looks like your boy is getting a mighty fine tree house. Is one of the hands helping him?"

The fact he thought Chase was a hand bothered her. "Ryan's helper isn't a ranch hand. Chase Landon is a Texas Ranger." That was all she was going to say.

The tall rancher stared down at her, then finally said, "I guess that about says it all. The ranger is a lucky man."

It wasn't a big deal Jerry thought she was dating Chase, she told herself. "It's still a new relationship."

"Well, he must be special if he got your attention. I wish the best for both of you."

She nodded. "Thanks, Jerry." Behind him she saw Ryan and Chase coming toward them. Oh, no.

"Hey, Mom. Chase needs to go back to the lumber-yard. Can I go?"

"Sure."

"Hi, Mr. Patterson."

"Hello, son," Jerry said, tugging on Ryan's hat. "Looks like you're getting quite the tree house."

Mallory knew Ryan had never cared for Jerry's teasing. "Yeah, it is."

She jumped in. "Ryan, go wash up, then you can leave." She nudged her son toward the house, but then saw Chase was approaching them. The day was just getting worse. He put on his shirt and was buttoning it.

Jerry smiled. "Looks like I get to meet the guy who finally caught Mallory's attention." He held out his hand. "Jerry Patterson."

"Chase Landon." He shook the offered hand.

"You're a lucky man to win a gal like Mallory."

Mallory's heart pounded as Chase's gaze caught hers. "Yes, I am lucky." He took two steps and stood beside her, then slipped his arm around her. "And Ryan's a bonus, too." He looked down at her upturned face.

Was he going to go along with her fib? "I was just telling Jerry that you came to visit." She shrugged. "He just sort of guessed something was going on." She laughed nervously.

"It's kind of hard to hide my feelings." He placed a quick kiss on her mouth. "Right, darlin'?"

"Well, I can see I'm not wanted here." Jerry tipped his hat then walked to his truck. Smiling, they both kept watching as the man climbed into the truck.

"You can let go," Mallory insisted, glued to Chase's side.

"Not yet," he told her. "We need to prove to him that you're taken." He turned her in his arms and his mouth closed over hers.

CHAPTER SEVEN

MALLORY'S HEART RACED as Chase's mouth captured hers in a hungry kiss. In an instant, she was lost in his arms, and wanting more. He didn't disappoint her. When he ran his tongue over the seam of her lips, her hands found their way around his neck and she held on for the wild ride. She loved his familiar taste, the feelings he invoked in her. Inhaling his masculine scent of soap, sweat and pure Chase, she felt alive.

Finally he broke off the kiss, but stayed close and whispered, "You think we convinced him?"

"What?" Mallory opened her eyes to see his smoldering dark eyes. "Oh—" She stepped back. "You shouldn't have done that."

He raised an eyebrow. "The kiss? I thought you wanted Jerry to think you had a boyfriend. Didn't you?"

"Yes, I did, but you didn't need to…kiss me," she stumbled over her words. "I was handling things just fine before you got here."

He folded his arms over his chest. "Maybe so, but now he knows you're taken." He leaned closer. "No need to thank me, it was my pleasure."

Before she could speak, Ryan came racing out of the house. "I'm ready to go."

"Good." He looked back at Mallory as Ryan ran off toward the truck. "Would you like to go with us? Maybe I can warn off any other guys who are interested in you."

She was fuming. "Thank you, but I can handle things from now on. I need to catch up on some work, so I'll stay here. I'm working on a list of horses for you to check out."

"Good. I'm looking forward to it. See you later." He hurried off to catch up with Ryan.

"Bye, Mom." Her son waved.

She watched the two of them and her heart soared. The sad fact was as much as she wanted both of them, she could only have one. And soon, she'd have to share her son's attention with his father.

Liz came up beside her. "So did Jerry decide on the colt?"

"Yeah. But you know Jerry, he doesn't make the sale easy."

"That's because he's sizing you up to be wife number three."

"I quickly nixed that idea."

"I know, I saw Chase." Liz tipped her hat back. "Nothing like a big, handsome Texas Ranger to ward off any unwanted suitors."

Oh, no. "I really didn't plan for Chase to get involved. I just led Jerry in that direction, then Chase showed up and took it another step."

"No kidding." She grinned. "That was quite a kiss."

Mallory was embarrassed. "It wasn't what it looked like."

"It looked like a kiss." She released a sigh. "Like a mouthwatering, heart-stopping, one that leads-to-other-things, kiss." She turned to Mallory. "Just admit you enjoyed it."

Mallory couldn't deny it. "Yes, I did." She sobered. "But it still isn't wise. Chase doesn't feel—"

"There you go again, overanalyzing everything. Believe me, Mallory, from what I saw, Chase Landon didn't act like that kiss was such a chore."

"He's still angry with me about Ryan."

They started walking toward the house. "He probably is. But I also see how he looks at you, and I think that anger is his protection against his feelings. I'd say go after that man, he's a keeper."

Mallory didn't want to think about starting up a relationship with Chase. He'd hurt her so badly before she couldn't stand it again. "I went after him once before, and look how that turned out."

Liz paused on the porch steps. "Yeah, you two got a great kid."

"Do you think Mom will like it?" Ryan asked as he paused from hammering a nail in the railing. His baseball cap was turned backward on his head, exposing a face smudged with dirt, and tiny beads of sweat across his nose.

"What's not to like?"

He grinned. "It's so cool."

Ryan raised his hand and they exchanged a high five.

"Yeah, cool." Chase glanced over the solid tongue-and-groove pine flooring. The two-by-four railing was up all around the sides. The structure had been reinforced so many times, he'd lost count. But he wanted it safe for the boy, especially when he wasn't around to protect him.

"Chase, when can the walls go up?"

"Not today. It's getting too hot to work much later."

Ryan looked disappointed. "What about tomorrow? Can we work on it then?"

Chase had been at the ranch for five days, and he'd counted himself lucky to spend most of that time with his son. "Sure. We'll get it finished before I leave."

The boy looked away, but not before he saw the sadness in his eyes.

"What's the matter?" Chase asked.

Ryan shrugged. "I wish you didn't have to go back to Midland. I like it that you're here all the time."

Chase liked that, too. "I have to go back, Ryan. I have a job. Just like you have to go back to school."

He sighed. "I know…."

Chase took off his hat and wiped his forehead on his sleeve. He sat down on the edge of the platform, then patted the spot next to him. Ryan took the offered seat. "We've talked about this, son." The endearment he called Ryan took on new meaning these days. "I'm only here for a visit. But I'll see you again when you come to your grandfather's ranch."

"I know…it's just that all my friends…Bobbie, Jason and Curt, they all got their dads around. I mean this is the first time I ever got to build something like this." The boy tilted his head up to Chase, his throat worked hard as he swallowed. "'Cause I don't have a dad."

Chase fought his own emotions. "I'm sorry, Ryan. I know what that's like. My dad wasn't around, either."

There was a long pause, then Ryan said, "You didn't have anyone, either?"

"I had my uncle."

The boy looked thoughtful. "I guess I have my grandpa, too."

They sat there for a few minutes, then Ryan said, "I saw you kiss Mom…and I thought if you really like her maybe you'd come back a lot. I mean she's really pretty…."

It was crazy, but Chase felt embarrassed. Not that he thought it was wrong to kiss Mallory. He just didn't know how to explain his feelings to the boy. Not when he didn't know himself.

The child went on to explain, "Mr. Patterson likes Mom, too, but I don't like him." He shook his head. "I'm glad you kissed her."

Chase couldn't help but smile. "I'm glad I kissed her, too."

Ryan's eyes rounded. "So are you going to be her boyfriend?"

Chase didn't want to deal with that question. He was still too mixed up about his anger. How could they start something, and keep it going when they lived so far apart? He tugged at Ryan's baseball cap. "You ask too many questions."

"I know, but I like talking to you. You know how guys talk." The boy looked down again and poked his finger at one of the knots in the wood. "You know what else— I wish? That you were my dad."

"Ryan…" Chase's chest tightened, his throat dried

up. He'd never experienced this feeling before. He wanted so badly to tell him the truth.

The boy still didn't look at him. "I don't remember my dad too much. I remember my mom used to cry a lot."

"You remember that?"

Ryan jerked his head in a nod. "I mean, I was just a little kid, but I sort of remember she got scared. But then we came to live with Aunt Liz and everything was better. Except one time Mom had to talk to the sheriff…she didn't let Dad come here." His gaze met Chase's. "You wouldn't do that, because I know you'd be nice to her…and me."

"Do you miss him?" Chase couldn't manage to say the word, *father*.

"No." His innocent gaze raised to Chase. "Is that bad?"

"No, it's not bad." He put his arm around Ryan's shoulders and hugged him close. "A father should be there for his kid." Chase was feeling his own guilt.

"I know. Mom says she's sorry he wasn't a better dad for me." The boy sniffed. "I used to be sad because he didn't want me…. Was it my fault that he didn't like me?"

"Oh, Ryan, don't ever think that. You're a great kid. Anyone would be proud of you."

"Really?"

Chase had to nod because he couldn't get the words out. If there was any doubt before, there wasn't any now. He loved this child.

"Hey, you two," a familiar voice called. "How come you aren't working?"

Chase looked down to see Mallory standing under the tree below.

Ryan stood up. "Hey, Mom. Look, the floor is done. But it's too hot to work anymore today."

"I don't blame you," she said. She glanced around at the structure, then turned to Chase. "It looks good."

Chase's emotions were still pretty raw, and a lot of it was directed at Mallory. "Does it meet your approval?"

"Yes, and it's even better. Can't wait to see it finished."

"A few more days."

"Well, since you're finished for today, how about a swim?"

"Sure, but where?" Ryan asked.

"Bobbie's mom called and invited us over for swimming and a barbecue." She paused. "All of us."

Ryan looked at Chase. "Wow. It's like we're a real family."

Later that afternoon, Mallory sat at the edge of the shallow end of the Everetts' pool. She was wearing a modest aqua-colored, one-piece suit, but she wasn't keen on swimming with a half-dozen splashing kids. She'd leave that to Chase and Bobbie's father, Robert.

"They should be exhausted by supper," Meg Everett said as she sat down beside Mallory and dangled her feet in the water.

She was a pretty blonde with a warm smile and a friendly manner. She'd married her high school sweetheart and had two great kids, and was probably Mallory's closest friend, outside of Liz.

"Oh, I don't know. Ryan's been going like this since school let out."

For a long time they both watched the antics in the pool between the fathers and sons.

Meg spoke first. "I've never seen a Texas Ranger without his hat and badge. I'm impressed."

It was hard not to be. Chase had wide shoulders and a muscular chest and that flat washboard stomach. A strange feeling stirred in her stomach. "They have to stay in shape," she answered honestly.

"He seems to care about Ryan. They're like father and son." Meg turned to Mallory. "It's really great, isn't it?"

Meg wasn't stupid. She could see the obvious, that the two were related. "So far, but it may not be down the road."

Her friend smiled. "If I were you I wouldn't let the man get very far away. It's easy to see he cares about Ryan…and you."

Mallory couldn't think about a relationship with Chase. It was her son who needed a father. She didn't need a man.

Suddenly a stream of cold water startled them. She looked out in the pool to catch Ryan and Chase smiling at her.

"Why not come in the water?" Chase asked.

"I'm fine right here."

Robert and Bobbie appeared. "Come on, Mom," Bobbie said, waving for Meg.

"I'm being summoned," her friend said and waded in as she pulled her hair up into a ponytail.

Envious, Mallory watched the other couple at play. It seemed she wasn't going to be left out as Chase came up to her. He stood in the shallow end, looking all tan and gorgeous. There was a swirl of dark hair on his perfectly sculpted chest. She had trouble breathing.

"If you won't come into the water, I guess I'll have to bring you." She gasped as he scooped her up in his arms. She could hear Ryan's cheers and laughter as Chase carried her to the deep end.

She ignored the cool water because Chase held her close. Too close. She could hear Ryan's cheers.

"You think just because you're stronger than me, you can manhandle me."

"I've never manhandled a woman in my life," he told her, then leaned in and whispered against her ear. "This is called gentle persuasion. Damn, but you feel good."

She pulled back and looked at him as the water rose to their necks. "Maybe you should put me down."

"No, you feel fine just where you are."

"Mom… Mom…"

She jerked around to see Ryan and the other kids wrapped in their towels at the side of the pool. "We're gonna go inside to play video games. You stay here with Chase and swim, okay?"

She managed a nod, then looked back at Chase. "Maybe I should get out, too."

"You should stay here," he told her. "Our son can entertain himself for a while." He let go of her legs and turned her to face him. "Wrap your legs around my waist."

"Chase…this isn't a good idea." She glanced at Robert and Meg. They were at the other end of the pool, cuddled together talking softly.

"Relax…just enjoy it." His hand circled her legs and

guided them around him. "We aren't doing anything wrong…yet."

Up close, she eyed him sternly. How could she relax with her body tucked against his? She found herself swaying forward as he pressed his hand in the small of her back, nudging her closer. Their eyes locked for a long time, his dark and smoky. Her fingers moved around his neck and locked together as his mouth dipped and pressed a kiss against her mouth. It was only a whisper of a touch before he pulled back.

"Hold on," he told her, then he caught her by surprise. He pushed off backward, causing her to end up on top of him. With a gasp, she managed to tighten her grip around his neck. A warm shiver surged through her as her body made contact with every inch of him…intimately.

His gaze locked with hers, telling her he felt it, too. "It's still there, Mallory. Whether we like or not, there's something between us."

She closed her eyes. At one time she'd have given anything to hear him say those words. "Please, Chase, just let it die. Too much has happened, too much resentment."

He moved them to the side of the pool, gripping the ledge. "How can it be too late, Mal? Not when I lay awake at night, thinking about you, remembering how it was to make love to you."

She sucked in a breath. "Chase, please…"

He didn't stop. His hand moved over her back, keeping their bodies connected. "I can't keep my hands off you. Even our son has noticed what's going on. He saw me kissing you the other day."

She glared at him. "What did he say?"

"He wants me to pursue you. He doesn't like Jerry. I don't either."

"Well, it's not your business." She started to pull away, but he held her tight.

"You made it my business, Mallory. So if Ryan doesn't like him around I don't either."

"So now you're dictating who I date?"

"No, but I can do something to make you forget any other man." His mouth captured hers in a hungry kiss. She wanted to protest, but telling herself that she didn't want to make a scene in the pool, she didn't stop him.

In truth, she wanted Chase to kiss her. And what did that make her? A woman still in love with a man who would never forgive her for not telling him about his son. She didn't blame him. How could she when she couldn't forgive herself.

It was after nine when the Everetts walked Chase and Mallory out to the truck. A giggling Ryan and Bobbie followed close behind.

Chase found he didn't want this evening to end. He'd spent a nearly perfect day with his son…and Mallory. He also knew that he'd taken advantage of her when they'd been in the pool. He didn't know what had come over him.

That was a big lie. Truth was, he'd never been able to resist Mallory Kendall. Nine years later, that hadn't changed. Except there was more at stake now. His son's future happiness.

Mallory turned to Meg. "Are you sure you want to keep Ryan overnight?"

"Yes, we do," the blonde told her. "Bobbie's been wanting this sleepover since Ryan got home." She glanced at Chase. "It seems he's been pretty busy with this secret project of his."

"I'm sure Bobbie will get an invitation when it's finished."

"I think we'd all like to see it," Robert told him.

"You will, right, Ryan?"

The boy came over to Chase. "Right. And I'll be home tomorrow…early. Mr. Everett said he'll take when me he goes to work."

"I won't start without you."

"Okay." Ryan glanced around at the group and motioned to Chase to follow him. Once alone, he said, "It looked like you and Mom had fun today."

So the little stinker had set him up. "Yes, we had a good time."

The boy grinned. "Now, you don't have to worry about me tonight. Maybe…you can take her out…if you want…."

Chase tried to act indifferent. "I think I can handle this part on my own."

"Okay, but if you need to know anything," the boy told him, "I know what Mom likes."

Chase was intrigued. "What does she like?"

He looked thoughtful. "Daisies. Her favorite color is pink. And she likes butterflies, too. A lot. She collects them. Her favorite is a glass one that has all these pretty colors inside. I can't even pick it up. She keeps it on the table next to her bed."

Chase's chest tightened. He remembered all those

vivid colors, too. He'd given her that butterfly for her birthday. So she still had it.

"Ryan," Mallory called to him.

They walked back. "What, Mom?"

"Just wanted to say good-night." She kissed him.

"Good night, Mom, Chase." He went to stand with Bobbie. Ryan's friend had curly blond hair and a stocky build. And according his son, they'd been best friends since kindergarten.

"Thank you for a great day and a wonderful supper," Chase said as he shook Robert's hand.

"You're welcome any time," Robert said.

Chase handed him a business card. "If you're in Midland stop by the office and I'll show you around."

Robert grinned. "You can count on it. Bobbie would love it."

With his hand against the small of Mallory's back, Chase escorted her to the truck and helped her in.

Funny, he'd never gone for much of the couples thing. Girls he'd dated in the past went with him to ranger parties as a group thing. Today was different. The Everetts saw them as a couple. Of course the way he'd kissed Mallory in the pool, he shouldn't doubt it. Door shut, he walked around to the other side and climbed in.

He started the truck, then turned to Mallory. "I think we need to talk about—" He suddenly noticed the soft hair floating around her face. Her eyes were intense with desire.

It hit him like fire in his gut. "You better stop looking at me like that, or we'll never make it home."

CHAPTER EIGHT

THE TRIP BACK to the ranch seemed to take forever, but Mallory was glad. She needed time to think. If she went with Chase to the cottage everything would change between them. She knew he wanted her body, but did he want her? Did he want her for a lifetime?

And was she ready for this?

Chase drove the truck under the archway and her heart pounded so hard she knew he could hear it. She would be foolish to go with him, but knew that wouldn't stop her.

Once in front of the cottage, he shut off the engine and turned toward her. Silence hung in the humid air. She knew what he wanted from her. He didn't say a word as he reached out and pulled her into his arms. When his mouth came down on hers, she knew she wasn't going to deny him…ever.

When he finally released her, she was almost dizzy. He climbed out of the truck and pulled her after him. On the ground, he wrapped his arm around her and led her up to the porch, then through the unlocked door. Inside, he closed out the world with the click of the door latch. In the darkness, he reached for her, then covered her mouth in another hungry kiss.

Her heartbeat quickened as her arms found their way up his chest and around his neck as he nibbled on her lips. She whimpered and returned his fervor. No doubt, she wanted him, she'd always wanted Chase. As his tongue slipped into her mouth, his skilled hands moved over her body, causing unbelievable sensations.

He broke off the kiss. "I want you, Mallory," he breathed.

She searched for the last of her common sense. "This isn't wise, Chase. We have so much to work out…."

He moved against her, letting her feel his desire. "Right now this is all I want to think about, just you and me." He kissed her tenderly, then raised his head. With only the moonlight, she saw his silhouette, felt his breath against her cheek. "This is a start, Mallory."

"What if… Oh, God—"

Her words died off as his hand moved under her T-shirt to her breast, stroking her through the lace. Her nipple hardened immediately and she pushed against his hand, aching for more.

He cupped her breast, then leaned down and drew the nipple into his mouth, sucking gently. She moaned and gripped his arms to keep from crumbling to the floor.

"Just tell me you want me to stop," he said. "And I'll walk you back to the house." He groaned and rested his head against hers. "Please…don't, Mal. I'll die… right here."

"So would I," she admitted.

He tugged the material over her head, then released the clasp on her bra and let it drop to the floor.

Her hands went to his shirt and pulled it from his jeans. "I'll need to help you catch up, so I can drive you crazy."

She could feel his grin. "Then let me help you, ma'am." He jerked the long shirttails from his pants, and she pushed the material off his wide shoulders.

She drew in a sharp breath. He was beautiful. Her hands went to his chest, feeling his solid heat, the rapid beating of his heart.

Chase sucked air into his lungs, trying to hold it together as her hands moved slowly over his skin. Mallory was like a fever in his blood. She'd always had that effect on him. But there was so much more at stake now. She'd been hurt badly, and they had a son to think about. He knew he had to earn her trust again.

She placed her lips on his flat nipple and sucked gently. That was it. He couldn't take it any more. He raised her head to greet her with a searing kiss. His hunger for her was well past the point of playfulness.

Once he released her, he lifted her in his arms, carried her into the bedroom and lay her down on the mattress. He flicked on the table lamp, filling the room with a soft glow, silhouetting her in the bed.

He searched her lovely body, and stopped at her face. "Never doubt that I never stopped wanting you, Mallory."

She blinked. "I never stopped wanting you, either. Oh, Chase, I wish—"

He stretched out beside her. "No regrets. No past. I think tonight it is just for us…the here and now."

She nodded and he smiled. But all he was thinking about was more and that he wasn't about to let her go again.

The next morning, the sun wasn't up yet, so Mallory thought she could make a quiet exit. Wrong.

"Trying to sneak out on me?"

She swung around. Chase was sitting up in bed, only a sheet covering the lower half of his magnificent body.

"Chase, I didn't want to wake you. I was just—" She pointed over her shoulder. "I should get back to the house. Ryan will be home soon."

"Our son isn't coming for another few hours." Reclining, he propped his head on his hand and smiled up at her. "You were running away, admit it."

Her face flamed. "Not exactly… Maybe this wasn't such a good idea."

"You mean us spending the night together making incredible love?" He sighed. "Oh, yeah, that was such a rotten idea."

Mallory couldn't help smiling. So did he. "I just thought it would be better." She sobered. "Everything is so complicated…with Ryan and…you."

He stared at her for a moment, then motioned for her to come to him. Foolishly, she did. He grabbed her hand and pulled her onto the bed. Before she realized what was happening, he pinned her body with his.

"What's the matter, Mallory, did I get to you?"

Yes! Yes! And yes! "Get over yourself, Landon." She tried to get free, but it was useless. "I have work to do."

"You couldn't even kiss me goodbye?"

"You were asleep." And he'd looked far too tempting.

"I'm wide awake now. So can I talk you into breakfast in bed?"

Pressed up against him, she felt the evidence of his idea of breakfast. She couldn't let this happen…again. She was in too deep as it was and needed to get away to find some perspective. To think.

"I think it's safer if we have breakfast at the house with Liz. So, please, let me go."

"Then at least give me a good-morning kiss."

She closed her eyes. "Chase, this isn't a good idea. Ryan is expected home soon."

"Our son would be tickled to see us getting along."

That was what she was afraid of. Ryan getting hurt when the two weeks ended and Chase went back to Midland. "And what about when you leave?"

Chase's sexy bedroom eyes locked with hers and she felt her insides quake. He leaned down and brushed his mouth against hers. "Who knows, maybe we can work something out…. Don't you want to see where this will lead?" Before she could say anything, he leaned down and this time captured her mouth in a mind-blowing kiss that had her aching for him and believing they could work this out. But she'd already given everything up for a man. She couldn't lose herself again. No matter how much she loved him.

With the last of her strength, she pulled away. "Stop, Chase. Please. I can't do this."

He let go of her and she climbed off the bed. She brushed her hair back. "I'm sorry. Everything is happening so fast. And what we really need to think about is Ryan." She paused, not knowing what else to say. She loved this man. And that was what had her frightened more than anything else. "I've got to go." She turned and rushed out, not stopping until she got to her bedroom at the house.

Closing the door, she collapsed on the bed. She had done it now. A tear fell. She had fallen in love with Chase again. And the pain would only be worse when he left her for the second time.

Two mornings later, Chase stood back to examine his work. It was finally looking like a tree house. The door and windows needed to be framed, along with a coat of sealer to protect the wood. But it was close enough to finished to satisfy Ryan.

"What did you do to my mom?"

Chase turned around to find an angry-looking Ryan.

"Why? What's wrong with your mother?" he asked. He hadn't seen her since the morning after they'd made love.

"She's sad again. And she won't tell me what's wrong. I thought you liked her."

This was crazy. He wasn't used to explaining himself to an eight-year-old. "I do," he admitted honestly. "But it's more complicated sthan just that."

The boy placed his hand on his hips. "I hate it when grown-ups say that. Why don't you just kiss her again and tell her how much you like her?"

"I've already done that," Chase said a little too angry. He lowered his voice. "I don't think your mom wants a man in her life right now. Outside of you, of course."

The child's expression turned sad. "But I want you

to come back here and see me. I want—" Tears flooded his eyes and he turned and started to leave. Chase grabbed him.

"Leave me alone," Ryan cried, fighting him.

Chase's heart was breaking. "I'm not going to leave you, Ryan. I'm never going to leave you, son."

Finally the boy wrapped his arms around Chase's waist and buried his face against his stomach. "Yes, you will. It will be just me and Mom. I thought you were different…. I wanted you to be my dad."

Emotions welled inside of Chase as he hugged him close. This was killing him, and it couldn't go on. "Ryan, we need to find your mother and talk about this. Is she home?"

Ryan wiped his tears away and stood back. "No, she went to Lubbock. She won't be back until late. Don't say anything to her…she'll just get sad again. Just forget I said anything…."

"No, I won't, Ryan. I care about you."

"Don't say you have to leave. I know that." Fresh tears spilled over. "I should have never started to like you because I knew this would happen…. I don't want a stupid tree house. I don't want you, either. I wish you never came here," he yelled then ran off.

"Ryan—" Chase went after him. He had to tell him the truth. "Ryan."

The boy shot off in the direction of the old pile of wood. He stumbled, but caught his balance, then suddenly he froze with a startled look on his face.

Leery, Chase slowed down and searched the area to

find the reason. His own heart pounded with fear when he saw the coiled rattlesnake about four feet from his son.

"Ryan, just stand there," he said in a soft calming voice. "Don't move, son."

"I'm scared…."

So was he. "I know, son. But believe me, I'm not going to let anything happen to you."

"Hurry."

Chase assessed the situation, and it didn't look good. He didn't have a gun, just a small knife on his belt. What he needed was to draw the snake's attention away from the kid. That could backfire, too. The sound of the rattle let him know the snake wasn't leaving.

He had one chance. Slowly, he came up behind the boy, talking calmly. "Ryan, I'm going to grab you, so don't fight me."

"Okay," the boy answered.

Chase couldn't even breathe, praying he was doing the right thing. He was about a foot from the child as he whipped his arm around Ryan's small frame, and pulled him up and away. He almost made it until he felt the sharp pain in the back of his thigh. Safely away, the snake was gone, but Chase fell to the ground.

"Man, that was cool," Ryan said. But his happiness died when he saw Chase. "What happened?"

"I don't think I'm as quick as I used to be. The rattler got me on the leg. You think you can find Liz? I should go to the hospital."

An hour later, Mallory rushed into the emergency room. Her heart was beating like crazy. It had been since she'd gotten Liz's voice mail that she'd brought in Chase because of a snakebite.

She glanced around to find Ryan and Liz seated in the waiting area and rushed over to them.

"Mom, you're here." Ryan ran to her. "Chase saved me from a snake, but it bit him. So Liz brought him here."

She hugged him tighter. "But you're okay?"

He nodded. "Yes, but it's my fault that Chase got bit. I was running away and he came after me."

She glanced at Liz. "How is Chase doing?"

"He seemed okay when I brought him in. I had the snakebite kit in the tack room." She sighed. "I guess we need to clear the area better so this won't happen again."

Mallory stood. "We live in Texas on a ranch. Snakes come with the territory." She looked at her son. "You have to be more careful."

"I promise. Just don't be mad at Chase. Okay?"

"I'm not mad, but the man seems to be rescuing you a lot." And Mallory owed Chase once again.

"Mom, will you go and see if he's all right?"

"Okay, but I'm not sure they'll tell me how he is." She walked up to the desk. "I was wondering how Chase Landon is doing."

The receptionist barely looked at her. "Are you family?"

She hesitated. "Yes…ah, I'm his wife."

The woman nodded. "I'll let you talk to the doctor." She led her down a hall into a cubicle with the curtain drawn. She stepped behind it and found Chase lying on his side, with his long leg exposed, a bandage on his thigh.

He tried to sit up. "Mallory…"

"Hi." She suddenly felt shy. "Ryan was so worried, he sent me back here. Are you okay?"

"It hurts like the devil, but the doctor says I'll live."

She edged closer to the bed. "Ryan also said you saved him from the snake."

He shrugged. "It would have been worse if the boy was bitten. We almost made it, too." He smiled. "I guess I'm getting slow in my old age."

"Oh, yeah, you're so old." She smiled, too. "Thank you, Chase. Thank you for taking such good care of Ryan."

Chase reached for her hand and laced his fingers with hers. She liked the connection to him. "He's my son, too, Mallory. Don't you know I'd do anything for him? I'll admit I never felt so helpless…and so scared…."

"That's how I feel a lot of times."

His dark eyes searched hers. "You don't have to do this alone any more. I'm here, Mal. I'm going to be a part of Ryan's life. And I want to be a part of your life, too."

She swallowed back her overflowing emotions. She wanted that, too, but her past caused a lot of doubts. "I don't know if I can handle that right now. I don't know if I ever will be…" She saw the hurt in his eyes. "I do know that we need to tell Ryan the truth."

He smiled. "I'd like that. I won't let him down, Mallory, or you."

She knew that in her head, but in her heart she was still afraid. Someone was bound to get hurt.

"You sure you're comfortable?" Ryan asked. "I can get you another pillow."

Chase nodded. "No, I'm fine." He glanced up at Mallory from the guest-room bed. Since leaving the hospital that afternoon, both Mallory and Liz insisted he come and stay at the house during his recuperation. And so they could keep an eye on him. He wasn't used to being taken care of.

Ryan ran out of the room.

"His energy is exhausting."

"You do that to him, Chase. I've never seen him take to anyone as quickly as he has to you. It's time he knows the truth."

He swallowed. "You sure?"

She nodded. "I'm sure. He already loves you."

Dressed in his pajamas, the boy walked back into the room carefully carrying a glass of water. He set it beside the bed on the table. "That's just in case you're thirsty in the middle of the night."

"Thanks, Ryan," Chase said and patted the mattress. "Here, why don't you come sit down next to me. Your mother and I want to talk to you."

The boy climbed on the bed, but was careful to stay away from the Chase's injured leg. "I'm sorry I got mad today, and I'm sorry about what happened to you."

"I know, Ryan, but that's not what we want to talk to you about." Feeling the emotions clogging his throat, Chase looked at Mallory for courage. "Remember when I told you that I knew your mom a long time ago?"

Ryan nodded. "Yeah."

"Well, we dated back then…and we fell in love."

The child looked back and forth between them. "Really?"

"And there's something else, too," Mallory joined in. "Alan wasn't your father," she told him, then took a breath. "Chase is…."

Ryan sat there a long time. His expression told her he was trying to take it all in. "I guess that's why he didn't like me so much, huh?"

Mallory's heart sank as tears filled her eyes. "I'm sorry, honey. I wish I could have made it better."

Ryan didn't seem to hear her as his attention was drawn to Chase. "You're really my dad?" he asked, his eyes rounded in hope and questions.

"Yes, I'm really your dad."

"Did you know about me before now? When I was little?"

Mallory could see that Chase didn't look happy having to answer that question. She sat on the other side of the bed. "No, Ryan. Chase didn't know about you. He went off to be a ranger, and I married Alan… because I didn't know how to find Chase."

He nodded and turned back to Chase. "Do you want to be my dad now? I mean do you want a kid?"

"Yes, and yes," he told him. "But I don't want just any kid, I want you, Ryan…Landon."

Ryan grinned. "Wow, I get your name, too."

"I'd like you to have it," Chase said.

"Sure."

"Do I get to call you Dad, too?"

Chase nodded and drew the boy into his arms. "I love you, son."

"I love you, too, Dad," the boy whispered.

Mallory looked on at the two men in her life. At least for them, all seemed right with the world. For now.

CHAPTER NINE

IT WAS AFTER TEN O'CLOCK when Mallory peered into the bedroom to see Ryan asleep. Finally. It had been a busy day and evening, especially for an eight-year-old.

She smiled, thinking about father and son together. They'd spent most of the evening in the guest room, talking. Only after Chase promised they would work on the tree house in the morning, had Mallory managed to get Ryan off to bed.

She walked down the hall toward her own bedroom, but seeing the light on in the guest room, she stopped to see if Chase needed anything.

Tapping on the door, she waited to hear his voice before she walked in. She paused when she saw he was propped up in the bed, shirtless, that glorious chest of his exposed to her. A hundred delicious thoughts came to mind and her pulse immediately shot off.

He smiled at her. "Well, this is a pleasant surprise."

She gripped the doorknob, trying to keep a safe distance from the man. "I just wanted to know if you needed anything before I turned in."

His dark eyes locked on hers. "Could you stay a minute?"

She hesitated, then walked in and closed the door. "Not too long, I have some work I want to finish up tonight."

"You seem to work a lot."

"Not all of us are on vacation."

He sighed. "And that's going to end soon. I'll have to go back to Midland. I don't want to leave Ryan...." His gaze searched hers. "Or you."

She wasn't ready to discuss anything between them. "Maybe you should just concentrate on Ryan."

"Is that what you want me do? Just forget the other night...us being together?"

She knew this would happen. "We aren't the main focus here, Chase. Ryan is. I don't want our son to get the wrong impression. We can't give him false hope that his parents might get together."

"Come here, Mal." He patted the spot beside him on the bed.

She shook her head. "Why? So you can prove that you can complicate things even more?" she said bravely. "I don't think so."

Chase knew he should leave her alone, but the hell with it, he couldn't. He jerked the sheet away and started to climb out of bed.

"Stop." She rushed to his side and pushed him back against the pillow. "You need to stay in bed."

With her leaning over him, he reached out and touched her cheek. He was encouraged when she didn't pull away. "God. You're beautiful."

She sucked in a breath. "Chase, we can't—"

Chase played dirty. Even knowing Mallory could complicate everything, he still wanted her. "Believe me, I'm controlling myself. If you knew what I really want to do with you…"

Those beautiful green eyes widened. "We can't let anything happen."

"We already have, Mallory. And we both enjoyed it very…very much." He leaned forward and brushed a kiss against her tempting mouth.

She sucked in a breath. "Chase…"

"I love it when you whisper my name…." He craved her like no other woman. Tempted, he nibbled her lips, then when her breathing grew rapid, he deepened the kiss and drew her closer. She tumbled into his arms, and he reveled in her softness against his chest. He feasted on her mouth, tasting her sweetness…her own hunger. Finally he pulled away and looked into those mesmerizing eyes.

"I've never wanted anyone as much as I want you. And if you want me to keep my hands off you, you better leave now."

"It would be the wise thing to do." Her hands moved to his chest, drawing an imaginary pattern with her fingers. "I mean, this can't lead to anything good."

"Oh, I disagree. The way we feel right now is a very good thing. Makes me happy." He placed a kiss on her nose. "And I'm planning on making you happy, too. Very happy."

"What about Ryan?"

"Sssh," he breathed. "Ryan has nothing to do with this. This is you and me, Mallory."

She glanced down at his leg. "What about your injury?"

He pulled her closer. "I'm a Texas Ranger, I'm tough. I can handle it." He grinned. "And you, too." He closed his mouth over hers and proceeded to show her.

The next morning, Chase woke with a jerk and sat up in bed. The sun was already up. He rubbed his hand over his face. His thoughts turned to Mallory and their night together. He glanced to the other side of the bed. Of course it was empty. She'd left him hours ago.

He remembered the soft kiss, then she'd slipped from his arms. He'd hated letting her go. It felt so right, her being there, curled up next to him. His body stirred in memory of their lovemaking. But it wasn't the physical response that bothered him, it was what he felt in the middle of his chest.

Mallory had gotten into his heart…again.

Thing was, had he gotten to her? Did she feel the same about him? Was she willing to work on a relationship with him? There were so many things they needed to talk about, and soon.

He grabbed the pair of neglected pajama bottoms off the floor. He slipped them on and stood. His thigh felt better today. Walking around the room, he found most of the soreness was gone, too.

And in a few days, he would be, too. He only had a little vacation time left. And a promised tree house to finish for Ryan. But first, a shower and some coffee. Before he could gather clean clothes and head for the bathroom, there was a knock on the door.

"Come in," he called.

It wasn't Mallory as he expected, but Jesse Raines. He was juggling two mugs. "Hey, Chase. Sleeping in, I see."

"Hey, Jesse." He went to him and took one of the mugs. "What brings you here?"

"I heard you tangled with a snake."

"Yeah, but he didn't get as much as he wanted." He shook his friend's hand. "Please, don't tell me Robertson sent you here to bring me back."

"No, the captain isn't asking for you. I just thought you'd want to hear what's been going on with Reyes."

Chase motioned for Jesse to sit in the chair. His partner wouldn't make the trip if it wasn't important.

"So what did Reyes have to say?"

"I went to Sweetwater with a ranger from UCIT to make it official."

Chase nodded, knowing protocol was to call in the Unsolved Crimes Investigation Team on this. "So what happened?"

Jesse leaned forward resting his arms on his knees. "Reyes's story is that he knows the man who shot Ranger Wade Landon."

"So who is it?"

"He says he'll only talk if the D.A. will make a deal."

Chase didn't like the sound of this. "Let's see, Reyes is a known drug dealer. He's in for armed robbery, then add on a kidnapping charge, attempted murder and… he's a horse thief."

"It was Jacobs who shot Buck Kendrick," Jesse clarified. "Also Reyes swears he's the one who kept Ryan safe."

Chase hated to think what could have happened to his

son. Ryan was safe now, and he was going to make sure of that. Men like Jacobs and Reyes needed to stay off the streets.

"Reyes says the drug dealer who shot Wade is big time," Jesse explained. "He also hinted that the man likes to collect trophies of his kills." Jesse's gaze never wavered. "Like guns…and a Texas Ranger's badge."

Chase froze. No one had that information but law enforcement. "What's your gut tell you about this guy?"

"Reyes is scum," Jesse said. "But…he's small-time scum. Reyes knows he's not getting out anytime soon. But he wants a deal where he can be moved to a facility closer to his mother so she can visit him…and take off the life sentence. He wants a straight twenty years, with the possibility of parole."

Chase shut his eyes for a moment. "What's the prosecutor say?"

"Nothing, yet. He needs a name and enough proof that he can bring in the killer and get a conviction."

Chase knew he couldn't ignore this. Over the years he'd followed too many leads that never went anywhere. He had to talk to Reyes. "I'll be back in Midland this afternoon. Tell UCIT I'll be ready to go first thing in the morning."

Jesse nodded. "We'll be ready."

Just then there was another knock on the door. "Come in."

A smiling Ryan stepped into the room and went right to Chase. "Mom and Liz want to know if you both want breakfast?"

The men exchanged glances and nodded. "Sounds good."

Ryan looked at Jesse. "Did you know that Chase is my dad?"

"Really?" Jesse exchanged a knowing glance with Chase. "How great is that?"

"And we're building a tree house, too. It's almost finished." He looked at Chase. "Dad, are we still going to work on it after breakfast?"

Jesse motioned for the door. "I'll head on downstairs to wash up."

"Tell Mallory I'll be down in ten minutes." After Jesse left, he looked at Ryan. "Sit down, son. I have a favor to ask you."

"Sure." The boy sat on the mattress next to his dad. "What's the matter?"

"Remember the guys who kidnapped you?"

He nodded. "Are they still in jail?"

"Yes, but the man named Reyes has some information about the guy who shot another Texas Ranger. Remember when I told you my uncle Wade took the place of a father who wasn't around?"

The boy nodded.

"Well, he was also a Texas Ranger. He was shot and killed about ten years ago." Chase felt a strange surge of emotion. He also felt Ryan's hand in his. "When I buried him, I promised that I'd find out who killed him. This man Reyes might know something. He wants to talk to me tomorrow morning."

"So you have to leave today."

"It's my duty, Ryan. I'm a Texas Ranger. If it wasn't important, I wouldn't leave you."

"I know." There were tears in the boy's eyes, and his lower lip trembled. "Are you coming back…to see me?"

Something tightened around Chase's heart. "So many times that you'll probably get tired of me."

Finally Ryan smiled. "I never will. You're my dad. I love you." He hugged him tightly.

"And you're my son. I love you, too."

He looked up. Mallory was standing in the doorway, and a mountain of emotions bombarded him. And they weren't just for Ryan. He wanted to enclose her in the same hold he had on his son, and keep them both close forever. The thought surprised him, but even more, it scared the hell out of him.

The realization suddenly hit him; he wanted it all. His son, Mallory…a complete family. Just how could he convince her to take a chance on him again?

Mallory fought to find her voice. "Ryan, why don't you go downstairs and help Liz so your dad can shower?"

"Sure." He turned back to Chase. "Don't take too long, we're fixing pancakes."

He smiled. "I'll make it fast." He mussed the boy's hair, before he took off, leaving them alone.

Mallory wasn't sure what to say to him this morning. Then Chase took it out of her hands as he walked to her, pulled her into his arms and kissed the daylights out of her.

By the time he released her, she had trouble catching her breath. "Good morning," he whispered.

"Morning," she labored to answer.

"I could have greeted you a little more up close and

personal, but you disappeared from bed before I got the chance."

"I thought it was better if Ryan didn't catch us…his imagination would run wild."

His lazy grin appeared and her heart began to pound hard once again. "I know the feeling. My own imagination is going a little crazy. Damn." He sighed deeply. "Last night was incredible."

Mallory could feel the blush rise to her cheeks as she thought about their wonderful night together. She'd done the unthinkable. She'd fallen hopelessly in love with Chase Landon. Again. Not a smart thing.

"Yes, it was, but…we have to think of Ryan, too." She pulled back. "It might be better—"

He placed a finger against her lips. "Don't create problems, Mallory. We can work this out."

She stiffened, then stepped back. "Working this out means exactly what? That you come on weekends to spend time with your son, and I'm a bonus."

She saw the anger flash in his eyes. "That's what you think of me…and what we shared last night?"

Mallory knew she had come on too strong. She was frightened, too. "I'm sorry. It's just that we've all spent an idyllic two weeks here…no outside problems to interfere with it. Real life isn't like that. It'll be a huge struggle, Chase, just for you to be able to spend time with Ryan. We don't even live in the same town."

He raked his fingers through his hair and walked to the other side of the room. The muscles worked across his broad back and shoulders. Her gaze moved to his pajama bottoms hung low on his slim hips. More memories flooded her and she wanted to run to him. Beg him not to leave. But she'd done just that nearly ten years ago…and he'd left her anyway. Tears pricked her eyes. She couldn't do it again. This time their son would be hurt.

The following morning, Chase and Hank Whiting from UCIT, along with a D.A., were ushered inside the prison visiting room to talk with Reyes. Chase knew that if this panned out, he could finally close the door on this chapter of his life.

His thoughts turned to Mallory. She'd tried to act indifferent when he'd driven away yesterday, but he saw something else in her eyes. Yet, he knew she'd been right. He couldn't give her any promises, not until his past was settled. And she still had ghosts that followed her, too. Her marriage to Alan had made her leery of giving herself to him…or any man.

Today would change that one way or the other. Whether there was evidence or not on who shot his uncle, he had to let it go. Wade wouldn't want it to take over his life. And yet, it had. Even years ago, when he couldn't commit to Mallory. He wanted so badly for today to change that….

For so many years Chase hadn't wanted any connections. To let people in. For a second time Mallory changed that, but was he too late? Too late for a family. All he knew was he wanted his son and Mallory and somehow he was going to find a way to get them all together.

Chase turned as the metal doors opened and a guard entered with Reyes. The prisoner didn't look happy. He nodded to Chase. "I only wanted to talk to the ranger."

"Cut the crap, Reyes, and get down to business,"

Sergeant Whiting said. "Ranger Landon is here to hear your big news."

In the end, Chase sat down at the table with the prisoner while the other men went to stand with the guard. "Okay, Reyes," he began, "Talk to me. Tell me who killed Wade Landon."

He pointed to the D.A.. "Is he willing to make the deal I asked for?"

"He's willing if you come up with a name and some proof."

Reyes leaned forward and lowered his voice. "Give me a piece of paper."

Chase removed a small pad and pen from his shirt pocket and slid it to the man.

Reyes wrote down something. "My cousin has all the information on this man." He pushed the folded paper over.

Chase opened it and saw a name, Sancho Vasquez. Chase tried not to react, but it was difficult not to. This man was a well-known drug dealer along both sides of the border.

"So why are you giving him up now?"

"He betrayed me," he said, his voice low. "I was a loyal *amigo,* then he hooked my brother on the hard stuff. He was supposed to look out for *mi familia* with me in here. I kept my mouth shut too long.

"Talk to my cousin, Cesar Reyes." He wrote down the information. "He'll tell you about the man's trophies. You'll find what you're looking for."

"You better not be jerking my chain, Reyes, or you'll be sorry."

The prisoner raised his cuffed hands in surrender. "You'll be happy. Just get me out of here so I'll be safe."

Chase stood. "As soon as we get our man."

"Then you'll come back and thank me." Reyes grinned. "Is the *niño* okay?"

Chase thought about his son. "Yes, the boy is fine."

It had been a long day by the time Chase turned in to the drive at his town house. After they'd left Reyes, he and Whiting had gone to find the cousin. Late last night, Cesar had met them in a secret location and handed over the information on Vasquez.

The day wasn't over yet. Jesse, Whiting and he were headed down to the border town of Presidio, Texas. Before dawn they were going in to search Vasquez's U.S. headquarters in the Chinati Mountains.

Chase hoped everything they'd been looking for was on this side of the border. It would sure make things easier.

He walked through the door of his home and into the empty silence. It suddenly hit him…along with a hard loneliness in his gut. Hell, he missed his son… and Mallory.

He picked up the phone from the kitchen and punched in the memorized number. By the second ring, it was answered by Mallory saying, "Mooney Ranch."

His throat went dry like a teenager's. "Hi," he managed.

There was a long pause. "Chase," she said in a throaty voice.

"I meant to call sooner, but…things got going and just didn't slow down. I hope I didn't call too late."

"No…it's fine. I just came upstairs to my bedroom."

He bit back a groan, thinking about her lying in bed. He shook away the thought. "How's Ryan?"

"He misses you, of course."

"Believe me, I miss him, too. I would have called sooner, but we were in a meeting most of the afternoon. And tomorrow I leave."

Another long pause. "So you got the information you were hoping for."

"Yes. We're still not sure if it's going to pan out. First, we have to find the man…" He stopped. He couldn't tell her any more, but surprisingly he found he needed to share everything, including his fears, with her.

"Chase…are you okay?" she asked.

He sank down on his oversized sofa, lifting his feet on the coffee table. "I could say I've been better."

"Wade meant a lot to you. I just wish there was something I could do to help."

His chest tightened and he closed his eyes wishing she was with him. "You're doing just fine, Mal. Just fine."

She paused. "Will you promise me something, Chase?"

Anything in the world. "If I can."

"Be careful. I know how much you want this guy, but he's a murderer."

"It's my job to bring him to justice." He didn't want to waste his time talking about Vasquez…he wanted Mallory. "Will you be waiting for me when I get back?"

"Are you coming back here?"

"My vacation time sort of ran out. I thought I'd save those few days." He paused. "Dammit, Mallory, I want to see you. I want to hold you…make love to you."

There was a pause. "I don't think we should talk about this now…."

"It's past time, Mal. We should have been together long ago." He released a breath. "Give us a chance."

"I don't know if I can," she said. He could hear the tears in her voice. "I've found a life I like, Chase. I'm my own person."

"And you can't share it with anyone?"

"I've tried, Chase. And if you care about me, please don't try and push me into anything."

CHAPTER TEN

FOR THE LAST twenty-four hours, Mallory had tried without success not to worry about Chase. She hadn't slept since she'd talked to him on the phone, since she'd lied and told him she didn't want a future with him.

Mallory leaned against her pillow and closed her eyes. She didn't know many of the details about the assignment, but that didn't stop her prayers to keep Chase safe. Although he was well trained at his job, he was still going after a known killer.

Suddenly regrets filled her. What if something happened? What if Chase never came back to her…to Ryan? Tears filled her eyes.

"Mom…"

She sat up and saw her son standing in the doorway to her room. "Ryan…what's wrong, honey?"

"I can't sleep. I'm worried about Dad."

She held out her arms and the boy came to her. He climbed in beside her and let her cradle him close. "It's going to be all right, Ryan. Chase is a ranger, he knows what he's doing."

"I know, but this is a really bad guy." Her son raised his head, and his dark eyes met hers. "He killed someone. Every time I close my eyes I see him shoot at Dad."

She tensed. "I wish I could say he isn't in danger, but we don't know that. Just trust that your dad knows his job, and he wants to come back to you more than anything in this world."

Ryan nodded. "He wants to come back to you, too. Mom, he loves us both."

She swallowed hard. Mallory wasn't so sure. She knew Chase loved his son, but was she just part of the package? He hadn't loved her enough to want her years ago. And she couldn't go through that kind of rejection again....

"Hey, why don't we go and visit Grandpa? You can be closer when your dad gets back home."

His eyes lit up. "Chase will want you there, too."

Mallory didn't want to burst her son's bubble right now. This was all too new. She just wanted them all to get through the next few days. She knew that Chase had waited for years to find his uncle's killer.

Then hopefully, she could get back to her life. But she knew with Chase Landon in it, things would never be the same again.

The next morning at dawn, Chase and Jesse hid behind a large boulder, staking out the Spanish-style house on the ranch compound. Nothing looked suspicious. To the untrained eye, it looked like any of the other ranches in the area.

This was supposed to be Sancho Vasquez's U.S. headquarters. All the big guns were out here today, the

DEA, the U.S. Marshals, along with the Texas Rangers and local law enforcement.

Reyes had better be telling the truth about this place being where Sancho ran his drugs operation across the border through Ojinaga, Mexico. There were several other buildings in the compound, probably housing the drugs. Word on the street was there was marijuana and cocaine stored here camouflaged by herds of cattle.

Chase should be happier about the possible drug bust, but he had one thought on his mind. To get his uncle's killer. Everything else was a bonus.

His phone vibrated on his belt. The text message stated all the men were in place and ready to move in. They had a search warrant in hand, but they knew Vasquez wasn't going to let them just walk in.

"It's time," he told Jesse. "Let's move."

They climbed into their vehicles, along with several rangers and some local law enforcement and drove toward the compound, breaking down the gate as they went. Once stopped, they drew their weapons.

Several of the workers scattered, some pulled guns, but seeing they were outnumbered, surrendered. Chase drove his jeep to the front of the house and jumped out. With Jesse following him, they kicked in the front door.

"Texas Rangers, come out with your hands up," he called. A lone housekeeper walked out, looking terrified.

Jesse spoke to her in Spanish and asked where Sancho was. Sobbing, she pointed down the hall.

Guns poised, Chase and Jesse took off, peering into several rooms along the hallway, before finding a library. Seeing scattered papers, they had a good idea Sancho had been there…and recently.

"Damn, how did he get away?" Jesse asked as he checked the locked windows.

Chase searched the perimeter of the room and found something odd about the built-in bookcase. One set of shelves was slightly ajar. He tugged it open to find a set of stairs and a long narrow tunnel. "He went this way," he said before walking cautiously down the steps, before waiting for backup.

Chase wasn't about to let the man get away. If Vasquez got through this escape route, he could sneak across the border in no time. And they were out of luck if the drug lord landed in Mexico. He could disappear for good.

Feeling his way along the narrow passage with its rough-hewn beams and dirt floor, Chase fought to find his way through the musty-smelling tunnel. There was barely any light, but he didn't care, he wasn't going to stop.

Finally he saw a soft glow of light and heard voices up above outside the end of the tunnel. Chase stopped behind a beam as Sancho rattled off orders in Spanish to two men. It was something about using explosives to close off the exit.

Jesse came up beside Chase and waited until Vasquez and his men climbed out, then the two rangers went after them. Outside in the grove of trees, Jesse called to them to halt, but one man fired at them. Immediately, Jesse's bullet took him down. The other surrendered, but Vasquez took off toward the jeep. Chase went after him and easily tackled the forty-something dealer to the ground, then handcuffed him before he could work up a fight.

Chase pulled the short man to his feet. "You're under arrest, Sancho Vasquez, for possession of illegal drugs and the murder of Ranger Wade Landon."

He frowned. "You are *loco*. I murdered no one," he said with a sneer. "I want to call my lawyer."

As he walked the man back to the house, Chase read him his Miranda Rights. Jesse was with him as they entered the home and were met by the sheriff and Captain Robertson.

"You got him. Good work."

"You can't hold me for long," Vasquez said as he looked around to see his home being torn apart. "You have no right to destroy my *casa*." He cursed in Spanish. "I demand you leave."

Another ranger came through the front door. "Captain, you won't believe what the DEA found in one of the barns. It's a drug warehouse." He looked at Sancho. "Looks like you're going away for a long time."

The man looked panicked. "I demand to speak to my lawyer."

"You'll get your phone call, Vasquez," the captain said, his voice low and controlled, as if trying to hold it together. "But you might want to tell your lawyer that in our search of the house, we've found a lot of evidence…evidence that will keep you off the streets for good."

The man straightened. "You have nothing on me."

"I have to disagree. We found something very interesting. A hidden room." The captain glared at the prisoner. "You're a sick man, Vasquez."

"What hidden room?" Chase asked Robertson.

The captain frowned. "There was another room off the tunnel."

Chase handed Sancho off to another ranger, then returned to Vasquez's office, not knowing if he was more afraid of what he wouldn't find...or what he would find.

He marched into the library to find DEA agents at the base of the steps. He saw the narrow door open. The hidden room that Reyes talked about...the so-called trophy room.

Heart pounding, Chase crossed the room and peered inside. A light illuminated the small area, and the items on display. He moved inside, drawn to the numerous gun racks that were mounted on the wall.

Chase had trouble controlling his breathing as he eyed the weapons. Right away he zeroed in on the familiar sidearm, a 45 caliber Colt automatic. It was exactly like the one his uncle carried in his holster when he was a ranger.

Chase had no way of knowing for sure until he checked the serial number. But in his heart, Chase knew this was Wade Landon's issued sidearm. Then his gaze caught the shine of silver. It was the familiar star badge. He sucked in a breath to see the name Landon engraved across it.

Emotions tore through him as painful as if he'd been shot himself. Sancho Vasquez had killed his uncle over ten years ago, and now he was going to pay for it. Rage nearly took over...along with the need to go and beat a confession out of the man.

Suddenly he felt someone else in the room. He glanced over his shoulder to see his friend, Jesse.

"You okay?" he asked.

Chase shrugged. "It hurts like hell, but it's nearly over." His thoughts turned from his past to his future… his son…and Mallory.

"Are you sure you're going the right way?" Ryan asked his mother from the passenger seat of the SUV. "I can call Dad and ask him the directions again."

"You will not call anyone," she told him. "I can get us there."

Mallory wasn't sure she wanted to find the ranch. She'd waited for three days to hear from Chase, but got nothing. Not a word. Then this morning at her father's house, he'd called her out of the blue. He asked her to bring Ryan and meet him at a place about forty miles away, nearly halfway between Midland and Lubbock.

"Did Dad say why he wanted to see us here?"

"Honey, you know as much as I do," she said, seeing the worry on her son's face.

The boy smiled. "I'm glad he's back and the bad guy is in jail." He turned to her. "I'm going to start a scrapbook. Did you save the newspaper?"

Mallory smiled and nodded. "Yes, I saved it," she told him, recalling how she'd reread the article and studied the grainy picture of Chase as he brought Vasquez in. She knew he'd downplay it, but his son wouldn't be able to contain his pride.

"Look, Mom. There's the sign." Ryan read it off the faded archway. "The Last Dollar Ranch."

Mallory drove further down the road to find a two-story clapboard house with a brick front. The green shutters needed painting. So did the rest of the place. She turned to see other whitewashed structures, plus a faded red barn.

A man came out the door and stood on the porch waving. It was Chase. Her heart kicked into gear as he smiled, and she knew in that instant she would never love anyone like she loved this man.

"Mom, look, it's Dad."

"I see him." She stopped the SUV and Ryan unbuckled and jumped out of the truck. She watched as her son ran off toward the man in the jeans, Western shirt and dark cowboy hat.

Chase made it to the bottom step as his son launched himself into his arms. Good Lord, the boy felt good.

"I've missed you, son," he told him, unable to let go just yet.

"I've missed you, too, Dad." The boy pulled back. "I was worried you might get hurt and not come back."

"Since I found out about you, I'm extra careful." He set his son down. "And we got the bad guy."

"I know, Mom and I have been reading about it in the paper."

"You have?"

"Yeah. Mom even read it twice."

Chase glanced at the woman coming toward them. She was dressed in those slim jeans that made her legs seem a mile long, giving him thoughts he didn't need right now. He redirected his attention to her face, shaded by her dark cowboy hat. She came closer and he saw her smile and that silky dark hair pulled behind her ears.

"Welcome back," she said.

He wanted to pull her in his arms, but resisted. "Thanks. It's good to be back."

Ryan looked up at him. "Dad, why are we here?"

"Well, because I wanted to show you my new home. The Last Dollar Ranch."

"Oh, boy. You live here?"

He nodded, but kept his gaze on Mallory. "I just moved in yesterday. I have a lot of work to do, yet, but the house is solidly built, and there's plenty of room."

"Will I have a room?" Ryan asked.

"Sure. We can go inside and you can pick the one you want."

Ryan cheered, then took off into the house.

Chase slipped his hands into his jeans pockets and turned to Mallory. "I've missed you."

"This last assignment had to be hard on you. How are you doing, Chase?"

He sighed. "A lot better since you showed up."

She glanced away. "Looks like you've been busy. I had no idea you were buying a place."

"I told you I was looking."

"I thought that was a story you just invented for Ryan's sake."

"No, it's something I've always wanted to do. Have my own place." He stepped closer. "I want you to like it, too." He reached for her and was encouraged when she didn't step back. "And I'm hoping you'll want to spend a lot of time here, too." He leaned down and brushed his lips against hers. He heard her soft gasp, and returned for more. This time he captured her mouth in a hungry kiss. He wanted to let her know how much he'd missed her. How much he wanted her. He finally let go.

"How about if we continue this later?" He took her hand. "I want to show you the inside."

Mallory wasn't sure what to do. Chase had her confused, and she desperately needed to keep her head. She'd made mistakes in the past, and wasn't about to jump into anything. Not even for Chase.

They went up the steps together and across the weathered porch floor. He opened the heavy oak door and led her into a huge entry with bare hardwood floors and a staircase to the second floor. There was an antique cut-glass chandelier hanging overhead.

"Oh, Chase, this is lovely." She walked into the living room with a tile and brass fireplace. There was faded wallpaper on the walls, but that could be easily removed and painted a warm color. There was a camel colored leather sofa, a matching chair and a large television.

"You haven't seen the bathrooms and kitchen yet. They need a lot of work. It's one of the reasons I got the place so cheap."

"I think you got a great deal. This house has charm, and great bones."

The sound of footsteps called to them upstairs. They went up to find four bedrooms, a large bath and then down the end of the hall was a master suite.

Mallory stepped into a huge room with a row of windows; underneath was a window seat. A king-sized bed was against one wall with rumpled covers and a long dresser against another. She peered into a side room which at one time must have been a dressing room, now converted into a bath.

"This is wonderful, Chase. This room looks new."

He came up behind her. "It was done about five years ago. Not my style. If I redo it, I'd like one of those spa tubs and a double shower big enough for two people."

Mallory didn't need to think about this man standing naked with water streaming over his body. Suddenly heat surged through her.

"Hey, maybe we should see about Ryan." She turned and walked out, finding her son down the hall in one of the bedrooms.

"Look Mom, I can see the barn and corral from here." He looked past her. "Dad, can I have this as my room?"

"If it's the one you want. Sure."

"Okay, when do I get to stay here?"

She wasn't sure how to answer that. They hadn't sat down and talked about the arrangements. "Your dad and I haven't had a chance to talk about that. And since he doesn't have much furniture."

"Then let's go downstairs and talk about it?" Chase suggested.

Downstairs, they went through the dining room that had a large mahogany table and six chairs with a matching sideboard. "This is yours?"

"My mother's. I had a lot of things in storage. There's some other things, too. I put them in the garage for now."

They ended up in the kitchen where there was a large pine table and four chairs. The maple cabinets were in good shape, the butcher block countertops were scarred from years of use, but Chase had moved in completely, bringing in his coffeemaker, toaster and can opener.

She glanced through the curtainless window, noticing the wind had picked up as dark clouds blocked the afternoon sun. "Looks like a storm is heading our way. Maybe we should leave, Ryan."

"And get caught in the middle of the storm," Chase said. "No way. You and Ryan are staying here."

As she started to argue, lightning flashed in the dark sky. "Why don't I fix us some supper and we can discuss the arrangements for Ryan to come visit," Chase suggested.

"Yeah, Mom. I want to stay here with Dad."

Chase looked at Mallory. "Do you need to be anywhere today?"

She shook her head. "No, but you aren't exactly ready for company."

He grinned at her. "Why do you say that?" He went to the big cupboard and opened it to show her his supply of canned goods, cereal and bread. "I went shopping this morning."

"So you don't have to work?"

He shook his head. "I'm off until Monday."

"Oh, boy," Ryan chimed in. "We can stay overnight."

Mallory tried not to panic. "We can't, honey. We can make it back to Grandpa's house. Besides, your father doesn't have any beds."

"I've got two sleeping bags," Chase argued. "And you can take my bed."

"Cool," Ryan said. "It's almost as good as sleeping in the tree house."

Mallory was ready to argue again, but a loud crash of thunder drowned her out. She glared at a smiling Chase. She was going to get him for this.

She turned her attention to her son. "How about we eat supper, then see if the storm moves on before we decide to stay tonight?"

"But I want to stay, Mom. It will be fun. I never stayed at my dad's house before."

"But I'm not prepared to stay. We don't have any clean clothes."

"I have a washer and dryer and new toothbrushes," Chase volunteered. "You could sleep in one of my T-shirts."

"Yeah, Mom. Please…"

The rain was now sheeting against the windows and they couldn't even see outside. This was definitely unusual weather for this time of year. A freak storm. She looked at father and son, both giving her the same charming grin. She couldn't resist.

"Okay, we'll stay the night, but we need to leave first thing in the morning. I'll call Grandpa to let him know our plans."

The two exchanged a high five, then took off to the garage to find the sleeping bags.

Okay, Chase Landon, you might have won this round, but you're not going to win again. No matter how much she wished she could, she just couldn't trust her feelings for the man.

The storm had cleared out by ten o'clock, but Chase knew Mallory wouldn't make Ryan leave. But lying on the hard floor in his son's bedroom, he wondered if this had been such a good idea.

"Maybe you should ask Mom out on a date," Ryan said into the darkness, then turned on his side and put his head in his hand. "You want to go out with her, don't you?"

The boy never quit. "I think your mother and I are old enough to handle that on our own."

"But you're not doing anything. I know you like her, and she likes you. She got really sad when you were away."

Chase was thrilled with that news. He also knew Mallory's first marriage had been the worst. Hell, the bastard had abused her. He tensed, hating the fact that he hadn't been around to help her. Well, he was now, and he wasn't going anywhere.

"Maybe you should tell her how you feel," the boy said, breaking the silence.

This wasn't something he wanted to discuss with an eight-year-old. "You ever think that your mom isn't ready?"

The moonlight shone through the curtainless window. "Then why does she look at you all the time? She kisses you, too."

And she made sweet-sweet love to him, Chase remembered silently.

"Dad? If I ask you something will you promise not to get mad?"

"You can ask me anything, son."

"Do you love my mom?"

Chase closed his eyes, feeling something grip his heart. He'd never stopped. "Yes, I love your mother. I love her a lot."

"Oh, wow! This is going to be so cool."

Chase raised a hand. "Just hold on, son. How I feel about your mother, and how she feels about me is between us. You have to promise to stay out of it."

"But, I want to help," he said.

He reached out and touched Ryan's shoulder. "Son, when you get older you'll learn that there are some things a man has to do on his own. And this is one of them."

"You mean when I like girls."

"Yes, when you like girls. Now, go to sleep."

"Okay…" The boy flopped back on the pillow and closed his eyes. Chase did the same, praying that he wasn't going to disappoint his son…or himself.

After a few minutes, he heard his son's even breathing and got up. In his boxer shorts, he walked out of the room and down the hall to his bedroom.

He gave a soft knock and waited until the door opened and Mallory appeared. She was wearing his white T-shirt and nothing else. Oh, boy.

"Is something wrong with Ryan?"

"No, I just wanted to see you to say good-night and give you this." He drew her into his arms and captured her mouth in an eager kiss. She moaned, and wrapped her arms around him. By the time he released her they both were breathing hard.

"Chase, we shouldn't…" she protested weakly.

"I know, but I just needed to see you…just to hold you for a little while." In the dim light he searched her face. "We need to talk about our future, Mallory. I just don't want to be in Ryan's life… I want to be a part of yours, too."

She started to speak, but he silenced her with another kiss. "Later, Mallory," he whispered. "Good
night." He touched her cheek, then turned and walked
away. Hopefully it was the last time he would walk
away from her.

CHAPTER ELEVEN

THE SUN WAS BRIGHT the next morning when Mallory got up and found her laundered clothes were neatly folded at the end of the bed. Chase.

She smiled. "I like the service at this hotel," she whispered. There was no denying her feelings for the man hadn't changed over the years, and seeing him with their son just enhanced them.

It could be so perfect….

She quickly stopped the train of her fantasy thoughts. She'd given her heart to Chase Landon once before, and it hadn't been enough…. He had left her anyway.

He was a Texas Ranger, and that would always come first in his life. His dedication had been one of the things she'd loved about him. The other was his love for his son. She just wasn't so sure there was room in his life for her. She'd learned that a long time ago when he'd so easily left her…and never looked back.

Now, she had to think about their son. Ryan deserved a life with his father, and if that became complicated by her and Chase's troubled past, it would ruin it.

Worse, she didn't know if she could survive losing Chase a second time.

Mallory grabbed her clothes and headed to the shower. She needed to get out of here. There were no more foolish dreams of her being included in his life. Sooner or later, Chase would come to realize that to have a good relationship with his son didn't have to include her.

And it broke her heart.

Chase stood at the old stove, spatula in hand. It was after nine and he was more nervous with every tick of the o'clock. He wanted Mallory to come downstairs. Yet, he didn't. He hadn't planned to ask her to share his life quite this soon, but he couldn't wait any longer. He wanted his family with him…always.

"You want another pancake, son?" he asked Ryan, still surprised that he'd discussed his future plans with the eight-year-old earlier that morning.

"Yes, please. They're really good. But Mom still makes the best. Her blueberry pancakes are the best." He took the last bite on his plate as Chase poured four more scoops of batter on the hot griddle.

"I sure hope your mother likes pancakes."

"She does," Mallory said as she walked in.

Chase smiled. All bright and sunny with her dark hair pulled back into a ponytail, she looked cute. Although her face was free of makeup, her cheeks were still rosy.

"But I'll just have coffee this morning. Then I've got to leave for home."

"Aw, Mom, do we have to?" Ryan asked, looking panicked. "Dad wants us to go with him to look at a horse."

Something had changed overnight. Chase could see it in her face. "I thought since you're the expert, you could help me," he coaxed as he took a mug from the cupboard, filled it and handed it to her. "What do you say, Mallory? Will you help me find a good riding mount?"

She took a sip of coffee, but never met his gaze. "I can, but just not today." She took another drink, and looked at Ryan. "I need to get home." She checked her watch. "If you want you can stay here, and I'll come and pick you up tomorrow afternoon."

Chase's stomach dropped. She wasn't staying at all.

Ryan didn't hide his confusion. "Sure… I want to stay…but not without you."

"Sorry, Ryan," Mallory began. "I can't today, but don't let me stop your fun. I'm sure your dad can wash your clothes for one more night." She set down her cup and kissed Ryan. "Now, I'd better go. Call me if you need anything."

Chase watched as she grabbed her purse off the counter and started out the door.

Ryan turned to him. "Do something, Dad. Mom is leaving and you haven't even asked her."

"How can I stop her?"

"Tell her you want her to stay." He climbed off his chair and started pushing him toward the back door.

Chase ended up on the porch as Mallory was getting into the car. "Mallory, wait…" He took off in a jog and managed to reach her before she got in.

She held up a hand. "Look, Chase, we spent the

night. Now, I have to go. You have Ryan here. That's what you want."

He touched her arm. "It's not all I want, Mal. I want you, too. I've always wanted you."

"Please, Chase, don't do this. We tried once, it didn't exactly work out." She drew a breath. "You deserved this time with Ryan…and a lot more." She finally looked at him, tears filling her green eyes. "I'm sorry that I never gave you the chance before—"

"Stop, Mallory. That's in the past. We both made mistakes." He pulled her against him. "So don't run off. We can work this out."

She shook her head, resisting. "And what happens to Ryan if we can't? He'll be the one who gets hurt. I've made some bad choices in the past. I can't do it again. Goodbye, Chase. I'll be back tomorrow to get Ryan."

Before she could get into the truck, Ryan came running out the door, calling her name.

They both waited as Ryan raced to them. "Mom, I changed my mind, I want to go home with you." He looked at his dad when she climbed in the truck and waited. "She needs me to go with her."

Chase was proud his son wanted to be with his mother, he just wished he could find a way to have them both.

"It's okay, son." He hugged him, knowing nothing was going to be okay at all.

"Chase asked you to stay, and you just walked away?" Liz asked.

Mallory sat at the kitchen table. "It's okay, Liz. I know what I'm doing."

"Oh, really. The man—who you love to distraction—asked you to stay and work out a future, and you left? Are you crazy?"

Mallory finally looked at her friend. "No, I'm practical. Chase wants Ryan. He wants me as part of the package. But in the end, we'll get hurt."

"You didn't even stay to find out." Liz pulled out the chair and sat down next to her. "Look, Mallory, not all men are jerks like Alan. You got the possibility of a future with one of the good guys, but you've got to give the man a chance." She sighed. "You love him...just admit it."

She couldn't. She shook her head. "It doesn't matter."

"Yes...it does matter, Mom."

They both turned toward the back door to see Ryan standing there. "Hi, son," she said, wiping her eyes and stood. "I bet you're hungry."

"No, I'm not."

Mallory knew he'd been upset since they left Chase this morning. He hadn't said a word all the way home. "You need to eat."

"And you need to tell the truth." His fists clenched. "You know Dad loves you, but you wouldn't even listen to him." He ran out of the kitchen upstairs, then they heard the slam of the bedroom door.

Mallory wanted to cry; instead she went to her son. She'd made so many mistakes by not telling Ryan the truth a long time ago. Somehow, she had to convince him that what she was doing now was for the best.

With an encouraging look from Liz, she made her way upstairs, then knocked on his door. Without waiting, she walked in to find her son on the bed.

It broke her heart to see him looking so sad. "Hey, honey. We need to talk about this."

He nodded, then went into her arms. "I'm sorry I yelled at you."

"I know, son." She shut her eyes. "Oh, Ryan, I know these last few weeks have been tough on you."

"For you, too. You've been so sad for a long time." He wiped his eyes. "Then Dad came here."

"It was because of you, Ryan. He loves you. That doesn't mean that your father and I have to be together."

"Why not? You love him and he loves you. Why is that so hard?"

Out of the mouths of babes. "Sometimes life is complicated."

"But Dad is trying to make it better. He bought the ranch so he can be close to us. And he wants to marry you so we can all live together."

Mallory's breath caught. Marry her? Her son climbed off the bed and went to his backpack. He reached inside and took out a black box. He brought it to her. "Dad got you this. He showed it to me this morning before you got up. He said he wanted to ask you to marry him."

Mallory's hands shook as he held the box. "What are you doing with it?"

"He asked me to keep it safe for him. It's really pretty." The child opened the lid to reveal a pear-shaped diamond ring in an antique setting. It was beautiful.

"I bet if you don't like this ring, Dad will buy you another one. He just had this one for a long time. Even before I was born. He said he was going to ask you to marry him when he got out of training."

Mallory swallowed the dryness in her throat. Oh, God. "What did you say?"

"I said that Dad was going to ask you to marry him before I was born. That's why he bought this ring for you. He said it was your favorite kind."

Tears clouded her vision as she reached for the ring. Then it dawned on her she had told him that she liked antique jewelry. "He remembered…"

"Please don't be sad, Mom. And don't be mad at Dad."

Chase had come back for her. He'd wanted to marry her all those years ago. She hugged her son. "I'm not mad, Ryan. But I did manage to make a big mess of things." She pulled back and wiped her eyes. "I think it's time I tell your father how I feel."

The boy finally smiled. "Just ask him, I did. He told me last night that he loved you."

Her chest tightened. "And I love him."

"Then go and tell him."

"I think I will, son. I think it's past time I tell him the truth."

Chase wanted to stay in bed, but the pounding in his head wouldn't let him. He sat up, feeling every beer he'd drunk last night. He needed some aspirin. Pulling back the covers, he went into the bathroom and took a bottle from the medicine cabinet. He turned on the shower and got in to soak away his misery.

But that wasn't going to happen any time soon. When the water turned cold, he shut it off and climbed out to dry off. He pulled on a pair of jeans and a black T-shirt.

He needed coffee, then a busy day of physical work

to help him forget his troubles. He'd already started on the barn yesterday, hoping to have a horse to board. Didn't look like that was going to happen any time soon.

In the kitchen, he managed to make coffee, then by the time he drank his first cup he heard a vehicle pull up.

Great. He didn't want any visitors today. He got up and saw it was a truck attached to a horse trailer. "What the hell…" He pulled opened the back door and walked outside in time to see Mallory climb out of the truck.

Dressed in faded jeans and a pink blouse, her cowboy hat was cocked back off her smiling face. "Good morning," she tossed at him as she continued to the back of the trailer and started to unhitch the gate. There were two horses inside.

He came down the steps. "What are you doing here?"

Her gaze met his. "I promised to show you some horses, but never got around to it."

What was going on? He took her by the arm to stop her. Mistake. He felt her warmth, even through her blouse. He released her.

"You just decided to bring two horses over here this morning…. Out with it, Mallory, because I can't take any more of these games."

She turned serious. "Okay, I used the horses as an excuse to see you."

His chest tightened, as did his gut. "Hell, Mal, you don't need an excuse…ever."

"Are you sure? I didn't think I'd be exactly welcome."

He'd had enough. "Dammit, woman. Just tell me why you've come here." He blew out a breath. "And don't say it was because of the horses."

She swallowed. "I came to ask you something."

"Okay…" He folded his arms across his chest to keep from reaching for her. "What is it?"

She went to the truck and came back with the black velvet box. "When did you buy me this ring?"

"Where did you get that?"

"Ryan said you gave it to him for safekeeping."

He closed his eyes momentarily. It seemed like another lifetime ago, the plans he'd made with his son. "What does it matter now? You told me there's no future for us."

"Please, Chase, tell me."

"It was the first weekend I had free during my ranger training."

"Nine years ago." Her eyes widened. "You were going to ask me to marry you then?"

He nodded. "But I was too late. I came by the ranch and learned you'd gotten married a few weeks before."

"You came back for me," she whispered. "Why didn't you tell me?"

He shrugged. "Would it have made a difference?"

"Yes. You said you had no room in your life for anything except being a ranger. I thought I'd always be second in your life."

"Never." He reached for her and she didn't resist. "I realized I was wrong. I came back because I didn't want to live without you. When I learned about your marrying another guy, I tried to hate you. If you loved me…you would have waited."

"And if you loved me you would have taken me with you," she countered.

"I did love you, Mallory. That's why I walked

away in the first place. You were so young. Then I found I couldn't concentrate, I wanted you with me… always."

Mallory knew she owed it to him to take the next step. "I loved you, too, Chase. Then and now. Forever." Her gaze met his. "Could you forgive me, and love me again?"

He blinked. "Oh, Mallory, you have no idea." His arms wrapped around her, and drew her closer.

"Tell me…" she whispered. "I need the words, Chase."

"I've always loved you, Mallory. For nine years, I've never stopped, and I don't plan to anytime soon." He kissed her, slowly, softly at first, but then it grew intense.

He finally released her. "Let me have the box."

She handed it to him and watched as he took out the ring. Then to her amazement, he went down on one knee. "This isn't exactly how I'd planned this, but I finally got you agreeable, and I'm not letting the chance slip by. I love you, Mallory Kendrick. I have since the day you went speeding by me. I want us to spend the rest of our lives together, raising our son, and having more babies. Will you marry me?"

Mallory was shaking as she managed to nod. "Yes, oh, yes, Chase, I'll marry you."

He slipped on the ring and kissed her hand. Standing, he pulled her into his arms and swung her around.

He finally set her down. "Dammit, woman. You made me work for this one." He grinned. "But you're worth it."

"I'm sorry—"

"No, no more saying that. We both have made mistakes. We'll probably make a lot more over the next fifty or sixty years, but just know I love you, Mal." He kissed her again. "Come on, let's go into the house so I can show you how much."

Mallory resisted being pulled away. "I'm not sure Beau and Scarlet would be too happy about that."

He frowned. "Oh, man. The horses." He immediately went to the trailer and lowered the gate.

Mallory waited for his reaction to the roan stallion and brood mare. "What do you think of my wedding present to you?"

Chase already had the stallion out of the trailer, then the mare. He stood back and looked them over. "They're beauties. Where did you find them?"

"I happen to have connections. And I thought this guy would sire some beautiful foals."

He grinned. "So we're going into the horse breeding business."

Together, they led the horses toward the corral. "That's one of the things I'd like to do." She led Scarlet inside. Unfastening the lead rope, she let the mare run off. Chase did the same with the stallion. "I was hoping we'd start with our own family…and a baby," she said.

Mallory knew she'd taken a lot away from Chase when she'd never told him about Ryan. She'd lost a lot, too. It had cost them both. No more. This was their time.

"Are you sure you want a baby right now?" he asked, looking hopeful. "We haven't even decided where we're going to live."

She smiled. "I thought we'd live right here. You can continue your work as a Ranger. And I can handle my business anywhere I have a computer. Liz is close enough and can visit us, and so is Dad." She stopped.

"Unless you have something else in mind… I just thought since you proposed to me…you wanted—"

He leaned down and kissed her again. "I want you and Ryan any way I can get you. Here, in Levelland…or Timbuktu. And, yes, I want you to be pregnant with my child…again."

She felt a thrill rush through her. "I feel the same way." She leaned into him. "We have a second chance…." She thought about how she'd almost lost him again.

He reached for her. "Come up to the house with me. We'll discuss our future…and how large our family is going to get."

"So are you going to use your power of persuasion on me?"

He grinned at her. "As a Texas Ranger, I am trained as an expert negotiator. And I feel it's my honored duty to work toward the best results for everyone."

She reached up and kissed him. "Just so you know that you're my Texas Ranger."

EPILOGUE

CHASE STOOD by his uncle's grave. *Lieutenant Wade Landon, Texas Ranger. He served Texas and his family with loyalty and honor.*

Months had passed since they'd caught and arrested Sancho Vasquez. Although the man refused to confess to murdering Wade, there were other witnesses eager to make a deal with the D.A. for a lighter prison sentence.

It didn't matter to Chase. He knew the man had killed his uncle, and with the drug and attempted murder charges against him, Vasquez wouldn't see the light of day ever again.

Chase rubbed his fingers over the silver star badge in his hand. The name Wade Landon was engraved across the front. It was over. He could close this part of his life.

"He was proud of you, Chase."

Chase turned and saw Mallory, his bride of three months. They'd had a small wedding at the Lazy K Ranch with friends and family.

"I hope so. I sure was proud of him."

"I'm proud of you, too," she said as she slipped her

arm around his waist. "You're a special man, Chase Landon. Father, husband...lover."

Mallory couldn't be happier if she tried. She touched her slightly rounded stomach. She was ten weeks pregnant.

"How are you feeling?" he asked. "Shouldn't you be sitting down?"

"No. I should be doing everything that I'm doing." She wouldn't take any chances with their baby, but she wasn't going to go to bed for the duration of her pregnancy, either.

"I think you should slow down a little."

"I have a business, Chase. I'm not overdoing it. And when the time comes, I'll stop." She smiled. "Gladly. There is nothing more important than my family." She glanced at her watch. "I think we'd better get home. Ryan is anxiously waiting for us."

They climbed in the truck and drove back to the ranch they'd renamed the Landon Ranch, Mallory K Landon Horse Broker.

They drove through the new gate and saw the freshly painted house. Flowers bordered the rebuilt porch and the trimmed lawn was lush and green.

After painting the inside rooms, Mallory had brought over a lot of furniture, filling the house with warmth and hominess.

Friends and family were coming from all around for today's festivities, Ryan's ninth birthday. The first Chase got to share with his son. And it was going to be the best...for everyone.

Chase reached over and took Mallory's hand. "I love

you." He squeezed it. "Even more for giving me this second baby."

"I love you, too. And I was thinking about names for the baby. If it's a boy how about the name Wade? And if it's a girl we could name her after your mother and mine, Sarah Pilar."

His throat worked to swallow. "I like that idea."

He pulled up at the house and Ryan came running outside. "Mom, Dad, where have you been? Did you get the cake and ice cream?"

"Son, chill," Chase said as he tugged the boy's hat down. "What do you think this is, your birthday?"

They carried the party items into the kitchen where Liz, Rosalie and Buck were busy organizing things.

Chase wanted just a few minutes with Ryan before things got crazy with the party. He took his son and walked him into the living room that had become the family meeting room. It was painted an olive-green. A brown area rug took away the echo and drapes added privacy.

"What do you want, Dad?"

He still got a thrill wherever Ryan called him that. "This is a special day for you…and for me, too."

"I know. It's my first birthday with you."

Chase nodded. "It's also an ending to something in my life. Your mother and I went to collect the things Vasquez had of my uncle's." He took the ranger badge out of his pocket. "This was his star he wore as a ranger." He handed it to his son.

The boy examined it with interest. "Wow."

"I want you to have it, Ryan. I want you to have something of the man I loved and respected."

"Really?" the boy asked.

Chase nodded. "He was part of your family, too. You should be proud of him, he was a great ranger."

Ryan looked at him with those dark eyes. "Thanks, Dad." He hugged him, then walked away, but stopped in the doorway. "You're a great ranger, too. And I'm proud you're my dad."

Chase felt his chest tighten. "Thanks, son. I'm proud of you, too." He released a long breath. "Now, let's get this party started."

Ryan grinned and ran off. Chase was following as he spotted Mallory standing in the dining room.

"A little father-son talk?"

"I just had a gift for him."

"Another one? The new saddle isn't enough?"

"It was Wade's badge."

She smiled. "Later, we might want to confiscate it for a few years to keep it safe."

He nodded and pulled her close to his side. His emotions were so raw. "Oh, God, it's so good to have you with me."

She hugged him back. "I love it, too." She looked at him. "One of the good things about us finding each other—even though it took a bad situation to get us back together—is we know what we've lost. And we appreciate what we've found again."

"All I know is that I never want to lose you or Ryan again," he told her. "You both mean too much to me."

"Don't worry, we're here for keeps."

Chase kissed her. Today, he wasn't thinking about

how many years he'd longed for this. There was no
room in their lives for regrets any more, there was only
a future of promise and love.

* * * * *

So you think you can write?

**Mills & Boon® and Harlequin®
have joined forces in a
global search for new authors.**

It's our biggest contest yet—with the prize
of being published by the world's
leader in romance fiction.

Look for more information on our website:
www.soyouthinkyoucanwrite.com

So you think you can write?
Show us!

MILLS & BOON

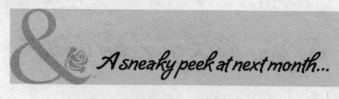

A sneaky peek at next month...

By Request

RELIVE THE ROMANCE WITH THE BEST OF THE BEST

My wish list for next month's titles...

3 stories in each book - only £5.99!

In stores from 17th August 2012:

☐ Three Blind-Date Brides –
Jennie Adams, Fiona Harper & Melissa McClone

☐ Top-Notch Men! – Melanie Milburne,
Margaret McDonagh & Anne Fraser

In stores from 7th September 2012:

☐ The Million-Dollar Catch – Susan Mallery

Available at WHSmith, Tesco, Asda, Eason, Amazon and Apple

Just can't wait?

0812/05